About the Author

Greig Beck grew up across the road from Bondi Beach in Sydney, Australia. His early days were spent surfing, sunbaking and reading science fiction on the sand. He then went on to study computer science, immerse himself in the financial software industry and later received an MBA. Greig is still involved in the software industry but still finds time to write and surf. He lives in Sydney with his wife, son and an enormous black German shepherd. *This Green Hell* is Greig's third novel.

Also by Greig Beck

Alex Hunter series
Beneath the Dark Ice
Dark Rising

Valkeryn Chronicles
Return of the Ancients

This Green Hell

Greig Beck

Momentum

First published by Pan Macmillan Australia in 2011
This edition published in 2012 by Momentum
Pan Macmillan Australia Pty Ltd
1 Market Street, Sydney 2000

A CIP record for this book is available at the National Library of Australia

This Green Hell

EPUB format: 9781743340578
Mobi format: 9781743340585
Print on Demand format: 9781743340592

Cover design by Jeremy Nicholson
Proofread by Tara Goedjen

Macmillan Digital Australia: www.macmillandigital.com.au

To report a typographical error, please email
errors@momentumbooks.com.au

Visit www.momentumbooks.com.au to read more about all our books and to buy books online. You will also find features, author interviews and news of any author events.

Hell is not hot, or cold.
Nor is it deep below ground, or somewhere
in the sky.
Instead it is a place on Earth filled with
sucking bogs, disfiguring diseases and millions
of tiny flesh-eating creatures.
Hell is a jungle, and it is monstrously
green.

Prologue

It had traveled for a billion years.

Exploded from its cold, black world by a massive meteor strike and scattered in a spray of diamond-hard matter throughout the universe.

Different-sized fragments would arrive at different times; some many millions of years before others. Some were folded deep below the primordial earth; others perished under a toxic sunlight.

It didn't matter. It had traveled for a billion years. It could wait a billion more.

ONE

Northeast Paraguay River, 1617

Father Juan de Castillo looked up from his journal, his eyes drawn once again to the small church being erected in the clearing. Only months ago the local Indians had cut the land from the jungle, and already the building's foundations were laid. A deep and solid basement had been sunk into the black loamy soil and now the workers were dragging heavy stones into place from one of the few quarries on the banks of the Rio de Paraguay. At this rate the church would be finished in a matter of weeks – days even.

Father Castillo smiled as a small girl ran up to drop an exotic flower on his table, scampering off before he could thank her. She stopped at the edge of the clearing and stood on one leg just under an enormous fern frond, watching the young Jesuit with large chocolate-colored eyes. The priest picked up the flower and twirled it between his thumb and forefinger – it looked like a large blue star with a triple stamen of the brightest vermilion.

'*Bello* – beautiful,' he said, loud enough so she'd hear.

He lifted the flower to his nose and recoiled with disgust; it smelled like rotting flesh. The girl giggled, clapped her stubby little brown fingers and disappeared into the deep green of the jungle behind her.

The Jesuit went back to his notes, describing the flower, its odor and characteristics, and then drew the face of the girl, spending considerable time shading in her large dark eyes as best he could with his charcoals and ink. He used a sleeve to wipe his face, which was covered in insect bites. It was only midmorning and already his body was slick with perspiration beneath the heavy black cloth of his robes.

He squinted through the rising morning steam to the clearing where his traveling companion, Father Alonso González, was on his knees polishing the huge bronze bell that awaited its home in a church tower that, so far, existed only in the Jesuits' imaginations. Father González was in his sixties but still tall and vigorous, the only sign of his age visible in his thick, square beard, which had a swathe of gray at his jawline.

Castillo slid his eyes from the senior Jesuit to a small group of elderly men sitting half-hidden in the shade. One sat like a stone and stared back at him through rheumy, smoke-damaged eyes. If not for an occasional tic in his left eye, the shrunken, teak-brown body would have been invisible among the jungle's dark shadows. It seemed that not all the Guarani Indians were happy to see the Jesuits – Nezu had arrived a few weeks back – a powerful medicine man from the upper Paraguay River. He locked eyes with the Jesuit and lifted a small gourd with the plumage of a dozen different colorful feathers tied to one end and shook it twice, making a rattling sound, before pointing it at Father Castillo.

'And God bless you too,' said Castillo softly. He closed his journal, put two fingers to his lips and then touched them to the ornate gilt crucifix pressed into the cover of the leather-bound book.

He looked up with a smile when he heard a small boy trying to speak in Spanish to his older friend.

'Com ... uhhh, como bello ... flor de oro, padre.'

'Si, una flor de oro gigante,' Father González responded.

Castillo nodded; the boy was right: the bell the older Jesuit was polishing did look a bit like a flower – *a giant golden flower waiting to bloom high in a holy tree*, he thought.

He wrinkled his brow and turned his head slightly – there was a faint noise, a whistling, little more than a whisper, just audible above the sounds of the surrounding jungle.

'*Allá! Mire, padre.*' One of the children with Father González was pointing a small finger up at the sky.

Castillo craned his neck to see beyond the foliage that was shading his table. Cutting across the heavens were flaming orange streaks, like long lines of fire, all heading down towards the jungle. More appeared, until eventually they filled the entire sky.

The faint whistling had become a scream. The young Jesuit stood and walked a few paces out into the middle of the clearing; he placed one hand over his brow and squinted upwards. Children were laughing and hopping around him in excitement at the strange spectacle, but many of the adults were shouting in alarm, and mothers ran to gather their babies into their arms.

Castillo could hear the grating voice of Nezu as he rattled his gourd at the sky; he was yelling something about the fingers of Tau reaching down for them. The priest knew that Tau was the local people's word for the Devil.

Just as Father Castillo was about to call out to his older colleague for advice, the gleaming bell rang with a loud, deep *bong*. Everyone froze and looked towards the golden dome.

Castillo was wondering how the bell could have tolled by itself when the high-pitched whistling ended and something thudded into the ground. Another crash came from one of the huts, a hole appearing in its roof. Seconds later, it burst into flames. A further object smashed into a tree trunk at the edge of the clearing.

'It's raining stones!' Castillo yelled to Father González.

More whistling, this time at a volume that startled birds from the green maze all around them. He saw Father González look up at the noise – in time to catch one of the speeding projectiles in his left eye.

The old priest fell flat on his back, blood and jellied optical fluid spraying the children who stood nearby. Castillo ran to his friend, gagging as he saw smoke curling from the ragged hole in his face. Father González gasped in agony as steaming fluid pulsed out of the wound and oozed down his cheek; then, thankfully, he shuddered and lay still.

The fiery streaks across the sky seemed to evaporate, and the strange whistling ceased. All that remained was the sweet smell of burnt meat filling the air.

*

Father Castillo sat next to his colleague, watching a girl fan the old man's face with a large, broad leaf. The slow strokes were almost hypnotic in their pace and tenderness. It had been two weeks and, though Father González continued to draw ragged breaths, he hadn't woken from his death-like sleep. His once-robust frame had fallen in on itself and his gray face and shrunken cheeks looked incongruous among the bright piles of sweet-smelling flowers heaped around him. The Indians replaced the blossoms daily, but Father Castillo knew they weren't delivered just as a sign of respect for the old man. From his position next to the bed he could smell the strange odor coming from Father González's open mouth – raw and rancid. It disgusted him.

He turned his head at the sound of breaking pottery. The Guarani had been sun-curing the hundreds of flat clay plates that would be used as roof tiles on the church. They were only days away from having a completed structure ready for furnishing and blessing. The massive stone altar had been carved and hauled into position, a task that had taken a full day. A previous block of granite sat discarded – a shallow face, perhaps of *Jesu Christi* had been started on the stone, but the block had proven far too hard and heavy for the stonemason's tools so it had been abandoned. It would take nearly every man in the village to remove it. *Other priorities now*, he thought.

'Padre ...'

Castillo flinched as the girl touched his arm, then placed a pile of clean cloths and a bowl of water on the table beside the bed. It was time to change the dressing over the old priest's eye. It was strange how he thought of González as an old man now – a few weeks ago he had seemed anything but – however, the damage to his head had seemed to absorb his life force and left him a foul-smelling skeleton.

He carefully unwrapped the damp, discolored bandage from around the patient's head. In the noon light, Father González's tight, gray skin looked almost reptilian. Up close, the vile odor wafting from his open lips was stomach-turning, even for a Jesuit who had endured more hardships than many men had seen in a dozen lifetimes. Father Castillo pulled back the old priest's top lip – the gums were black and also seemed to be shrinking. His teeth looked strange … longer perhaps, and the tongue behind them lay like a fat, dead worm in the back of his mouth. He couldn't help secretly wishing that the Lord would take González and free him from his rotting bonds.

He soaked one of the clean rags in the water and wiped away the sticky fluid that was still leaking from around González's eye socket. The ruined eye seemed lumpy and uneven behind its closed lid. He gently bathed the mucus-smeared lashes, then reached with his thumb to pull back the lid to check for further infection. As he lifted the delicate skin, he felt a movement behind it. He leapt back, landing on his rump and sending the small clay water bowl flying. He grabbed for it, too late, and managed to cut the skin between his thumb and forefinger on the broken shards.

There was something *in* there. Something small and gray that had wriggled and shifted from the light as he lifted the eyelid. Perhaps some strange parasitic vermin had managed to worm its way into the wound. Bile rose in the young man's throat.

After a few seconds he gathered himself and approached Father González again. His heart hammered and his hand shook as he lifted the eyelid once more, steeling himself to make a grab for whatever creature had invaded his mentor and friend. There was nothing. He leaned forward over the wound, peering closer; still nothing. Perhaps it had just been the light, or his fatigue and anxiety for the old man had made him see something that wasn't there.

He was about to gently probe the empty socket for anything foreign in the wound when the old priest dragged in a large breath and slowly opened his other eye. Its once clear brown iris was now indistinct, as though a layer of slime had grown across it. The muddy orb fixed on Father Castillo, then on the bleeding cut on his hand.

The nostrils in the cadaverous face flared as the older priest inhaled again, and his lips turned up slightly in a brush of a smile. Then the expression vanished and the eye closed again.

Father Castillo should have been elated at this sign of consciousness from his holy colleague. Instead, he felt a terrible coldness spread from his stomach through his entire body. He hadn't recognized the man who had stared up at him.

*

The church was finished, but there were no celebrations.

The previous night, all the animals in the village had been slaughtered. Their bodies had been found shredded, as though whatever had attacked them had rent them to pieces in search of their precious fluids. Some of the animals had been taken while tethered close to the villagers' huts – yet no one had heard a thing. It worried Father Castillo that whatever had attacked the animals so viciously had crept silently among them while they slept – and was clever enough to untie knots.

When he went to check on Father González, he found the old man had color in his face again and his cheeks seemed fuller than they had in weeks, which was amazing as he had been given nothing but water dripped into his open mouth.

Father Castillo peeled back the eyelid of the ruined eye, steeling himself as he remembered his last experience of cleaning the wound. It was a miracle: there was once again an eye in the socket. Still shrunken and a milky gray color, but an eye nonetheless.

Father Castillo leaned closer and placed his hand on the old priest's cheek but Father González didn't wake. The younger man noticed the smell from his mouth had changed. Now it was rawly metallic and musky; and unsettling.

*

Father Castillo felt he had aged a decade in the last few hours. They had woken to find they had been visited again in the night – but this time several children had been taken. The sleeping infants had been silently pulled from their mats and spirited away in the dark.

The villagers had been frightened following the killing of the animals, but now, with the children missing, their fear turned to panic and anger. The children had to be located quickly, and alive.

By midmorning, a single child had been found wandering incoherent through the deep green maze of the jungle. The small boy had turned his red-veined eyes on Father Castillo's black robes, screamed the Guarani word for devil, and sobbed until bloody tears ran down his face. Father Castillo did what he could but the child had lapsed into a deathly blankness and had never woken again.

Now, the young priest exhaled wearily and looked at the faces surrounding him. Not since he and Father González had first arrived had he seen such mistrust among the Guarani. And now there was something more in their eyes – fear … fear of him.

A dry rattling behind him caught his attention and he turned to see the medicine man, Nezu, shaking his gourd and pointing it at him, his creased lips moving in a chant and his eyes full of hatred. A small crowd had gathered, and this time they listened to his every word.

*

Father Castillo decided to move Father González into the church. It was cooler within the stone structure, and far more secure. The tribe's superstition was like a river that ran strongest just beneath the surface, and now that undercurrent was bubbling upwards in a surge of panic. It would not be long before it turned into savage action.

Father González groaned as he was carried across the clearing. Steam seemed to rise from his sweat-damp skin wherever the dappled sunlight touched it. Despite the way the old man's body shivered, Father Castillo thought it looked fuller, more fleshed out.

The faces of the men carrying the stretcher were twisted in disgust. None of the Guarani wanted to be near the old priest, or even look at him. It was if they believed he was somehow responsible for the turning fortunes of the village.

Garbled words bubbled up from deep inside the man and Castillo leaned close to his lips to hear. *'La estrella nos quema.'* Castillo frowned: *the star burns us* – the words didn't make any sense.

The old man's mouth hung open behind his damp beard and strange squeaks and half-words continued to tumble out.

'What is it, Father? I am here.'

Castillo wiped the man's brow and whispered a silent prayer when he felt how cold his flesh was. He held his hand over González's face to shield him from the sunlight.

'*Nos libre ... Nos alimente ...*' Then more soft squeals and liquid-sounding moans.

Free us, feed us. Castillo was confused. 'Are you hungry, Father?'

Castillo grimaced as the man's face blistered in the light and he tried to keep his hand over the steaming skin as his body writhed and squirmed.

The old Jesuit's mouth closed with an audible clack, then slowly opened again like a trap being reset. More words came forth although his lips behind his beard did not seem to move. '*La piel de este mundo debe estar abrirse para que seamos libres.*'

Castillo turned away from the smell emanating from González's mouth as he tried to decipher his meaning. *This world's skin must be opened for us to be free.*

He shook his head. 'I don't understand, Father – we *are* free.'

The men placed the cot at the base of the massive stone altar and Castillo sat on the ground beside it. He should have been thanking God for the miracle that had restored the old priest, but now he wasn't so sure it was God's hand at work. González was almost glowing with vitality ... which should have been impossible considering he had survived on nothing but water dripped between his flaking lips.

Father Castillo made the sign of the cross over his old friend, closed his eyes and said a silent prayer. As he opened them, a tear ran down his cheek. Placing one hand on the priest's forehead, he said, 'What is happening to you, Father? Is it really your soul still in there?'

*

The screams ripped him from his sleep, leaving him disorientated with a pounding headache. Father Castillo sat silently in the dark, listening for a few seconds, feeling the perspiration running down his face as the night heat of the jungle steamed his skin. His fingers clutched at the damp bedding, hoping the sounds had just been a fever-dream – a dreadful remnant from his exhausted and overworked imagination.

A shout and the sound of running came from just outside his hut, and his hope that it had been a dream fell to pieces. He swung his legs out from under the clinging sheet and wiped his face with his hands. The clamour was now rising all over the camp, and he could hear only Guarani words – no one spoke Spanish anymore. In among the shouts of terror and confusion, he could make out that the remaining children had been taken – some from within the arms of their mothers. He went outside and tried to ask some of the Indians questions, but they shrugged him off or just hissed angrily at him.

The village fire was relit and flaming torches spread out quickly through the jungle, looking like flaming birds as they darted from tree to ground to fern and then flew on again.

Father Castillo saw the medicine man, Nezu, standing in the clearing. His was the only face that didn't contain fear, anger or confusion; instead, he looked triumphant. It was clear he was blaming the Jesuits for the missing children. Castillo groaned as he noticed the harmless gourd in Nezu's hand had been replaced by a war club – two feet of fire-hardened wood, sharpened on one side so it looked like a cross between an axe and a paddle.

Castillo grabbed a torch and headed quickly for the church. Pushing open the large wooden doors, he crossed himself, then walked to the center of the solid stone room. He felt an immediate sense of dread: Father González was gone.

He held the torch higher and saw that the basement trapdoor was open. He crept lightly towards the black pit. Passing the altar, he snatched up the brass crucifix and clutched it to his chest as he stared down into the stygian darkness. A smell rose from the opening like nothing he had ever encountered before, ranging from sharply metallic to thickly corrupt. He shuddered and gripped the crucifix a little tighter.

'Father González? *Padre* … are you down there?'

He crossed himself again, drew in a breath and straightened his back; he would be safe in the house of God. He leaned across and lit one of the lanterns beside the altar, then dropped his burning torch into the pit. Instead of the sound of it hitting dry packed earth at the base of the steps as he expected, it splashed thickly, as though falling into mud, then fizzled and went out.

'*Mierda!*' he cursed, then quickly crossed himself for profaning in a house of God.

'Father González, are you hurt?'

He paused for a few seconds, looking up towards the altar and the face of the Savior carved above it. He knew he didn't have a choice.

He licked his lips and spoke softly into the mephitic darkness. 'I'm coming down, *padre.*'

Father Castillo descended the rough stone steps on stiff legs, concentrating on his foot placement and breathing through his mouth so he wouldn't have to taste the fetid air. It was a difficult descent as he refused to relinquish his grasp on the items he carried: in one hand he held up the brass crucifix; in the other, a shaking lantern, grasped so tightly his knuckles stood out like white knobs. He prayed softly, his lips moving rapidly with the words and also because of the trembling of his chin.

His first foot left the steps and he felt himself sink into a soft rubbery wetness that slid from under his feet and oozed up between his toes. He lowered the lantern and looked down; a sob escaped his lips as he beheld the ruination beneath him. He had stepped into a pile of ropy tendons, fat, tissue and fragments of bone.

He put the hand holding the crucifix across his mouth to stifle any sound, but still a combination of strangled gurgle and execration leaked out. He had found the missing children – or what was left of them. He was in a charnel house of humanity: all around him were strewn arms, legs, bodies with their skin rent from their bones, chewed or drained and discarded like leftovers from some mad demon's banquet.

Among the mutilation, a small lifeless face stood out, its beautiful dark brown eyes still open – little jewels that had flashed with such gaiety and mischief when the child had given him the flower. That moment seemed a lifetime ago.

Above the sound of his frantically beating heart, Father Castillo heard a vile sucking coming from a darkened corner. He lifted the lantern. '*Ay, Dios mío, Dios mío.*' Bile rose in his mouth and he fell to his knees, holding the cross to his forehead as he prayed with lips cold and wet from fear and the tears that streamed down his face.

A darker shadow loomed over him and he crushed his eyes shut as the crucifix was torn roughly from his fingers. In his head came a voice he recognized: *We need you.* He opened his eyes one last time and couldn't hold back the shriek that burst from his lungs to bounce around the small stone-lined basement.

There was a deep grunt, the sound of something moist being roughly torn, and silence for a few seconds – then the vile sucking began again.

TWO

Mining Base Camp, Paraguayan Northern Jungle; Present Day

Aimee Weir squinted up at the supply helicopters buzzing through the air like prehistoric dragonflies. From her pocket she pulled a damp handkerchief and used it to mop her brow and cheeks, wincing as the material passed over the rash of red lumps dotting her skin. The gallons of bug repellent that needed to be applied twenty-four hours a day were playing hell with her complexion. *Great choice*, she thought, *either I get little itchy lumps from the poison I'm covering myself in, or I leave off the bug spray and get eaten alive resulting in big itchy lumps. Welcome to tropical paradise.*

Truth was, she had lotion to apply to the rash, but couldn't be bothered. Besides, who cared how she looked down here. She blew strands of her dark hair out of her eyes and leaned back against the doorframe. The distant clank and whirr of the drilling machinery had fallen quiet days ago, to be replaced by the living buzz and thrum of the jungle. Drilling had been shut down for forty-eight hours now, with the men refusing to travel out to the drill site because of the bandits that had been raiding the platform. At first, they had just stolen equipment, but then several workers had been shot and one killed. And just last week, explosives had been discovered on the rig itself.

But now the US cavalry had arrived: six Green Berets, each man twice as big as the local Paraguayans. They were preparing to leave the camp for the drill site, and Aimee watched them as they got their gear together. Each man wore black and green camouflage fatigues and a green flat cap pulled down on his head. The soldier leading them out had removed the sleeves from his uniform – either due to the heat, or to give an enormous pair of biceps more room to move. Aimee noticed a blue crucifix tattooed on one upper arm and a grinning devil's head on the other. *Covering all bases*, she thought.

Bringing up the rear was their fireteam's leader, Captain Michaels. He turned and gave her a thumbs-up. He had short dark hair and an easy smile, and, for a brief moment, in the right light, he reminded her of someone.

She kept her gaze flat and uninterested. Out of the side of her mouth she blew more hair out of her eyes and ignored him, and he gave up with a shrug and turned back to his comrades. Aimee shook her head as if to clear away an annoying irritation; *no more army guys for me*, she thought.

*

'But why do I need to be down here?'

Aimee had the phone wedged between her shoulder and ear as she talked to Alfred Beadman, the elderly chairman of the company she worked for.

While she listened to his response, she picked up mud-stained pieces of clothing, rolled them into a ball and flung them into the corner of the small pre-built cabin, pulling a face at their dampness and smell. She *hmm-hmmd* every now and then, nodding as she listened to the avuncular chairman's words before cutting him off when she caught sight of movement below one of her particularly soiled T-shirts.

'Hang on, Alfred.'

She put the phone on speaker and placed it down on the small folding table, then lifted the T-shirt with the toe of her boot and bent to pick up an ugly brown bug the size of a matchbox that lurked underneath. It hissed and vibrated its abdomen as she held it between thumb and forefinger and she curled her lip in disgust as she opened the door and flung the heavy insect outside. She stuck out her tongue at the creature as it opened large translucent wings and fluttered away with a sound like a deck of cards being shuffled. She watched as it alighted on the trouser leg of one of the drill workers standing in the mud. *Oops*, Aimee mouthed and silently closed the door.

'Aimee, are you there, my dear?'

Alfred's cultivated baritone sprang from the phone, sounding way too civilized in the hot cramped room in the middle of the Paraguayan jungle.

'I'm back, Alfred. Just had to see someone out … Yes, you're right, the gas is in a very impure state and will need a lot of scrubbing, but I could have told them that from my lab at home if they'd just sent me a small sample.'

Beadman sighed with good humor. 'My dear, your petrobiological arm of the company leads the field internationally. You came highly recommended to the Paraguayan energy minister and, well, who were we to refuse such an important request from a friendly neighbor? Believe me, America can do with all the friends it can get right now. You're doing your country a great service, you know.'

Aimee pulled a face. She picked up a bottle of water, sipped and swallowed, and was about to respond when Alfred continued.

'You know it's exactly what you've been waiting for: a young gas – there could be viable bacterial DNA – it could be the key to your synthesis tests. A sample might have decomposed in transit. Much better to get it *fresh*, as it were.'

Aimee expelled a long breath and dropped into the clothing-covered chair beside the small table. Alfred was right. Most gases were created over millions to hundreds of millions of years, but this deposit was young and very dirty – it was perfect. It contained everything: mercury, butane, ground water and all sorts of other base impurities, which meant it wasn't yet fully cooked. There could still be evidence of bacterial methanogenesis occurring – her holy grail for energy synthesis. Carbon-hungry bacteria in the rock digested the trace hydrocarbons, leaving behind pockets of natural gases. She had worked for years with older samples from the Powder River Basin in Wyoming and Antrim shale deposit in Michigan, but these had been mature samples. The bacteria had long degraded down to nothing more than gases themselves. For years, her company had proposed the idea that if they could extract viable DNA from these specialised bacteria they could actually bioengineer them to digest polymers and return clean natural gas. In effect, it would be possible to create a cheap fuel source from waste plastics. All she needed were some deep-rock samples from the gas pocket with living bacteria, or at least with identifiable DNA strands. So far, no one had ever found any living microorganisms or even any complete DNA strands – the methanogenesis process was still a mystery.

Aimee sighed and rubbed softly at a smudge on the table with her thumb. They had almost broken through into the subsurface chamber when the drill site had been closed down; it still hadn't re-opened, even though it had been a week now since the Green Berets had headed off into the jungle to see off the bandits.

She stopped rubbing as she felt a tickling vibration run from the soles of her boots to her stomach. Aimee shook her head and got to her feet – another small tremor. More drilling complications she needed to worry about.

She kept the phone on speaker and carried it with her to the door. As she opened it, a thick wave of air that smelled like decomposing flowers washed into the cabin. She wrinkled her nose; it had rained again last night and the red mud throughout the camp was ankle deep in some places. A warm mist hung over the ground and everything that wriggled, jumped or crawled was heading towards the gathering of humans for a free meal. Aimee took a long swill of water, then pursed her lips and directed the stream at a small red and black snake that was slithering towards her across the muddy ground. It changed course under the bombardment and headed back towards the dense green jungle.

'Aimee, I understand the drill site is not yet open and you're all still confined to the camp. Am I correct?'

Alfred's tone suggested that he already knew the answer.

'Yep, Camp Boggy's still home. By the way, did you know it's the start of the rainy season down here? Or that we seem to be having ground tremors daily? Alfred, I knew the Nazca Plate was close, but never thought its movement might actually affect us. A week ago there was a 5.2 shock in Chile, and it broke a shitload of stuff even over here – we get one like that just a little bigger or closer, and the gas bed will be gone for good … So, hot, wet and shaky; you should really come for a visit, Alfred, you'd love it.' Aimee paced in a small circle, before turning to stare back out the open doorway. 'And no, before you ask, I don't know where the GBs are – still out playing soldiers in the jungle, I guess.'

They ended the call, but, despite Aimee's light tone, she was concerned. She knew a little about Green Berets and they shouldn't have had any trouble with a few South American mercenaries, no matter how well armed.

*

Aimee's camp was over a mile from the drilling site, and, like the drill-rig infrastructure, the pre-built cabins and tents, equipment and nearly one hundred men had all been choppered in. It was a large upfront investment but it cut set-up time by seventy-five percent and also ensured there were no roads left behind to be reused by loggers or settlers. This way, when they finished, all that remained was a small scar and a pristine jungle – much better for public relations.

Aimee squelched across the muddy camp to the manager's hut. The groups of men standing around stopped talking to watch her pass. Most of the workers had come from a scattering of local villages, with the mining and engineering specialists from the capital, Asunción.

She spotted Francisco Herrera, the camp doctor, and waved – he returned the salutation, looking impeccable in a linen suit and manicured silver goatee. She smiled back and stepped around another group of idle men. When the drilling stopped, the men got bored. The clearing for the camp wasn't huge for the number of men on site, and was only slightly larger than half a dozen football fields. Its size, combined with the period between nightly rains becoming shorter, meant the time spent out in the open was shrinking. Beyond the camp, a hundred foot wall of the almost impenetrable jungle presented little alternative to days spent watching the sporting channels on satellite television, smoking cigarettes that smelled like burning underwear, or playing a card game whose rules, so it seemed to Aimee, appeared to change at every single hand. Some of the men had resisted the enforced idleness by hunting for fresh meat for their *barbacoa*. Now, none even bothered with that; it seemed all the animals had disappeared.

Aimee joined Alfraedo Desouza, the mining manager, and Francisco, for a satellite link-up with the Paraguayan government officials who had recommended the shutdown. They needed to discuss the impact of the delays and the potential risks of restarting the rigs.

The city bureaucrats were sympathetic at first, acknowledging that the mining company was spending millions of dollars on 'sit-down money', but it soon became clear that they had little intention of cooperating. They were co-funders of the venture and subject to public scrutiny, they said; they felt their hands were tied. At least until they had proof that their investment was safe and the bandits were out of the area.

Aimee could understand their position, but she was also bored and homesick. The sooner she could get a sample of deep rock and help the engineers clean up and compress their gas, the sooner she'd be going home. Besides, with a bunch of Green Berets patrolling the jungle, she figured they were safe. She decided to create a little political competitive tension over the satellite link … just to move things along.

'What concerns me is that your neighbouring states know of your gas discovery,' she said with a sigh. 'The stratigraphic imaging of the vast underground chamber showed it resided completely on Paraguayan territory. However, its northern-most chamber is very close to the Bolivian border.' She let the information hang for a moment in the air. 'Gentlemen, are you aware of the advancements in directional slant drilling? An amazing technique – it is now possible to drill for many miles at angles of up to ninety degrees. Be a real shame if you found your energy source of the future was being bled away from across the border while we sat on our hands down here.'

She grinned at Francisco, who nodded and raised his silver eyebrows at her. There was a muffled discussion on the other end of the phone, then Alfraedo cleared his throat.

'*Señors*, there have been no attacks for days, no sign of any bandit activity in the area, and we have a team of American Green Berets patrolling the jungle. I think to wait any longer brings a risk of losing more than we gain. Don't you agree?'

He sat back and folded his hands across his enormous belly. The unanimous decision to restart drilling was made within another three minutes.

*

Aimee pulled on a pair of khaki pants, still stiff with traces of red mud up to the thighs, and tucked a gray T-shirt into them. Thick socks and damp work boots were next, the boots lacing over the pants and halfway up her calves to seal her off from anything that decided to hitch a ride. Last to go on was a belt with a black holster. Their small security contingent had machetes for the jungle, but only Alfraedo, Francisco and Aimee had sidearms. Aimee hoped Alfraedo never needed to reach for his in a hurry as it was almost fully obscured by the paunch that hung over it. For that matter she hoped he never had to reach for anything down there in a hurry. *Errk*, she thought briefly.

They set off just after eight in the morning, along a walking track the men had cleared through the jungle. Once outside the camp perimeter, Aimee was reminded why they didn't bother bringing vehicles – the wetter it got, the deeper the mud. Eventually the trucks would sink to a point where they would need to be dug out. Best just to use leg power.

The small army of twenty riggers, half a dozen security men, manager, supervisors and Francisco and Aimee plodded along without speaking. The jungle was waking around them and the squelch of their footsteps seemed unnaturally loud in the dark green tunnel. As the sun rose, it lifted the moisture from every tree, bush and blade of grass, forming a thick, hot blanket that resettled over the jungle for the rest of the day. Aimee was breathing heavily and aching from knee to groin – the thick, viscous mud fought to steal their boots with every step. A single mile had never felt so draining, and when the rig superstructure came into view she almost whooped with delight.

The framework of the rig had been dropped into place by giant helicopters and pieced together on the ground. It stood like the skeleton of a blue and white ship in a sea of red mud, its hundred-foot mast the core of a metal framework over a central pipe that ended in a conventional rotary drill, that with all its spikes and knobs, looked like a colossal insect's feeding apparatus, ready to puncture the earth's skin and suck out its blood.

Aimee sighed with relief as she stepped up out of the mud. She scraped what felt like pounds of the stuff from her boots against the steel grid platform that extended all around the machinery, then stamped her feet and stretched her back.

While the riggers set about checking the equipment in preparation for restarting the drilling, Alfraedo ordered the security team to make a sweep of the surrounding jungle – just to be sure there were no bandits waiting to place a bullet between someone's shoulder blades. Aimee could tell by his relaxed manner that he wasn't expecting any trouble; after all, it'd been quiet for days now.

With a whine of the generators and a deep thump, the machinery restarted and the drill began its descent once again. Due to the depth at which they were drilling and the dense matrix they were encountering, the speed of penetration had slowed to around a dozen feet per day. At the time they had been ordered to stop drilling, they were already a mile down and not far from their target depth. Their seismography readings had shown they were within a few dozen feet of the gas chamber. Unless they encountered any deep-mass obstruction, they should be into the gas pocket by the early evening. Once there, they would withdraw the penetration drill tip and replace it with a drill head dotted with unlockable perforations that would enable the gas to flow into the pipe.

Alfraedo had promised that the final penetration drill bit was to be brought to Aimee, untouched and uncontaminated, before the gas began to fully flow. She needed a sample of the rock from the inner skin of the chamber, away from its center, or floor, where the more mature and heavier gases would have settled over the millennia. She knew that if she were to find a viable sample of living microorganisms, it would be in the thin crust at the roof of the cavern where, theoretically, methanogenesis would have last occurred. Or, if she was really lucky, was still occurring.

Aimee had set up her equipment under a sheet of canvas stretched between metal poles at the outer edge of the rig. A table and single chair completed her South American office. Soon, after weeks of advising, she would finally be hands-on. First, she would need to ascertain how much gas scrubbing was required to bring the natural product up to international standards, and then she would need to supervise the compaction work. The gas had to be compressed 600 times to a liquefied state for shipping – a process that was extremely dangerous, but necessary to get any sort of economy on cost of transportation.

'I've got something for you, Dr. Weir,' said Francisco Herrera.

She hadn't noticed him approaching and jumped at the sound of his voice. He bowed slightly and Aimee wondered how he managed to stay so spotless. She only had to walk twenty feet outside her door to have red mud splattered up to her knees and perspiration stains like a football player. She looked down: his boots were only slightly reddened by the mud; and his crisp white shirt was as dry as if he had been on a gentle stroll through a Boston park in springtime. Aimee, on the other hand, felt and looked a wreck.

From behind his back Francisco produced a cream-colored woven fedora with dangling seedpods strung around its brim. He placed it on her head and touched the pods so they swung back and forth, creating a nearly impenetrable barrier for the insect hordes.

'I hear it works for the Australians,' he said, giving her a smile that wrinkled his perfect little silver moustache.

Aimee laughed. 'I love it, and thank you.'

The elderly doctor, from the tiny town of Rosario, was the only person she really spent any time with in the camp. His olive skin was an indication of his local Indian heritage, and she had enjoyed hearing the stories he told her about his people and their culture. Despite their friendship, however, he just couldn't help being inordinately formal all the time, to the extent of refusing to call her by her first name. But rather than making him seem stuffy, it just made him more likeable.

She flopped back down onto her chair, her arms flung out at her sides and exhaled slowly. She pulled off the hat and pushed more of her stray hair back under the brim before replacing it and looking up at him.

Francisco looked at her for a moment longer and then became serious, leaning forward as if about to tell her a secret. 'Something troubles you, Ms. Weir?'

'It's nothing. I'm tired and homesick, and thoughts of old friends keep whirling around in my head.' Aimee gave him a crooked smile.

Francisco's eyes twinkled. 'Hmm, something tells me this friend is a man, and not so old, yes?'

Aimee's eyes slid away from the small dapper man, and though she seemed to look out at the jungle her vision was focused on something a lot further away. 'Yes, a man, and no, not so old.'

A yell from the edge of the jungle and the sound of sloshing feet brought Aimee's head around quickly, causing the seed pods strung around her face to clack together. It was the security detail, yelling in rapid Spanish to the foreman and Francisco. Even from a hundred or so feet away from where she sat, she could see their faces were pale and their eyes were as wide as those of startled horses.

Francisco walked across the gantry to meet the men, holding up one hand to slow them down. Though Aimee had undertaken a crash course in basic Spanish before departing, all she could make out was something that sounded like '*un jaguar muerto*'. *A dead jaguar?* she thought. *What's the big deal?* She got to her feet, and strained to hear more.

After a few minutes, Francisco returned and explained that the security detail had found something at the edge of the jungle that they believed might be the result of an attack by a jaguar.

'It would be best if you stayed here for a while, Dr. Weir. Just until we make sure the animal is not still in the vicinity.'

Francisco seemed slightly embarrassed to be so solicitous towards her, especially as Aimee was nearly half a head taller than most of the Paraguayan site workers and also taller again than himself.

Aimee smiled and put a hand on his shoulder. 'Francisco, an old friend taught me how to shoot, throw a knife and a good punch. He also took me to places a lot more dangerous than a jungle with a few big pussycats hanging from trees. I'll be fine, you'll see. I may even be able to help.'

There's that *old* friend again, she thought and couldn't help a lurch deep inside as she recalled the times she had spent together with Alex Hunter. Even if they were over, the memories, and the skills he had taught her, would stay with her forever.

Francisco shrugged. 'Somehow, I knew you would want to come. Just be aware that this area of the jungle is very dense and very dark. People rarely venture into its depths; for that reason it has been known for hundreds of years as *La oscuridad verde* … the Dark Green.'

Aimee pulled a comic spooky face. 'I'm not afraid of the dark, so lead on.'

Her face grew serious again as she followed the small doctor off the platform and into the red mud. *And believe me, I know dark.* Despite the intense humidity, she shivered as she recalled the dangers she and Alex Hunter had faced deep under the ice of Antarctica.

Alfraedo's security men led the way through the dense jungle to a clearing. Even before pushing through the last of the foliage, Aimee could hear the mad zum of millions of insects in the open area. The security men stood back to allow her, Francisco and Alfraedo to enter first – and she noticed none of them looked in a hurry to follow.

The clearing, little more than twenty feet across, was a riot of color and movement: the ground crawled and the air seethed with an insect horde in a feeding frenzy.

Aimee almost gagged. What she smelled wasn't just decomposition, it was also the smell of torn-apart bodies, viscera, urine and faeces. In the humidity of the jungle, odors got trapped and concentrated in small areas – like this clearing. She couldn't just smell the stench; she almost tasted it.

'*Jesucristo!*' Francisco crossed himself, then turned to one of the men and spoke in hurried Spanish before pulling an immaculate handkerchief from his pocket and folding it over his nose and mouth. The man nodded and raced back along the trail.

In a few moments, he returned with a small chemical fire extinguisher and sent a freezing white cloud into the clearing. The insects disappeared instantly, even the scavengers on the ground heading for the cover of the underbrush.

With the insects gone, the raw carnage was laid out before them. To call it a massacre would imply some force had overcome these humans, beaten them into submission and then to death. But this went beyond anything one human could possibly inflict on another, Aimee thought; it was complete physical annihilation. The bodies had been obliterated in a mad frenzy.

Francisco was the first to step forward. As he did so, his boot squelched, not in the ever-present mud but in a carpet of shredded flesh and bone.

'*Dios Padre Todopoderoso* – oh my.'

He looked around, obviously unsure of where to start – there was no single body left intact to examine. It was impossible to tell if there were two or ten bodies in the mess. Even the skulls had been cracked and opened, pieces of cranial bone thrown around like shards of broken pottery. Francisco used a stick to lift a lump of flesh, his eyes narrowing at the strange marks at its edges.

Whoever the men were, they had been armed. Aimee could see guns flung around the clearing; several were bent nearly in half. Her eyes traced a line of bullet holes up the trunk of a particularly broad tree – and stopped at a pale flap plastered against the wood about ten feet up from the ground. She frowned and stepped a little closer. It was a square piece of flesh, still streaked with blood, but intact, and showing a tattoo of a crude blue crucifix. Aimee felt acidic liquid rise at the back of her throat. She knew that tattoo – she had seen it on the bicep of the big Green Beret. She remembered the self-assured Captain Michaels and the almost cocky thumbs-up he had given her. Was he here too? Had he also been reduced to … this mess? She closed her eyes and held her breath for a moment.

When she opened them, Francisco was beside her. His eyes had found the scrap of skin in the tree too, and when he looked into her face again, Aimee could tell he was probably thinking the same thing she was. That fragment and its placement was no accident. It was … what? A warning, a trophy? She shuddered.

'Could your Green Berets be this savage, Dr. Weir?'

Aimee backed up a step as the insects started to descend once again. She shook her head. 'No, Francisco, this is the Green Berets. And I don't think any human being could inflict this … this insanity on another.'

Francisco looked back at the chaos, his pallor telling her that he was finally seeing it for what, and who, it was.

Together, they backed out of the clearing, the doctor's eyes bulging slightly above the handkerchief that he held over his nose and mouth as a barricade against the returning swarms of insects. For the first time, Aimee noticed that his permanently immaculate trousers were stained red to the knees.

*

The short trek back to the rig was made in silence. Aimee pushed her new hat to the back of her head so she could dab at the greasy perspiration on her forehead. The deep background thrum of machinery reminded her of the hurricane of insects that had boiled over the pile of flesh in the small clearing. She felt sick, and a long, long way from Connecticut.

Francisco appeared beside her and held a silver flask under her nose, the top already unscrewed. The peaty smell of whisky rose up and Aimee took the ornate little bottle from his hand with a whispered 'Thank you'. She took two good gulps of the fiery liquid, feeling it burn a path down her throat to settle in her stomach with a warm, pleasant bloom.

She handed the flask back. 'What could have done that to those men, Francisco? I don't believe it was a jaguar.'

Francisco took a small sip of whisky himself and carefully screwed the crested lid back into place. He pursed his lips before responding, his perfectly trimmed silver moustache bunching at its center.

'I've never seen, or even heard of, such butchery, Dr. Weir, and I also find it hard to believe sane men were responsible. Even brutal torture could not inflict such damage. I also do not think a jaguar was responsible.' He paused. 'It is known that some of the drug dealers from the north keep tigers and bears as pets, and sometimes free them into the jungle when they tire of them. Even so, the creatures would have had to find their way through a lot of jungle; and besides, I think there was too much … anger in the attack for it to be an animal.' He sighed and rubbed the silver lid of the flask with his thumb before holding it out to her again.

'Will you send the men's remains home?' Aimee asked after taking another sip.

He shook his head without looking at her. 'Impossible – little will remain in a day or so. The jungle is very good at cleaning up after itself.'

THREE

Offutt Air Force Base, Nebraska; US Military Space Command

Colonel Jack Hammerson sat behind an oak desk the size of a small Buick and lifted the progress report on Captain Alex Hunter. He pinched his bottom lip between thumb and forefinger as he read the details.

Newly promoted to the rank of colonel, after fighting against it for months, Hammerson – or the Hammer as he was known friends and colleagues – was beginning to enjoy the new pay grade and larger office now that it was confirmed he would still have direct line of command over his beloved HAWCs. Colonel Hammerson had been in the military all his life. His rise to his current position had been largely due to a mix of intelligence, competence and ferocity in various Special Forces operations – first as a participant, then as a leader. The Hammer now headed up one of the most lethal and covert teams in the world: the elite Hotzone All-forces Warfare Commandos, or HAWCs for short – a select few drawn from the ranks of the Green Berets, Navy SEALS, Special Forces Alpha and the Rangers. When the HAWCs were deployed, the job got done, no matter how bloody or brutal. It was a tough unit, and there were very few functioning *old* HAWCs – Hammerson being an exception. Most lasted fewer than five years – usually rotated out before psychological burnout, or their good luck came to a sudden end and they finished up as an unidentified corpse in a bloody hotspot somewhere on the globe.

Hammerson's eyes traveled back and forth over the charts, images and small print of the report and gave a half-smile. Its subject, Captain Alex Hunter, was one of his most experienced HAWCs and by far the most mystifying. The young man hadn't so much been born for the job as manufactured for it by circumstances. Alex Hunter had been changed, and Hammerson had authorized it personally. The genesis had been an assassin's bullet; comatose, with the bullet buried in an inoperable position in the center of his skull, Hunter looked to be heading for an existence dependent on artificial respirators and feeding tubes, immobile and unresponsive, until his once giant frame transformed to a living cadaver before their eyes. Hammerson owed his life a hundred times over to taking risks, and he had taken one with Alex Hunter. The secretive USSTRATCOM Medical Division, or UMD, had been testing a new treatment that was years away from human trials. A chemical restorative that had the potential to get soldiers back on their feet and able to keep fighting while they were literally being blown to pieces. The new batch had been ready for testing, but no one expected it to work.

Hammerson had hoped it would at least give Alex some sort of life; perhaps assist in a basic form of recuperation. But within weeks of the treatment starting, he got a call: Alex Hunter was awake. But there was more: he was awake ... and *well*.

Preliminary scans had shown that his brain had dealt with the trauma by enfolding the bullet and rerouting blood to sections of his brain that science categorised as unused or unknown. Over time, the changes had become more significant. Hunter's brain had begun to increase its neocortical mass by refolding along both sides of his interhemispheric fissures. His body changed too: normal cells acted more like stem cells; and his chemical engine room went off the scale, producing natural steroids, adrenalin and interferons on demand. His system was like a biological powerplant.

Alex Hunter had been returned to life – but as a different kind of being. He had been wounded and broken a hundred times, and each time he emerged stronger, more powerful, than ever. Captain Hunter was now a project; a secret file codenamed 'the Arcadian'.

The treatments had continued even after Alex's recovery from the initial trauma; UMD had convinced Hammerson that stopping would risk a total regression to his former vegetative state. But with further treatment came further change. Alex developed new abilities – some, perhaps, that evolution had allowed to dull in mankind through its immersion in modern life. Others that may never have been meant to become apparent for another millennium.

At first, Hammerson had been delighted by the strength, speed and enhanced mental acuity his young HAWC had displayed. However, the more Alex changed, the more Hammerson became aware that the UMD regretted returning him to the HAWCs. Attempts to create another Arcadian subject had failed. After several years, Alex was looking more like an accident – a perfect collision of physical change caused by the bullet trauma and biological enhancement through the treatments. Individually, either may have resulted in nothing but coma or death; together, they had turned a dying man into something unbelievable.

Jack Hammerson had been around long enough to save a few hides and develop a circle of friends in very high places. Through bullying and bargaining, he had been able to keep Alex in the field. But the deal was not infinite, and UMD were impatient for their prize. Hammerson had been told Hunter had one more year until he was to be … retired.

Bastards, Hammerson thought as he flipped another page of the report. *Trying to engineer reasons to pull him in early, aren't you, you sons of bitches.*

He ran his eyes down the diagnostics on Alex's alpha, beta and delta waves, and the summary that was included below. He rubbed his brow and compressed his lips for a second; there were those words again: 'lethal instability'. It seemed that Alex Hunter's heightened brain activity had a price: the cyclone of electrical impulses occasionally triggered hurricanes of rage that were physically terrifying. Alex had learnt to master the rages through psychological conditioning, using his conscious strength to contain and even focus his furious impulses. But deep down within the man, there was no control. When that subconscious boiled up and ran free, Alex Hunter became potentially lethal. Another phrase caught the Hammer's eye: 'psychopathic potential'.

Not everything goes to plan, he thought as he exhaled and closed the report, asking the empty room: 'Who will win, Alex? You or the furies?'

He rubbed his eyes hard with a thumb and finger. He couldn't keep lying to the soldier forever, and damned if he was going to let them cut him up in some military lab.

He blinked a couple of times to refocus, and picked up the next folder. It was titled 'Operation Green Shield – Eyes Only', dated and time-stamped just hours ago. He took out a small disc and pushed it into the sleek computer on his desk. The image on the screen – the lightning bolts and fisted gauntlet of the US Strategic Command – dissolved as the hard drive accessed the information, and the menu for the operation dropped down. Hammerson selected the overview to read.

Seemed the friendly government in Paraguay had discovered an enormous gas field with a potential 50 trillion cubic feet of natural gas a few miles below its surface. It would make the small country one of the region's energy superpowers. They were planning to extract the resource and pipe it to the coast, where it could be sold into a fuel-hungry world economy. Good news for America, as the friendly relationship meant trading would be open, honest and long term. Good news for America, but obviously bad news for some of the less friendly neighbours, like Venezuela, Bolivia and a half dozen others that had tried to claim that the gas bed extended under their own country's borders. When this was proved false in the international courts, a different kind of pressure was exerted. Bandits had been disrupting drilling, and when the bodies began to pile up, Paraguay had asked for help – first from a team of energy experts to assist with the identification and rapid extraction of the gas, and then recently for something a little more covert and muscular.

It was a typical political–military skirmish situation. The rebels could strike and run; if they retreated across the border into a neighbouring country, then the Paraguayan troops couldn't follow. The USA had regular army bases down in South America, but for domestic political purposes it couldn't be seen in any way to be governing, co-opting or even influencing the gas-bed economics. Worse would be to deploy an active ground troop operation within another foreign country – even if requested. Still way too much baggage after the Middle East for that. So the classified decision had been to deploy a small six-man unit of highly skilled Green Berets. Should have been more than enough to deal with a small rebel interaction … but that's where things got real strange.

Hammerson clicked on some audio transcripts from a Captain Michaels out in the field and turned up the volume. At first he thought he was hearing white noise, then recognized the sounds of the jungle – the hum of millions of insects and animals going about their hectic, crowded lives. And then, oddly, total silence, as if the jungle had held its breath. Hammerson frowned and turned up the volume, only to turn it back down quickly when the automatic gunfire rang out. After a few more seconds there was heavy breathing – either exertion or fear. The jungle slowly began its buzz again, before a man's voice could be heard – a barely coherent, hurried staccato. 'It's out there … it's coming back … we can't stop it.'

More gunfire, and a roar that immediately hushed all the noises of the jungle. Only the sound of the captain's swallowing and rapid breathing remained. Hammerson narrowed his eyes and listened intently. In those small sounds, he could sense the man's abject fear — the juddering breath, the slight wetness of the inhalations, as if his nose was running. He knew adrenalin was coursing through that body – fight or flight. *Come on, soldier, this is what you trained for,* he thought, willing the young man to pull himself together.

There was a tearing sound, then a thump that could have been a tree falling, and then a roar so loud that it made Jack Hammerson sit up in his seat. It was close, and followed by the panicked yell of the young captain. 'Anybody, if you're there – they're all dead. Come in … please, come in.' There was a pause and then what could have been sobbing.

Hammerson wished he was there. He knew battlefield panic – without someone taking immediate control, things would quickly go to shit. The sobbing stopped only to turn into a shout – 'This goddamn green hell!' – and then more gunfire. There was another roar, a grunt of pain and the sound of cloth or something soft being ripped, then nothing but the real white noise of severed communications.

The recording stopped and the menu reappeared. Hammerson's brow furrowed and he said angrily to the screen, 'What the fuck was that?'

The final menu item displayed was titled 'Current Operational Status'. Hammerson read it quickly; it was a brief information squirt from command: *All contact severed. Green team 1 assumed neutralized.*

An advanced VELA satellite had been redirected and, although it was partially blinded by the thick growth of the jungle, it had used its thermal, motion and energy signal scans to confirm no movement and no intact human heat signatures from the potential skirmish zone.

Thankfully, the local and American scientists and advisors were well away from the hotzone, but they would eventually need to enter it to continue drilling. Hammerson ran his eyes down the list of names and came to one he immediately recognized: Dr Aimee Weir – Independent Petrobiological Consultancy.

'Ohh, shit.'

The Hammer knew what was coming. When a squad like the Green Berets were taken out, you didn't just send in more GBs. Instead, you changed the extent or category of force. There were three options: one, send in about a hundred regular army with heavy ground support; two, burn the entire zone from 10,000 feet; or three, send in the HAWCs.

Hammerson also knew that once Alex Hunter found out Aimee was in a hotzone, nothing would stop him going in, with or without authorization. And if anything happened to Aimee down there, burning from 10,000 feet would have looked like the soft option.

He picked up the phone. He didn't need to dial, and the call was answered immediately. He spoke slowly, not taking his eyes off his computer screen. 'Find Captain Alex Hunter and get him in here, immediately.'

FOUR

Alex Hunter crouched at the tree line and sucked in a deep breath of pine-scented spring warmth. Using his hand as a shield, he squinted into the distance at the crystal, tumbling waters of the French Broad River – wouldn't be long before it had a fly fisherman or two in its shallows. Asheville this time of year was magnificent, and with the national park close by, a small population of folks who were more than happy to mind their own business, and plenty of white-tailed deer, elk and rabbit, it was a place where you could really live. And, if you wanted to, it was also a place you could get … lost. Perhaps that's why his mother had settled here after his father passed away. The property at the foot of the Black Mountains was a lot of acreage for one woman, two horses and an enormous German shepherd, but Alex guessed she was happy to let nature share it with her; if it decided to intrude from time to time, so be it.

Alex kept his eyes narrowed. Though the sun was behind him, he was a mile from the property and even his enhanced vision had trouble picking out the details. He pulled a small scope from his pocket and thumbed the resolution button. As he'd expected, his mother was on the front porch, a magazine open on her chest as she lay snoozing on her favorite swing bench. Her dog, Jess, lay in front of her – close by as always.

His mother looked content, peaceful – maybe a little grayer than he remembered, but otherwise no different. He wished he could talk to her. His father had been gone ten years now, and a few years back she had been told that Alex, her only son, had been killed on a mission overseas. She probably thought she had lost everyone, but she hadn't. Alex was very much alive, and every day he longed to tell her that she wasn't alone.

But it was impossible. After his accident, the treatment and his recovery, and the resulting physical and mental changes, his entire existence now belonged to Hammerson and the HAWCs. His fighting force was one of the most lethal and covert that had ever existed – they were ghosts. Hammerson once described them as 'cleaners' – someone makes a mess and the HAWCs clean it up before it gets any worse. No headlines or applause.

In Alex's line of work, friends were rare, but enemies were numerous. Enemies who would think nothing of wiping out an entire family if it meant an opportunity to bring pain, even indirectly, to a HAWC. His abilities made him nearly untouchable, but his mother …

He gazed at the sleeping woman and dog on the sunny porch, his face a mix of regret and resignation. While he was dead, she was safe.

The German shepherd waggled her ears to bat away an over-attentive bee and lifted her head. A bit more silver in the muzzle, but at about a hundred pounds of muscle still formidable enough to see off the largest intruder – four- or two-legged.

Look after her, Jess, Alex thought.

The dog raised her head and tested the air, then looked towards the tree line where Alex crouched. He froze, keeping his eyes on the house. His comm unit vibrated once in his pocket and he ignored it, but in another few seconds it double vibrated – urgent. He pulled the small silver box free. On its screen were just three letters: HIR.

Alex grunted: HAWC-Immediate-Recall. He melted back into the trees.

*

Alex listened to the recording in silence.

'Play it again,' he said, and this time he leaned in and closed his eyes.

Colonel Jack Hammerson sat back in his chair with his hands behind his head. 'Sounds like a grizzly attack.'

'Not a bear … not any animal. That sound came from a human throat.' Alex opened his eyes and looked at his superior officer, his face unreadable. 'It's not a language, Jack, or not one that I know of. Human vocal cords definitely produced it, but there's something wrong with the throat – it's warped somehow, or there's something stuck in it.'

Hammerson knew Alex's hearing was acute enough to pick up the super and subsonic ranges. If he said the noise came out of some guy's mouth, it did.

'Captain Michaels and the rest – we believe they're all dead. Something down there surprised them and took 'em all out – and that isn't easy to do to six heavily armed Green Berets.' Hammerson was sitting forward in his chair now, his fingers locked together.

'And now they want us to take a look?' Alex said.

Hammerson gave a humorless half-smile. 'Yes and no. I've requested this one, for a number of reasons. First, it's a critically important project for the USA, and as the whole region down there is a little anti-Uncle Sam we need to deal with this delicately – and be mindful of how others see us dealing with it. We can't park the seventh fleet off the coast of Brazil and fly low-altitude sorties over the jungle, or march 200 marines in there. Paraguay is a small pool of friendship in the midst of an ocean of distrust and aggravation – we have to respect their sovereignty and requests. At this point, they want us to help but to be delicate about it.'

Alex nodded. The rationale didn't really matter to him. If his friend and mentor asked him to lead a team into hell, he would oblige. 'I haven't caught up with the teams yet. I'll need to find out who's available. I'm not sure who's on base or still out in the field.'

Hammerson grinned. 'It's already done. I've pulled in Mak and Franks, and I believe Sam has just completed his rehabilitation. He's still sore, and probably needs another few weeks of physical therapy, but you know Sam – he'll be ready to go whenever we say.'

Alex nodded. 'What about Adira? She could be useful.'

Hammerson shook his head. 'Not ready yet, and I want to keep an eye on her for a bit longer. Just to make sure she's serving the HAWCs first; Mossad, and anyone else, after that. I think we both know she didn't join us because she wanted to be a HAWC.'

Alex raised his eyebrows. 'She says she's my guardian angel. She's not going to be happy to be left behind, Jack.'

Hammerson gave Alex a my-judgment-is final look. 'Team's picked. I'll deal with Captain Senesh. I agree it's not a big team, but after you find and neutralize what hit our GBs, it'll probably end up as a babysitting mission for a week or two.'

Alex chuckled. 'The last time you used the words *babysitting* and *mission* in the same sentence, we spent some interesting time under a certain southern ice cap being chased by something I still have nightmares about.' The smile fell away as Alex sensed something else behind his superior officer's rough features. 'What is it, Jack? You didn't have me pulled in from some downtime for a simple search and secure. What's the urgency? Wait a minute – you said *first.* What're the other reasons?'

Hammerson looked at Alex for a few moments, weighing what he should tell the young man and what he should hold back. He said slowly, 'Only one other reason, son.'

He pushed the Green Shield personnel folder across the desk for Alex to read, and saw his eyes stop where he'd expected.

Alex slid the folder back and stood up, his face like stone. 'Yes, I see. I need to go now.'

'Sit down. She's okay. I spoke to Alfred Beadman at GBR – you remember him? He tells me her job down there will be wrapped up in the next few weeks, and she's not in any danger. *But* I thought with her involved, you'd like to oversee this one personally. You leave in twenty-four hours.'

'Sir, I can *be there* in twenty-four hours.'

Alex began to pace the office and Hammerson could tell what was happening. He was feeling frustration, which would soon build to anger, and then … Hammerson knew he needed to bring him down, quickly.

'Sit down, soldier, that's an order. Beadman's talking to her daily, and I've recalibrated a VELA satellite so we can have a little look-see. You need to be —'

'No! We need to go in right now. She's in trouble – I can feel it.' One of Alex's hands had curled into a fist.

'Arcadian!'

At the shout of his codename, Alex stopped pacing, shook his head slightly and rubbed one of his temples. *Another headache, I bet*, thought Hammerson. He watched the HAWC for a few more moments, assessing him. He was on edge … volatile.

'When was your last visit to Medical Division?' he asked.

'Ah … three weeks ago. I'm due back again at the end of the month.'

Hammerson nodded. He had already known the answer before he'd asked the question. 'Anything interesting? What did Captain Graham have to say?'

Alex fell back into his chair and exhaled. 'Same as usual – the migraines should ease off eventually – nothing to worry about. Gave me some stronger codeine; some sedatives for the nights if I feel I need them.' He held up his hands in a brief gesture of resignation or weariness. 'He gave me some shots, took more blood, looked pleased with the latest scans of my brain – didn't say why. I asked again about the unusual physical manifestations, the accelerating extra-sensory symptoms. He thought they might slow down, stop or even reverse at any time. Said I should be patient.' Alex looked directly into Hammerson's eyes and gave him a lop-sided grin. He shook his head very slightly as he said, 'They're not slowing down, Jack. What happens if they never stop? What will I become?'

Hammerson sat in silence. He knew there was more the younger man wanted to say.

Alex rubbed one hand across his forehead, then back up through his hair. 'Fact is, I can take the pills, spend my nights in a drugged stupor, visit Medical once a month for the treatments, and every week something still changes inside me. I'm not sure I even remember what it's like to be normal anymore.'

Hammerson knew that Alex had been questioning his treatments for some time now. Many times he had asked for leave to get a second opinion – and every time he had been denied. Whatever was happening to Alex Hunter could never be discussed with anyone else, anytime, anywhere. That sort of information could cause someone to … disappear.

Hammerson also knew that Alex's relationship with Aimee had ended because of his physical and psychological changes; and the sight of her name on that list had obviously made the raw memories come flooding back. Normally the Hammer wouldn't give a damn for any of his soldiers' relationships – they rarely lasted anyway; after all, who wanted to date someone who couldn't tell them what they did, where they went, and sometimes came home all busted up … or not at all? Aimee Weir had been different. She knew about Alex, and had seen firsthand what he was capable of. Hammerson doubted she'd ever stopped loving Alex, but she couldn't bear knowing that eventually he was likely to hurt someone outside of the job, maybe even kill them. She had blamed Hammerson, as Alex's commander, and had called Alex 'Hammerson's Frankenstein monster'. *If only she knew how close that description comes to being fact*, he thought now.

'I think I really should get a second opinion,' Alex was saying. 'Even another military doc would do. Look, Jack, what happens if we stop the treatments … just for, say, three months? If something started to go wrong, anything, I'd tell you immediately. I give you my word.' Alex held out one open hand, as though offering something to Hammerson.

Hammerson knew Alex was prepared to take a risk on ending up back in a coma, but he wasn't. All that would achieve would be to shorten his time to the dissection table – and Hammerson was miles away from allowing that to ever happen. He wasn't so worried about what Alex would eventually become, or longer-term effects. His concern was that he knew the Medical Division had other, more finite plans for his soldier.

'A second opinion? Not necessary, son. I know Bob Graham – he's the best there is. I trust him, and so should you. He saved your life, Alex. I've seen the medical data; without the treatments, you know damn well you could lapse back into a coma, or die.' He sat forward. 'Is that what you want?'

'No …'

'Do you think that's what Aimee would want?'

'No.'

Hammerson hated himself for his manipulation of Alex. Fact was, he already knew what Aimee wanted: a second medical opinion for Alex – one not influenced by the military. But he had played this game with Alex before; and he would continue to play it for as long as was necessary.

'Believe me when I say this, Alex: I understand the changes could slow and uniformity may be regained. You could be back to normal, be —'

'NO!'

Alex leapt to his feet, his fist raised. He brought it down like a sledgehammer on the edge of Hammerson's heavy oak desk, shearing off a large chunk.

Hammerson sat immobile, looking at the damage to the thick wood, then back up to his soldier. Alex slowly raised his hand, showing the smashed knuckles and broken metacarpal bones. As Hammerson watched, the skin moved as the bones slid beneath the flesh. The knuckles popped back into place, and Alex flexed his fingers – good as new.

'Back to normal, Jack? Is that really what you believe?' Alex looked into Hammerson's eyes and held them.

The colonel knew Alex was trying to read him. He cleared his mind, kept his face impassive, didn't breathe or even swallow. He just waited.

Alex's brow furrowed and he dropped his gaze. He sank back down into his chair. 'Sorry, it's not your fault. I guess I'm just … not … thinking clearly …' He trailed off.

Hammerson exhaled and felt a bead of perspiration run down beside his ear. 'It's okay, Alex; you'll be fine. You're getting the best medical assistance in the world. Just go with it for now. The aggression is being monitored, and your physical capabilities have meant you've been able to save a hell of a lot of lives. Think of it as a gift, not a curse.'

Alex nodded slowly. 'A gift.' He kept his eyes on the floor.

Hammerson watched him for a second longer. 'Hunter: focus.' Alex nodded his acknowledgment and Hammerson went on. 'You and the team need to be terrain ready. We've got some new kit for you. Go and check on the team, then report back at ...' He looked at his watch; it was just after midday. 'Fifteen hundred.' He handed Alex the folder and the computer disc. 'See if there's anything else you can learn. Dismissed.'

'Fifteen hundred, confirmed.'

Alex saluted and went out the door. He still hadn't looked his commanding officer in the eye. Hammerson wondered what Alex was thinking. After a few seconds, he lifted the phone and pressed one of the speed-dial numbers. He was immediately connected to USSTRATCOM's Research and Development division.

'I'll be sending four down for some light suits, and I'll also want an ice gun prepped.' Hammerson listened for a few seconds, his teeth grinding as he looked at the damage to his desk. 'Son, I'm not in a negotiating mood right now. Just have a portable unit ready for demonstration. Out.'

He hung up without a goodbye, and sat with his hand on the phone for another second. He lifted the receiver again and spoke softly. 'Have First Lieutenant Samuel Reid come to my office.'

He sat staring ahead for a few moments before leaning back in his chair and groaning. 'Hunter's not going to thank me for this.'

FIVE

Ramón Reyes brought his blade down again. He and his cousin, Hector, had been struggling through the Paraguayan jungle's mad tangle of vegetation, slashing with heavy machetes to clear the wrist-thick vines that blocked their path. Their soiled T-shirts and mud-streaked pants were already wet with perspiration, and both had plant debris and insects stuck in the streaks of sweat that ran down their faces.

Ramón stopped to lean against a tree and wondered whether his large cousin was as fatigued as he was. The drilling shutdown had left the men bored, and while most of them were content to play cards, listen to football on radios, or argue, Hector had seen it as an opportunity to explore – he always liked to explore.

He hadn't told Ramón what he was looking for, but each afternoon, Hector had dragged him along a new quadrant of his compass, and together they had hacked for hours out, and just as many back; each time returning with little more than strained shoulders, and new and more painful insect bites.

Ramón muttered under his breath. Ever since they were small boys, he had done what his bigger and older cousin had told him. One day it would get him into trouble, for sure.

'How much further?' Ramón called now, blowing sweat from his upper lip. 'I'm tired.'

Hector stopped chopping vines and turned to shrug. He pulled a canteen from his rear pocket, unscrewed it, swirled some of the brackish water around his mouth and spat it out. 'Hour, maybe more.' He looked at his cousin from under lowered brows. 'You have somewhere you need to be, Ramón?'

Ramón shrugged in return. 'Just mindful of the evening coming.'

Hector replaced his canteen and withdrew a small brass compass, flipped its lid up, swiveled on his heel for a few seconds until he must have felt he had his bearings, then snapped the lid closed. He looked above his head, obviously seeing what Ramón had – the setting sun was turning the jungle a burnt orange as it fell towards the horizon. Twilight's purple wave would catch them soon, along with the mosquitoes.

He looked back at Ramón, and then dipped his hands into his front pockets, replacing the compass in one, and pulling a small plastic bottle from another. He uncapped it and tapped a small mound of white powder onto the back of his hand. He pushed his hand under his cousin's nose. 'Sniff. C'mon – for energy.'

Many of the men in the camp used cocaine. Some for fun, others to relieve boredom, and some, like his cousin, to be able to keep working long after others had given up. Ramón shrugged and inhaled hard through his nose – a punch of light almost kicked his head backwards. Immediately he felt warm, hot, horny … and less fatigued. He smiled, and then laughed.

Hector licked the remains from the back of his hand, and smiled back. 'Okay, just a few more miles. *Vamos.*'

More hacking, more bites, and then Hector vanished from Ramón's sight. When Ramón caught up, he found his cousin standing in a clearing, hands on his hips, sucking in long breaths and staring in awe at the sight before him.

'*Santa Madre de Dios,*' Ramón said softly, slowly shaking his head as he saw what held Hector spellbound.

A giant banyan tree held in its titanic embrace an old stone building that looked like a church. The tree's muscular roots had grown over most of the building, and flowed down from its peripheral limbs to create a hanging curtain effect over the back and sides of the stone structure. The wooden doors must have rotted away long ago, but a black opening was just visible at the top of a few stone steps behind the hanging root screen. Along the ground a long crack zigzagged across the dry clearing towards the building, split the steps, and continued on up in through the dark aperture.

'The lost church of the Jesuits – it must be,' said Hector. Trancelike, he walked slowly forward in the twilight. 'At last, we have some luck.'

'It cannot be possible; it's just a myth,' Ramón whispered.

All Latin Americans knew the legend of the lost Church of the Jesuits. It was believed that after the fall of Vilcabamba, the last hidden city of the Incan empire, the ruler, Tupac Amaru, had ordered his people to carry the last treasures of his empire off into the jungle so that the Gold-Eaters – the Incan name for the Spanish invaders – could never feast on his wealth.

Ramón raked his mind for more of the ancient story. According to the legend, the Incan gold and jewels had been moved around for decades, before being either buried or taken in and finally being hidden, in the 1600s, by some priests in the basement of their church. Like most of the Jesuits that marched into the jungle between 1600 and 1750, they disappeared, along with their church, or any record of where it might have been. The missing church was rumored to contain an underground vault that held something so fantastic; it would surely outshine even the boy king's tomb in Egypt.

Hector marched forward quickly, and Ramón had to scamper to keep up with his larger cousin's longer strides. Getting behind the structure was impossible, as the enormous trunk of the tree engulfed the back of the church and extended deep into the thick jungle. It seemed it was the only thing that dared put its roots down into the unusually dry soil around the ruined structure.

Both men threaded their way through the hanging tree roots, ducking below spiderwebs that, judging by the size of the dried corpses hanging within them, had been built by creatures strong enough to capture birds and small animals. Eventually they stood before the black doorway. Hector reached out with his long-bladed machete to drag aside a particularly thick web. As he did so, something scuttled away from his blade into the tangle of roots above the door. Ramón hoped it was a rat; the thought of a fist-sized spider dropping onto his neck made his stomach quiver.

'Look at this.' Hector was pointing at some carved writing beside the door. 'It says something about gold, I think … *debajo de … la flor de oro* – what is that? "Below" or maybe "beneath the golden flower". What does it mean, do you think?'

Ramón shook his head and dusted the carving with his fingers. 'I think it is *cuidado debajo de … la flor de oro* – "*beware* below the golden flower".' He grinned, satisfied with his improved translation, even though they were no clearer on its meaning.

His smile evaporated when Hector motioned with one hand for him to go first into the dark hole. He looked left and right, trying to think of an excuse, but none came to him. His heartbeat, already speeded up from the powder Hector had given him, leapt again. Ramón reached inside his shirt and pulled free a small gold crucifix on a slim chain. He held the sweat-slicked cross to his lips for a second, then looked quickly at Hector, who nodded and tilted his head towards the opening. Ramón hesitated a moment before ducking under the web-matted vines.

'Give me the flashlight,' he said. 'It is too dark; I can't see.'

Hector grunted impatiently, sheathed his machete and pulled free the medium-sized axe hanging from his belt. He spent the next few minutes chopping away the roots that hung over the doorway. This, combined with the angle of the setting sun, allowed weak illumination into the building.

This time, Hector followed Ramón inside.

The floor was littered with broken clay tiles, probably from the roof, which had been replaced by a ceiling of massive tree trunk. Its heavy, gray body looked like a living thing, Ramón thought, with coiled, gray-brown muscles just waiting to unwind and drop down upon them.

'Look here.' Ramón pointed at a huge slab of granite propped at the wall just inside the doorway. In the dark, a bearded face carved into the stone could just be made out, its features almost lost to the gloom.

Hector sighed with approval. 'One of the Jesuits maybe – God bless you *padre.*' He patted the image and then moved ahead into the dark space behind a heavy screen of root fibers, calling to Ramón, 'Come quickly, *amigo,* I've found something.'

He stood before a waist-high blackened dome that had been toppled from a once finely carved slab of stone split by the recent earth tremor's crack, and strangely, its two halves slid many feet apart. When he tapped the dark shape with the iron head of his axe, it responded with a deep metallic *bong* that vibrated the air around them.

'The golden flower maybe … or perhaps a golden bell?' he said.

He flipped his axe blade around and chopped at the bell, first at one place then another. It was no use: the metal was hard; too hard to be valuable. Ramón grimaced; he knew that even the lowest grade of gold would have yielded to his cousin's blade.

Hector kicked the bell, eliciting a duller peal. '*Mierda!* Must be fucking brass.'

Ramón turned his machete blade sideways to scrape the side of the metal, removing a six-inch crust of oxidation and ancient soot. It seemed the bell had been in a fire at some point. Underneath, the brass shone through, reflecting the weakening light from outside back at him.

'At one time it would have *looked* golden,' he said. 'But not worth anything now, unless you have friends at the museum.'

'*Bastardo!*' Hector kicked out at the bell.

The loud curse in the small tomb-silent room made Ramón jump, and he took a step back as his cousin muttered more profanities, looking like he wanted to hit something else. He lunged at the large bell, grabbing it and tugging savagely, causing it to roll a few feet. Hector moved around behind the solid dome and put his shoulder to it, and grunted. The bell rolled some more, grinding small stones to powder beneath its rim, before picking up speed as the large man gave it one last push.

Ramón expected it to stop there, but instead it kept rolling, out through the opening and into the clearing, where it settled heavily in the dry soil. The movement shook loose centuries of oxidisation to reveal the bell's golden hue in places.

Hector stared at the path the bell had taken, breathing in loudly through his nose and exhaling through gritted teeth. His noisy breathing suddenly broke off and he clicked his fingers, looking at Ramón with his eyes wide. 'Not the bell; it's not *the bell* – remember the words outside? It was *below* the bell we needed to look.' He brought the beam of his flashlight back to the floor, and traced the path of the rolling dome.

The circle of light waved back and forth, and then came to a sudden stop. 'Oh, *gracias Jesús.*' Hector took a few steps and then went to his knees, keeping his light on the object in the ground. 'A door.'

Ramón stood back and watched as his cousin laid his flashlight on the ground and used one large hand to brush away loose debris. He grimaced at the thought of climbing down somewhere that could be even darker than where they were.

'Remember there was also a warning outside,' Ramón said. 'I think we should come back with some more men … and also maybe in daylight.'

Hector curled his lip in a sneer. 'What are you afraid of, *estúpido*? Look, there might be nothing under here but more tree roots, or the graves of the Jesuits. Or it could be something more – something that could make you, me, our families, richer than a Hollywood movie star. Forget about the stupid words outside – every ancient treasure room in history had some sort of warning or curse written somewhere. It's a good sign – there must be something down there they wanted to keep people away from.'

Hector reached out to take a swipe at Ramón's thigh. 'There are no real curses or evil eyes, *amigo*, no horn-headed beasts, or devil-demons. Unless you count the ones you've seen after too much sangria.' Hector smiled disarmingly. 'Now come on and help me.'

Ramón shook his head as if clearing away his moment of indecision, and took another step forward. 'All right, I'll help you. But you are wrong, *Señor Ignorante*. There are bad things in this world; things my mother has told me about. I just wish she was here with us now.'

On his knees, Hector clapped his hands once and waved Ramón over. He motioned to the other side of the door, and finished brushing away debris.

Ramón looked at the square trapdoor with a large metal ring at one end. In the beam of light from the flashlight, he could see the crack running across the stone blocks in the floor, halting at the door, and then continuing on after the wooden frame once again. He frowned for a second in puzzlement, as the door didn't carry the patina of age that the surrounding stonework did, and his eyes moved to the large slab that was broken and shoved aside.

Hector grabbed the light and held it up. 'You pull.' He pointed the beam of light and waited.

Ramón reached down with one hand and took hold of the ring. He immediately dropped it, and held his hand up to his face, to check his fingers. They were wet with something slick and slightly greasy. He sniffed, and only detected a hint of something salty and metallic. *Rust and grease maybe*, he thought and wiped his hand, getting ready to try again, when Hector barged him out of the way.

'Too heavy for you little cousin? Let me.' Hector spat on his hands and grinned in the dark. 'There must be a hidden room underneath us. This is it, *amigo*: prepare to be rich.'

He hunched over the trapdoor and pulled on the ring with two hands. Nothing happened. He grunted, invoked the names of several saints, and strained. Still nothing. He changed position, counted three deep breaths and yanked quickly. The trapdoor groaned against the floor's stone edges and then rose an inch. Hector stood up, pressed his hands into the small of his back, cursed softly, then bent back to his task. With the next tug, the door squealed open, and he let the heavy wooden square drop back flat against the ground. A set of steps led down into the blackness below.

Hector flung himself down on the floor and looked into the pit. Ramón stood back slightly, reluctant to get too close to the black hole. The inside edges of the opening were abraded, as if they had been scratched by some great beast, and he could see that the bottom of the trapdoor was also covered in the same deep gouges. He reached out his hand and spread his fingers, placing them in some of the ancient grooves – they fit almost perfectly. He frowned for a moment, then shrugged and went back to straining his eyes down into the darkness.

Hector snatched up the flashlight and extended his arm down into the pit. Ramón took a few steps closer but couldn't bring himself to lie down and look over its edge. There was a smell, a feeling … *something strange*, he thought.

Hector slid the weak yellow beam across as much of the vault as he could see from his limited angle of vision.

'There's something down there,' he said. 'I think it's gold. I knew it, *amigo* – we've found the treasure room.' He scrambled to his feet and stepped onto the stone staircase. 'Well? Are you coming?'

Ramón shook his head and rubbed the cross around his neck again. 'I'll keep a lookout. Come back and tell me what you find.'

'Okay, but remember: *La suerte favorece a los valientes.'*

Hector laughed at his own wit and started down into the thick darkness.

*

The small stone-lined room seemed to absorb the torchlight, giving nothing back in return. Hector moved quickly, as much by feeling as by his limited sight, to the golden object he had glimpsed from above. He pulled it free from several inches of what looked like flakes of mud and dried fruit skins. As he broke the crust, a pungent odor rose up, like a ripe fungus.

The golden object was a crucifix. Hector held it up and squinted at it in the weak light – the arms had been bent and screwed up like wadded paper, and the body of Christ nailed to its center was crushed flat. He was glad Ramón had remained upstairs – he would have taken the deformed crucifix as a bad sign. He tested its weight in his hand and shook his head. It was too light to be made of a precious metal, and there were no significant stones anywhere on its surface.

'Jesuit rubbish!'

He flung it to the ground and continued his search, waving the flashlight from side to side and squinting into the darkness. The room looked to be empty, except for a skeletal body propped up in a corner, covered in some sort of black webbing. In the weak light, it looked moist and greasy – almost as if it was still putrefying. Hector approached the remains and his brow furrowed. The head looked wrong; the jaws and teeth were misshapen. He brought his light closer and thought he could just make out something in its skull, something that quivered when the weak beam touched it. *A mouse?* he wondered as he leaned in to peer between the jaws.

Something swivelled and repositioned itself, shivering in reaction to the movement or light. Hector reached for his blade, intending to poke it at the small moving creature. When he looked back, the thing had shifted again – he could see it clearly now, and it wasn't a mouse, or anything he recognized.

He grunted in distaste and used the blade to pry open the jaws.

In an explosion of movement, the thing launched itself at Hector's face.

*

Hector's scream blasted up out of the dark, causing the small hairs on Ramón's neck to stand upright.

'*Madra Dios!* Hector? Hector, answer me!'

Ramón sucked in a deep breath and lifted the small crucifix to his mouth, placing it between his lips to hold it there. *He must have fallen, or got stuck in something. He must be hurt. That must be it … that must be all.*

He edged closer to the pit and called to his cousin again. There was no sound but his own rapid breathing. He peered down the staircase and saw a weak yellow beam across the floor – not moving and low down. Hector must have dropped the flashlight.

Mierda; there was no choice – he would have to go down.

Ramón crossed himself twice and put one foot onto the first step, hesitated, then silently inched down the remaining steps. At the bottom, the ground was soft and spongy. He called again, but in a whisper, as if fearful of being overheard. It was hard to judge the size of the room in the blackness, but his voice bounced back in a cramped echo, suggesting it was fairly small. Still no response. He couldn't understand it. There was nowhere for his cousin to go, unless he had found another way out. He must be in here somewhere.

Ramón picked up the flashlight and edged along the wall towards the back corner. There was a mound there; maybe Hector was behind it. His foot touched something hard. He bent to see what it was: some kind of book. He pulled it free of the crusted floor and rubbed away some of the black sticky substance that coated its thick leather cover. There was a gold-leaf crucifix on the front, but no title. *A Bible perhaps?* He tucked it under his arm and waved the flashlight around again. The gouges he had seen above were more pronounced down here: deep furrows in the wall and ceiling stones, as if some great beast had been clawing at its enclosure.

Like it was trapped here.

He blinked away the frightening thought and brought the beam back to the strange lump.

'Hector? Is that you? Are you hurt?'

His hushed tones seemed unnaturally loud in the small space. His steps got shorter, his feet seeming to deny him the forward motion his brain requested. He stretched out his arm instead, holding out the light. Even with its beam directed on the mound, he still couldn't make sense of what he was seeing. The mass seemed to move and glisten in the flickering flame – *something covered in moss, perhaps*, he thought.

He took another step and saw his cousin's mud-streaked pants just showing from under the sticky-looking lump. The whole pile looked unclean and he was loath to reach out and touch whatever it was, so he stepped to the side and crouched, extending the flashlight as far as he could. There was definite movement – the thing shifted. He could see now. His cousin was curled up on the ground, a grotesque black figure crouched over him, pressing its face into his, as if kissing him deeply. But this was no gentle caress; instead Ramón could see rows of needle-sharp teeth hooked into Hector's cheeks, while long skeletal fingers restrained him. As Ramón watched in horror, he saw his cousin blink once, very slowly, as if the effort of the tiny movement was almost beyond him.

The glistening skeletal head seemed to burrow further into Hector's face. Ramón could see rivulets of red running over the thing's bony mass, as though its veins and tendons were filling with the life fluids it was sucking from his cousin's rapidly thinning body.

There came a scream so loud it hurt Ramón's ears. Only when his throat rasped with strain did he realize the sound was emanating from his own mouth. He stopped himself, not wanting to draw the creature's attention, and instead moved his cold lips in prayer. But it was too late. The monster stopped its revolting sucking and detached its head from Hector.

Ramón saw something slither back between the thing's jaws as the long face swung towards him. Hot wetness splashed his groin as his bladder released in revulsion and fear. He fell backwards and scrambled on his back along the floor to the steps, his hands still clutching the book. The flashlight remained where he had dropped it, casting a yellow halo over the monstrosity in the corner.

The creature rose up, pieces of wet blackness falling from its frame as it flexed strings and bulges of flesh that were becoming muscles and skin. *We need you*, it said, its voice dry and dispassionate, and sounding not in the room but within his mind.

Ramón hit the steps with his lower back, ignoring the pain. The thing moved out of the light and was now invisible in the darkness. Ramón edged up the steps, trying to pray, but only small squeaks came from his dry throat. He held the book up in front of him, brandishing its gold-leaf crucifix like a shield.

His head breached the rim of the pit. He scrabbled his way out, then turned and ran.

It took him hours to find his way back to the mining camp. Once there, he did not speak of what he had seen. Who would believe him? He had no proof – he had dropped the book during his flight. Besides, it had probably been a hallucination; a result of the powder his cousin had given him. There was no ruined church, no foul beast lurking below it in its lair. He had simply got lost in the jungle and wandered until he had come upon the camp again. And Hector? He would turn up. He always did like to go out exploring on his own.

SIX

Aimee sat quietly in the shade of the stretched canvas sheet that was doing little to block out the pervasive humidity. Her eyes followed the activity of the men as each worked smoothly, but noisily: changing pipe segments, calibrating penetration force or drill speed, or simply yelling out data to Alfraedo on the other side of the platform.

Her stomach roiled from the impatience she felt over the time it was taking to break through into the deep cavern, and also from the images of the ruined bodies just past the jungle's edge. She thought she could still smell a hint of the ripped and torn flesh as it sat slowly baking in the sun and heat, and a tiny shot of bile hit the back of her throat; wishing she could have another sip of Francisco's whisky, she swallowed hard.

Aimee grimaced when the acidic taste refused to leave her mouth, and began searching for the small doctor just as the background noise of the drill thumped, startling her, before taking on a smoother sound for a second or two, then stopping as its rotational brakes were applied.

A shout went up from the rig foreman – they had broken through into the gas chamber.

Aimee got to her feet. Her stomach still threatened more discomfort, but she was thankful for some action at last. She strode a few feet closer, but had been cautioned to keep her distance from the heavy machinery while it was being operated, and settled for hovering just behind the workers and their furious exertions.

The drill head had to be carefully extracted and the toothed bit drawn back up inside the drill shaft. It was a tense procedure: the pipe remained sealed, but with trillions of cubic feet of gas under thousands of pounds of pressure, any mistake could be disastrous – causing either an explosion that would crush hundreds of feet of expensive pipe, or destabilization and fissuring around the penetration site resulting in gas leakage over a huge area.

Aimee paced back and forth while the last few hundred feet of pipe were withdrawn from the well. Finally, the end hissed free in a white cloud of raw gas and micro-fragments scraped from the walls of the shaft. She held her breath – primitive gas contained sulfur, methane and a number of other revolting-smelling compounds that always made her imagine dinosaurs farting.

Ignoring the warning that she should stay well clear of the drill zone, she pushed forward. She had to get the encrusted drill tip before surface bacteria contaminated it. What she sought came from an environment so different from their own that it might as well have been from another planet – so fragile that it could be destroyed on contact with the air. Assuming there was even anything there in the first place …

*

Ramón used a twenty-pound wrench to unscrew the drill bit, then let it drop gently onto a padded sheet so the soil and rock caught in its teeth wouldn't shake free.

He stood and rolled his shoulders – his whole body was sore and he had a headache. He hadn't slept properly since his trip into the jungle, and he was tired – deathly so. Nightmares continued to boil away his sleep at night, and his cousin, Hector, hadn't returned. Still Ramón refused to take seriously the dark images that filled his dreams; to accept them as real memories, rather than some sort of drug-induced hallucination – to do that, would surely lead to madness.

The American woman stood behind him, watching his every move. She was attractive enough, but not his type; like most foreign women, she was too tall and much too aggressive.

The encrusted drill head glistened darkly in the sunlight, like the feathers of a water bird fouled by an oil slick. Ramón lifted it in his thick rigging gloves and held it out to the woman. She looked pleased, but refused to take it in her hands. Instead, she asked him to return it to the sheet and make a kind of carrying sack by lifting the fabric's edges, so it could be moved to her tent office.

After Ramón had placed the sheet and its contents on the small folding table, the woman said something to Doctor Herrera, who then turned to Ramón.

'Please get some new gloves, Ramón,' he said. 'There could be contaminants on that pair now.'

Ramón nodded and walked away, pulling off first one glove, then using his bare hand to remove the other. Black, oily sludge now stained his fingers.

*

Aimee scraped a tiny speck of the glistening debris onto a glass slide before placing the drill tip in a clear isolation box. With experienced hands, she added a few drops of demineralized water to the sample and placed it under the lens of a high-power microscope. Then she unwound a small length of cable and inserted one end into a free port on her computer; the other end fitted neatly into the back of the microscope. Aimee clicked an icon that informed her the scope was successfully connected, and immediately her screen expanded to show a seething gray ocean of microbial life. She grinned and punched the air – success! It was exactly what she had been hoping for: living bacteria from a primordial gas chamber deep beneath the earth.

In among the whirling, flicking and spinning life, flecks of silver shimmered. Aimee recognized the material immediately: iridium. *Must be where the K-T layer extended in this region*, she thought. She had come across the mineral many times in her work. The rare substance was in abundance in two places that she knew of: the first place was a thin sedimentary layer that dated back over 65 million years and separated the Cretaceous and Mesozoic eras; a global skin that separated humans from the dinosaurs. The theory was that iridium was the pulverised remains of a massive meteor strike – which was where the second common form was found: in meteors, meteorites and astral bodies that made Earth landfall.

Aimee moved on from the mineral to the microscopic animals that crowded the screen. She clicked her mouse to create a square border around them, then enlarged and rotated the captured images. Many she was able to identify as well-known, simple anaerobic life forms, but others … they refused to fit into any recognisable categories. She was sure she'd seen something like them before – long spherical bacteria in chains – but not from miles below the ground.

She suspended another image on the screen and scrolled down to the description box, her cursor blinking at her as she sat thinking for a moment. She remembered Alfred's words about the bacteria being a potential key, then smiled and typed: *Clavicula occultus*; Latin for 'hidden key'. *And hopefully that's what you might be*, she thought as she added a standard taxonomic descriptor for spherical bacterium.

She flipped back to the live images and was surprised to see that some of the chains had increased slightly in size. *Hmm, hungry little fellows, aren't you?*

She continued to examine the bacterial life forms for a while, their shape nagging at her memory. Finally, she saved the images and shut down her computer. She'd know more after she ran some tests back at the camp.

She smiled again, her earlier dark memories and fears swept away by the realization that she may have hit upon an inexpensive, and limitless, source of fuel for the world. *Today is a good day for mankind*, she thought.

*

Ramón was having the strangest dream of his life. He was in a black pit full of twinkling stars – pinpoints of light that landed on him like angel dust and tickled his skin. His hands were the most thickly covered, and they wouldn't work. He felt as light as a feather, but just as weak.

He came awake slowly, as though rising through water to break the surface on a gloomy landscape. His nose was running into his mouth and the taste was strange, like dirt and tar. He tried to sit up in the dark tent, moving quietly so his three companions would not waken – all were bigger than Ramón and would not take kindly to being roused unnecessarily after a long day's work and an early start the following morning. But he couldn't move his arms to place them on the ground. The darkness was velvet black and made it impossible to see even outlines. Still, he knew something was terribly wrong: his arms didn't just feel numb, they felt … gone.

The tingling sensation turned to pinpricks of fire and he knew he was going to have to wake his co-workers. He would risk their harsh words or blows; he just needed to ensure he was okay.

'*José, lo siento,*' he called softly into the dark, beginning to sob as he felt the prickling sensation moving to his shoulders. He called again, a little louder. 'José.'

This time he was answered by a grunt in the dark, then a deep and sleepy voice beside him. '*Qué quieres, Ramón?*'

Ramón sobbed out his request for light.

The larger man swore softly under his breath and reached for the mud-caked flashlight they kept near the door of the tent. A small click and the beam lit Ramón up like a ghastly performer on a stage.

Jose's scream was high and piercing and immediately wrenched the other two men from their sleep. On seeing Ramón, all three pressed themselves to the back of the tent.

Ramón's body was coated in a black oily mucus that ran from every orifice in his body, even from the very pores of his skin. The most shocking aspect was his upper limbs – or lack of them. At his shoulders were dripping stumps. The wounds weren't bloody and ragged, as would be expected if the arms had been hacked off by a knife. Instead, the limbs were frayed, as though something had dissolved them into a tattered mess. As the men watched, a piece of gray-black flesh fell away from Ramón's shoulder and plopped into the pool beside him, melting away like butter in a hot pan.

Ramón's vision was clouding, but he could see the horror on the men's faces and knew it must be bad. He tried one last time to sit up, but all he managed was to rock forward a few inches and then flop back down, splashing into the pool of viscous liquid that surrounded him. It splattered the other men and they cried out in disgust, holding damp sheeting or clothing over their lower faces.

Ramón sobbed and turned his face to the canvas roof to pray, his voice now a wet, guttural sound. He coughed, and a plume of dark spray flew from his throat and swirled around inside the tent.

His three colleagues had seen enough. They fell over each other as they scrambled outside, screaming for the medic as if the devil himself had appeared to them.

*

By the time Francisco called Aimee, all that remained of Ramón was a blackened head and neck, a pair of glistening feet, and a mound of jelly-like substance steaming in between.

'Oh my God, what the hell did this?' Aimee asked. 'Some sort of industrial solvent?' She pulled the front of her shirt up over her nose. 'Smells like boiled vegetables and … something like tar.'

Francisco shrugged and shook his head. His eyes were locked on the remains and his normally light brown complexion looked sallow and waxen. He raised a handkerchief to cover his nose and spoke through the incongruously spotless cotton. 'There are no chemicals used on this project that could cause that type of damage to the human body. Do you think it could be a disease? There are recorded virus types that exist in jungles that can cause extreme cellular disintegration – like Ebola or Marburg?'

Aimee narrowed her eyes at the mess on the sleeping mat and spoke through her shirt. 'Yes, you're right, but I don't believe there's been any recorded incident on the South American continent. Anyway, they don't cause total disintegration, just cell-wall destruction leading to organ failure and bleed-out. No, this is something different – and very weird.'

She kneeled for a closer look, still keeping her distance from the corpse. 'It's still active – it's breaking down rapidly. Let's get some photos of the remains before there's nothing left. I'll take some samples too.' She paused. 'This tent should be off limits to everyone.'

'Yes, I agree. I also think the men who were with this poor soul should be disinfected and kept in isolation until we know what it is we are dealing with.' Francisco pulled the handkerchief away from his face for a moment, and tilted his head. 'It seems the more we erode the jungle, the more it fights back. There have been extreme contaminations in Latin America, Dr. Weir. Two hundred people were infected with hantavirus in the Boquerón region. Many recovered, but our government takes any outbreaks very seriously now.' He looked at Aimee, his face still very pale. 'I will have to report this to the Paraguayan Communicable Diseases Unit in Asunción.'

Aimee nodded and followed him out of the tent. She regretted entering the enclosed space without a mask. If the contaminant was a microorganism, and was airborne, she was also now at risk.

SEVEN

Alex knocked, then pushed open the door. Jack Hammerson was standing by the window, talking on the phone and looking out over the base grounds. On seeing Alex, he nodded and motioned towards the lounge chairs in the corner. He said a few more words, hung up without a goodbye, then joined Alex and sat down.

'How's Sam shaping up?' he asked.

'First Lieutenant Reid is A-okay. His ribs are still painful, and he's got a few less teeth so his modeling days are over, but he's ready for duty. We're *all* ready for duty.'

Alex kept his face expressionless as he reported on his second-in-command's mission fitness. He'd seen Sam leaving the Hammer's office earlier that day, but when he asked about the meeting, Sam had been evasive. All he would say was that the Hammer was checking on his physical status. It was unusual for Hammerson to do that personally and not simply trust Alex's review. At the same time, Alex wondered if he was suffering from paranoia. He felt he was starting to mistrust everyone and everything a little too much. Was it yet another side effect of his treatments?

Hammerson chuckled. 'Good. You leave tomorrow at 0800 hours. You'll need to get your team down to supply today for kit-out. I suggest the new hothouse jungle fatigues – black and green tiger-stripe camouflage. Two-layer Kevlar weave – tougher than steel but with full

59

flexibility and maximum strength without the added weight. You're going into a wet zone, so you can expect humidity between eighty and
a hundred percent. The suit's first layer will pull the water away from
your body; the second layer's durability can defray a knife strike.'

Alex nodded. 'Additional body armor?'

'No. Even the lighter ceramics would trap too much heat.
However, there are optional gloves with zirconium dioxide knuckle
protectors. If you have to hit something, it'll give it a real nasty headache.'

'We'll take 'em. What about offensive armaments – is the
KBELT laser still available?'

Hammerson shook his head. 'Way too much humidity in the air
for it to be useful; the high-energy pulse would fray in only a few
feet. But we do have something that we've perfected for high-hu-
midity terrains.' He glanced at his watch, then got to his feet. 'Let's
get down to the range. I've got something to show you – I think
you'll like it.'

Alex grinned. 'You just don't trust me near your furniture anymore, do you?'

Hammerson laughed and looked at his desk. 'Hey, you're getting
the bill for that, mister.'

*

It took nearly half a minute for the secure lift to drop eight levels
below the camp and reach USSTRATCOM's operational research
facilities. It was probably one of the most secure and invisible facilities anywhere on the planet, with almost as much ionised shielding
as the President's Mole Hole.

The lift door opened to a blank metallic wall containing a tiny
silver grate at head height. Both Alex and Hammerson stated their
name and rank into the small opening and waited while their voice
patterns were analyzed and the DNA extracted from their exhal-
ations. The wall slid back to reveal a long, brightly lit corridor.
Approaching them was a young man in a mid-length lab coat. He saluted and gave them a friendly smile.

Hammerson ignored the smile and started walking quickly, forcing the man to almost skip to keep up. He spoke without turning his head. 'All set up?'

'Yes, sir, absolutely. Range five. If you need anything else —'

'That'll be all.'

Hammerson increased his pace and the young man slowed to a halt, obviously aware that his usefulness had expired.

Another barrier, another code; this time the door opened onto a long room, like an aircraft hangar.

'Good,' Hammerson said when he saw his orders had been carried out correctly.

Mounted on a tripod was a piece of equipment that looked like a gauntlet. Fifty feet away, a row of figures were lit from spots above, the lights illuminating their translucent amber torsos. Hammerson stood behind the device for a second, looking down the room to the targets. Then he stepped aside and motioned for Alex to take his place.

'Portable Solidified Moisture Projectile Device,' he said.

Alex grinned. 'Ice gun will do just fine.'

Hammerson pushed a stud on the back of the gauntlet and a small blue light came on. 'Clever use of technology. The problem we found with extremely humid environments was that the armaments gummed up from too much moisture in the air. Even the bullet casings tended to corrode and swell. So, a few years back, we set the lab guys a simple task – give us something that's light, doesn't corrode, doesn't need a lot of ammunition, but is deadly as hell.' Hammerson lifted the device and slid it over his forearm. 'They gave us this …'

He pointed flat-handed towards the targets, then made a fist. A stream of particles hissed from the gauntlet and cut a ragged hole into the central torso at the end of the room. Hammerson relaxed his hand and the hissing stopped.

'Fires between ten and fifty high-velocity ice projectiles per second,' he said. 'Number of deliveries depends on the available moisture in the atmosphere. We based the volume and speed on the metal storm concept – rapid continuous dispatch. The advantage of this device, other than its size, is that it doesn't need to store its rounds – it actually creates them from the moisture in the air.' He rubbed his shoulder. 'Got a bit of a kick.'

He pointed to three separate units on the device. 'Ignition and powerplant, projectile factory and, lastly, delivery. All miniaturized to under half an inch in height so there's little physical bulk or weight.'

Alex placed his hand on the gauntlet. 'Wow, cold. What about freeze burn?'

'No chance – shielding on the inside. Though the power plant uses a helium mix, which has a lower liquefaction temperature than nitrogen, it only starts the freeze on ignition. As soon as you press the ignition, a pellet gets punctured, allowing the chemicals to combine, and you're ready to go. The pellets are under enormous pressure and have a dual action: they release the gas to snap-freeze and shape the moisture in the delivery chamber, then act as an explosive thrust to push the spike out – bit like a high-speed blowdart.'

Alex nodded. 'Nice. What's the capability duration?'

'As long as there's available moisture, you probably have about twenty minutes of high-speed delivery. There are backup pellets – and one more thing.'

Hammerson pointed his arm towards the dummy again and made a fist. This time, when the projectile stream started up, he opened his hand, sticking his fingers in front of the stream. It immediately cut off.

'Sensors. Got some pretty smart technology built-in to control the speed of delivery and make sure each part of the manufacture-to-delivery process is working in harmony. Also ensures you don't take your hand off by accident.'

Hammerson lowered his arm and rotated his shoulder.

'Drawbacks, other than the obvious recoil?' Alex asked.

'A few, but I doubt they'll affect you. The other users, maybe. The technology has been miniaturized, but you still need a wrist-to-elbow length of at least eleven inches to support the carriage – can't pack it down any smaller than that. Also, the recoil is tough. The projectiles are pushed out at approximately 3000 feet per second, and once you have a firing stream in motion the pushback is *significant.*

The lab boys recommend short multisecond bursts rather than long streams.'

Hammerson slid the gauntlet off and handed it to Alex. He weighed it in his hand for a moment before pushing it up his arm and strapping it into place. He turned his arm over and then back again.

'What's the trigger?' he asked.

'You are – brachioradial muscle extension.' Hammerson smiled and stepped back.

Alex nodded and turned to face the half-dozen ballistic gel torsos at the end of the room. He raised his arm flat-handed as he'd seen the colonel do, then made a fist. The hiss of the ice gun filled the room and a white stream of needle-sharp darts flew at the target dummies. Alex destroyed the first two rapidly, then moved on to the third – this time he just removed the head. Then the next, and the next, until they were all just piles of shredded gel on the floor. As Hammerson had expected, the recoil didn't affect him in any way.

Alex relaxed his hand and smiled broadly at the damage. 'Oh yeah, very nice indeed.'

He concentrated his gaze on one of the ravaged torsos. Hammerson realized he was using his extraordinary vision to study the trapped darts before they melted. Each was about an inch and a half in length, and a bit thicker than a toothpick. In another second they would all be gone without a trace.

There was a slight chemical smell in the air and the room was a few degrees cooler, but, other than some water on the floor, there was no debris around the men.

'No casings, no evidence left behind, very tidy,' Hammerson said as he helped Alex to remove the gauntlet. 'You get three – one each for you, Sam and Mak. And you get the fun of telling Franks there isn't one to fit her.'

Alex pulled a face of mock horror. 'Oh, great. That's going to be one pleasant conversation.'

Hammerson raised his eyebrows. 'I didn't pick you as one to be afraid of girls, Arcadian.'

'Sure I am, and for lots of good reasons,' Alex laughed.

Hammerson replaced the gauntlet on its stand, slapped Alex on the shoulder and they headed for the door.

'Any more news from down south?' Alex asked.

'Nope … and no news is good news. Say hello to her for me, will you?'

Hammerson's tone was light, but, as he looked at Alex from the corner of his eye, he felt a knot in his belly. Alex was worried for Aimee, but he didn't know the walls were rapidly closing in around himself. He wondered if he should simply tell Alex to grab Aimee and just keep going. Not to return to USSTRATCOM and its Medical Division.

Maybe next time, he thought, as the door slid closed behind them.

EIGHT

A imee lifted the small glass tube that contained the sample and shook it. The fragment of flesh she'd collected had totally degraded into a viscous black liquid. She frowned, both horrified and astounded at the speed of the decomposition.

With something this corrosive, she knew she should have the sample under glass and be wearing some form of bio-suit. But here in the jungle, the best she could muster was two pairs of gloves, overalls and a surgical mask from Francisco's medical stores. The extra clothing was only moderate protection, but made her so hot that the headband she wore was already sodden with perspiration.

She dipped a thin glass rod into the putrid liquid and smeared it onto a slide, then quickly placed it under her microscope viewer. This time she had the computer ready to accept the image, and as soon as she tuned back to the screen the dark pool was already in focus.

'Whaaaat?' Aimee softly breathed out the word in confusion.

She typed some commands and the screen split: half showed the live images from Ramón's sample; in the other she called up earlier pictures from the drill head. In the drill sample there had been a community of different life forms whirring, whipping or floating in the tiny sea she had created for them. But in Ramón's sample there was just one life form: spherical and joined in chains like a segmented worm – unmistakably the same bacteria she had extracted from the drill head.

Aimee knew it was far too soon to be postulating any theories, but this organism definitely should not have been in Ramón's body. Other than in her own samples, this sub-terra lifeform shouldn't have been *anywhere* else on the surface of the Earth. She sat back and mopped her eyes with her sleeve. It was impossible. Only yesterday this microorganism only existed solely a mile underground, and now it was in abundance in what remained of the man's flesh. She went to place a hand on her chin, then changed her mind. Somehow, Ramón must have got some of the black material on his body and become infected.

She held up the glass tube again and swirled the liquid. How did it manage to degrade the flesh so quickly? Maybe there was something else at work; something she couldn't see with this micro-scope's level of magnification. As well as the bacterium, there could be some sort of underlying viral bloom, or perhaps even a unique chemical interaction occurring. Could be a hundred things she hadn't even thought of yet.

She placed the tube in a rack and sat back for a moment, folding her arms and biting the inside of her cheek. She felt like she was dig-ging for gold with a spoon. She needed help – from someone with a lot more scientific knowhow than was available to the local author-ities. *I need the big guns*, she thought. *I need the CDC.*

Problem was she didn't know anyone at the Centers for Disease Control and Prevention, and the thought of spending hours wrestling with government bureaucrats, trying to find out who she should *really* be talking to, and being put on hold time and again, was over-whelming when she was already so fatigued. But although she didn't know anyone there, she knew who would.

She swivelled to her computer and started typing. 'Always nice to know someone with connections.' She finished her quick message to Alfred Beadman, attached her images and pressed *send*. The mes-sage took several minutes to be dispatched as it had to pass through a relay booster station the mining crew had brought with them. This deep in the jungle, even satellite uplinks needed a springboard.

*

Aimee opened the screen door of the cabin that had been hastily converted into an isolation ward. Thick industrial plastic sheeting hung over the windows and down in front of the doorway. She pushed the sheeting aside and entered the room where three men lay on cots, their arms and legs tied to the railings to stop them trying to flee. Each man's exposed skin glistened in the artificial light of the cabin. One seemed to be asleep, perhaps unconscious. Another stared blankly at the ceiling. The last wept softly, black tears streaming from dark-veined eyes to stain the pillow under his head.

'I think there is no doubt that they are now also infected,' Francisco said from behind his paper mask. His eyes were red and drooped with fatigue and sadness. Even his proud little silver moustache had lost its vigour. 'As a general practitioner, I am lost on this, Dr. Weir. Do you, perhaps, have any ideas?'

Aimee pursed her lips tightly behind her mask and gave a half-nod, half-shake of her head. 'I have a few thoughts, but they're too way out to share just yet. I've sent some images back home. Hopefully the experts can give us some clues as to what we're dealing with.'

'Good.' Francisco looked at the men on their beds. 'I think we should burn their tent.'

Aimee nodded without taking her eyes from the three bodies slowly decomposing before her.

*

'Of course they're scared … and so am I, Alfred.' Aimee paced back and forth in her cabin, kicking clothing out of the way to create some space, as she talked to her boss on the other side of the world. 'We're trying to keep things quiet, but …' she paused to listen for a few seconds before continuing. 'Yes, Alfred, we've got the men who shared the tent with the primary contamination victim in isolation, but down here everyone seems to know everything as it happens. It's such a small community – you can't keep secrets. Francisco says he's overheard some of the men talking about leaving.'

'Aimee, there's no evidence that the disease, or whatever it is, is airborne or that there are any vectors involved – you said that yourself. As long as you use basic sterilization procedures, everything will be okay. It's usually you telling *me* this stuff, not the other way around.'

'Alfred, you didn't see the infected body – it literally dissolved in front of our eyes. It was horrible. I should be wearing a full biohazard kit, not a sweaty T-shirt and paper face mask.'

Alfred's warm, deep voice rose slightly. 'Okay, okay, stay calm, my dear. Do you really think it's your little *Clavicula occultus* that's culpable? I like the name, by the way. But how could it be? I doubt one microbe could be responsible for converting hydrocarbons to oil and gas and also somehow cause the human body to simply fall apart. I think we need more information, and you need some help. As you suggested, I sent your data to the CDC; they were very interested and have dispatched two of their specialists.' He cleared his throat and then sounded as if he'd leaned in closer to the speaker. 'I had another call this morning, Aimee. Someone I hadn't heard from in ages. You remember our friend Jack Hammerson?'

'Jack?' Aimee remembered Jack Hammerson only too well – Alex Hunter's commanding officer. He had always been in the background, controlling, overseeing Alex's treatments, and advising him. As her relationship with Alex had started to change as he became more secretive, as he worried more about the uncontrollable rages that would shake him from his nightmares in the middle of the night, and finally as he had confided to her his fears that he wasn't sure he was even human anymore, Jack Hammerson had always been there. She had begged Alex to get a second opinion from doctors outside the military. But Jack had refused to allow it. She knew the colonel had saved Alex's life – brought him back from the dead – and Alex would never forget it, even though by doing so he had allowed the HAWC commander to turn him into a killing machine – at the mercy of what seemed to be an unstoppable anger; an inner demon that threatened his sanity.

It had seemed to Aimee that Alex had chosen Hammerson and the military over her. Her concern for his safety and mental state, or perhaps it was her pride, had driven her to refuse to accept his decision – and that had been the end of them. She would never forgive Hammerson for not giving him the chance to start a new life outside the Special Forces. *Yes, she remembered Jack Hammerson very well.*

'Good, I knew you'd remember him. Well, he's sending in some of his people to follow up on some military matter,' Alfred went on.

Aimee grimaced as she recalled the horrific scene in the clearing. She hadn't told Alfred about her and Francisco's grisly discovery, or their suspicion that it had been caused by something other than a jaguar. Hammerson had clearly been charged with finding out exactly what had happened to the Green Berets.

'I believe he's sending Captain Hunter – he should be with you in a day or two. I'm going to see if the CDC team can jump a ride with them. Stay safe, Aimee dear, talk soon.'

Alfred ended the call in a hurry, obviously not wanting to deal with Aimee's reaction to the news.

She switched the phone off speaker, and sat back with her legs splayed. She lifted the water bottle from the table, sipped a little, then let a good stream pour over her forehead and neck. It ran over her lips and she blew out, causing a plume of spray to fan out above her. She watched it settle to the floor as she allowed her mind to drift.

In the time they had shared together, Alex Hunter had taught her to ride a horse, shoot a gun, deep-sea dive and more. She recalled the time he had taken her rock climbing – she had slipped and twisted her ankle, but Alex had caught her and carried her down the cliff and then for five miles back to their cabin as if she weighed nothing at all. Her lips turned up at the corners as she remembered what else had happened in that cabin, the intimate times they had shared there and in many other locations she could never have imagined herself visiting. The few men she had dated since had seemed so ordinary, so ... boring.

When she had walked out on him, it had seemed the right thing – for both of them. But now she wasn't so sure. She was confused and nervous at the thought of seeing him again. Confused, nervous ... and a little angry.

She put her hand up to her cheek and ran her fingers over the red rash bumps. *The first time I see him in two years and I look and feel like shit*, she thought. *Just great.*

A cough at the doorway interrupted her thoughts. She looked up to see Francisco standing there looking worried.

'What is it?' Aimee asked.

'The government has ordered the gas well to be capped,' Francisco said. 'I am so sorry, but they have locked us down. They suspect we have some form of hantavirus burning through the camp. No one is allowed to leave and no one will be coming in.'

'We're in fucking quarantine?' Aimee was on her feet, her blue eyes drilling into the small doctor, who backed up a step at the ferocity of her tone.

'I am sure it is just temporary, Dr. Weir. I'm so sorry this has happened.' Francisco was wringing his hands together, and his eyebrows turned so far down they looked as though they were about to slip off his face.

'Those assholes! I don't believe it. I don't fucking believe it.'

Aimee was building up to another onslaught when she realized she was taking her frustration out on the only friend she had in the camp. 'Ohhh, God. I'm sorry, Francisco. I'm tired and I don't know what's happening. This is well beyond the limit of my expertise.' A sudden thought panicked her. 'Are they allowing the CDC specialists through?'

'*Si*, I believe so. The bureaucrats say it is at their own risk.'

Aimee nodded and sat down heavily. She lifted her shirt front and used it to rub her face free of grime. 'At least it's stopped raining. Any more infections?'

'I am afraid so. There are now five men in the quarantine hut. I do not expect them to survive past tomorrow.'

'It's spreading,' Aimee said. 'I don't think it's airborne – there's not enough nasopharyngeal irritation to produce aerosolising of the bacteria – the men aren't coughing or sneezing to give it lift-off. There must be a vector – the water, insects, something else we're sharing ...'

'I agree. If it was fully airborne, we would all have been infected by now. I will have the camp checked for vermin and ensure all the men are using insect repellent.' Francisco paused then added, 'The well needs to be capped now, but the men are refusing to go back out to the drill site until they know what is causing the infection. They are calling it "the melting death".'

Aimee leaned back in the chair and shut her eyes. 'I don't blame them,' she said. 'Nope, don't blame them at all.'

*

That night, three more men were taken. But not by the disease.

In the darkness, something glided through the jungle and came to a halt at the edge of the camp, drawn there by the seed that had been brought to the surface. It sensed the sparks of growth that had been ignited. Now, they needed to feed. It needed to feed.

It moved quickly across the clearing towards the back of one of the tents. It could sense the three men inside – could hear their heartbeats, smell their blood. It needed them, all of them, every bit of them. It needed to be strong to protect the growing brood.

Under a single, long, sharp fingernail, the tough waterproofed canvas parted as easily as if it was being unzipped. The creature reached out to the first man and wrapped a long, taloned hand almost entirely around his throat. The man's eyes shot open and his tongue bulged, but no sound escaped his lips as soft tissue and his upper spinal cord were swiftly crushed together. His head flopped onto his shoulder, attached only by an empty tube of compressed skin.

The creature moved to the next man and crushed his neck in the same manner, careful not to spill any fluids or cause any damage to the surroundings. The tissue ruptured slightly and it was forced to bring its mouth down to the blood that was seeping from the split in the crushed skin. The flow subsided quickly as the heart stopped pumping and the blood settled in the man's lower extremities. The creature lifted its head slightly and sniffed, savoring the tangy smell of the ruptured flesh.

As it bent over the third man, he woke. The long fingers circled his neck like hot cables and it brought its face close to look into his eyes. There was no compassion, or even interest, in the creature's gaze; it was the look a hunter would give a dying hare as he held it up to check its weight. The man's eyes ran with tears and he dragged in a last strained breath as the pressure around his neck increased.

The wide mouth pulled open further, black gums receding to reveal rows of needle-like teeth encircling the entire ring of the oral cavity. A long tongue lolled out to lick at the man's tears. It squeezed tighter and watched the eyes bulge and become glass-like. The man's head flopped to the side, his face a deep purple from the trapped blood.

The creature gathered the three men in its arms and stepped from the tent. If anyone had been awake to see it re-enter the jungle, they would have thought its passage little more than a breeze stirring the foliage.

NINE

Alex looked out the porthole window of the massive Talon Blackbird, and down at the patchy green landscape and the giant runway that had been scraped out of it. The secret base at Mariscal Estigarribia, northern Paraguay, was one of America's best-kept secrets. Four hundred US personnel were permanently stationed there, their role to closely observe what they believed to be regional rogue governments determined to destabilize the entire South American continent. The base was in a prime strategic location due to its proximity to Brazil, Argentina and Bolivia, as well as the fractious Venezuela.

Though Alex appeared outwardly calm as the plane made its descent, impatience churned within him, knotting his stomach. He thought of Aimee somewhere in the Paraguayan jungle, and remembered the unidentifiable roar on the recording of the attack on the Green Berets. Now, the Paraguayan government had placed the camp under a quarantine order. Aimee needed his help. Why was it taking so long to get to her?

The aircraft touched down smoothly and, even before the rear ramp had fully opened, the four HAWCs and the two CDC scientists were leaping onto the tarmac. The CDC had sent one of their leading scientists from their infectious diseases division: Maria Vargis. Alex guessed she was in her fifties, but she was still a very handsome woman with an olive complexion, thick wavy dark hair with silver streaking back above her ears, and a figure that could be described as Rubenesque. Her large brown eyes showed a sharp intellect and what was either a sparkle of humor or an impatience just as keen as Alex's own to get to the drill site. Accompanying her was her son, Michael, also a scientist. Hammerson had assured Alex that the man deserved to be there in his own right, not merely as his mother's assistant.

It didn't take long to unload the HAWCs' gear: each soldier traveled with a compressed backpack that carried most of what he or she would need – the bulk of the carry-weight was reserved for weaponry. For this mission, that meant knives of varying lengths and thicknesses, each in a scabbard, plus a powerful H&K USP45CT pistol on each hip. The smooth, matt-black sidearms were made of a moulded polymer with a hostile environment coating and had a variant trigger for faster discharge. Finally, each HAWC had been issued with a stripped-down XM29 dual munitions burst rifle. The top barrel was a light cannon that fired bursting munitions using a ballistic computer to program the round, telling it where to explode. The bottom barrel was a 5.56mm assault rifle with integrated laser rangefinder, thermal- and night-vision capabilities, and up to 600 percent telescopic magnification. The plastic stock and polymer-cased ammunition made it lightweight but with all the lethality intact.

The scientists had more equipment and the HAWCs helped with the unloading.

'Fuck!' Casey Franks grunted as she hefted one of the smaller boxes. 'What the hell have you got in here – freakin' house bricks?'

Michael Vargis laughed. 'Sorry, I should have said something. It's our batteries – six 3R12 zinc-chloride dry cells – just in case it's the only power we can get access to. Very powerful but also very heavy – about fifty pounds altogether. Let me help you.'

'Nah, just give me room, baby face.' Franks's forearms bulged as she lifted the box. 'Took me by surprise was all.'

An ex-SEAL, Franks had been a HAWC for a number of years. Standing five eight in her combat boots, she had ice-blue eyes and a snub nose. Her face might have been called attractive once, but a cleft scar running from just below her left eye down to her chin pulled her cheek up slightly, giving her what looked like a permanent sneer. Her green and black tiger-striped uniform was tight across her chest, but not because of a cleavage like Maria Vargis's; rather, taut bands of pectoral muscles gave Franks the shape of a female body builder. She had multiple tattoos on her forearms – daggers, dragons, names of high-power motorbikes, and a rose with the name *Linda* written in curling calligraphy underneath.

'I expected it'd be hotter,' she said as she looked around, the unloading completed.

'Not much of a jungle either,' said the tall, dark-skinned HAWC who had come to stand beside her. He pulled a monoscope from a side pouch and focused it on the high mountains just visible to the northwest.

Makhdoum Basasiri Safieddin, Mak for short, stood at nearly six foot four, his wiry frame like corded wood. He had been one of the elite Republican Guards in Iraq and had worked with the Americans after the war. For that, his entire family had been wiped out by one of the local militias. Mak had come to Hammerson's attention when Alex had met the Iraqi after the completion of the Dark Rising assignment in the region. The US had been looking for good men who could train up local defense personnel. Mak had learnt quickly and with purpose. Now, he couldn't wait to get back to Iraq – there was a certain militia he looked forward to revisiting.

Sam took Mak's scope and scanned the nearby peaks for himself. 'We're about 1000 feet above sea level here, basically at the foot of Bolivia's Cordillera Mountains. But don't fret, children, where we're going it's roughly 800 feet *below* sea level. Down there we'll be getting into some of the densest, darkest, most impenetrable jungle on the face of the Earth. Plus all the heat and humidity you can suck up. Enjoy the cool breeze while you can.' He tossed the scope back to Mak.

'I love the heat,' the Iraqi said. 'The sun's warmth is a gift from Allah.'

'Yeah, but according to you, everything is a gift from Allah,' responded Franks.

'Ha, and so it is!' Mak turned his face to the sunshine and smiled, showing strong white teeth.

Alex looked up and down the runway, then did a 360 turn. His jaw was set in annoyance.

'Something bothering you, boss?' asked Sam.

'Something's missing – where's our chopper?'

Alex looked at his watch and swore. Their visit was top secret, so they hadn't expected a parade, but they had expected to pick up some supplies and then head out immediately on a waiting helicopter that would drop them into the drill site. All up, no more than another six hours of traveling.

'Best laid plans, huh?' Sam said, turning his own face up to the sun.

Alex spun again as he heard something on the other side of the runway. Two men had emerged from one of the small flat buildings in the distance and were jogging to meet them. One was in the jungle-striped camouflage of the Paraguayan military; the other wore nondescript drab green coveralls. *American*, Alex thought. He knew none of the US men and women stationed here wore rank badges or identifying insignia.

'Action at last,' Maria Vargis said, putting her hands on her hips.

'Maybe, maybe not,' Alex said.

He stepped forward as the men halted before him.

The Paraguayan saluted and held his hand out. He had a close-cropped beard and wasn't particularly tall. 'Captain Hunter, I assume? I am Captain Fernando Garmadia. I will be taking charge of your team.'

Alex ignored the display of authority. He didn't return the salute, just took Garmadia's hand briefly, then turned to the other man.

'Sergeant Banks, sir,' he said. 'Glad you and the team could make it.'

Alex nodded in response. 'I don't see our chopper, Banks. I assume you know we're in a bit of a hurry.'

Captain Garmadia spoke before the American sergeant could respond. 'There has been a complication that has necessitated a slight change of plan. Please follow us for new instructions.'

Alex felt the knot of frustration in his belly tighten. He turned to Sam, discontent plain on his face. 'Lieutenant, get the team ready to leave on my return.'

'You got it. Want me to tag along?' Sam raised his eyebrows.

Captain Garmadia smirked slightly at Sam and took a step towards him. 'Stand at ease, *soldado*, this is just procedure. You and your superior need not be alarmed by my request.'

Alex shook his head at Sam and set off at a brisk pace towards the buildings, not waiting for the other two men. He heard them break into a run in order to catch up.

*

Garmadia put on a sprint to get ahead of Alex so he could lead him into the building and down to a meeting room at the end of the corridor. Banks followed in what Alex thought was amused silence.

A man in his late fifties stood up when Alex entered the room and gave him a flat smile. He didn't bother saluting, just held out his hand. Alex could see by the insignia on his uniform – three gold stars with red circles underneath – that the man was a colonel either in the artillery or infantry. *A working soldier; good*, he thought.

'Colonel Eladio Lugo,' the man said. 'You must be Captain Alex Hunter. An old friend of mine speaks very highly of you; Cabeza Dura, we used to call him – it means "hard head". Many years ago he trained some people for us.'

By that description, Alex guessed he meant Jack Hammerson.

Lugo gestured to some chairs around an enormous walnut desk and spoke briefly to Garmadia in Spanish, who nodded in reply and turned to smirk briefly at Alex.

'I believe Captain Garmadia mentioned there has been a complication,' Lugo said. He turned a map around so Alex could see it. A red circle had been drawn around a dark green zone roughly halfway between the cities of Asunción and Concepción and close to the Paraguay River. There were no markings for towns, roads or any other sign of human habitation.

Lugo sat back and folded his hands across his flat stomach. 'This complication is something far more dangerous to us than bandits or mercenaries, Captain Hunter. The area has been closed by an extreme quarantine order from the highest level. Even our people cannot go in, neither can our vehicles, aircraft or helicopters – nothing. Until the source of infection has been identified, or has burned itself out, we must wait.'

He leaned forward and brought his hands together on the map, looking hard at Alex, perhaps expecting anger or some other type of outburst. Alex, however, barely reacted to the information. His voice was even and unemotional.

'My team will be completing its assignment. We are going in, whether I have to buy or steal an aircraft. We leave in thirty minutes.'

One of Lugo's eyebrows went up and a small smile touched the corner of his mouth. 'Are you sure you are not related to Cabeza Dura?'

Sergeant Banks finally spoke. 'There *are* no planes, Captain Hunter, or choppers. They've all been deployed to the Bolivian border for security exercises. Even if there were, you'd probably be shot down if you tried to fly across the exclusion zone. I'll do what I can to help, but we're a little restricted on foreign soil.'

Colonel Lugo had turned the map back around and was examining its green lines and swirls. He spoke without looking up. 'It is a problem we are becoming more familiar with, Captain. As we push further into the jungle, we are seeing more and more sporadic outbreaks of disease – such as the hantavirus hotspots. We fully intend to keep such infections out of populated areas.'

'You North Americans need to be reminded that you must follow the rules while you are guests here,' Garmadia said with a self-satisfied grin. He allowed his eyes to drift across to Banks. 'While *all* of you are guests here. The United States needs this base; you don't have too many friends in Latin America anymore, Captain Hunter.'

Alex could feel the blood surging in his chest and a small bloom of pain in the center of his head. He sat immobile and tried to keep his breathing calm. His eyes remained, unblinking, on Garmadia. The smaller man swallowed, perhaps thrown off by not getting the reaction he had expected. He went on, this time sounding a little less sure of himself.

'You probably think you will walk out of here, make a phone call and go over our heads, but be warned that it could be *us* phoning *your* superiors.'

Alex's eyes slid across to Colonel Lugo. He saw that the man's face had gone a deep shade of red.

'That is enough, Captain Garmadia,' Lugo said. 'North America is like a big brother to us. There will be no insulting of family – especially while I am in the room.'

He held Garmadia's eyes a moment longer, the glance carrying a warning, then returned to the map and the HAWCs' destination. He opened his mouth about to speak, but Garmadia was there before him.

'If I may remind you, Colonel,' he said, raising his finger, 'even the Minister for Foreign Affairs has said that we must look to our own neighbours for our security in the future, rather than bowing before fading superpowers —'

'That's enough!' Lugo exploded and slammed one hand down on his desk. He squeezed his eyes shut for a second then opened them again, a roguish smile creeping across his face. 'Captain Garmadia, I was about to send you out of the room, but I believe you may be of assistance on a little trip I am about to authorize.'

He turned to Alex. 'It is true what Sergeant Banks has told you. There are no aircraft available to you now, and the zone is under mandatory quarantine. However, I believe your CDC scientists should be allowed to enter the area to assist our country with any diagnoses and, we hope, the containment of this health hazard.' He smiled and pointed at a red line running down the interior of the country. 'This is the main road all the way to Asunción – and you can't be shot down traveling by vehicle, can you? You have two choices. First, leave the highway at Pozo and head towards Concepción, where you can obtain a boat and travel down the Paraguay River to this spot close to the camp.'

Alex did some quick calculations: just over 200 miles by truck, forty by boat, then another forty-mile trek. A lot of distance over some tough terrain. He wasn't sure how the scientists would cope.

'But if it was me,' Lugo went on, 'I would be tempted to drive to a point just past Pozo and obtain a guide there to take you through the jungle to the camp. This way you avoid the river altogether, which is unpredictable coming into rainy season. Two-fifty miles by truck, then about twenty miles through some dense jungle – should take maybe two days, or less if you have a good guide.'

Alex looked up from the map and nodded.

'Good. How long until you can be ready?' Lugo asked.

'We're ready now, Colonel.'

Lugo looked over his shoulder. 'And you, Captain Garmadia?'

'What?' Garmadia's smirk vanished.

'I think you would be of enormous assistance to our North American friends in providing translation services, obtaining a guide and generally showing them some real Paraguayan hospitality,' Lugo said. 'Only a few days. I'm sure your wife will not miss you. Get yourself a light field pack and be out front in twenty minutes. That's an order. Dismissed.'

Garmadia looked as though he had just received an electric shock.

Lugo rose from his desk, clapped the Paraguayan captain on the shoulder and walked him to the door. As the two men left, Lugo leaned in close to Garmadia's ear. Alex could hear the colonel's muted words as though they were whispered into his own ear.

'You may have the ear of the minister, but I have the ear of the President. Take care, Captain, and take care of them, or I will make sure you are stationed deep down in the jungle permanently.'

TEN

Twenty minutes later, Captain Garmadia roared up to the waiting team in a camouflaged Humvee. The cigar between his lips pointed forwards like a small brown diving board as he seemed not to want to make eye contact with any of the HAWCs.

Sam walked around to the front of the enormous vehicle and had a quick look underneath. 'Thought so. Armor's been stripped out to make it lighter, and the suspension's been raised for better ground clearance. Jungle Hummer – this'll do nicely.'

He looked over his shoulder at Alex, who was staring in the direction they would be going. His face was slightly raised, as if he was trying to catch a scent on the breeze. Sam guessed what he was thinking.

'Aimee'll be fine,' he said, walking up beside him. 'She's tougher and more resourceful than most of us put together.'

Alex half-smiled. 'We need to get there, Sam. Something's not right; I can feel it.' He stood there a moment longer then drew in a deep breath through his nose and slapped his second-in-command's shoulder. 'Let's load it up, Sam. You and Dr. Vargis in the front with Garmadia; everyone else in the back – double time. And, Uncle, I'm not sure our Paraguayan captain is fully on board with our little vacation. Keep him honest, will you?'

Sam chuckled. 'No problem. I'll tell him my best jokes … and use satellite positioning to check his route. We'll stay on track, I guarantee it.'

He started to turn away then stopped. 'Gauntlets?'

Alex shook his head. 'Not till we're in deep jungle. Carry on.'

'You got it.' Sam walked off towards the team, leaving Alex still staring at the horizon.

*

Alex dozed in the cooled rear cabin of the Humvee, trying to unwind the coils of impatience that threatened to overwhelm him. However, rest was not coming easily to him; strange images formed in his head, and phantoms whirled and screamed through his subconscious. Some he might have recognized from previous missions, but others made him shift uneasily in his seat. Anyone watching him would have wondered at the way his brow creased, and his eyes moved rapidly behind their lids.

He saw a landscape, its plains dominated by dark and greasy looking protuberances that lifted and swelled like trunks of limbless trees. They were alive, but were not familiar.

There was a sound – a calling that grew louder. The lumpy mass opened hundreds of eyes, and saw him. The calling became screams.

He opened his eyes with a start, and shook his head to clear it. He noticed Franks looking at him and she raised her eyebrows. He nodded to her once, then turned away to check his watch and scan the jungle.

*

The vehicle, packed with the HAWCs, the scientists and their equipment, sped along the partially sealed road, only slowing when it had to leap across loosely packed gravel and swerve around water-filled craters. Alex noticed Garmadia never let the speed drop below seventy miles per hour.

The sparse bush and patchy grassland from the higher altitude gradually grew and thickened to become a wall of green either side of the road, sometimes up to a hundred feet high. In a few areas it was hard to determine individual trees as thick vines sewed them together in a mosaic of different hues.

Garmadia changed gears and accelerated across yet another wooden bridge in need of repair. Some of the short spans crossed shallow gorges that made Alex think of surface wounds slashed into the body of the jungle; others dropped hundreds of feet to streams of milky green water. Alex watched rotting fragments of timber fall away as they roared over the bridge and wondered how many more crossings it could take before a vehicle ended up tumbling into the green abyss.

Ramshackle shelters began to appear in clearings along the road. Small bands of stocky, brown people gathered inside and around them, talking and smoking long-stemmed pipes. With their colored shawls and small round hats woven with bright feathers, they reminded Alex of flocks of exotic birds settled to feed.

Garmadia slowed the Humvee as they passed the shelters and most of the locals waved. Few smiled, however, and Alex wondered briefly what their relationship with the local military was like.

Several miles back, he had ordered Garmadia to turn off the air conditioning so there would be less of a temperature differential when it came time to leave the truck. The open windows let in the sounds and smells of the jungle, and, as they shot past another campsite, the delicious fragrance of roasting chicken.

'I'm hungry,' said Franks, leaning a little further out the window.

Michael Vargis rolled his eyes at her. He turned to wave to some small children who'd backed up when the vehicle approached. As he put his elbow on the window edge, the Humvee hit a large hole and his teeth came down on his bottom lip, cutting it slightly. 'Ow.' He placed his fingers against his lip and brought them away with a smudge of red.

Franks took his hand. 'I know; it's tough out in the field, honey. But don't worry, Mommy can put a band-aid and a kiss on that for you later.'

She smacked her lips together in a mock kiss and Michael pulled his hand away from her. Even Alex had to turn away to stifle a laugh.

After another hour, the breeze coming into the truck cabin was thick with the smell of damp vegetation and decay. Garmadia pulled off the road and onto a small hump of dry ground, killing the engine and leaping from the driver's door almost in one smooth motion. He stretched his back.

'This is as far as we can go by road. Now we enter the deep jungle. But first we find a guide – or, rather, they find us.'

The HAWCs stepped from the vehicle. Alex looked across to Sam, who gave him a small nod. *Good*, Alex thought; Garmadia had taken them in the right direction. He had no real reason to think the Paraguayan officer wished them ill, but he didn't think the man would be all that unhappy if the HAWCs ended up lost in the jungle.

'Let's unload and take a few minutes to orientate ourselves,' Alex told his team.

He looked at the emerald barrier in front of them. He could sense the crowded life force emanating from the dense, crazy tangle. The noise was amazingly loud: it seemed that everything that could buzz, thrum, croak or screech was trying hard to outdo its neighbour. His senses were almost overwhelmed by the crushing waves of movement and sound. He took a deep breath, exhaled, and ran his hand up through his damp hair. It was only about a hundred degrees, but it was impossible to cool down in the high humidity. The heat stayed with you, on you, all over you. It blanketed, suffocated and drained you.

He turned back to the team. 'Any more questions about lack of heat and humidity, Franks?'

'This'll do just fine, boss. I'll cool down in the hotel pool later,' Franks said as she pulled her webbing pack onto her back and threw her XM29 over her shoulder. She methodically patted each of her pockets and belt pouches, and opened and closed holsters, checking on the clasps and the smoothness of the draw.

Alex smiled as he watched her professional movements. He liked Casey Franks. She made him laugh with her evil sense of humor, but also instilled confidence in her teammates with her I've-always-got-your-back attitude. Her only problem was she liked to fight way too much. The scar on her face was the result of a brawl in a bikers' bar when she ended up on the receiving end of a broken bottle. Alex had heard that she'd left plenty of broken bodies behind before her face was finally opened up. Franks needed to learn when to stand and fight and when to walk away – and Alex wasn't at all sure he was the right person to give that lecture.

She had cut the toughened suit sleeves from her jungle camouflage and he could see the muscles bulging in her arms as she worked smoothly through her tasks. Her five foot eight inch body carried a lot of coiled muscle power – Casey Franks was no lady and she'd be the first to tell you that. She finally pulled her plated gloves back on and punched one hand into the other to test the fit and knuckle impact. Satisfied, she headed over to Sam and Mak, laughing as she greeted them with a joke.

'Ahhh, here we go …'

Alex turned at the sound of Garmadia's voice and saw a small Indian boy standing just behind the first wall of trees. The kid looked about six or seven years old, and had skinny brown legs that poked out from oversized shorts. His feet were bare and muddy, and his small chest was covered by a huge T-shirt that just retained a faded image of Superman's 'S' shield.

The Paraguayan soldier crouched down, took a small silver coin from his pocket, flipped it in the air, and then held it out to the boy. Tentatively, the kid stepped forward. He looked from the coin to Garmadia, then up at Alex and the HAWCs. Eventually his desire for the money outweighed his fear and he darted forward. Instead of releasing the coin, Garmadia held on to it and spoke to him calmly. When he had the boy's full attention, he pointed to the jungle, then to the HAWCs. Alex heard the word *norteamericanos* several times. The boy looked at the HAWCs again with his eyebrows raised, nodded enthusiastically and said a few words back to the Paraguayan captain.

Garmadia nodded and released the coin, and the boy darted back towards the tree line. Halfway there, he looked back at the group and yelled, '*Norteamericano*,' then pointed at his chest. When he had their attention, he looked at the HAWC soldiers in their striped battle fatigues, smiled and held his thumb up. '*Superman, Batman, excelente!*'

Garmadia chuckled. 'To most of the children here, in the cities or the forests, North America is the country where the superheroes live.' He dusted his hands together and stood up. 'All right, now we wait. Either he will bring us back a guide ... or not.'

Franks yelled to the kid as he sprinted into the jungle: 'Up, up and away!'

He turned one last time to smile then slipped deeper into the green.

'About three hours until nightfall,' Garmadia said to Alex. 'If we can make a start tonight, and march for most of tomorrow, we may reach the drill site by late evening, or very early the next day. Provided we are not surprised by a storm, or attacked by a jaguar, or fall into a sinkhole, or our guide doesn't get us lost ...'

'Good enough.' Alex turned to his team. 'Okay, people, let's assist Dr. Vargis with her equipment.'

Michael Vargis had removed all of the medical boxes and packs from the truck and stacked them on the grass. Most were small compact field-equipment cases holding computers, microscopes, centrifuges, and several portable batteries in case there was no generator out in the field. There was also a single, reinforced brushed metal case. Alex picked it up and the tips of his fingers tingled. *Strange, I can sense radiation*, he thought.

'What's in here, Dr. Vargis?'

'Michael can carry that, Captain Hunter,' Maria Vargis replied. 'It contains micro field X-ray equipment, which is pretty delicate, so please be careful when you're putting it back down.' She turned away, indicating the conversation was ended.

Alex knew she was lying, but he could wait to find out why. Instead, he lifted the box that contained the battery packs. It was heavy and he knew that carrying its weight for over twenty-four hours would just about kill anyone else. He thought of some of the miniaturised technology he'd worked with in the HAWC labs – weapons and comm device power packs that contained ten times more power at about a hundredth the size. *Guess there's more money in war than in medicine*, he thought as he strapped the heavy box to his back.

Twenty minutes later, the boy emerged from the jungle with another slightly older youth, who, judging by his facial features, was probably related to him. The younger boy walked up to Garmadia. '*Él es mi hermano Saqueo*,' he said, then indicated himself with his thumb. '*Yo soy Chaco.*'

Garmadia turned to Alex. 'His name is Chaco, and this one here is his big brother, Saqueo – he will be our guide.'

Garmadia pulled a map from his pocket, spread it on the ground and pointed to their current location, then at a red circle about forty miles inland towards the river. He asked Saqueo several questions and the boy nodded to each, replying in a language that Alex thought sounded sometimes like Spanish.

'It's a mixture of Guarani, Tupi and Spanish,' Sam said softly, appearing beside Alex and squinting while he listened.

'Can you understand it?' Alex spoke without turning.

'Some. The Spanish, no problem, but the Tupi and Guarani, just a word here and there. Only had a few hours to pick up the basics on the plane.'

'Okay. Make sure our captain's playing it straight, but keep your language skills quiet for now,' Alex ordered.

Garmadia took two bank notes from his pocket and showed them to Saqueo. He gave one to the boy and made a show of putting the other one back in his pocket. The gesture was clear: *this one now, the other when we get there.*

'He can take us to the drill site,' Garmadia told Alex. 'And he's confirmed it's a 24-hour trek – maybe a bit longer seeing we are not local.'

'Good. Tell him we want to leave immediately. How long until they can be ready?'

'Two strong legs and a jungle full of food – they turned up ready, Captain Hunter.'

Garmadia folded the map and got to his feet. He said something to Saqueo and pointed to the piles of equipment. Alex watched as Chaco darted over and lifted one of the small packs onto his shoulder; he'd obviously decided he was coming as well.

'No. Tell him he can't come.'

The boy looked up at Alex in shock, understanding the near universal negative. He started to argue with Garmadia, his older brother joining in. The pair of them created a high-pitched chatter that had the captain covering his ears and waving them away.

'I cannot stop him,' Garmadia said with a shrug. 'He will come anyway.'

Alex thought for a second. The two boys stood frozen in anticipation, waiting for a decision from the man who was clearly the group leader.

'Okay, just to the river. But neither of them is to enter the camp,' he said.

Though neither boy had a grasp of English, the word *okay* was obviously universal as well. Chaco was beaming again.

'*Gracias, señor.*'

'What about the truck?' Michael Vargis said as he shouldered his pack.

Garmadia spoke without turning. 'It will be safe where it is. We are far from any of our borders, and the Indians have no use for something this large. Just make sure the doors and windows are closed so nothing can take up residence in it.'

'Let's move. Chaco, Saqueo, after you.' Alex made a sweeping gesture towards the tidal wave of vegetation that looked like it was about to crash down on top of them.

Saqueo went out at lead point, but Chaco fell in next to Alex, looking first up at his face, then down to the belt circling his waist with its strange mix of metal objects and pouches. His eyes alighted on the green and black gloves with their hardened ceramic armor. He reached across and tapped one with his small brown hand, feeling the toughened plates, then looked back up at Alex. '*Como Batman, si?*'

Alex shook his head and said, 'HAWC.'

Chaco's eyebrows shot up. '*Hawkman?*' An even more excited look lit his face.

Alex groaned. *It's going to be a long trek*, he thought.

ELEVEN

'Where are they all going … and in such a hurry?' Maria Vargis looked puzzled as yet another small group of Indians hurried past them in the opposite direction.

'I was wondering the same thing. They look spooked by something.' Alex called to Garmadia. 'Captain, why are the locals leaving?'

Garmadia shrugged and called the question to Chaco, nodding towards the retreating Indians. 'They are more likely to tell him than they are me,' he said to Alex.

Chaco scampered after a woman with a huge pile of brightly colored clothing strapped to her back. Alex watched the boy's eyes widen as she spoke to him, and he hung onto her arm and pumped it, as though the action would keep the information flowing. He returned to Garmadia speaking rapidly and gesturing towards the jungle. Garmadia shook his head and dismissed the boy with a sweep of his hand.

'Well?' asked Alex.

'It's nothing. They are moving to find a better campsite, that is all. These people are still quite nomadic, Captain Hunter.'

'That's not what he said,' Sam whispered. 'It was something about a golden flower … and missing children.'

Alex gave a small nod.

'Everyone take a break,' he ordered. 'Captain, a word, please. Lieutenant Reid, can you join us?'

Alex walked a few paces away from the group and called to Chaco. He nodded to the jungle and repeated one or two of the words he'd heard the boy use. Chaco replied quickly, pointing towards where the people were coming from, then making his eyes wide and holding his fingers in front of his mouth, mimicking long teeth.

Alex nodded, pretending to understand, then turned to Garmadia as he approached. 'Sounds like a little more than poor geography causing the exodus, Captain. It's important that we have all the facts heading into any type of hotzone. As a soldier you should know that.'

Garmadia went slightly red at the rebuke, but also frowned at Alex's apparent ability to understand the local language. 'Pah! It is nothing but a myth,' he blustered. 'They say there is a bad feeling in the jungle and so they have decided to leave. You must remember these people are still very superstitious and easily mix a Christian saviour with a bird-headed god that brings them rain. A bad storm with lightning can necessitate the sacrifice of a goat… or tell them it is time to leave and find another camp. You do not understand what you are hearing, Captain Hunter.'

'Really? Educate me then – tell me about the golden flower and missing children.' Alex's eyes bored into the Paraguayan soldier's.

'*Mierda santa*,' Garmadia said under his breath and rubbed his forehead. 'It is nothing. It is as I said —'

Frustrated, Alex held his hand up and nodded at Sam to talk to the boy.

Sam dropped to one knee and smiled at Chaco. '*Amiguito Chaco. Cuándo hizo esto sucede?*'

The boy nodded and the two of them talked quickly for several minutes. Sam gave Chaco a stick of gum, ruffled his hair and stood up.

'The Indians believe something called the Tau, "the evil one", is in the jungle. They are leaving before it eats them all. Seems a few young men disappeared during the night first off, then children were taken from their beds. The woman Chaco spoke to told him about a legend about a golden flower – when it blooms again, a great evil will be reawakened in their land. She thinks it is either an evil spirit, or perhaps Luison himself, the Great Devil.'

'Eaten by the Devil? Hmm,' Alex said and looked at Garmadia. 'We must operate as a single team in the field, Captain. Is that understood?'

The captain returned Alex's gaze from under a furrowed brow, his expression a mixture of hostility and embarrassment. His compressed lips bent into a tight smile and he walked away to light a cigar.

Alex watched his back for a moment, then returned his attention to the small boy. 'Sam, tell Chaco there's nothing to worry about. But his brother must go faster – we have to hurry.'

The light was just about gone. Alex thought of the unearthly roar he had heard on the recording from the Green Berets. *Eaten by the devil.* He thought of Aimee alone in the jungle. They could get another few hours closer if they left immediately.

'We're moving out, ladies and gentlemen. Now!'

*

Francisco and Aimee watched the wooden hut burn. Its six inhabitants had died, their skin, muscles and bones liquefying until they were nothing more than putrid black puddles on and around their cots. With no biohazard clothing or materials to hand, neither the Paraguayan doctor nor Aimee could bring themselves to clean out the cabin in preparation for any future inhabitants. They had decided their only course of action was to burn the site and use another hut for isolation. It already had its first occupant – strapped down and weeping black tears onto his pillow.

Aimee found the flames on her face surprisingly soothing; she closed her eyes and tilted her hat back so she could feel the heat dry the perspiration at her hairline. The corks around the hat's brim banged softly against her forehead and she remembered when Francisco had given it to her – just a few days ago, but the insane events unfolding around them made it seem so much longer. She opened her eyes and saw that her friend stood almost in a trance as he watched the flames. Tiny flecks of orange were reflected in the centers of his dark, watering eyes.

The men had gathered in clumps at the fringes of the blaze. About eighty of them remained, trapped in the jungle by both geography and a government order. More disappeared each night – always an entire tent of them, as though some unanimous decision had been made and acted upon. Aimee couldn't understand why they never took their belongings, meagre as they were; surely they would have wanted their machetes, food, photographs of their families? And why did some of the tents have slits cut into the back? *Nothing's making sense anymore*, she thought.

The cabin blazed furiously and was quickly reduced to a mound of ash, glowing nails and twisted metal fastening strips. The mud surrounding it was blackened and dried to a pottery hardness by the heat of the fire. Aimee looked up at the darkening sky and closed her eyes again. That morning, Alfred Beadman had told her that Alex Hunter's HAWCs and the CDC specialists had arrived in the country and were on their way, but he had been vague about when they might arrive. She hoped it would be soon – they were all feeling the strain of being under quarantine. With the rig shut down, men running away, a hideous disease burning through their camp, and something out there in the jungle that had butchered a squad of Green Berets, she felt like running off into the dark herself. *That was no jaguar attack.* The thought made her exhale slowly.

Aimee opened her eyes and watched the shadows lengthen – she knew within an hour, night would collapse on them like a warm wave. The day's sapping heat would be swapped for night's humidity – a shitty trade, and the oily feeling of fatigue never went away. She rubbed her cheek; with her red-rimmed eyes in darkening sockets, an itchy rash, and lank hair that seemed to be constantly damp, she knew she looked how she felt. *Nothing a hot shower and ten hours sleep in a cool hotel room couldn't fix*, she thought with a crooked smile pulling up one spotted cheek.

Aimee's reverie was broken as she became aware of raised voices, followed by Alfraedo's deeper tones, first conciliatory, but quickly lifting in volume as he obviously felt the need to assert his authority. The big man had managed mine sites all his life and knew how to stay in control of his most volatile resource – manpower.

Some moments later, he came to join Aimee and Francisco. 'The men are angry and bored; they are demanding a date when they can go home. I hope your friends can give us some answers, Dr. Weir,' he said. 'I also wish we had more security. For now, the men listen to me, but soon …' He shrugged his meaty shoulders.

'Yes,' was all Aimee could manage. Her vision blurred with exhaustion, but she was loath to use her hand or sleeve to wipe her face in case her clothing was contaminated. Instead, she squeezed her eyes hard shut and blinked twice. When she opened them, there was a man, dressed all in black, standing at the edge of the jungle.

She nudged Francisco. 'Who's that?'

Francisco followed her gaze to the stranger. 'I do not know, Dr. Weir; I have never seen him before. He is certainly not part of the drilling team. He is too tall for a local man. I would have assumed him to be one of Captain Hunter's team, but he looks to be wearing the cassock of a priest.'

Aimee squinted; there were now just a few bars of weak sunlight streaked across the clearing, and in the twilight gloom it was hard to make out the man's facial features. Francisco was right: he looked like a priest, but his cassock was old-fashioned – rough and heavy. He came towards them smoothly, almost gliding across the mud. He stopped to talk to some of the men, who stood quietly and nodded at his words. He touched the top of one man's head, as though blessing him, then turned to where Alfraedo, Francisco and Aimee stood.

Aimee shuddered; the man's gaze was so intense it seemed to penetrate her skin and see her soul shrinking within her. He came towards them again with that strange gliding motion. The men surged behind him in a rough horseshoe shape. About ten feet away, he came to the last weak strip of sunlight and halted, appearing to collect his thoughts. Aimee could see him a little more clearly now: a tall, robust-looking man in his fifties or sixties, with a thick square beard covering a strong chin. A line of iron gray at his jawline and temples gave him a look that was a combination of scholar and screen star. He smiled without opening his mouth, causing his cheeks to pull up slightly.

The last rays of sunlight thinned to a slit and then finally vanished. Halos of light appeared around the clearing as the generators whined into life. As soon as the lights ignited, their cyclopean heads were assailed by squadrons of flying insects of varying sizes, their bodies ricocheting off the thickened glass lenses.

The man glided closer and stopped a few feet in front of Aimee. He nodded respectfully then spoke in a voice that seemed to well up from deep within him. Aimee frowned slightly as she recognized some of the words curling from his barely opened mouth.

Alfraedo placed a hand on his chest and responded in Spanish, gesturing to all three of them.

Francisco whispered to Aimee, 'He is speaking in an old Spanish dialect and also using some Latin words. He says his name is Father Alonso González and he is a Spanish priest sent here to bring enlightenment to the indigenous population.'

'I *thought* I recognized some Latin,' Aimee whispered back. 'Who the hell speaks that anymore? Ask him where he's staying.'

The priest had turned to Aimee, seeming to watch her lips as she spoke. He repeated the question, '*Where* he's staying, where *he's* staying, where he's *staying*', trying different inflections as though tasting them on his tongue. After a few seconds he responded to Aimee directly, in a voice that contained only a hint of an accent.

'Forgive me, *señora*, I have not heard the language of the English for a long time. I am Father Alonso González, and, to answer your question, I am staying just a few miles to the northwest of your camp. I only became aware of your presence in the last few days when I spoke to some of your laborers ... who seemed in a great hurry to leave.'

He held out his hand. Aimee looked at it for a moment, then grasped it. It was only later that she realized the grip had been cool and dry, unlike everyone else's, whose skin was warm and slick with perspiration.

'I'm Dr. Aimee Weir – pleased to meet you, Father. Have you been in the jungle long?'

'Longer than I can remember, Dr. Aimee Weir, but I am patient, and my work is eternal. I bring the God's Word to the Indians of Paraguay, and perhaps, one day, to this entire world.'

He brought his hand up to his face, seeming to smell his palm and fingers where they had pressed against Aimee's hand. Aimee thought she saw his mouth working and had a disgusting impression that he was licking the traces of her perspiration.

Alfraedo cleared his throat. '*Padre*, the men that left the camp – are they with you now?'

González dropped his hand and glided a little closer to the site manager. 'I'm afraid not. I gave them my blessing and some supplies, but they were in a hurry to be on their way. Is there a problem here? If I may be of assistance, please let me know. At least allow me to conduct an evening mass at my church for the men. I detect a strong desire for spirituality here; I think they need me.'

Francisco cut in before Alfraedo could respond. 'I'm not sure that is a good idea just now, *padre*. The men must not be allowed to leave the camp while we are under a formal quarantine order. Also, it may not be safe for you or your followers if some of our men are carrying the infection. It would be best if those who have left were strongly encouraged to return to us here at the camp.' Francisco's fine silver brows knitted for a moment, before he spoke again. 'How far exactly are you from here, Father? If you have a sizeable group, I'm surprised that our initial surveys didn't pick up your settlement when we were doing our initial aerial mapping.'

Aimee was convinced one of the priest's eyes bulged and swivelled to look at Francisco while the other remained fixed on Alfraedo.

What? Must be a trick of the light, she thought as the priest's head turned and both eyes fixed normally on the small doctor.

'I'm not too far away, and my flock varies in size,' he said. 'The children of the forest come and go and need much guidance. I have been ill and not very active for a time, but I am healed now. I feel strong again; as if my own stone has been rolled back and, like the God, I have been reborn to carry on their work.'

Aimee felt the priest was both smoothly evasive and a little too fervid, and what was with *the God* reference? She'd never heard that expression before. There was something about him that made her feel very uncomfortable.

González gave another closed-mouth smile and turned his hands palm upwards. 'I would be happy to come here if that is your wish, but I assure you that any man in my care will be safe. I would like to suggest they come in small groups in the evenings for mass. Simply being in my church will be spiritually beneficial to the men.'

Francisco remained expressionless but his tone was a little terse. 'We found evidence of a terrible attack by a large animal on a group of men just a few days ago. I feel it is too dangerous for our men to enter the jungle at night, and you shouldn't be out there either. Perhaps, for your own safety, you should move into our camp temporarily. Then you could perform a morning mass for the men —'

González cut him off abruptly. 'My days are extremely busy, and if there were any large animals they have surely moved on by now. The jungle is safe, I assure you. I feel you are in more danger from your own men, who grow angrier and more fearful every day. Such emotions can be soothed through prayer.'

The priest glared at Francisco, and Aimee noticed that his eye seemed to bulge again.

Alfraedo cleared his throat and gave an apologetic little bow. 'Thank you for the offer, Father. We can talk again tomorrow evening. Please may I ask of you one thing? If any more of our men come to you, could you please tell them to return to the camp … for their own safety?'

The priest looked around at the circle of men craning to hear the conversation. 'I am sorry, I cannot do that. These men have the gift of free will; they may choose to exercise it by staying with me or traveling back to their own homes.'

Aimee heard Francisco *hurrumph* under his breath, before continuing to needle the priest.

'I must warn you *padre* that I will need to inform the authorities of the men's potential movement back to the cities … and of your providing assistance to them in violation of a formal quarantine order.' He held the priest's gaze.

Aimee could feel the tension building between the two men, and decided to ask a question before the doctor finished with one of the sharp but polite insults she had seen him use on boorish bureaucrats.

'Father, did you see any sign of bandits in the jungle?' She made a sweeping gesture with her arm to indicate the dark wall of green around them.

The priest tore his eyes away from Francisco and looked at her for a few seconds as though trying to see behind her eyes. 'There are no bandits out there, there are no soldiers out there, there is just us.'

There was a hint of a smile on his lips as he looked at each of them individually, before letting his gaze rest on Francisco for a final few seconds. Then he turned and glided smoothly back into the jungle.

Aimee noticed Francisco shivered despite the evening's humidity. She was feeling pretty spooked herself. *Who mentioned soldiers?* she wondered.

TWELVE

The scream of tearing metal woke the camp at around midnight.

Aimee sat up and blinked in the inky blackness. The camp lights were out and, as the moon wasn't directly over the clearing, the darkness in her cabin was total. She sat still and listened ... it was if the whole camp was holding its breath. She lifted her damp pillow, used it to wipe the perspiration off her face, flung it down and then threw back the mosquito netting.

She got unsteadily to her feet, feeling groggy, and staggered a little as she groped around on her table top for a lantern. She had to screw her eyes shut for a moment against the sepia yellow glow; her eyeballs felt swollen and grainy.

By now Aimee could hear shouts and running footsteps throughout the clearing. She pulled back the elasticized curtain at her window to peer outside. Electric lanterns darted across the muddy clearing like a swarm of giant fireflies, all drawn towards the southern end of the camp.

She pulled on her boots and was about to head out the door when she remembered the insect repellent. Nighttime was the worst for bugs; she wouldn't make it ten feet without getting bitten, sucked or injected by some multi-eyed thing that saw her as a moving bag of food. She sprayed herself all over and also some on her hands, wiped her face with the fluid, then spat a couple of times to rid her mouth of the bitter taste on her lips.

Yelling men careened past her in the dark, their panic filling her with a sense of urgency. As she jogged past Francisco's cabin, she saw it was empty, so continued on to the camp's version of a command center. Aimee heard Alfraedo before she saw him. He was bellowing in Spanish, and then she saw his large head above the men as he yelled and pointed at them as though accusing them of some crime. Francisco was standing next to him. When he caught sight of Aimee, he held up his hand for her to stop, and stepped around the crowd to join her at the rear.

'Some more men have disappeared, but unfortunately it seems they didn't leave quietly in the dark like the others.' Francisco looked over his shoulder as some of the men started shouting back at Alfraedo. 'This time there has been damage to the camp,' he continued. 'They destroyed our generator – that's why we have no lights.'

'But why would they? Why ...' Aimee stopped as she realized the full extent of the damage. No power meant no lights, but it also meant no refrigeration and no water purifiers. 'You'll have to tell your government ministers that we can't stay here now; they'll need to supply another generator or move us to a new quarantine site closer to the city.'

Aimee knew that once the Paraguayans agreed to move the campsite, she wasn't going to let them quarantine her again; she was going to keep going, all the way back home.

Francisco took her hand. 'I'm afraid we cannot inform them of anything, Dr. Weir; we cannot inform *anyone* of anything. It seems the men also destroyed our communications room, the satellite uplink and even the computer equipment.'

'What? They've blinded us ... why? Why would they do that?'

'Most of the men are very angry about being stuck here; and, though they will be paid for the time spent in quarantine, they will miss out on their performance bonuses. Also, there is great fear of the melting sickness. But still, that is no reason to make it difficult for us to communicate with —'

Francisco stopped as a man rushed up to Alfraedo and gestured to the jungle behind the mob. Alfraedo listened for a moment with gritted teeth, then roared to the men, pointing at individuals in the crowd. They cheered and rushed off, looking overjoyed at having some concrete task that they could channel their anger or fear into.

Francisco turned to Aimee. 'They have found a trail leading into the jungle that is strewn with broken machinery parts. Alfraedo is organizing a party to bring the men back. I am sure he will deal with them harshly.'

Alfraedo waded through the remaining workers like an icebreaker pushing through bergs in the Arctic. He nodded at Aimee and Francisco. 'These men cannot have more than thirty minutes start on us. If we hurry we can bring them back to face justice for destroying the company's equipment. I think we may need some extra guns, Doctor, and you would be most welcome as well, Dr. Weir.'

'No.' Francisco stepped in front of Aimee waving his hand back and forth. 'No, we do not need Dr. Weir. She needs to continue her work on the disease. I am happy to accompany you and your men, Alfraedo, and bring my weapon, but I will not condone anything other than *accidental* injury during the apprehension of these men.'

Alfraedo thought for a moment, then said, 'Okay. But I think it best we have all of the weapons with us, Doctor. These men have proved that they can be violent, and it is very dark in the jungle at night. I would prefer to have the guns and not use them, than need them and not have them.'

Francisco exhaled slowly through his nose and nodded. He turned to Aimee with an anguished look on his face, and raised his silver eyebrows as if pleading for her consent. 'I am sure Dr. Weir would be happy to give us her weapon.'

Aimee was frozen with indecision. So far she had given little thought to the gun, but now realized that she felt secure with it hanging at her hip. She didn't want to give it up. She looked into Francisco's eyes and could tell he really didn't want her to trek into the jungle at night. For that matter, neither did she – the thought of it made her shudder.

'No problem,' she said, undoing her belt buckle and sliding the holster off the leather strap.

She handed it to Alfraedo, who nodded his thanks, unbuckled his own belt and threaded the holster onto his hip. He then spun on his heel and started to yell in Spanish to the assembling men.

*

Aimee watched the line of lights bob out into the jungle – Alfraedo and Francisco, both with powerful flashlights, and four men carrying battery lanterns.

She thought of the hurried conversation she'd had with the dapper little doctor just before their departure. She had thanked him for intervening on her behalf and asked how he had known she didn't want to go. His reply still made her feel uneasy. *Because something is not right in this jungle, Dr. Weir. Something ripped apart those soldiers and I do not believe it was a jaguar. Furthermore, I believe that whatever it was is still out there.*

Aimee shivered despite the thick heat and hugged her arms around her body. As she turned back to her cabin, she saw one of the workers sitting at the jungle's edge weeping. Even from a distance she could see the tears that splashed onto his knees were an oily black. A small cloud of mosquitoes whined around his head and shoulders.

*

Francisco could hear his own breathing – a rasping combination of exhaustion and nerves. Louder than usual, it was true, but he still shouldn't have been able to hear it above the sounds of the jungle. *Where are all the forest creatures? Have we frightened them into silence?*

Alfraedo called a halt just over two hours into the search. The trail they followed was faint, but the scatterings of machinery parts and sections of broken foliage were a useful guide. Francisco could not shake the unpleasant suspicion that it was almost too easy to track the men. Alfraedo reached out his hand to a broad leaf at head height – it came away sticky with blood. He pulled free one of his revolvers and held it up beside his face as he whispered over his shoulder, '*Silencio.*' He hunched down and carefully moved forward.

Francisco noticed the men had bunched up – no one wanted to be too far away from the main group. Even he found himself walking so close behind the large and reassuring frame of Alfraedo that he accidentally kicked the man's heels several times. The foliage they pushed through was wet; even in the dark, Francisco could see glistening blood and gore. It was everywhere: on their clothes, their skin; it dripped down on them and squelched beneath their feet. It was clear to Francisco that someone was very badly hurt, or dead.

Francisco knew he was breathing harder and faster, and Alfraedo half turned to him to slowly bring the muzzle of his gun to his lips, before waving them on. Francisco's mouth immediately dried, but he gulped anyway.

The moon broke from the clouds and lit a clearing just behind a thin veil of tangled vines and ferns. A figure sat naked and alone in the center of the silvery open space. The powerful frame seemed misshapen, and was hunched over what looked like a large, skinned monkey. The creature held the object to its face, jaws working, burrowing.

Alfraedo made a guttural sound and parted the curtain of green. He took a single step forward, straightened his back and trained his light on the figure. It seemed oblivious to the shaking beam and continued to gorge itself on the carcass in its hands.

A floating sensation filled Francisco's head, as if it was disconnected from the rest of him. He realized his knees were shaking and his heart pounding. He too moved forward, just one small step, barely aware of the movement.

The other men entered the clearing, forming a line either side of Alfraedo, their lanterns illuminating the space with a yellow glow.

'Hey, *señor* ...' Alfraedo's usually strong voice sounded small and frightened, and ended with a little quiver. He swallowed and tried again. '*Excúseme, señor.*'

This time the naked figure looked up. Francisco gasped as he recognized the face: the priest.

The man's long colorless face, the stark eyes, could have been a carnival mask floating in the torch beams. Blood and viscera coated his arms to the elbows and also his beard, as if he had pushed his entire head into the corpse he held. As Francisco's gaze fell on the carcass in the priest's hands, he recognized it as that of a human being.

Bile rose in his throat as he recalled the desecration of flesh that had once been the American soldiers. *So this is our jaguar*, he thought as he opened his eyes once more on the terrible scene. *Santa Madre de Dios*, he whispered and crossed himself with a shaking hand.

The lifted lanterns also served to illuminate the forest behind the bloody figure. Several carcasses dangled from branches, their ankles bound and throats crushed. The faces of some were bloated and darkened by settling blood, indicating they had been hung upside down while they still lived. With others, it was impossible to tell, as the skin had been ripped from their bodies and flung into higher branches to hang there like drying garments after washing day.

'We have been waiting for you.' The voice seemed to well up from deep within the man, as though his vocal cords had receded into his core. He smiled, showing row upon row of needle-like teeth, still coated with flesh and gristle from the feast he had been enjoying. He turned his head to look at the bodies hung behind him and smiled again. 'Yes, we took them all … we needed them.'

He turned back and his eyes bored into Francisco. 'As we need you. As we need *all* of you.'

Francisco could smell the acrid tang of sour sweat and urine among the men he stood with. *This is what fear smells like*, he thought, as two of the men holding lanterns fled back into the jungle. He would have liked to run as well, but his legs refused to do anything more than shake.

There was a roar like thunder that shook the trees around them and made Francisco cringe and cover his ears in pain and terror. The priest vanished, and Francisco felt a breeze pass by him. He assumed González had entered the jungle in pursuit of the men.

Without the priest's physical presence, the spell was broken and Francisco felt his legs return to him. Just as he was contemplating his own escape, the priest reappeared, both men clasped in his hands.

One hung by the ankle, moaning, his leg clearly broken, a shard of bone extruding through the flesh. The other was held by the throat, the priest's hand compressing flesh and bone to about a quarter of its normal size. The man's head wobbled as if held to the torso by skin alone.

González dropped the men onto the pile of human debris at his feet. 'I am sated now,' he said. 'They will be for later.' He looked at the hanging bodies again. 'All are needed; all will join with us by being consumed.'

Alfraedo lifted his gun and fired five shots. Despite the close range, he only managed three hits; the bullets making a damp *thwacking* sound as they struck the priest's chest. González made no move to dodge them; *it was as if he welcomed them*, Francisco thought; as though he wanted to test his body against them – and found himself to be superior.

González opened his mouth and roared again. It was an inhuman sound that conjured images of hell and cold and darkness, and made Francisco's bowels loosen in terror. In a blur, the priest was in front of Alfraedo, his hand around the large man's throat. He lifted him in one hand, and Francisco heard squeaking noises come from the mining manager's nose and mouth.

Francisco was weeping with dread now. He retched, bile spilling onto his silver goatee. The men with him had fallen to their knees; they looked as though they were praying to the priest, even though he was now something very different. González brought Alfraedo's face close to his own and smiled, his needle-sharp teeth glistening red in the moonlight. He dug his taloned fingers into the meat of Alfraedo's neck and ripped away a large flap of skin from the front of his throat. Arterial blood spurted over the priest's face and shoulders. He opened his mouth, wider than seemed humanly possible, and the red fountain sprayed into its black cavity. Even before the body was drained, González opened his hand and let Alfraedo flop to the ground, his legs and arms still twitching as though being touched by an electrical current.

Francisco was running – he didn't know how – his legs must have just taken over. He hadn't even thought of reaching for his gun;

it remained in its holster, forgotten. He had dropped his flashlight – he couldn't remember when or where – all logic had been washed away by a tidal wave of fear, revulsion and panic. He had made it through the first barrier of ferns when he was knocked from his feet by a blow so powerful he heard the sickening crunch of the large bone in his thigh breaking before he felt it. Then the pain came and it was excruciating; mercifully, he passed out.

Consciousness returned too soon. His ankles were bound together and he was being dragged along the ground, tied to other bodies in some ghastly procession of cadavers and weakly struggling men. He didn't bother fighting; like a small animal in the jaws of a predator, he knew he was without hope. He knew his fate: he and the others were little more than sacks of food to be consumed at leisure by something that was no priest, was no man at all really. Indeed, it was something probably older and infinitely more powerful than any mortal. *Perhaps demons do exist after all*, he thought in his near delirium.

The moon glowed above as they broke into another clearing. In the silvery light, Francisco could make out an enormous banyan tree and a stone building enfolded in its heavy embrace. As he and the other men were dragged up the steps and into the darkness, he smelled the charnel-house odor from inside. His body convulsed in one last desperate act of resistance and he began to yell and struggle.

The procession stopped and the priest looked back at him briefly, gave his needle-sharp smile and licked his lips. Then the movement started again, the column of writhing flesh dragged into the stone building.

Francisco wailed as they entered the pitch darkness. There would be no rescue, no merciful angels coming to save him because he had spent his life aiding his fellow humans. No, he would come to his end in a foul-smelling dungeon at the hands of an evil that was too horrible to contemplate.

Francisco finally remembered the gun still at his hip. He pulled it free and placed the barrel in his mouth. As he felt himself being tipped into a dark, acrid cavity in the floor, his last thought was that he was being pulled down into the very depths of hell.

He pulled the trigger.

THIRTEEN

A imee sat in her cabin staring at the mobile phone and computer on her desk. Both were useless as communication devices now that the uplink to the satellite had been destroyed.

Things were unraveling quickly and she wished Francisco and Alfraedo would return. She almost hoped they hadn't managed to find the saboteurs; there was enough tension in the camp without having to look after prisoners as well.

She switched off the lantern in her cabin and peered through the thin curtains out to the clearing. A few shapes moved about, some ambling, some darting. In the dark, the jungle itself seemed closer, thicker, more menacing and malevolent. She shuddered and dropped the curtain.

She undressed, dragged a damp T-shirt over her head and lay down on the rumpled bed. *Things will be better in the morning. They always look better in the morning*, she thought. She closed her eyes. A bead of perspiration tickled her temple as it ran from her forehead, her feet itched, and the still air felt like warm syrup as she dragged it into her lungs. She put one arm behind her head and immediately smelled her own sour body odor. *Nice*, she thought as she exhaled noisily through compressed lips.

Dawn wasn't far away, but sleep wouldn't come. There was something nagging at her, whispering to her in the dark, just out of focus, refusing to become clear to her fatigued mind. Aimee groaned as she pulled herself up and swung her legs over the side of her bed. She rubbed her face, and sat in silence for a few minutes holding her head. She grabbed her canteen from the table top and sipped loudly – the water tasted like plastic. She wished she had a metal container – they always made the water seem cooler. But you couldn't use metal in the jungle; it rusted, everything rusted. The germ of a thought bloomed in her tired mind.

She stood up and felt in the darkness for her computer. She hesitated a moment at the thought of using up its remaining battery power, then shrugged and switched it on, going immediately to her results for the bacterial DNA match. She had found close approximations to a number of microbial forms with many genus similarities, but her strange bug was stubbornly eluding that final step towards identification.

The effect the microbe had on living tissue was extraordinary and frightening. She had never heard of that level of biocorrosion in anything other than … *Corrosion* … Her fingers leapt across the keyboard as she pursued the thought. She dived into old research papers and mining notes – and found it. Her eyes flew over the notes as she read furiously. Just last decade, there had been a serious pipe failure on the North Slope of Alaska. It transpired that microscopic organisms were eating through the toughened pipes, leading to leakage and finally total failure. *Could it be …?*

She skimmed down the pages looking for clues. She knew that the microorganisms she had been looking for, responsible for converting carbon to natural gas, were anaerobes – they did their job without oxygen or light, which was how they could function so deep below the earth. The biochemistry of their metabolisms was extraordinary and, by their very nature, they were carbon hungry. In simple terms, they ate carbons – that was how they instigated methanogenesis.

Aimee sat back for a second, before switching her screen images to the sample data from the infected men. *Holy shit.* She sat back again, placing both hands on her slick forehead. *Of course, of course, of course.* The bacteria ate carbon, all carbon. It was just doing what it existed to do – and had turned out to be very good at it. Carbon was the fourth-most abundant element in the universe and was present in all known life forms – including the human body, where it was the second-most abundant element after oxygen.

'Oh God, no.' Aimee pushed her hair back wearily. 'It's fucking eating us.'

Clavicula occultus – her 'hidden key' to the world's energy problem – wasn't just converting prehistoric carbon into oil as she'd assumed; it was also consuming the carbon it found in the human body and literally converting it to something else. Maybe even something that may become petroleum in a few hundred thousand years.

Aimee looked up at the ceiling and the golden halo of light thrown by the lantern. She felt heavy, drained of all energy. The depth of the oil and gas chamber meant the microbes had been imprisoned, locked away from the upper world of light and air. The mile-thick barrier had been the human race's first line of defense. *Perhaps, while we've been looking for them, they've just been patiently waiting for us.*

She crushed her eyes shut for a moment, then said softly, 'What have I let loose upon the world?'

She needed to speak to someone but the phone on her desk was useless. *Shit!* Anger welled up inside her, then dissipated to leave a small knot of fear and frustration deep in her belly. She thought of Alex Hunter – he had once been her antidote to fear or loneliness. She needed him right now – his advice, and his strength.

Once again, her last days with him came back to her. She was the one who'd decided it would be best for both of them if he gave up being in the Special Forces; settled down, became more normal. At first she'd asked him, then, towards the end, she had demanded it, and had taken his refusal as him choosing the HAWCs over her. She hadn't even had the courage to say her final farewell in person. She could still remember every detail: the floral notepaper, the blue ink, the words: *You've made your choice, and it's a bad one. I think it's best if I don't see you again ... Goodbye forever, Alex.*

She looked back up to the halo of light and spoke softly. 'I wish I'd never said that.'

*

'I can't reach Aimee.'

Jack Hammerson took the call from Alfred Beadman just after four in the morning. The normally urbane and relaxed chairman of GBR was in a state of high agitation. Hammerson rubbed his face with his free hand, feeling the stubble on his chin, and let the man speak on, allowing himself time to ease into full wakefulness.

'Now there's a quarantine order. The Paraguayan government has issued a no-go directive over that whole area of the jungle and they won't say why. Something's wrong, Jack, Aimee needs help. Is Captain Hunter down there yet?' Beadman was breathing like a marathon runner.

'Yes, Alfred, we know about the Q-order.' Hammerson kept his voice calm, hoping to influence the older man. 'Surprised us a bit, and did slow us up by a day or so, but we've made secondary plans and expect to be there by first light tomorrow. Now, when did she go offline?'

'I don't know exactly. She was supposed to call me about 10 pm. When I didn't hear from her, I tried her phone, then her voice over internet link, then email, then even the site manager's number – nothing's getting through. Seems their satellite link is broken; and then when I called the government official in charge of mining and energy, he told me about the quarantine order. Would the quarantine order necessitate a blackout? Why? Jack, do you think you can use one of your satellites to check on her? I know you can zoom right in these days.'

Hammerson sighed. Why did people think he had some sort of satellite joystick in his top drawer that he could use to swing around a multi-billion-dollar piece of orbiting telemetry at a moment's notice? Still, he couldn't get angry with Beadman for trying all avenues. He knew that Aimee was like a daughter to him.

'Alfred, satellites are almost useless for vision down there – too much green for us to see anything clearly. But I know where the HAWCs are, and I think you know what Alex is like – he'll find her, no matter where she is. He and his team are less than a day from making contact. We all just have to be patient. I'll call you as soon as I get any further information. Now get some sleep. Good night, Alfred.'

Hammerson heard the chairman splutter a bit more, but hung up anyway. There wasn't anything further he could share with him. He looked at the clock: 4:14 am. He'd give it a few hours then get another field update. Wouldn't hurt to have Alex and the team punch it up another level.

*

Adira Senesh slowly pulled the tiny receiver from her ear. Her hand shook slightly and her eyes burned as she considered the implications of the conversation she'd just overheard between her superior officer and the chairman of the company that Aimee Weir worked for.

She spoke softly in Hebrew, cursing Jack Hammerson for holding her back from accompanying Alex Hunter on the mission, and for refusing to keep her informed of his operational status.

As a Mossad Kidon agent, Adira had believed she was the best in the world – until she had worked with Captain Alex Hunter on a recent mission in the Middle East. He had saved her life several times in the space of a few days; he had fought with her and for her, and he had kept her safe. She had vowed to do the same for him – and she *would* do the same for him. She always repaid her debts.

Her mind worked furiously on ways to join the mission – but each option was discarded as being impractical or seen as treason. She cursed again; someone would pay dearly if Alex was killed. She gritted her teeth and lifted her arm; a small dagger appeared in her hand and she brought it down on the desk top with enough force to embed it several inches into the hard wood.

FOURTEEN

A lex had slept little during the night. His mind had refused to shut down, and he didn't know whether the images he'd seen were the result of an overactive imagination, or whether he was receiving some sort of forewarning about Aimee's current predicament. He closed his eyes for a moment and tried to ignore the throbbing in his head.

He realized Garmadia had slowed and was closely watching Saqueo and Chaco. Both boys were moving ahead cautiously, peering left and right into the jungle.

'Why are we slowing?' Alex asked.

Garmadia motioned with his head. 'These are animal trails we are following, Captain Hunter. There are no people here, no tracks or paths. We could be the first people to walk along here in many years, and we need to be cautious as it is the beginning of the wet season. This area is honeycombed with subsurface limestone caves. The more water that passes below us, the more chance there is of a new cave opening up. The caves can be very deep and can swallow a platoon whole.'

More caves and underground lakes, thought Alex. *Just great.*

Up ahead, Saqueo yelped in surprise as a small striped pig belted from the undergrowth, shot between his legs, then slipped back through the vines and fern fronds. Chaco leapt after it, pulling a small blade from his belt and shouting excitedly to Saqueo who yelled something angrily in response. After a second of indecision, the older boy ran off in pursuit of his brother, leaving Alex and the team stranded on the narrow trail.

Alex heard the boars before they broke from the jungle.

Razorbacks, he thought, marvelling at their size. Wild boars were only introduced to South America in the early twentieth century, but already their population had flourished. There were stories of full-grown male boars weighing up to 800 pounds. The larger of these two was more like 600 pounds, but a terrifying sight nonetheless, with long yellow tusks curving up either side of a long blunt head, and a coarse coat that looked as though it was fashioned from wooden spikes and splinters. Alex thought it looked more like a hair-covered rhino standing in the gloom of the undergrowth.

Maria pulled Michael behind the HAWCs, whose hands immediately went to their sidearms. Time seemed to stop for a few seconds as the elite soldiers and two wild animals contemplated their next moves.

A squeal from deeper in the jungle pulled the massive animals' heads in the direction the baby boar had bolted. Both leapt into the forest, bulldozing a path in their haste to reach their offspring. Alex dropped his pack and sprinted after them. He knew the damage these beasts could do to a man, let alone to the two boys in their path.

He caught up to the female quickly, his long powerful legs easily keeping pace with her. Her head reached the top of his thigh and Alex watched her powerful shoulder and neck muscles bunch as she knocked undergrowth out of her way. The male was still hundreds of feet in front, and the more dangerous of the two, but Alex decided he could reduce the threat by dealing with them one at a time.

He really didn't want to kill either animal for protecting its young, so he lifted his arm up high and brought his armored fist down on the flat forehead of the charging animal. The ceramic plates of his gloves, coupled with his enormous power, felled the animal immediately. Its 340-pound body brought down a small tree before it slid to a halt.

As Alex increased his speed, he heard Saqueo's voice yelling frantically and saw the boy sitting high in a tree. He slowed long enough to guess at Saqueo's meaning – he was screaming and pointing down the path. Alex could hear the massive male boar smashing the undergrowth out if its way up ahead – it must have been almost upon the smaller boy.

Alex leapt forward as he heard a shrill scream.

In another few paces he broke into a clearing that was totally free of any vegetation. The sunlight boiled through to the ground, creating a low mist over the bare, and strangely dry, earth. He spotted the boy – Chaco stood at the center of the clearing – and the boar had already commenced its charge. The outcome was going to be catastrophic for the youth.

Alex knew he couldn't make it to Chaco, but he could make it to the animal. He lowered his shoulder, increased his speed and headed on a collision course with a creature made of material a lot tougher than human flesh. Chaco screamed, and Alex heard another yell that he realized came from his own throat as he collided with the boar. The thud of the impact and its shock wave made the boy sit down hard. The boar must have sensed Alex's approach for it had managed to turn its head just enough to get a tusk into his upper arm; blood spurted onto the ground at Chaco's feet. But the beast had taken the full force of Alex's weight, which, combined with his velocity, was sufficient to roll it into the thick ferns, where it lay still.

Alex got to one knee and placed his hand over his torn arm. It hurt like hell, but nothing was broken. It was the pain returning to his head that concerned him more.

He lifted the boy to his feet. 'Are you all right?'

Chaco quickly wiped tears from his dirty face, and looked from Alex to the still hindquarters of the giant boar, then back at Alex. His eyes were wide in disbelief and his face broke into a smile. Saqueo was yelling to them from the edge of the clearing, his jubilant chant blocking out the sounds of the jungle all around them. '*El capitán Hunter es Super*—'

The boy's words turned to a scream. Alex felt the ground tremble and turned quickly, but there was no time to avoid the boar's charge. Recovered, it raced towards them, its small red eyes filled with a murderous rage.

Alex only had time to pull Chaco behind him and hold up an arm, hand out flat.

The impact was like an explosion – then the ground gave way and they were falling – Alex, Chaco and 600 pounds of furious mammal plunging through a thin crust of limestone into a shallow pool of water thirty feet below.

As Alex hit the water, he remembered Garmadia's warning about the caves: *they can swallow whole platoons. No wonder nothing is growing here*, he thought.

Unfortunately, Alex wasn't the first to his feet. The impact knocked the wind from his lungs and tossed him through the air to smash against the slick wall of the large, bowl-shaped crater. He heard the boar squeal in rage, the sound eardrum-shattering within the small cave, then came Chaco's voice calling his name.

Alex groaned in pain. A melon-sized piece of stone fell from the ceiling to splash into the water beside him, and he glanced up at the hole above. They had come through at a weak point, but the whole canopy could only have been a few feet thick. He knew the entire roof of the cave was in danger of shaking loose, and any loud noises could result in them being buried alive under tons of stone.

The boar was gouging the shallow water with its head, throwing up plumes of liquid as it worked itself into an even greater rage.

Chaco had climbed onto the base of a stalagmite and was trying to shinny up the slippery stone as he would a tree trunk. For every foot of the water-smoothed stone he climbed, he slid back down the same amount. He yelped in frustration and the beast turned its head, trying to locate the sound. When it found Chaco, it charged.

Alex reached into the water and retrieved a fist-sized rock to throw at the maddened creature. It bounced off its shoulder and thudded into the wall, where it exploded, causing dust and smaller fragments of stone to rain down on them from the ceiling. Alex reached for his gun, then had second thoughts. He couldn't chance the discharge echo bringing down the entire roof. Instead, he pulled out his longest Ka-Bar blade; the laser-sharpened black steel a deadly tusk of his own.

By now Chaco had managed to climb about six feet above the water and was hanging on grimly. The boar tried to climb the base of the stalagmite, its blunt mouth open and showing rows of dog-like canines at the front and flattened yellow crushing molars deeper in. Alex knew what it wanted: wild boars were omnivores and meat made up a large part of their diet.

The sharpened hooves skidded again and again on the slick stone, unable to get purchase. Chaco slipped down a few inches and yelped. The beast opened its mouth wider. Alex needed to act.

The boar heard him running towards it and turned its head, utter-ing an ear-blasting squeal that would have frozen any normal man. Alex heard Chaco's wail as he and the beast came together in a thud of flesh and bone that echoed around the small cave. Alex had enormous strength, but he was easily outweighed by the boar, and its thick neck and shoulders gave it immense power. He drove his blade deep into the band of muscle across the beast's shoulders, but, as the animal tossed its head in pain and surprise, he lost his grip on the knife.

He grabbed the creature by its two, foot-long curved tusks and tried to keep its jaws away from any soft tissue on his body. Its crushing maw was easily capable of pulverising bone or tearing free large chunks of flesh. Though Alex planted his legs and strained with all his energy, the creature's huge bulk pushed him back again. He skidded a foot as the boar started to gain traction, and re-membered something his father used to say when he was a boy: *Catching a tiger was easy; deciding what to do with it after that is the hard part.*

The blade wasn't far from his grip, but he would need to release one hand to reach up for it. He knew he was quick enough – then he could aim for a more vital area of the boar.

Just as he was coiling his muscles to act, there was an explosive splash behind him.

'Cuidado! Allí viene el jabalí!'

Chaco's high-pitched voice was frantic, but Alex was locked in a death struggle and couldn't chance looking at the boy to try to work out what he meant. *I really hope you're telling me that my friends have arrived,* he thought. The boar dipped its head and lifted it quickly, nearly wrenching itself from Alex's grasp.

The boy was yelling again. '*El otro, el otro.*'

Alex knew only a little Spanish, and by the time he'd registered the words, *the other one,* there came a crushing blow to his back that forced all the breath from his body and pushed him into the face of the male boar.

The female razorback had obviously regained consciousness and had come in search of its mate, leaping down into the sinkhole. Now it joined the battle, and Alex found himself sandwiched between two stinking pigs, both determined to rip him to pieces and probably devour the remains.

The female's massive teeth clamped around his upper arm and started to grind together. Alex yelled as pain burst through his body in a red-hot wave. He had to let go of the male or the flesh would be ripped from the bone of his arm. His body was on fire: his arm burned, and his ribs were agonizing bands across his back. But nothing was as intense as the inferno of rage that consumed his brain.

He yelled into the male boar's face and, with a massive burst of strength, twisted his hand sideways, snapping off its deadly tusk and swinging it up and into its eye. Any thought of sparing the creatures' lives had evaporated the moment the rage had taken him.

The male screamed in pain and threw its head up and away. It gave Alex enough time to swing his free elbow around and into the side of the female's snout, stunning it long enough for him to pull his arm free and turn to grab its head. In one motion, he swung the 350-pound beast around and brought its body down on the back of the male. The weight of the female, combined with massive G-forces, flattened the male boar into the water.

Alex leapt at it, pulled his knife from the male's shoulder, and used the hilt like a club as he punched down with all his strength onto the center of its skull. The deep crunch bounced off the walls of the cave and the massive animal didn't pull its head up out of the water again.

Still, Alex continued to rain blows down on the broken skull until the head was a flattened mat of coarse hair, shattered bone and gore. The limestone smell of the cave was replaced by the coppery scent of blood.

The female hobbled over to one side of the underground chamber, its frame bruised and battered after the encounter with Alex.

For Alex, a red haze blurred everything. He turned to the smaller animal, the black blade still in his hand, and felt a mix of triumph and exhilaration at the thought of delivering it the same fortune as its mate. The boar turned and faced the wall, standing quietly – probably not wanting to see the alpha predator that was about to bring its death.

Alex gripped the blade harder. *Kill it. Tear it in two!* a voice screamed in his head.

He lifted the blade; he would bring it down in the center of its head. Penetrate the skull and brain in a single powerful blow. No, that was too quick, he wanted the beast to feel pain. He would disembowel it first.

The boar grunted and lowered its blunt snout even further.

Alex took another step closer to the animal. *While it lives, it's a risk. Kill it. Exterminate it, annihilate it ...* The voice was getting louder. Alex put one hand up to his head and pressed his knuckles into his temple.

The red haze engulfed him. Images flashed through his mind like a movie projector stuck on high speed. *Who is that? Hammerson's Monster. Kill it ... now!*

Over and over again the voice roared in his head. Alex felt outside of himself, a spectator watching from a back row as squeals and screams bounced around the walls. Fists rose and fell time and again. Like machines, blurring with speed and ferocity. The warm, coppery scent intoxicated him, but then came the more disgusting odors of freshly torn flesh, viscera, and opened bowels.

The squeals stopped but the screams continued. Alex blinked as blood stung his eyes. The screaming was coming from behind him, not from the boar. He looked down: the beast was barely recognisable. Its limbs and flesh were rent, but not by a blade ... more as though it had been torn apart.

Alex looked down at his hands: they were soaked in blood. He could see grazes and cuts crisscrossing the skin the gloves didn't cover.

No witnesses. The boy ... finish it.

'No!'

He screamed the word aloud, feeling a shock wave pass through his body as he rebelled against his subconscious. The chaotic storm of impulses in his mind started to calm and his breathing slowed. He knew he should feel revolted by what he had done. Instead, he felt a sated glow deep inside that troubled him.

Chaco slid down from the stalagmite, but when Alex looked at the boy he flinched and wouldn't come any closer.

'I'm okay now,' Alex said, holding out his hand and motioning the boy nearer.

Instead, Chaco moved to the cave opening and looked upwards, then quickly back at Alex, fear on his ashen face. Then he called out his brother's name, his voice watery and tremulous.

Alex glanced down and caught sight of his reflection in the still water around his legs. He grimaced at the mask of blood and gore that stared back at him. He kneeled down and washed his face and chest, and rubbed the mess from his gloves. He got to his feet and stood for a few moments, staring into the darkness. What were the military doctors doing to him in his medical sessions? Why was he becoming more like this – enjoying the blood and the death, even revelling in it? He would speak to Hammerson, and to the doctors, Graham and Marshal, when he got back. This time, they would answer him, or else.

*

'Sam, are you reading me?'

Alex's communication was immediately picked up by his second-in-command at the surface.

'We're at the edge of the clearing, boss. Been here for a while, wondering how to get you back up to us. Captain Garmadia's warned us not to get too close to the edge of the hole as it may collapse the entire area on top of you. What's going on down there? We've heard plenty of shouting and squealing. I hope you aren't anywhere near those giant bacon trucks that went after the boys.' Sam paused for a moment, then said more quietly, 'Are you okay in the cave, boss?'

Alex smiled grimly in the dark. Sam was only a few years older than Alex but acted more like a big brother some times. He knew of Alex's distaste for dark caves following his Antarctic mission beneath the ice; Alex had been one of a few survivors but ended up with deep psychological scars that still woke him up in sweats and violent rages. Aimee Weir had also survived – Alex often wondered what her burden was.

'Yep, I'm fine, Uncle. The pigs are … gone.' Alex looked at the mountains of flesh bleeding into the water.

'Kid okay?' Sam knew about Alex's rages too; how, when they took him over, it could be extremely dangerous for anyone close by.

Alex looked at Chaco, who stood silent and still like a small ghost at the rear of the cave. 'Yeah, he's fine too. Just thinks it's time to leave … like me.'

'How you want to do it?' Sam asked. 'As I said, the captain here gets real jittery if we step out into the clearing.'

Alex looked up to the cave ceiling. 'How much rope have you got? We're about twenty feet down under a lip of weak limestone – some areas more solid than others. You'll need to stay well clear – at least forty back.'

'We've only got about forty feet of rope overall. We need to tie it off to one of these tree trunks, or sink a ground anchor, then run it across the open space and drop it down to you – I reckon we need about sixty at least. I could crawl across and try to anchor it a bit closer to the edge, but that's about it.'

'No, stay clear; the roof's already raining down on us in some areas.'

Alex heard Sam check with the CDC scientists for more rope. The reply wasn't promising. Then he heard Garmadia's voice speaking Spanish, probably to Saqueo.

'Hold for five, boss,' Sam said. 'Garmadia has an idea.'

While he waited, Alex held his hands up under the column of light pouring into the cave. Where they had been cut and battered moments ago, they were now streaked with pink scars. He grunted to himself and looked at the boy. Chaco was shivering in the dark, his thin arms wrapped around himself.

After another moment, Sam came back online. 'Seems this jungle is a toolbox as well as a lunchbox for the locals. Saqueo has brought some vines that look like intertwined horsehair, and plenty strong too. Should give us an extra thirty feet. Be on its way down to you in two minutes.'

Alex nodded to Chaco and pointed to the hole in the ceiling. 'Time to go, son.'

The boy wouldn't move. Alex swore softly. He recognized shock when he saw it.

'Was it that bad – was I that bad?' He shook his head. 'Sorry, kid. I guess I'm not a superhero, after all.'

Sam's voice: 'Heads!'

The rope, tied to a fist-sized stone, came hurtling into the pit. Alex shot out a hand and caught the rock before it hit the water.

'Good work,' he called back. 'We're coming up.'

The climb was harder than he'd anticipated. He had to bind Chaco to his back, as he kept trying to break from Alex's grip. Now he hung there motionless, but continued to call to his brother. In addition, their combined weight caused a sawing motion on the broken edge of the roof. The rope started to smoke and fray, and pieces of stone rained down on them – some the size of a truck tire. Alex tried to keep the debris from the boy's exposed head, batting the stones away, but that meant having to suspend the climb and hang one-armed. As they got closer to the lip, more stones broke away, many striking Alex on the shoulders and face.

He felt the boy wriggling on his back, then the rope he had used to bind him loosened. The boy had freed himself. The fraying rope could not be used a second time, so Alex reached around quickly with his free arm and grabbed Chaco as he started to slide away. He flung him upwards and out through the opening.

As he no longer had to protect the boy, Alex could concentrate on climbing, and the slight loss of weight meant he reached the top of the hole almost immediately after Chaco. He saw the boy was already up and running to his brother, who grabbed and hugged him. The small boy cried and chattered rapidly, and Saqueo frowned and stared over his head at Alex.

Alex wiped his hands on his pants, then slowly bent to retrieve and wind up the rope. *Another great day at the office*, he thought, as he walked over to a grinning Sam Reid.

FIFTEEN

Aimee sat on the floor of her pre-built cabin and leaned back against the wall. She stared at the skirting board and the line of mold that had started to grow there. It hadn't rained again last night, but she knew the respite wouldn't last, and if the damp and humidity were bad now, just wait until it was bucketing down outside. *Ugh*, she thought, a heavy weariness settling over her.

She surveyed the room. Piles of soiled clothing created small islands on the floor, and a pair of very muddy boots with their tongues out lay beside the door like a pair of dirty sleeping dogs. She needed to urinate, but couldn't bring herself to step outside. She looked up at the empty washbasin, considering it.

It was midmorning and Francisco and the men still hadn't returned. Deep in the pit of her stomach she knew they never would. *The jungle ate them*, she thought miserably. She lowered her head onto her arms. She was beyond tired and had a headache that extended from behind her eyes all the way down to her neck and shoulders. She closed her eyes and exhaled; sleep seemed like something that had happened to her in another life.

A loud bang on the door made her jump, and she laughed out loud. *Perfect, I'm a nervous wreck as well as a physical wreck.*

A voice in Spanish muttered an apology then the banging started again. Aimee placed the heels of her hands in the sockets of her eyes and rubbed hard until they ached. *Get up, Aimee Louise Weir.* She wondered what Alex would say if he saw her sitting on the floor in a giant lump of dirty clothing, mud and sweat. She stood slowly and groaned.

She looked out the window and saw a group of younger workers standing just beyond the door, apparently debating whether to knock again. It was hard to tell: nearly everything sounded like an argument in the rapid local language.

'If you've brought me a cheeseburger and a soda, come on in,' she muttered.

When the men spotted her, they waved and stood back from the door. She should have expected this to happen. With Alfraedo and Francisco missing, she was the remaining member of the *gerencia*, the management. She needed to tell them something, or at least be strong for the men who were sick and dying.

She lifted her water bottle and tipped it to her lips; its contents were warm and not refreshing at all. She tipped the rest of it over her face and let it run down the front of her T-shirt to mix with the perspiration that beaded between her breasts.

She sucked in a breath and pulled open the door.

'*Habla inglés?*' she asked.

Her Spanish was weak, and the thought of trying to keep up with the lightning-fast language made her feel even more exhausted. She needed someone to translate for her. 'Uhhh, *habla cualquiera inglés?*'

Towards the back of the group, a small, wiry man tentatively put his hand up and smiled, displaying a mouth missing its front teeth.

'*Fantastico.* Your name …? Aahhh, *qué es su namo?*'

Blank stare; the men looked at each other.

'*Es su namo … su nombre?*' Ah, forget it. 'What's your name?'

'*Mi nombre es Tomás, señora Weir. Si* … yes, I speak tiny English.' He held his thumb and forefinger an inch apart and grinned broadly, seemingly oblivious of the vampire effect his lone canines had on his smile.

Aimee nodded in relief. 'Thank you, Tomás. Can you please tell the men what I am saying?'

'I try, *señora* Weir. But please, not fast for me.'

Tomás threaded his way through the small crowd towards Aimee. Some of the other men slapped him on the back, as though he had just been elected mayor, or had scored a date with her. Aimee couldn't help grinning at the thought: she was the tallest person in the camp and towered above the locals.

She put out her hand for Tomás to shake. He looked at it for a moment, then grasped it, pumping it hard and turning to grin over his shoulder. Aimee was sure a small blush appeared on his weathered cheeks.

'Tomás, please tell everyone that Alfraedo and Francisco are still out in the jungle scouting for the men who recently fled the camp. They wish to bring them back, or at least make sure they are all okay.'

She waited while he translated. He seemed to use unnecessarily long strings of words, but she had no reason not to trust his translation. A few of the men asked questions, and Tomás nodded and turned to Aimee. She already knew what he was going to say.

'The men, they already know this, but they say to me, when will they be returning?' He gazed up at her, waiting for an answer.

Returning? Never. The jungle ate them – didn't you know?

Aimee smiled, or at least lifted her lips and cheeks into the semblance of a friendly and confident expression. She thought quickly. Best if she responded as she did in board meetings when asked a detailed question that she didn't have an answer for: camouflage it by giving a bit of information then changing the subject.

'Alfraedo and his men will only be in the jungle for as long as necessary. I believe this will only be for a short time. I'm sure he would not want you to worry about them. There is, however, another team of doctors arriving either this evening or tomorrow.' *Please be true*, she thought. 'They are coming to assist us and tell us when we can go home.'

She nodded at Tomás, signalling she had finished. He was quiet for a moment, obviously thinking over what she had said, then he turned to speak to the men. They talked among themselves, some looking at Aimee with expressions of disbelief or resignation, then the group started to break up and head back to their tents.

Aimee now noticed that the tents had been moved. The majority were packed tightly together, almost in a ring, at one end of the camp – close to one another for security, but as far away from the isolation cabins as they could get without actually being in the jungle.

Aimee looked at Tomás. His face was a mix of annoyance and frustration. 'What did the men say?' she asked.

The small man looked briefly over his shoulder at the retreating men, then turned back to her and spoke without looking up into her face. 'They are afraid, *señora* Weir. Many wish to track back to the river, where they hope to find transport to the city. They do not care that this may cause them to lose their bonus pay, or that there is a *cuarentena* order.' Tomás looked over his shoulder again, as if to check the men were out of hearing range. 'They are frightened of the nights here now. They say a *demonio* is loose in the jungle.'

Oookay, a demon now. Great, Aimee thought. She had enough real problems to worry about without agonizing about imaginary ones. She pulled her tired face into another smile, hoping to show she empathised but without acknowledging there was anything to fear.

It must have worked. Tomás smiled his vampire smile at her and said, 'They are young, and most have families. But I am not afraid … and I am not married.'

Aimee laughed at his bravado and small attempt at flirting. She patted him on the shoulder. 'I am not afraid – or married – either.'

The sun inched above the tall tree line, bathing the campsite in its yellow rays for the first time, even though it was already mid-morning. Aimee turned her face to the warmth and inhaled. The sunlight banished the last of the jungle's humid shadows – for a time. Momentarily, she could almost believe everything was normal.

'Stay close to me, Tomás,' she said. 'You are promoted to communications manager.' He looked confused so she tried again. 'Uhh, you are now *director de comunicaciones, si*?' She patted his shoulder once more.

'*Si, si*, thank you, *señora* Weir.'

Tomás wiped his hand on his shirt and held it out to her, trying to stand a little straighter. Aimee smiled and shook it. He made a gesture with his hand, as if writing in the air. Aimee watched him for a moment before catching on.

'Oh, you want me to write the title down for you? Sure.' She nodded and Tomás beamed once again.

*

As Aimee approached the isolation cabins, she could hear sobbing – *tears of despair from the damned*, she thought before shaking the morbid impression from her mind. They had two cabins full now, and there would be need for another shortly. As before, once all the men died, they would seal and burn the cabin. It was a waste of a finite resource, but there was no one to clean them, and they could not risk further infection from the liquid debris.

Aimee had found coveralls, latex gloves and surgical masks for them both. When helping Tomás pull on his protective clothing, she noticed he had pinned her note to his dirty T-shirt. He had insisted on transferring his new job title to the chest of his coverall and it hung there now, like a creased paper sheriff's badge.

As they stood at the door of the first cabin, she saw the fear in Tomás's eyes. Everyone in the camp knew of the disease and what it meant to enter the *muerto cabana* – the death cabin: there was no return.

She pushed through the door and under the plastic sheeting. The smell that greeted her was both acrid and faecal – like shit and diesel fuel mixed together. She saw that Tomás was shivering and touched his shoulder. He looked up briefly and nodded. His eyes were very large and his brown face was tinged yellow from fear.

There were four beds, all occupied. Two of the men recently brought in were conscious and had needed to be tied down to prevent their escape when they learned they had the melting disease. Now they lay still and sobbed black tears onto stained pillows. Plastic sheeting had been hung between the beds to shield the men from seeing the progression and effects of the disease on the poor soul lying next to them.

Aimee indicated with her head towards the two conscious men. 'Tell them help is coming.'

Tomás nodded and spoke softly, his voice weak with fear. As he stepped closer to the beds, one of the men started shouting and jerked against his bonds. He spat at Tomás, and Aimee only just pulled him out of the way before the black gobbet struck the plastic sheet in front of him and slid slowly to the floor.

Tomás's hands were up and pressed together in prayer and she could see his mouth moving behind his mask. *Good idea*, she thought. *We could definitely do with some help here.* She took him by the arm, led him to the exit and held open the plastic. 'Wait out here for me, Tomás.'

She closed the door, drew in a strained breath through her mask, and turned to the last two beds at the rear of the hut. Her eyes watered and she blinked to clear them. The man on the first bed was little more than a torso, black column-like stains the only sign of where his arms and legs used to be. The restraints that had bound him sat limply on the discolored sheets. Aimee moaned before thinking and his head slowly turned towards her. She couldn't tell whether he actually saw her, as his eyes were totally black, from sclera to pupil. But she felt as if he was looking at her and his despair darkened her soul.

I'm goddamn helpless, she thought. *I have no idea what to do.* The more she found out, the more she realized how little she knew. She still had no idea how long it took between initial infection and the liquefying symptoms; she knew it was fast – faster in some than others – but just how fast? The lingering question that bothered the hell out of her though was how many infected and infectious people were walking around outside without knowing it?

What she did know was that once the symptoms were apparent, the disease was irreversible. It seemed the nerve endings died first, so the necrotic symptoms were not accompanied by pain – at least, as far as she could tell. Perhaps the brain just refused to believe the signals it was receiving, or became infected itself.

So many questions, she thought. Without power to access the internet or radio communications, she could do little more than record the data and then watch the men die. *Just as these men are going to die*, she thought miserably.

She backed up a few steps and stood in the center of the cabin, staring at the floor as her mind worked. She noticed black liquid from one of the beds oozing into the cracks in the wooden flooring. She would have to seal off the cabin soon. Better still, burn it, but she doubted if she could find the strength to do that alone.

She needed to prepare another isolation hut, but she was running out of cabins. And what happened then?

*

Below the cabin, the black fluid continued to drip to the ground. Once the rain stopped, most of the clearing dried out quickly, but under the cabins small pools of moisture remained, teeming with mosquito larvae. The growing puddle of black fluid was located next to one of these pools. Its surface surged, as though disturbed by a small wave, and the black fluid slid into the natural pool. The jerking and spinning waterborne larvae within it stopped moving, then, one after another, they all turned black.

SIXTEEN

Alex and Sam walked together in silence, listening to the chaotic commotion of the jungle all around them. It was still only mid-morning and the temperature hadn't yet reached anywhere near its peak, but the humidity had already begun to climb as the evening's moisture lifted into the air as a heavy vapor. The steam dragged with it all the smells of the jungle, from the living to the recently dead – rich, dark soil, heavily scented flowers, rotting plants and hidden carcasses. The cycle of life and death was speeded up here: animals and plants died brutally and quickly, and decomposed back into the earth just as rapidly.

Saqueo and Chaco weaved in and out of the foliage just in front of the HAWCs, keen to stay close since the boar attack. But the younger boy avoided even looking at Alex.

The communication stud in Alex's ear pinged twice: headquarters. He held up a clenched fist and the HAWCs stopped immediately. Sam called to the two boys, and Michael Vargis caught on after bumping into Franks's back.

Alex walked a few paces ahead. 'Arcadian,' he said.

The call was unexpected, which usually meant something new, something bad, or something worse. The studs only had a short range, and the communication satellite had to be focused to allow them to pick up a long-range transmission. Alex's regular check-ins with headquarters were timed for when the communication bird was doing a sweep over the continent. Seeing this wasn't a designated intersect time, Alex guessed Hammer deemed whatever information was coming to be critical.

As always, the colonel wasted no time on introductions or pleasantries. 'Be advised, Arcadian, mining camp has entered an unexpected communications void. VELA is being rerouted and will be "eyes on" in approximately 260 minutes. No detonation heat signature, no prior communication warnings and no new hostile activity encountered – there's a high probability the problem is technical. No other information until visuals. Over.'

'Understood. Over.'

Alex exhaled and turned around to look at the team. All their eyes were upon him. He motioned to Sam, who immediately walked forward with eyebrows raised.

'News, boss?'

'The mining camp's in blackout – they don't know why.' Alex's eyes ranged over the jungle surrounding them. 'But the Hammer wouldn't rotate a VELA if he thought all was okay. We're moving too slow, Uncle; we need to pick it up.'

Sam shook his head slowly. 'We could, but they can't. We'll burn them out and then either have to carry them or leave them behind. We can drop the toy soldier, but we'll need the CDC when we get there.'

Alex stared at the non-HAWCs for a moment, then swivelled to look at Chaco and Saqueo, then back into the jungle.

Sam must have guessed what he was thinking. 'Boss, I reckon it'd be best if we didn't split up right now – won't do a lot of good if you get there hours before us. And if it *is* a biological outbreak, those bugs could be even tougher than you. You're not helping anyone dead – think about that.'

Alex slowly turned back to Sam. 'You're right. Hammerson said he'd have visuals in a few hours – nothing we can do till then anyway.' He nodded towards Michael and Maria Vargis. 'Let's grab their packs and push it up another gear.' He squinted into the thick vegetation again and made a decision. 'Let's put the gauntlets on – I think we're getting close. Inform Mak.'

'You got it, boss.' Sam walked back to update the HAWCs.

Alex turned back to the jungle and swore under his breath as he thought about Aimee. *That girl sure knows how to find trouble.*

Maria Vargis came up to him, wiping her hands together, then rubbing her face, ears and neck. She handed him the small plastic bottle she'd been holding under her arm. 'Insect repellent – our own brand – CDC strength.'

'Thanks,' Alex said. He'd removed his torn sleeves after the boar attack and saw that she was frowning at the scar tissue that had formed over the top of injuries that were only hours old. She looked about to ask a question so he interrupted her.

'Michael your only son?'

She nodded.

'And where is Mr. Vargis?'

'Dead, I hope.' She swore under her breath in Greek before changing the subject. 'What's this for?' She pointed to the dark gauntlet that extended from the top of his armored glove to just below his elbow.

'Wild boar repellent – our own brand.' He winked at her.

She mouthed *okay* with raised eyebrows, then motioned with her head at the bottle. 'You should get your team to apply repellent every few hours. Believe me, in an equatorial rainforest environment, there are things that don't care how big and tough you think you are. To them, you're just a moving bag of food.'

'Nice thought.' Alex chuckled and slathered the lotion over his exposed skin. He knew she was right to be concerned about insects – they were very efficient parasites and disease carriers. In fact, he'd been wondering about them himself.

'You think the disease in the drill camp may be spread by bugs?' he asked. 'That's where it might have originated?'

Maria shook her head. 'Down here, the percentage of insects that are haematophagous – blood drinkers – is a large part of the total biomass. Most of them inject an anticoagulant to keep the blood flowing as they feed. A large grouping of warm-blooded mammals, like the campsite, will attract millions of biting and sucking organisms. So I would say, yes, they are my definite suspects for vector transmission. But do I think that's where the disease came from?' She sucked in a deep breath as though steeling herself for a distasteful thought. 'No, I don't think so. I hope I'm wrong, but I think this could be an incidence of something I have only seen once, via some CDC archival photographs.'

Alex's eyes were on his team as Maria spoke: Sam had portioned most of the contents of Maria's and Michael's packs between the HAWCs and Captain Garmadia. He had set aside the heavier objects, and pointed to them and then to Alex when he saw him watching. Alex nodded; he would take those things himself.

Maria seemed to be thinking of a way to phrase what she wanted to say next. 'If the information we have been sent by the scientist on site is accurate …' She stopped and looked up at him. 'Captain Hunter, do you know Dr. Weir? Is she competent?'

Alex walked over to the pile of extra gear and started to incorporate it into his pack. 'I know Aimee very well,' he said without looking at Maria, 'we're old friends. She's the best in the world at what she does.'

He felt Maria staring at him; he guessed she was probably smiling.

'Well, of course she is,' she said. 'Okay, now I see why we need to hurry, yes?'

Alex didn't answer; he wouldn't be drawn on his and Aimee's past relationship. Just the thought of her in danger made him want to charge ahead of the group and make sure she was safe. *If she's sick or in trouble, I'll never forgive myself for taking so long to reach her.* He felt his body surge forward of its own accord and had to consciously keep himself in check.

'Hey!' Maria was jogging to keep pace with him.

He slowed down slightly and allowed her to catch up, then spoke without turning. 'Tell me where you saw the disease before.'

'It's rare, or we think it's rare as we've only come across it once before – in the 1920s, when South Africa was digging extraordinarily deep mines to keep up its production of gold. But that one time was enough to scare a lot of people and put it straight onto our Biohazard Level 1 watch list – in fact, probably as our first inglorious member. The miners went down a long way – miles, in fact – and without all the fancy digging and drilling equipment we have today. Some of the mines were so deep they built donkey stables down there, and even installed beds so the men could sleep between shifts without going back to the surface. As they went deeper, the mines got hotter and the rocks became more pressurized. Did you know that at that depth stone can shatter like glass?'

Alex nodded, his eyes grim. 'I know a little about working in caves.'

Maria searched his face for a moment then continued. 'Well, they found more gold, and also diamonds, but also something else. The most famous mine at the time was the Egoli, the great Golden Well. They dug through into a cavern about two miles down that contained a type of stone never seen before, and the sedimentation striations above it were all crushed – as if the new stone had punched through the layers above it and come to rest where it was found. The men decided to take a look inside … and that's when things went bad. According to the one remaining record, "the stone bled" where they dug into it, dripping a "tar-like substance that stung the eyes and stuck to the skin". Within a few hours, there were instances of horrifying biocorrosion in both the humans and pack animals. Within a few days, twenty men were dead. Again going by what was said in that one remaining record, the men "just melted away and disappeared between the cracks in the rocks". Whatever that tar-like substance was, it contained a biological residue that was inimical to living tissue.' Maria shivered.

'Jesus Christ. How did they cure it?' Alex didn't want to believe this may be the same thing that had closed down Aimee's camp.

Maria looked at him, her face devoid of emotion. 'They didn't. They dynamited the mine and sealed it, with over one hundred men, or what was left of them, still below ground. The mine entrance was bulldozed over, and, to this day, the site is off limits to everyone. We don't know what the hell that disease was; or if it even was a disease. It may just have been some exotic chemical enzyme that reacted with the salt or oxygen in the human bloodstream. There were no samples taken, and no evidence other than the mine manager's written records and a few grainy black and white images of the victims, or what remained of them.'

Maria must have seen something in the set of Alex's jaw. 'Yes, I know. I'm sorry, but I really hope that your friend *isn't* competent. I hope that she's made some mistakes in her assessment, and this is nothing more than another hantavirus emergence.' She shrugged her shoulders and went on. 'The information sent by Dr. Weir about the organism's characteristics immediately set off alarm bells. This potential microbe is on an international risk-assessment watch list for highly communicable diseases. Anything with that level of bio-lethality, anything that fast and transferable, is watched by a number of nations. The CDC watches the Congo, Zaire, Mozambique, the Green Asian Belt and the entire greater Amazon – mainly for the bleed-out viruses. But this type of infection is moving up on our radar because of the depth of new mines. Unfortunately, we may have just come across it again.'

She stepped around in front of him, forcing him to stop. 'This is critical for both of us – the CDC and the military. You see, we need to understand the disease before we can safeguard against it. But there are other interested parties … Well, you can imagine what would happen if you inserted some of that microbe into a detonating warhead over a densely populated city.'

Alex nodded. 'I can assure you, I'm not down here to try to find a new weapon, Maria. And I think you're pretty confident that the Paraguayans drilled this infection up to the surface, and that's what's responsible for the quarantine.'

She held his eyes for a moment longer, then gave another shrug of her shoulders, stepped out of his path and walked alongside him again. 'Unfortunately, that is what I believe, Captain Hunter. Planet Earth has plenty of secrets – hidden in dense jungles, in deep waters, and buried far under the earth. We just keep tripping over them and tearing them out. The Paraguayan site is a fairly deep drill, over a mile, so it fits the historical profile. The images Dr. Weir sent were the first we've actually seen of the microbe's physical profile. The accompanying descriptions of the total cellular destruction and necrotising effects on human tissue, its transmission rate … yes, at this stage I have little reason to doubt.'

Maria nodded, apparently more to herself than to Alex. 'You know, these diseases are usually old. Primordial really. They should never meet us, and they infect humans only by accident. But when they do, their effect on life is usually devastating. It's strange; it's like they don't belong on our world at all.' Maria's eyes looked to carry the fatigue of experience when she spoke.

Alex felt the knot in his stomach grow tighter. 'With our current medical technology, can it be stopped, or cured?'

'Stopped? Yes, probably. I'm here to see to that, and to ensure it never makes it to the wider population. But cured, inoculated against, denatured, attenuated ...?' She stopped and searched Alex's face for a few moments, her lips compressed as if she was fighting to keep a secret. After another long moment, she said in a hushed voice, 'Have you heard of the Ten Protocols, Captain Hunter?'

Alex's brow furrowed and he shook his head. 'No.'

'I'm not surprised. Your commanding officer probably doesn't even know about them. Hell, not even my son is authorized for that level of information clearance and he works closely with me.' She drew in a long breath as if deciding where to start. 'There are real threats to our way of life. Not just the guys across the water building a bigger or dirtier bomb, but sometimes from the very planet itself. There are terrestrial threats, and sometimes even extraterrestrial threats.'

She looked over her shoulder to see where everyone else was, before going on.

'In the mid-1950s, a small asteroid fell to Earth off the coast of Japan, just a mile out from a small fishing town called Minamata. Within a few weeks, the population had developed physical deformities, retardation and eventually full cellular mutation. The public story was that a chemical factory had polluted the region's waterways with heavy metals, but that was a cover story to buy time. Japan, with the assistance of the United States, sterilised over fifty miles of ocean. It worked ... that time. Whatever it was that came down in that meteorite, and somehow leaked out, was cauterised, for good. After that, the five permanent members of the United Nations Security Council developed a secret set of rules – a blueprint to deal with extraordinary threats to the human race. They're called the Ten Protocols, and are known only to prime ministers and presidents and anyone at the rank of three-star general or above. The only one I know about is Protocol 9, which deals with extra-, intra- and inter-terrestrial biological threats.'

Wheels within wheels, thought Alex. 'And what do these protocols mean for our mission down here, Maria?'

Maria's jaw tightened and she donned a more business-like persona. 'My job is to review the situation and provide a risk assessment on the contagion. If the biohazard represents a threat to a populated area, any populated area, and is deemed intractable, uncontrollable, hopeless, then …' She stopped and swallowed.

Alex waited for her to go on.

'Then … total evacuation and total human isolation,' she finished. 'Miles of forest classed as a no-go area for a generation.'

'That's it?' He looked hard at her and saw that her eyes were watering. Something about all this didn't feel right.

'Yes. Let's hope it doesn't come to that, so these people aren't deprived of a chunk of their land.'

Alex grunted and gave a small nod.

He walked in silence for a while, his mind turning over what she'd said. No-go zones were notoriously hard to enforce – more so in a third-world environment. He'd leave it for now … but still … it just didn't sound right.

He had one more question. 'Could the quarantine order be responsible for the camp's communication blackout?'

She made a face. 'I can see why a blackout might be ordered or requested in certain circumstances, but as we're still in an investigatory stage and all information is vital …' She rocked her head from side to side, as if mulling it over. 'No, if I were a betting person, I'd put my money on a technical malfunction or something a lot bigger than a microbe … maybe with two legs.'

'I agree,' Alex said. 'I think we both need to get there as quickly as possible. Can you manage?' He looked down at her and smiled.

Maria wiped her nose and winked at him. 'Anything you can do …'

SEVENTEEN

'*Señora* Weir! It is the *padre*, he is back!' Tomás shifted his weight from foot to foot, looking as though he wanted to scamper over to the tall priest like many of the other men were doing.

Aimee couldn't blame him. The Paraguayans were devout, and after what Tomás had seen in the isolation cabin, she wasn't surprised he felt he needed a spiritual top-up. By now, all the men would probably be delighted to attend a mass and have an opportunity to pray for anything that would get them home. Or, at least, get them anywhere but here.

She watched the priest enter the camp – there was something about the way his body moved, unnaturally fluidly, that made her feel uneasy. Or maybe it was the way he spoke that gave her the creeps, lowering his jaw just enough to allow the words to dribble out from behind his beard. The priest sighted her and stared for a few seconds before turning back to talk to the men. Aimee could have sworn that one of his eyes remained on her as his head turned, acting independently of the rest of his body. She recalled the same effect the last time he had visited the camp.

The light was fading now, and some of the men moved around the edges of the camp lighting small fires to give comfort from the coming dark. They, too, stopped what they were doing and wandered over to Father González. He moved from group to group, nodding and listening as he went, sometimes reaching out to take a hand or touch a man on the head as though giving a blessing. Aimee could tell by the way the men reacted that he was winning them over. If he said to them, *we are all leaving*, they would all follow and she would be powerless to stop them.

At last, González made his way around the camp to appear in front of her, his hands tucked up into his sleeves. 'I wish to take the men back to my church so I can conduct a mass for them,' he said. 'You are welcome to join us, *señora* Weir.'

I knew this was coming, she thought. And then: That's odd, he didn't ask where Francisco or Alfraedo are, or whether he should consult with them.

'I'm sorry, I can't let the men leave the camp, Father. This area is in quarantine, and you are putting yourself in danger by being here. I suggest you wait until the medical specialists and their armed escort arrive shortly, then we can decide where and when it's best for you to hold your mass. I'd hate you to be held personally responsible if any of the men leave while they are sick. Leaving now would also cause the men to invalidate their work contracts.'

Aimee kept her gaze steady but she was bluffing. She thought the men would go with him if he asked, and be damned their pay and the medical specialists. But as González remained silent, she thought that perhaps he hadn't realized that yet. She decided to press her case.

'I'm the senior science specialist here and it's my call, I'm afraid. You see, Father, men are still dying, and until we know more about the disease that is killing them, everyone in the camp must remain under quarantine. You wouldn't want the men passing anything on to your other parishioners, would you?'

She could hear Tomás translating for the men gathered behind the priest.

Gonzáles turned to them himself and spoke in Spanish in a clear, strong voice. Tomás again started to translate, this time for Aimee.

'Only the God can forgive your sins, and He will hear your voices loudest on hallowed ground. Only He can comfort you, and heal you, and save you.'

The priest turned to Tomás and put his finger to his lips before continuing with his speech to the men. Tomás immediately stopped his translation and froze in what looked to Aimee like fearful indecision.

When González had finished his little sermon, he glided closer to Aimee. Though she was tall, he had to bend slightly to come close to her face. Aimee could smell his mouth. *The breath of a carnivore* – the revolting thought came out of nowhere.

'You are right, Ms. Weir. The sick must stay here and be tended to. But all others will come to my mass. That is *my* call, I'm afraid.' His bearded cheeks briefly pulled up in the semblance of a smile.

The entire camp had now gathered to witness the exchange. *So here it is*, Aimee thought. She had a decision to make. If she said no, there was a high probability the men would go anyway and her authority would be the only thing to evaporate in the humidity of the Paraguayan jungle. Or she could agree to let them leave ... temporarily. After all, she expected – she hoped – it was only for a few hours. She agreed.

González didn't say thank you; he simply turned away and threaded back among the crowd, touching a man here and there on the shoulder and speaking to him softly. Those he passed without touching dropped their heads slightly and Aimee guessed the priest had deemed them unfit to attend the mass. When he reached Tomás, he touched his shoulder too. Aimee was confused: the men he had left behind looked no different healthwise from those he had chosen to take with him. She couldn't see any biological reason for the choice, other than the men he had selected looked younger and slightly larger than those he'd left behind. *With the exception of Tomás*, she thought. *Strange. Can he tell who's infected?*

The camp quickly cleared as the men followed the priest into the jungle.

Tomás remained where he was, watching them go. 'I can go to the next mass, *señora* Weir,' he said and looked away shyly.

Aimee nodded. 'Thank you, Tomás. Thank you for staying with me. Umm, *tú eres mi amigo.*' She smiled at him and put her hand on his shoulder; the physical contact as important for her as it was for him.

While they talked, neither noticed that one of the workers who had been refused the mass crept out after the long train of men.

*

Felipe found it hard to follow the group as twilight turned to darkness. Soon it would be pitch black until the moon rose and threw some shafts of silver through the jungle's green ceiling. He didn't think he was that far behind – maybe a few hundred feet – but it was difficult to hear the men as sounds were gobbled up by the normal noises of the jungle. Broken twigs, small depressions in the mud and other signs of humans passing were soon swallowed by the night. Felipe scampered ahead blindly and hoped he was on the right path.

He felt he had been traveling for hours when at last he broke into a broad clearing and saw the last of the men being herded into a small stone building that was almost totally engulfed by a mighty tree. Felipe sprinted, although he wasn't sure what he would do when he got to the door. The padre had not chosen him, and he was afraid the holy man would be angry. But then again, his mother would be even angrier if he didn't pray in the house of God when he had the chance. Even if the priest just allowed him to sit in the doorway, he would feel better. *Of course he will permit it; he is a man of forgiveness, after all*, he thought.

When Felipe got to within a few feet of the church, he heard a strange grinding noise and saw an enormous slab of stone slide across the doorway. It didn't swing or close like a normal door; rather it seemed to be lifted from the inside and jammed across the entrance. He leapt up the steps, ducked underneath the sheet of hanging roots and placed his hands on the cool stone. He had missed his opportunity. He placed his forehead against the stone and was about to pray anyway, when he heard faint sounds.

They became louder – voices – were they praying? No, they were screaming. Although muffled by the thick stone, the absolute terror of the wails was clear. He made out more and more voices, along with dull thumps, as though bodies were being thrown against each other. What could it be? Were the men fighting among themselves?

Felipe banged his fist against the stone, but knew the small thud wouldn't be heard over the din on the other side of the huge block. He stepped back and placed both hands against its flat surface and pushed, but the mighty stone must have weighed several tons and probably would have take five men to shift. He was about to shout again when there came a deep roar from inside the church, an in-human sound like nothing he had ever heard. Felipe felt his skin prickle. He backed down the steps – tripping over the last few and landing on the dry soil.

Santa Madre de Dios, the padre and all the men must be trapped inside with some beast from the jungle.

He heard more screaming, but nearer than before. *Is that me? Be quiet*, he thought, and closed his mouth to shut it off. His legs felt like rubber as he tried to run. He fell and crawled for a few seconds before getting back to his feet.

He was at the tree line when another sound rolled across the clearing – the deep grind of the stone slab being hauled from the doorway. Felipe didn't turn; he knew what it meant. Whatever was in there with the men was now free.

He sprinted blindly into the jungle, and straight into the mossy trunk of a tree. He scrambled groggily to his feet, one of his arms dangling uselessly after the impact. He was dazed and his face felt wet; he licked his lips and tasted blood. Despite his injuries, he knew he had to keep moving. To stay meant meeting whatever it was that had roared like a hundred demons and made the men scream in terror. He staggered a few more feet, not knowing where he was, hopelessly lost in the dark.

He just had time to notice that the jungle around him had fallen silent when a large hand closed on his neck. At last, Felipe re-membered to pray.

EIGHTEEN

It was just on dawn when Alex looked through the scope into the camp. Tents were zipped up and cabin doors closed tight. There was no power, the fires had died to embers around the camp's perimeter, and there was absolutely no sign of any current human habitation.

Garmadia placed his hand on Alex's forearm and looked sternly into his face. 'We will stay here until we receive further orders, Captain Hunter.'

Alex ignored him and continued to scan the campsite. He and Garmadia were both captains, but Garmadia still believed he had been put in the charge of the mission. Sam rolled his eyes, probably expecting someone was about to receive a small broken bone.

Garmadia dropped his hand and spoke in a lowered voice. 'I will check in with Colonel Lugo when he wakes. Until then, we hold our position. I don't need to remind you, Captain Hunter, that this site is under an executive quarantine order and —'

'Call who you like, Captain Garmadia, but we're going to take a closer look,' Alex said.

He dropped his pack and pulled his rifle down from over his shoulder. The three HAWCs immediately did the same. Alex spoke over his shoulder. 'Sam, left flank; Franks, take the right. Mak, you give us some rear cover and stay with the doctors.'

Just as they were about to step forward, Alex held his hand in the air. No one moved. Seconds passed then a zip went up on one of the tents and a man staggered out and walked to the edge of the jungle. He lifted one leg of his shorts and urinated into the foliage, tilting his head back, obviously enjoying the relief. He finished with a fart so loud it made a colored bird screech back at him from the tree overhead. Both Chaco and Saqueo sniggered from behind the HAWCs.

'Well, that looks a little more normal,' Sam said.

'Can we wait a second for that gas to dissipate?' Franks asked, seeing the man was on her right-side flank.

'Negative. Just hold your breath, soldier. Remember: war is hell.' Sam grinned as he checked the slide on his gun.

Alex held a finger to his lips then pointed with a flat hand into the camp. Sam and Franks fanned out left and right just behind the tree line as Alex stepped into the clearing. Although a large man, he moved quietly and with sure-footedness on the lumpy wet surface. Every ten feet he paused to listen, but it was difficult to pick up individual signs of life as the jungle was a cacophony of sounds, smells and small movements. It was like a living thing surrounding them and testing all of their senses. Alex knew Aimee was here – and alive – he could feel it. But he also sensed the presence of something else – something almost primordial, repellent and powerful.

He walked past the zipped tents and sensed the men inside. Some of the tents were full, and some only contained one person. *Strange*, he thought. *If there are supposed to be around one hundred workers, there's an awful lot of them missing.*

One of the tents' zips came down and a small brown head popped out. The man and Alex stared at each other for a few seconds. Alex smiled and winked, but the man's eyes went wide and, like a magic trick, his head disappeared and the zip flew back up. Perhaps the sight of a giant in green and black camouflage clothing, carrying a lethal-looking gun, was a bit much first thing in the morning.

Alex could sense Aimee clearly now – he almost smiled with relief. He moved quickly towards one of the cabins and stopped twenty feet from the door. He hesitated, unsure why he didn't just walk up and push the door open.

*

Aimee pulled back the curtain and felt shock run through her body. Alex Hunter stood a few feet from her door like a green and black statue. He hadn't changed a bit – same thick, black hair, same unwavering gaze from gray-green eyes. *No*, she thought as she looked harder, *he has changed*. His eyes were sadder, held more pain than she remembered.

A smile split her face and she went to launch herself at the door. Then something inside her yelled, *Stop!* She and Alex hadn't seen each other for years, and *she* had walked out on him. He'd probably moved on by now, maybe even had another girlfriend. All she was likely to do was embarrass herself, and him. Her heart beat hard in her chest, and her stomach flipped and danced. *Shut up, stay cool*, she wanted to shout at them.

She raised her hand to her cheek and felt the rash pimpling the flesh. Suddenly she became very aware of her body odor and the greasy strings of black hair that hung over her eyes. Alex, as usual, looked perfect … at least to her.

She sucked in a deep breath of humid air, squared her shoulders and pulled the cabin door open calmly and slowly.

I'm going to be relaxed and wait for him to come over to me. I'll just shake his hand and maybe kiss his cheek, like old friends do. After all, that's what we are now.

She stood on the top step, fidgeting. She felt as if time had slowed down. *Oh, fuck it*, she thought, and stepped to the ground with a casual smile and her hand outstretched. Her bare foot sank into a mud puddle. *Yech, forgot the boots, didn't you?* She stretched her smile even wider.

*

Alex's extraordinary senses were concentrated on the woman coming towards him, and as she approached he absorbed every bit of information about her – her eyes, her mouth, her heartbeat and breathing. She swallowed, then swallowed again. Her heart was racing in her chest.

She was as beautiful as he remembered, but tired; she looked so very tired. He probably should have expected that – the quarantine order, the power failures, the heat and humidity. But there was something else he could sense within her: fear. Not of him, or the jungle, but of something else – an instinctive fear of something dangerous. The same thing Alex could feel all around them – a hopeless dread hanging over the camp.

He kept looking at her, trying to see deeper into her, trying to read the woman who had once shared his life. Sometimes he was able to pick up potent mental images created by strong emotions. Unfortunately, Aimee's mind was clouded with fatigue, fear and stress.

Alex flipped his gun over his shoulder so it hung at his back, prepared to fold her in his arms – a reflex from their past time together. He quickly adjusted the action as her hand came up for a formal greeting. Surprised, he took it but didn't shake; he just held her hand and looked into her eyes, their familiar soft blue.

'Aimee,' was all he said, all he could manage. She had once been the most important woman in his life. A bond had formed between them in the ice caves in the Antarctic, and it had grown stronger during the time they'd spent together after that. Even though their relationship was over, that bond refused to break, at least for him. It was still so strong that he would have sensed her death as keenly as if he had lost a limb.

'Thank God you're okay,' he said, continuing to hold her hand.

She just stood there looking up at him, her mouth opening then closing without any words coming out. Seconds passed before they both heard someone clear their throat at the jungle's edge.

Alex got the message. 'Okay, come on in,' he called.

The HAWCs stepped out from the jungle and Alex saw Aimee's smile when she saw his second-in-command.

'Samuel Jackson Reid, he dragged you down here as well?' she said in delight.

Sam had become a good friend to Aimee when she and Alex were a couple, and later had offered a rock-solid sounding board for her anxiety about Alex's rages.

'Of course I came, young lady. The boss here said something about nature walks, tropical fruit and sunshine – and, well, who could resist?' He gave her a wink and a smile.

The scientists and the two local boys had followed the HAWCs into the clearing.

Aimee turned to look at them, then nodded to Maria Vargis. 'I'm hoping you're Dr. Vargis. Thank heavens you're here.' She stuck her hand out, but Maria had looked away and seemed to miss the gesture.

Alex introduced Aimee to the rest of the team. He noticed that Michael Vargis blushed slightly when he shook her hand, and that Casey Franks also looked at her with admiration and interest.

By now many of the workers had poked their heads out of their tents, and their curious murmurs were waking the others. In a few more minutes, the camp's remaining residents surrounded the HAWCs. A man wearing a creased piece of paper pinned to his T-shirt approached Aimee.

Maria Vargis's shout startled them all. 'Keep them back!'

Captain Garmadia seemed to take it as an instruction. He shouted in Spanish and put one hand on his sidearm, waving his other hand at Tomás and then at the rest of the men encircling them.

'Leave them alone!' Aimee shouted at the Paraguayan soldier. She waved Tomás closer. 'He's okay. He translates for me and has been very helpful.'

Tomás looked from Aimee to Garmadia, who kept his hand on his gun.

'At ease, cowboy,' Alex said softly.

When Garmadia didn't immediately relax, Alex turned to lock eyes with the man. Garmadia slowly took his hand from his holster and folded his arms.

Maria brought her hands up in a placating action. 'Sorry, I didn't mean to startle anyone. It's just that until we have a chance to examine the men, we have to remember we're in a biohazardous area and everyone and everything is potentially infectious – including Dr. Weir here. We should continue to live off our own food and water for a while.'

Aimee gave the scientist a flat smile. Like Alex, she probably now realized that Maria Vargis hadn't missed her outstretched hand earlier. She turned to Tomás and said quietly, 'It's all right. Could you please ask the men to return to their tents and the doctor will come to examine everyone a little later?'

Tomás frowned for a moment, then nodded slowly and turned to speak to the men. Most shrugged and turned to leave, but a few continued to stare. Tomás spoke to them again, but they ignored him, talking rapidly to each other. Garmadia yelled at them in Spanish and Alex noticed Tomás cringe, as though shielding himself from a blow. The remaining men moved away quickly, but Tomás merely retreated twenty paces.

Alex had counted the men as they left. He examined the clearing: the dried mud churned up by hundreds of footsteps, the surrounding deep jungle, the burnt-out cabins at the rear – his eyes missed nothing.

'Aimee, where is everyone? There's supposed to be almost one hundred men down here. I count twenty-five, give or take.'

'There are twenty-seven still here, counting myself. Another twenty dead or strapped down in isolation, and the rest ...' Aimee looked out into the surrounding green. 'About a dozen ran off into the jungle; we don't know where they went. The other forty or so went with the priest, and never came back.'

Garmadia looked both perplexed and annoyed. 'Forty of the men went with a priest? What priest? We know of no current mission here in the jungle basin area.'

Aimee shook her head wearily. 'I don't know. He looked and acted like a priest, sort of. He said he had a mission nearby. He offered to hold a mass for the men, and they went with him last night, and they haven't come back yet. That's all I know.'

'My orders are to ensure that the gas-extraction operation goes back online. How is that possible without any men? *Mierda*! Where is Alfraedo Desouza, the site manager?'

Garmadia's voice was getting sharper as he addressed Aimee. Alex's eyes narrowed slightly, but he kept quiet. He'd cut the Paraguayan a little slack; the man had a job to do, and it looked like it was going to be a lot harder than he'd expected.

Aimee sighed. 'Alfraedo's gone too. He went into the jungle to look for the men who destroyed our equipment, and he never came back. They're all … just gone.'

She needs to sit down, thought Alex. He put an arm around her shoulders and guided her to the step of her cabin. He felt her lean into him slightly as they walked.

Garmadia followed them. 'Have you looked for the missing men yet, Dr. Weir? Have you questioned the *remaining* men? They may know —'

'Fuck off,' Aimee said, sitting on the step and letting her hair fall over her face.

'That's enough,' Alex said to Garmadia, who looked as if he was about to get into interrogation mode. The edge to his voice pulled the Paraguayan up short and he backed off a step.

Alex kneeled down beside Aimee and spoke softly. 'So, how's the holiday going?'

Her mouth turned down and she shut her eyes for a second. 'The margaritas are warm and the swimming pool is too cold.' She wiped her nose and gave him a watery smile. 'I'm glad you came.'

'I'll always come for you. Are you up to helping us?'

She nodded.

Alex mouthed *good* to her, then, still half-kneeling, turned to the group. 'Sam, you and Mak check the communications and power – I want the generator back up before dark. Franks, you assist Dr. Weir and our CDC friends in setting up, and get them anything they need. Captain Garmadia and I will walk the perimeter. One more thing: re-member your quarantine procedures.'

This last was greeted with a 'Yes, boss' and the HAWCs dispersed.

Alex noticed Chaco edging forward to get a better look at Aimee's face. He turned to Garmadia. 'Captain, please pay the boys what we owe them and send them home.'

'Sorry, they're not going anywhere,' Maria Vargis said. 'Captain Hunter, this is a quarantine zone. You enter, you stay, until *we* give the all-clear.'

Alex realized he should never have allowed the boys to enter the camp. He thought briefly about arguing with the CDC woman, but she held his gaze and tilted her head, perhaps welcoming any challenge. He sighed and nodded. 'You're right.'

To Garmadia he said, 'Cancel that order. Just tell the boys to stay out of trouble and not to touch anything.'

He looked around the camp again and spotted Tomás. When the man noticed Alex's eyes on him, he looked as if he were about to flee. Alex gave a friendly smile and waved him over.

'*Señor* Tomás, I am pleased to meet you. I am Captain Alex Hunter, a friend of Dr. Weir's.'

Tomás's eyes slid to Aimee. She nodded to him, and he looked back at Alex.

'I want to thank you for helping Dr. Weir,' Alex went on. 'Now, we're going to see what it is that's making the men sick, and also try to get the power back on. The sooner we work out what's happening here, the sooner we can all get back to work, or go home. Okay?'

After a moment, Tomás gave a small nod. Alex held his hand out and Tomás grasped it, flashing a quick, near toothless smile.

Alex glanced at the uneven muddy ground, then at the red stains on Tomás's and Aimee's legs. He scanned the camp perimeter, then looked back at Tomás. 'I need your help, *señor*. We cannot work on this surface. If it rains again, we will be up to our knees in mud. We need to cover the cleared ground with some matting. Can you organize the men to cut down some fronds and branches to create a thatch … er, like a mat, a cover, over the ground?'

Tomás looked around the clearing and raised his eyebrows. 'All of it, *señor*?'

Alex just nodded and smiled.

Tomás gave his best grin in return. 'Yes, this is a good idea. The men have been complaining about the mud; it coats everything. This will give them something to do and take their mind off the sickness.'

Tomás squelched over to the tents and clapped his hands to call the men together. He seemed to be relishing his authority, Alex thought.

He turned back to Aimee. Maria and Michael Vargis had joined her, and Casey Franks stood a little apart watching the jungle, her weapon cradled loosely in her tanned, bulging arms.

'We've got a bit of work to do, but we'll get things back online and then see about flying us all home,' Alex said to Aimee. 'Maybe a hot shower first. How's that sound?'

She nodded and opened her mouth, then glanced at the two scientists and paused. She gave Alex a small smile and said, 'Sounds good. Let's catch up later.'

NINETEEN

Aimee felt a lump in her throat as she watched Alex disappear with the Paraguayan soldier into the jungle. The green closed around him so quickly it was as if he had been consumed before her eyes.

Maria Vargis stepped up next to her and followed her gaze. 'Strong, handsome man. You are close friends – lovers once, I think? But not anymore?' Maria raised her eyebrows and gave Aimee a half-smile.

'Yes, no … I mean, yes, we used to be friends and still are, but no, not that close anymore. Not like that anyway.' Aimee exhaled and rubbed her face.

Maria folded her arms under her large breasts and nodded slowly. 'Good. We all need clear heads now.'

Michael Vargis stepped forward as Aimee rose slowly to her feet. 'Dr. Weir, we've reviewed all the information on the *Clavicula occultus* microorganism you sent us. I have to say, we found it fascinating. We've had no up-to-date data since you went into a communication blackout though, so it's critical you bring us up to speed on anything else you've learned.'

Aimee laughed mirthlessly. '*Clavicula occultus*, my little hidden key – what a joke. It would've been better named something like *Infernum morbus* – the Hades Bug – much more appropriate for this little beast, considering the hell it's causing us. I can't tell you how happy I am to have someone I can share this with. I don't have the equipment or the training – it's gotten way beyond my capabilities now. Let's get to work. I've been saving my computer battery's energy so I can show you the results of my latest analysis. Then we can take a look at the subjects we have in isolation.'

She stepped up into her cabin and reached for a towel on the ground that was already stiff with the reddish mud of the camp. She scraped as much of the stuff off her bare feet as she could, then threw the cloth down beside the door again. 'All right, come on in, but be warned – it's going to be a bit cramped.'

Maria and Michael scraped their boots on the edge of the step before entering the tiny cabin. Casey Franks poked her head inside, looked left and right, then stepped back down. 'It's okay. I'll wait out here, Dr. Weir.'

Aimee's desk was covered with empty water bottles, dirty T-shirts, notebooks marked with red-mud fingerprints. 'Maid's day off,' she said, and swept the lot of it to the floor. She sat down, lifted the lid of her computer and switched it on. After a few seconds, it gave the warning for low battery level.

'Let me start at the beginning,' Aimee said, selecting a document from the list onscreen, 'and quickly bring you forward to where we are now. My work is in petrobiology. I specialise in seeking alternatives for our rapidly diminishing fossil fuels. I came down here for a number of reasons. My primary objective was to assist a friendly nation confirm a significant natural gas cavern and advise on its safe extraction, super compression, and plan for its delivery to the coast. My secondary objective was a little less official.'

She opened another folder and brought up images of molecular chains breaking apart and recombining with each other. 'We know that at least twenty percent of the world's natural gas is generated from microbial activity. This process, called methanogenesis, represents the key to a possible renewable resource. To date we know a lot about the high-level process, but the *actual* microbial-related elements of the conversion are still a mystery.' She flicked though some more screens. 'To find trace evidence, let alone a sample, of the methanogenesis key could lead to the solution for synthesising the microorganic fuel-production process in a laboratory. Cheap and unlimited natural gas for everyone – the golden fleece of microbes for a petrobiologist.'

'Impressive,' Maria said, standing behind Aimee's chair. 'But let me guess. You found your golden fleece and it turned out to have sharp teeth.'

Aimee nodded slowly and switched to the samples from the drill head. 'You could say that. I needed a primordial sample – deep, dirty and not yet fully cooked – to be able to detect and extract any living microbes.' She sat back and ran her hands through her hair before swivelling to look at Michael and Maria. 'Yeah, it has teeth all right. Turned out to be very efficient at converting polymers and hydro-carbons to the base components of petroleum and natural gas. Has a huge appetite for hydrocarbons. In fact, it turns out it has a taste for *all* types of carbon, even biological. One of the men must have gotten some into his system somehow – it literally ate him down to nothing. I'm not talking about a bleed-out or even severe necrosis; it was more like some type of biocorrosive got into his body and con-verted him into … something other than flesh and blood.'

Aimee stood up, stretched her back and indicated that someone else should take her seat. Michael sat down and immediately in-creased the magnification of the bacterium on the screen. He studied it closely for a few seconds, frowned and leaned his chin on his hand.

'Well, it's got a weird protein coating, but there are certainly bacterial chains … and we've seen that primitive strep-type organ-isms are similarly linked.' Michael shrugged. 'After all, one of the haemolytic streptococci is responsible for necrotising fasciitis symp-toms, and once that little monster gets established under the skin, its sole focus seems to be to liquefy flesh – at a rapid rate too.' He looked up at Aimee. 'There are documented cases of it destroying flesh at nearly one inch every six hours.'

'An inch over six hours, huh?' Aimee nodded wearily at the screen. 'Well, this thing fully dissolved an entire grown man down to some type of black liquid in under twenty.'

Michael stared at her. 'That's ah, around one inch every fifteen minutes … definitely not strep-based then; and maybe too fast to treat by the time infection is identified. And, in any case, treat with what?' He turned back to the screen and traced the outline of one of the microbes with his finger. 'These are strange – the spheres are just slightly more oval than spherical, and there seems to be a rigid mobility filament.' He swung around in his seat and looked at Aimee again. 'Your Hades Bug is aggressive and seems in a hurry.'

'For every attack there's a counterattack,' Maria said. 'We just need to learn more about our little invaders. Let's have a look at the men in isolation and draw some samples. Then we can do some further analysis. Is there somewhere we can set up, Dr. Weir?'

Aimee thought for a few seconds. Cabins were becoming a scarce resource now the sick were multiplying and their infirmaries eventually became their funeral pyres.

'You can use Francisco's cabin,' she said eventually. 'He's the camp doctor. I'm not sure when he's coming back.'

She sat down on her cot and pulled on her mud-encrusted boots. There was no point bothering with socks; all she had were dirty ones – stiff, they'd be more abrasive than the tough leather. She gathered her gloves and mask, and glanced at the hat with corks that Francisco had given her. *Not sure when he's coming back? I don't think he's coming back at all*, she thought. *None of them are.*

*

Aimee felt underdressed as she accompanied Michael and Maria to the isolation huts. The CDC scientists were covered head to toe in disposable coveralls and wore fitted gloves, a hermetic mask and perspex laboratory goggles. Aimee was in her usual biohazard uniform: stained and mud-crusted clothing, cotton surgical mask, rubber gloves and sunglasses.

Casey Franks followed at the rear, chewing gum. When she saw Aimee glance back at her, she nodded towards the two scientists and said, 'Happy Halloween!'

At the entrance to the first isolation cabin, Aimee hesitated; it was quiet inside. Usually there was moaning or swearing. She looked at Michael Vargis. He was very pale behind his goggles, and

154

where the suit met his skin a line of perspiration glistened. *For a disease specialist, he's pretty scared*, she thought.

Maria Vargis looked much more in control. She raised her eyebrows behind her goggles and nodded towards the door. *Get on with it*, the motion implied.

Casey Franks went to enter first, but Aimee stopped her. 'Sorry, you can't go in without some form of bio-protection.'

The HAWC looked at Aimee's clothing and pulled a disbelieving face. She drew some wrap-around sunglasses from a pocket and put them on. 'Happier?'

'No. I mean it, Franks; you're not coming in.'

Aimee stared hard into the brawny woman's face; she could tell Franks was thinking it over. Her job was to guard the medical team, but Aimee knew her brief didn't extend to fighting with them over an area that wasn't within her expertise. After another few seconds, Franks reached into her left sidearm holster and pulled out a handgun. She spun it in her hand and handed it butt first to Aimee.

Aimee took the gun without hesitation, checked the slide and number of rounds expertly, then sighted along the short black barrel. When she was done, she stuck the gun in her waistband.

Franks nodded with approval. 'Pretty cool, Doc.'

'Thanks. We won't be long.' Aimee turned back to the door, feeling strangely more secure now she was armed.

'Okay, but first sound I'm coming in – germs or no germs.' Franks noticed Michael watching and winked at him. 'Hey, anyone ever tell you you look kinda cute when you're terrified?'

Aimee took a breath through her nose and pushed aside the plastic sheet to get to the door. She wished she had a proper bio-mask filter like Michael and Maria – it was always the smell that first revolted her. With the doors and windows sealed tight, there were few places for the gases to escape, and the odor particles created an airborne soup that mixed blood, faeces and stomach gases with a strange oily, toasted scent that defied biological classification.

As Aimee felt the rank humidity on her skin, she worried again about whether the microbe was able to become airborne. She decided to get the task over with as quickly as possible and moved to the first bed.

'This man was admitted just over twenty hours ago,' she told the scientists.

She pulled back the discolored plastic curtain that surrounded the bed. There was no body left to see. The sheets were stained dark red, black and gray, and the floorboards below looked as though several buckets of ink had cascaded over them. The blurred outline of a torso on the sheets was the only proof that a human had once lain there. *Our own personal Shroud of Turin*, Aimee thought as she held her breath.

There was nothing to examine, nothing to sample. She let the plastic drop. The next three beds were the same.

At the final bed, she hesitated before pulling back the thick plastic. 'This man came to us just twelve hours ago.'

Aimee kept her eyes on Maria and Michael instead of looking at the bed; she had seen the horrific sight too many times already. The Vargises' eyes widened behind their laboratory goggles. Aimee could see the reflection of the remains of the man on the cot in Maria's protective lenses. His arms were gone. His legs were stovepipe-shaped stains leading to a dark jellied substance that oozed from his steaming chest cavity.

Maria blinked twice behind her glasses. The second time, she kept her eyes closed for several seconds.

As the junior attending scientist, it was Michael's job to collect the samples. His shaking hands came up holding a glass vial and a small spatula. But that was as far as he got. Aimee could see he was having trouble convincing his legs to propel him forward. He rocked slightly and Maria put her hand up to stop him.

'I'll do it,' she said.

She took the implements from Michael, squeezed his wrist briefly, and stepped towards the mess on the bed. Slipping into professional scientist mode, she began to talk through her actions as though conducting an autopsy. She was breathing hard as she spoke and Aimee could tell the process was her way of coping with the situation.

'Subject appears to be in final stages of total bacterial disintegration. Flesh, blood, osseous material, all physical substance seems to be …' Her voice trailed off as she moved up the bed towards the man's head. His entire face was blackened and glistening as the skin and skull beneath dissolved. Maria shook her head slightly before going on. 'Simply amazing. I've never seen anything like this, anywhere in the world.' She prodded the man's cheek with the spatula, and looked down at the liquefying flesh below the chest. 'I'm unable to determine if the biological degradation is the result of some type of protoplasmic conversion or is simply an excreted waste product – the end result of a digestion process.'

As she prodded the man's face again, a glob of black jelly plopped onto the sheet from the top of the chest cavity. A few drops of the black fluid splashed into the air but didn't land on Maria. Nevertheless, Aimee saw her freeze and draw in a sharp breath. Biohazard suit or not, no one wanted anything this dangerous touching them.

Maria took a scraping from the man's cheek, coaxed it into the small vial, then sealed it tightly. She did the same with the gelatinous mound at his chest cavity, and finally took a smear of the black liquid that was dripping from the bed to leak between the cracks in the floor.

She carried the three vials to Michael, who was ready with a small silver suitcase. The hiss it made when he opened it told Aimee that it was a hermetically sealed portable unit for chem-bio sample containment. The lid hissed again when he shut it.

'We should be working on this agent in a level-4 biohazard laboratory,' Maria said, checking her gloves and her arms for any residue. When she'd finished, she looked across at Aimee in her dirty clothing and simple cotton mask. 'Well, at least you've got a gun, darling.'

Aimee smiled tightly behind her mask.

Maria took a last look around the small cabin then back to Aimee. 'Okay, Dr. Weir, I think we've got all the information we can gather. Any further exposure now is just inviting more risk. This isolation room needs to be sterilized.'

Aimee nodded; she'd been thinking the same thing. *Time for another bonfire.*

*

The contents of the isolation hut had shaken the three scientists. But if they had looked below the hut, what they would have seen would have frozen them in disbelief and horror.

Long, black, greasy-looking stalactites hung from the underside of the cabin's floor, dripping into the pools that hadn't yet dried out into the dark red mud. At first, the drops sank to the bottom of the shallow puddles. Then, as if heeding some inner call, they began to roll along the bottom of the pools and coalesce together.

As the dark mass grew, it also started to move, straining and stretching towards the life it could sense above. It sank back into its small liquid world; not large enough or strong enough yet.

Where the other huts had stood, small black stains on the mud below the charred ground attested to the matter's previous attempts to free itself from its prison. These dried residues lay trapped among the fine silt.

Trapped, but only temporarily.

TWENTY

'I'm not ready to come home yet, General.'

Adira could hear the old man's rasping breath and the scrunch of leather as he shifted in his favorite chair. She could picture him as clearly as if she was sitting across from him in his office over 5000 miles away. General Meir Shavit, the head of Metsada, Mossad's Special Operations Division, and her uncle, was not a man to be easily swayed by speculation or sentiment. The old man's spirit was fire-hardened by war, grief and the witnessing of many atrocities. He could be stubborn, uncompromising and quick to anger – all traits she too possessed. But Adira had an advantage – she was his favorite niece.

She could imagine his expression – countenance creased in an amused smile, one eye slightly squinting as smoke curled up beside his face from his cigarette – as he listened to her argument.

'Your friend Jack Hammerson keeps me in training even though I have more skills than the frontline HAWCs,' she said. 'And I can't get near the son of a bitch to complain. He only talks to Captain Hunter.' Her hand tightened on the comm unit as she thought of Alex Hunter out there in a hotzone. 'And now Hunter's taken a team over to South America … I should be there with them. And I would be if not for that Hammerson.'

Her uncle gave a slow, dry chuckle. 'He's on to you, Addy – maybe from the very first day. "That Hammerson" is no fool.'

She ground her teeth. 'Maybe, maybe not – he is not as clever as you think, Uncle. But I'm close, I know it. Their Deep Storage facility is buried many levels below the base. I can't get to it yet, but Hammerson or Hunter are my keys. I just need more time.'

There was a long pause, and Adira heard the general sip something before he spoke again. 'This man Hunter, his name comes up a lot when we start to talk about the Arcadian, hmm?'

Ach, stupid slip, and he misses nothing, Adira thought. She had avoided revealing that Alex Hunter was the soldier with the extraordinary skills that General Shavit had sent her to find out more about. If he discovered her subterfuge, uncle or not, he'd send other agents who may not be as careful in their information-collection procedures. Adira's aim was to find out as much as she could about the underlying genesis of Alex Hunter's skills and capabilities – after all, why deliver up a single man when she could deliver the means to make a thousand of them? She cursed silently; so far, however, she knew very little. It was if Hammerson was anticipating her moves, and keeping her close so he could watch her.

That said, she felt she still had a few cards to play.

'Information is the greatest weapon we can possess, Uncle. Information on the Arcadian Project is invaluable to Israel. I just need more time, and then it will all be yours.'

'Hmm, anyone else and I would be suspicious of their motives, Captain Senesh, and perhaps their … manipulations.' She heard him sip again. 'You can have your extra time, but bring me something soon … or I'll send *you* something, Addy.'

The line went dead, and Adira pulled the small PDA comm away from her head. She tapped her chin with it for a few moments, musing for the hundredth time on how she might either get into the deep facility or get Hammerson to talk, or perhaps even ask Alex Hunter to tell her about the Arcadian blueprint.

If she had been sent on the mission to South America and been able to spend time alone with the man, she might have found out what she needed. There was a connection between them; they were friends. He may even have told her about it voluntarily.

She slid the back off the PDA, pulled the small chip free and replaced it with its standard HAWC chip. She put the removed chip between her back teeth and bit down hard, crushing it, then spat out the fragments.

As she headed back to the barracks, her mind was still working furiously. Being *inside* the tent wasn't working; maybe it was time to try going *outside*. She cursed Jack Hammerson again – he was her greatest roadblock to success.

Two of the recent HAWC recruits fell in behind her and started making comments. The term *Jewish princess* floated in the air, spoken deliberately for her to hear. Her fists balled. *You do not want to piss me off today*, she thought.

The men trailed her into the barracks. Adira pushed open the doors into the large, relatively empty rec room. The catcalls from behind became louder as she went to the center of the floor, rolling her shoulders and flexing her hands, still keeping her back to the men.

Normally, she would have ignored them – they were insignificant, little more than a distraction to her mission plan. But her anger was already at boiling point following her conversation with the general and the knowledge that she had limited time to achieve her aim. Alex Hunter, her reason for joining the unit was being kept from her; the information she needed on the Arcadian Project was out of reach; and Jack Hammerson was holding her in an operational suspended animation. And now she had to deal with a pair of silly children who might have distinguished themselves as SEALs or Rangers, but would probably last an hour in the deserts of Southern Lebanon, and less in a Gaza spiderhole.

She heard them getting closer, their footfalls loud and clumsy. *How could these fools ever work with Alex Hunter? They aren't worthy of him.*

A hand alighted on her shoulder.

When she turned, she didn't see two young men; she saw Jack Hammerson laughing at her. Her anger boiled over and she acted.

*

When Zac Ingram regained consciousness, he tried to move but couldn't. Vision slowly clearing, he realized he was looking through one eye only. His face, chest and groin all hurt. In fact, there were few parts of his body that didn't.

Slowly turning his head to the left, he could hear the metronomic hiss and pump of a respirator. Denny Wilson was in the bed next to him, purple-bruised eyes taped shut, a breathing tube taped into his mouth. Both arms were in casts and he seemed to be missing a chunk of skin from his forehead.

Zac groaned and looked up at the hospital ceiling. Slowly, a picture drifted into his mind.

The Jewish woman turning – the ferocity on her face – the speed with which she moved. She had knocked them both down, then allowed them up – just to knock them down again.

He moaned as a wave of pain rippled across his bruised diaphragm. 'Who the fuck is she?' His voice sounded funny as he spoke the words aloud, and he realized all his front teeth were missing.

TWENTY-ONE

The scientists made their way to the makeshift laboratory that had been set up in Francisco's old hut. Aimee pulled the gun from her waistband and handed it back, butt first, to Casey Franks.

Franks shook her head. 'Keep it.' She pointed her thumb over her shoulder back towards the isolation hut. 'Bad in there?'

'Thanks,' Aimee said, tucking the pistol back into her pants. She looked at the tough woman, wondering what she should tell her. Franks raised her eyebrows in anticipation of an answer.

Fuck it, Aimee thought, *we're all in this together now.*

'Casey, there's an alpha-terminal micro life form at work here – one that literally breaks down the human physiology. The symptoms are unmistakable – human biological material conversion to a lique-fied substance in a matter of hours. We don't really know what it is, how it spreads, or how to stop it. What we do know is it's infectious as all hell. So if you see anyone weeping black tears, stay the fuck away from them.'

Casey stopped walking for a second, one side of her face pulling up in a grin. 'Ooookaay; I'm guessing it's pretty bad then.'

Maria and Michael had already entered the lab. Aimee paused with her foot on the step. 'Best if you stay out here, Casey. Don't want you weeping black tears if anything goes wrong.'

Casey spat out her gum. 'Not a chance. Didn't you know? HAWCs don't cry.' She winked and followed Aimee into the small room.

The Vargises had already unpacked the samples and set them up in a portable isolation cube: a collapsible perspex square with side-attached gloves, and a lens fitted into the top so either a camera or microscope could be attached. Maria fixed a single large electronic eye onto the top of the cube then fed the cable back to her computer. Michael busied himself with the samples, dripping and scraping specimens onto slides and lining them up so Maria could pass the lens over them.

Aimee moved some of the scientists' other gear out of the way to make space for herself and Casey. '*Oof...* wow, what's in here?' she asked when she tried to lift a metallic suitcase.

'Leave it,' Maria said. 'It's X-ray material – the lead shielding makes it cumbersome.'

She watched Aimee put the case down before turning her attention back to the microscope.

'Good to go,' Michael said, pulling his hands from the cube's gloves and sitting down in a chair close to his mother.

Maria typed a few commands and the wriggling, spinning life forms jumped into focus. She moved across the different samples, enlarging, clarifying. The forms became more animated the more liquefied the flesh samples became.

Maria folded her arms and sat back. 'Well, your little Hidden Key is bacterial all right, and it's big, perhaps one to one-point-five micrometres. I'm guessing peptidoglycan bacterial walls given the cross-linked polysaccharides. Michael, take a look – see the protective rigid S-layer covering the outside of the cell? Going to be a tough little bastard with all that organic armor plating.'

She increased the magnification slightly on a section of one of the microorganisms and shook her head. 'You know, just when I think I know what I'm looking at, I see something else that makes me think this thing doesn't belong here at all.'

Aimee frowned. 'You mean, on the surface?'

Maria shrugged. 'No. I mean anywhere.' She pointed at the screen. 'Look, a single flagellum gives it mobility, but only when in suspension ... And there, another smaller one; rigid – not sure what that's for – could it act as a potential virulence factor?'

She sat back again and Aimee crouched down to look at the computer screen. 'Well, it's big enough that we can trap it,' she said. 'Filter it out maybe?'

Maria and Michael talked together in rapid Greek, completely ignoring Aimee for a few moments. At last, as if suddenly remembering the question, Michael said over his shoulder, 'You're right; it's enormous – way too big to pass through skin. It'd need to enter via the respiratory system, the eye or any other orifice, or perhaps an open wound. A vector could probably inoculate it directly into the body – and round here there's no shortage of biting insects. But the stiffened filament … strange … it's too highly developed to be a superfluous vestige.'

Aimee crossed her arms. 'Maybe direct epidermal introduction …?'

'Hmm, interesting … You're thinking maybe that rigid filament is some sort of delivery mechanism – like a genetic injector? Could be used for some type of nucleic material transmission … acting like a virus? No, no, no, that's impossible for a bacterium.'

Michael shook his head. Aimee could tell that his mouth was turned down behind his mask.

Maria clapped her gloved hands together, making a dry, muffled sound. 'Why not? It could attach to the skin surface and simply inject its biological or genetic material into the cell. Michael, think … Remember chlamydia – it's a bacterium but in some ways it acts more like a virus. It *is* virus-like, because it's dependent on molecules from its host organism to reproduce. When it enters a host cell, it uses supplies from that host to make copies of itself inside the cell. The new bodies can grow, divide and metabolise, and once there are enough copies they burst the cell open and escape to infect new cells or new people – just like a virus.'

She swung around in her chair, opened another case beside the desk and withdrew a couple of items. The first – a small, flat black square she stuck to her chest – *digital flash recorder*, thought Aimee. The other was something smaller that she kept in the palm of her hand. She looked first at Aimee then Casey.

'You, soldier girl, come here.'

Franks just looked at the CDC woman, her only movement the slow chewing of her gum. Aimee knew Casey Franks wouldn't follow any command given to her that didn't directly parallel the orders she had received from Alex.

'What do you need?' she asked the scientist.

Maria scowled at Casey and slid her eyes to Aimee. 'A blood sample, and these suits need to remain unbroken. Come on, quickly, this is vitally important.'

Aimee could see now that the object in Maria's hand was a lancet. 'I'll give you one,' she said, 'but give me the lancet and I'll do it back in my cabin where I can clean up.' She knew the lancet was sterile and sealed, but needed to ensure she had a sterile solution to slap on the skin immediately after it was pricked.

She held out her hand to Maria. Maria grabbed her wrist and, in one swift motion, pricked the skin of her forearm. A spot of blood welled up like a small polished ruby.

'Hey!'

'Be a big girl now, Dr. Weir – you know this is important.'

Maria wiped a glass slide over the blood, then released Aimee's hand, ignoring her intense glare. She handed the slide to Michael, who took it to the isolation cube.

Aimee grabbed a bottle of iodine from the table top and splashed some on the red dot.

Casey Franks leaned in close. 'That's why I gave you the gun, toots.' She sniggered softly and went back to chewing.

Michael pushed the slide into a small chamber on the side of the cube, inserted his hands in the mounted gloves, retrieved the slide and moved it up to the small raised work surface.

Maria focused on the new medium and spoke over the top of her screen. 'Add in a small amount of the bacterial fluid in the D-900 lateral quadrant.'

Michael did as he was told. Maria's screen now contained gridlines cutting the sample up into defined quadrants. She touched the black square on her chest to turn it on, then began a commentary as she focused in on the sample.

'It's not red,' Casey Franks said.

Maria swivelled in her chair to look patronizingly at Franks for a few seconds before turning back to her screen. 'That's right, dear. Blood at this magnification is more a pinkish-yellow. That's because the red blood cells are suspended in plasma, which is about ninety percent water. Here we are: plenty of healthy corpuscles, nice shape, though a little pale.' Maria turned once more, this time to Aimee. 'You need to eat more red meat, and get some rest; you're low on iron, and oxygen as well, I'd say.'

She gave a small smile and pulled back on the magnification so the near-transparent, biconcave circular discs could be seen floating within the fluid. She moved her cursor around and navigated to the upper left quadrant of the screen where Michael had placed the bacterium.

'Dr. Weir's Hidden Key – although I think I prefer Hades Bug as well, Hades for short. Anyway, it survives deep below ground and therefore measures its life in geological terms. After being locked beneath miles of stone, in the dark and heat, it probably finds us as alien as we find it. The only difference is, where we see it as a lethal little germ, it sees us as an accidental or opportunistic food source. No malice, no planning, it's just doing what it has evolved to do – ingest carbon, and … oh, my God …'

It appeared as though a shadow was falling across the screen as a black stain moved across the field of small red discs. The Hades' small filaments whipped them furiously through the serum towards the blood corpuscles, just like semen rushing to fertilise an egg. Once they made contact, they rotated until their smaller rigid spike was lined up with the red blood cell wall, then punctured it. Instantly, the blood cell's pink turned to gray, then black, before exploding to release a stain of black fluid into the pool of blood.

Michael screwed up his brow. 'That's odd; I was expecting a bacterial plume to be released. It doesn't seem to be using the blood cells for replication. It's just destroyed them without any defined outcome.'

'Not quite,' said Maria. 'Look at the Hades Bug that just ingested that cell.' She pointed the cursor at a body of the bacteria that was vibrating inside and wrestling with itself. After another second, a small dot appeared on its side. 'Replication bubble – it's hiving off some of its DNA and preparing to launch a daughter cell. So this is how it multiplies, by binary fusion. It's not acting like a virus and using the cell as some form of brood nest to create duplicates from within. It doesn't live within the cells either; it's way too big for that. Instead, it's raiding the contents of the cell and sucking out what it needs to use as an energy store for its own growth. It's using Aimee's blood cells as a grocery store ... and doing it very efficiently.'

The bacterium had finished splitting; now two dark cells existed where only a few seconds ago there had been one.

Michael was literally on the edge of his small chair. 'No wonder it can spread so quickly through our physiology – it's using our bodies as a highway and a food source at the same time.'

Aimee peered over Maria's shoulder to better see the detail. 'Move to the lower quadrant,' she said. 'There's always a shepherd to guard the sheep – let's see if we can find it.'

Casey Franks stepped up behind her. 'What are you looking for?' she whispered.

Aimee nodded at the screen. 'White blood cells – our last line of defense – humans have billions of them: some coded for specific invaders – fungi, parasites; and the most powerful reserved for viruses and bacteria. What type is it, Maria – an NK or neutrophil?'

'Looks like a lymphocyte ... nice big NK ...'

'NK – Natural Killer cell,' Aimee translated for Casey.

'Yeah, that's my type of cell; game on.' Franks pushed her gun up over her shoulder so it rested against her back and leaned in to look at the screen.

The NK cell was twice the size of the red blood cells and looked slightly granular around its edges. They all watched in complete silence as the black stain raced towards it. The explosions of the tiny cell walls as it advanced made the screen look like a battlefield, with all the heavy artillery stacked in the invader's favor. When the battle line reached the large white orb of the NK cell, everyone held their breath.

The first of the Hades Bug cells crowded up against the white blood cell. It attempted to swivel its spike around, then stiffened suddenly as though it had received an electric shock. The entire cell body shuddered, and crumpled like an aluminium can in the hand of a giant. More NK cells appeared, seeming to have been called to arms by their single advance soldier.

Aimee smiled and folded her arms. 'Chemical warfare on a micro scale – the NK have a battery of armaments, the most potent being an ability to release specific cytotoxic granules that target invading cells. Think of it as a mother ship sending out attack drones to destroy a target.'

Aimee's smile broadened as more and more of the dark bacteria crumpled and floated away in the yellowish medium. The NK cells crowded in, almost forming a solid wall against the black tide. More of the Hades cells crumpled and drifted away as micro-fragments.

'Chalk that up as one for the good guys,' Franks said. 'Hey, you're pretty tough on the inside, Dr. Weir, as well as —'

She cut off as, on screen, the black invaders overwhelmed the white blood cells' defenses. The familiar internal storm began within some of the NKs' own walls, then a round of soundless micro explosions tore the infected white blood cells into a cloud of dirty liquid. After another few seconds, the inky blackness spread further across the screen. Of Aimee's blood cells, nothing remained other than some cell fragments floating freely in the dark, cloudy fluid. The small one-sided war was over as fast as it had started.

'Ahh, shit.' Aimee's smile had vanished. She leaned back and exhaled.

'So much for our shepherds ... and last line of defense,' said Maria. 'I'm afraid it's what I was expecting, and I'm surprised you weren't as well, Dr. Weir. Why do you think that no one has recovered once infected? Eventually the body's defenses are overwhelmed by an ever-growing invading force – there could only ever be one result.' She gave Aimee the kind of look a college professor gives a student who shouts out a dumb answer in class.

Aimee crossed her arms. 'I don't agree. In fact, the immune response was good considering the advanced state of infection from a totally unique bacterium. It just wasn't quick or powerful enough, that's all. If we could boost it somehow, or maybe catch the infection earlier …'

'*If, somehow* and *maybe* are not words we use often at the CDC, Dr. Weir. Our fields of science … and expertise are obviously vastly different.'

As Maria Vargis turned away, Franks nudged Aimee's arm and motioned to the pistol in her belt. Aimee rolled her eyes and mouthed back a silent curse.

Michael glanced at Aimee then turned to his mother with a look of indecision on his face. 'Maria, Dr. Weir is right – to a degree, that is. I agree it looks bad, but not all bad. It *is* good news that our body recognizes the Hades Bug as a foreign body. And I agree that one line of investigation could be to somehow give our immune system a little help to marshal its troops faster and in greater numbers. Perhaps —'

Maria leaned towards him. 'That *may* be possible given enough time and appropriate facilities – neither of which we have here. So that's bad. But what's *very* bad is that this thing delivers total cellular destruction in a matter of hours, not days. By the time overt symptoms are manifesting, it has already destroyed a significant amount of the organic matrix. If it got to a vital organ or the brain in the first few hours, the immune response would be too late. The last time I saw something this lethal and infectious was in a military biohazard laboratory. From my reading of the data, once infected the patient is as good as dead.'

'Yes … *once infected* …' Michael let the words hang in the air.

Maria narrowed her eyes and pursed her lips together, obviously thinking. After a moment she raised her eyebrows and began to slowly nod at her son. Michael smiled, as if some form of communication had just passed between them.

'Okay, okay, I see where you're going. You're thinking we might be able to mount an immune response before it takes hold – create some sort of vaccination shield against it?'

Michael sat forward. 'Why not? It's big and aggressive, but our body recognizes it as being foreign. The problem is, by the time we're ready for it, the bugs have already scaled the walls and blown up our armory. If we can create an immune system memory, then as soon as it enters the system, we'll be already taking aim.'

'Of course, you're right,' Maria said. 'I've been so caught up in the lethality and uniqueness of the microbe, I'd forgotten that it's just another bug. After all, we've done it successfully for cholera, bubonic plague, polio, hepatitis A and numerous others. Yes, it's just another bug, Michael.' She patted him on the leg, as though rewarding a puppy for good behavior.

Aimee noticed there was no apology coming her way, even though it had been her idea. *Oh, well*, she thought. She was way too tired to really care.

Michael flexed his fingers, as though itching to start but not really knowing where. 'Okay, it's going to have to be a primary prophylaxis – a vaccine that prevents the *development* of the disease. Once it's established into the system, any secondary measures would be too late. We need our NK cells to be ready and waiting.'

Michael half-turned to his mother as if seeking approval of his method. Maria just nodded.

'An attenuated vaccine would be best,' he continued, 'but we just don't have the facilities or the time to engineer a less virulent microorganism. Given the constraints, there's only one option: generate Hades relics – pieces of the dead bacterium.'

Maria mouthed *yes*, as if happy with her pupil.

Aimee knew a little about vaccine creation through her biology research. She also knew Michael was right about their options. Vaccines could be created in a dozen ways these days, from bioengineering to synthesizing artificial dumb-bugs to trigger the desired human immunological response without any of the detrimental consequences. Nearly all required significant lab space, equipment and time – and even then, most only produced a minuscule amount of useful vaccine. *Still in this situation, any amount would do*, Aimee thought.

'How are you going to terminate the bacterium? Do you have the necessary equipment?' she asked.

'Standard techniques are heat and chemistry. I thought I'd try heat first as we're not exactly sure what to use on the chemical side just yet.' Michael was scribbling notes as he spoke.

'Don't worry, Dr. Weir, we know what we're doing,' Maria said.

Aimee found her air of superiority both unwarranted and annoying given how little they really knew about the bacterium. Even though Aimee knew Michael was using the correct logic and procedure, she couldn't resist needling the older woman a little.

'Heat? I'm not so sure. This thing came up from over a mile below the surface and actually needs heat to trigger its own micro metabolism to degrade and digest the trace hydrocarbons from the rock. Exposing it to more heat could, in fact, cause some sort of aggressive metabolic acceleration.'

Michael looked from Aimee to Maria, who rolled her eyes. 'Given the time and facility constraints, there are no other options. Proceed, Michael, using heat as the first choice attenuation trigger.' She folded her arms and looked squarely at Aimee, daring her to object.

Michael gave Aimee a look that could have been a plea not to get in a fight with his mother. 'Umm, Dr. Weir, I don't think even the hardiest extremophile could withstand prolonged exposure to a naked flame. Then again, I don't want them incinerated, just dead, so I can use their shells.' He compressed his lips into a tight, nervous smile and tilted his head, obviously hoping she would agree with his logic.

Aimee couldn't bring herself to give up just yet, even though, deep down, she knew the two disease experts would make the better decisions. 'Look, I acknowledge you two know much more about this than I do, but at this point none of us know what this bug is capable of doing or withstanding. You brought some nuclear material for the X-rays – why not try it first? In fact, I've read about research work undertaken by the National Institute of Allergy and Infectious Diseases that proved radiation attenuation worked far more effectively in the trials on an aggressive strain of Listeria. Basically, the irradiated bacteria was found to retain the properties needed to evoke a broad immune response – and it proved vastly superior to other methods of killing infectious pathogens.'

Maria's eyes slid to the silver suitcase in the corner of the room, then narrowed as they returned to Aimee. She spoke in a soft voice that carried a hint of steel. 'Dr. Weir, not only have I *seen* the research, it was one of *my* teams that was responsible for it. And just what do you suggest we use as shielding while we work with the radioactive material?' She looked Aimee up and down. 'Dirty linen and sunglasses?'

Aimee felt her face going red-hot, and not from embarrassment. She glared at Maria, her mind working furiously. Perhaps she was overly sensitive because she was tired, or perhaps she was envious of the woman's calm professionalism and authority while all she felt was panic – the infection, the men dying horribly, the heat, the quarantine ... the list seemed endless. Whatever it was, something made her want to stand and fight.

Maria pressed the back of her hand to her forehead. 'I'm sorry, Dr. Weir ... Aimee. We're all tired and on edge. We'll see to the attenuation process – it's our job – that's why we're here. It'll take us a while to set up, so ...' She made a shooing motion with her hands.

Aimee looked at Michael, who made a small placatory gesture behind his mother's back. Deciding that her anger wouldn't help the situation, Aimee shrugged and turned to leave.

'Wait,' Maria said, 'before you go, is there anything else you can tell us about the bacterium – its behavior, where it came from, its condition when you uncovered it? Anything and everything is vital now.'

Aimee searched her memory. 'Only that we must have pierced the K-T layer to enter the gas cavern – there was a lot of iridium in the sample matrix.'

*

Outside the cabin, Casey Franks turned to Aimee and said, 'What's up, Doc?'

Aimee caught the joke, but ignored it because she was so tired and pissed. 'I don't understand,' she said. 'A senior CDC scientist who's worked with micro agents all her life and has some radioactive material with her – why *wouldn't* she be interested in using it to create a higher-value terminated bacterium for a vaccine? That's some big call she's making.'

'Maybe she's just being a bitch, or … she actually knows what's she's doing,' said Franks.

Aimee's fists were balled as she responded. 'Yeah, maybe – to all or none of the above.'

*

Back in the cabin, Maria pondered the last piece of information Aimee Weir had given her – the presence of iridium in the original sample. Iridium – the footprint of the cosmos. She shivered even though the temperature was still well over a hundred degrees.

TWENTY-TWO

Alex and Captain Garmadia returned from their check of the perimeter just as Aimee and Franks were coming down the steps of the makeshift laboratory. Both men watched the women, and Garmadia turned to study Alex's face for a moment.

'She is your friend. The reason why you came personally, I think.'

Alex continued to look at Aimee as he spoke. 'She's not the reason I came.' It wasn't strictly true, but he wanted to remind the Paraguayan captain of the legitimacy of their mission. 'A team of our Green Berets Special Forces personnel sent down to provide perimeter security for the mining camp disappeared without trace. We believe an unknown assailant, or assailants, attacked them. We also believe this camp is still very much under threat, and not just by bandits or the disease outbreak. We're here to determine that threat, whatever it is, and counterbalance it, so the people working here can get on with their jobs.'

'I'm sure my own men could have dealt with the problem, Captain Hunter. It may have saved you a trip down here. I think you'll find that we are not all cane cutters and coffee growers waiting for the *norteamericanos* to come and save us.'

Captain Garmadia pushed through the last stand of ferns, leaving Alex by himself behind the dark green curtain of the jungle.

Alex needed Garmadia; the last thing he wanted was to get off-side with the man who had all the contacts on the ground. Plus, if he wanted to, he could make life hell for the hundreds of American men and women at the base in Mariscal Estigarribia. *Ahh, politics*, he thought as he walked from the jungle, intent on catching up with Garmadia.

His foot alighted next to a patch of black in the mud that sparkled faintly, as though oil and powdered glass had been mixed together, spread on the ground and allowed to bake into the red surface. He was about to take another step when his senses screamed at him; he halted with his foot suspended over the mass. He kneeled and examined the dark shimmering matter, then used a twig to scrape at it. The black substance was a fingernail's depth on the surface of the dried mud. He brought the twig to his nose and sniffed; it was slightly organic, a bit like gasoline and bad fish. It looked harmless, but his senses tingled as if in the presence of danger. He stood slowly and flicked the twig away into the undergrowth.

Alex could see Tomás and his men had nearly covered the entire campsite with broad leaves and branches. He had originally requested the work primarily to keep the men busy, although it would be useful not to have to wade through mud whenever it rained, but now he had another reason to be glad he had made the call. Something about the black matter was unsettling.

He was about to continue on after Garmadia when he saw Sam and Mak waving to him from the other end of the camp. He changed course towards his two HAWCs, and saw Chaco and Saqueo fall in behind him, the younger boy keeping a safe distance.

'What've you got, Sam?'

'We've managed to get the generator working at about twenty-five percent capacity. Means we'll have some perimeter lights for restricted times; also, water purification and refrigeration units are online. But the communication uplinks are dead – we need new parts. We're pretty happy considering the extent of the damage and what we had to work with.'

Sam stopped speaking but Alex could tell he hadn't finished with his briefing. He and Sam had been on some hair-raising missions before, but he hadn't seen his large friend looked this concerned for a while.

'What did they use – axes?' Alex asked.

Mak jumped in before Sam could respond. 'I don't think these guys, whoever they were, used axes, or even needed them.'

Alex frowned. 'Tell me.'

'Picture's worth a thousand words,' Sam said. 'Best if you take a look – it's a little weird.'

The three men walked quickly towards the electronics and generator shed. Alex noticed that Mak continued to look left and right at the surrounding jungle, and Sam rested his hand close to his firearm. Sam held the door and Alex entered the room. A couple of fluorescent bulbs shone with a cool hospital whiteness that was incongruous in the sticky heat of the jungle. He could see the damage immediately: heavy generator units had been upturned and the metal casing peeled back. There were dents in everything. The floor was littered with hundreds of feet of cable of varying lengths. In the midst of it, he could see his men's work – some of the generator units had been rewired, and pieces that obviously weren't part of the original design had been jerry-rigged to complete circuits or connections that had been torn free in the attack. Not a bad job given the maelstrom that had obviously been unleashed in the small space.

He looked from Sam to Mak and raised his eyebrows. *Well?*

Sam nodded to Mak, who bent down and retrieved a large sheet of heavy-gauge steel that had obviously been part of the main generator's external shielding. He grunted with the effort of holding up the heavy plate and turned it around for Alex to examine. At first all Alex noticed were several large, deep dents in the quarter-inch thick steel. Then Mak turned it slightly and Alex realized what had unnerved Sam and the large Iraqi: the central dent, penetrating to a depth of about half an inch, was unmistakable. Alex raised his hand and curled his fingers into a fist – it fitted perfectly into the imprint. Someone had punched the steel with more force than a pile-driver. Alex knew that, other than himself, no human could have made that indentation. They might have tried if they were totally hyped on speed or ice, but they'd be left with a hand that was little more than a bag of shattered bones and still wouldn't have achieved that depth.

He looked around the room again and, with fresh insight, saw the damage to the equipment in another light. Now he could see the fist strikes, the finger-grip marks, and imagined the steel being torn apart like cardboard by something, or someone, with enormous strength.

Alex looked at Sam; his face was etched with concern. Sam had also heard the recording of the attack on the Green Berets and Alex figured his cool-acting second-in-command was thinking the same thing he was: was this what had taken out Captain Michaels and his Special Forces fireteam? He needed to speak to Aimee about the GBs; they were the prime place to start an investigation.

'Things just got real interesting,' Alex said, looking at his watch. 'We've got another few hours before sundown. I'm going to talk to Aimee, find out a little more about what's been going on, and then we'll meet at 1600 for a briefing on our nighttime defenses. Tell Franks, and stay alert. And good work on the generator.'

Sam and Mak nodded, and Alex pushed open the door and left the building.

*

When Alex knocked on Aimee's door, Casey Franks pulled it open.

'Boss.' She nodded but didn't salute her superior officer – in the field, rank was never visibly acknowledged.

'Go and get something to eat,' Alex told her. 'Sam will update you on some new information and then we'll be having a full briefing at 1600 hours.'

'You got it.' Casey looked back at Aimee and nodded goodbye.

Alex watched her go, keeping his back to the room for a few seconds to allow himself thinking time on how he was going to start the conversation with Aimee. Out of the corner of his eye he saw a pillow land on top of a pile of dirty underwear in the corner of the room; he tried hard to suppress a smile.

He didn't have to start; Aimee spoke first. 'I'm glad you came.'

He turned. 'They couldn't have kept me away when I found out you were down here.' He pulled up one of the two chairs in the room and sat down, straddling it. 'You certainly know how to pick your holiday spots.'

She laughed wearily. 'Holiday? Now that would be nice. But I'll settle for just getting out of this green hell. I'm tired, I feel dirty and I want to be home.'

He sat forward and took her hands in his, looking into her eyes. 'Tell me what's been happening down here.'

Aimee expelled a long breath, pulling free of Alex's hands as she sat back. She screwed her eyes shut and Alex could tell she was picking a place to start, organizing her thoughts. It looked like it hurt.

'They've all been leaving and not coming back. First the Green Berets; then Francisco and Alfraedo went looking for the men that wrecked the equipment; and then a group of the remaining men followed the priest out. You know we found the Green Berets …? It was horrible. If you hadn't come when you did, maybe I'd have walked out into that deep green madness and disappeared as well.' Aimee looked towards the ceiling, her eyes welling up.

Found the Green Berets? Alex wanted to ask more, but Aimee started talking again.

'And the rest of the poor saps still stuck here? They'd probably be better off out in the jungle as well, 'cause I dug up some bad shit that's turning them all to a black mess – they're leaking away like ice left in the sun. Do you know what they're calling it? The Melting Death – yep, one horrifying way to die brought to you by Uncle Sam care of Dr. Aimee Weir. Hey, maybe they'll name it after me … Weir's Weirdness … how's that?' She exhaled through compressed lips, then began to laugh and cry at the same time.

Instinctively, Alex reached out and embraced her. He felt her relax. After a while, she pushed against him and sat back, sniffing on her tears. He kept his hands on her upper arms and looked into her face, focusing her attention.

'Aimee, tell me about the Green Berets. We've had no contact. Do you know what happened to them?'

She sat back and stared. 'You didn't know? Oh, God.' She shook her head and shuddered. 'Alex, it was horrible – they were ripped to shreds. We think it was all of them, but we couldn't really tell – there was nothing left, nothing to bring back, or even bury. The men think it was a jaguar. I doubt it. But I also can't see bandits, or any human beings, being so savage.'

Alex felt like he'd been struck a physical blow. He had worked with many Green Berets in the past – they were good people, good soldiers and ultimate professionals. He dropped his hands from her shoulders and sat back to think.

Aimee reached down and picked up a soiled T-shirt and wiped her face with it, then blew her nose. She threw the T-shirt into the corner and folded her arms. 'So, how have you been? Read any good books lately?' She began to laugh again.

Alex recognized the symptoms of stress. She was wound wire-tight, and starting to internalize the problem as being all her own.

He gave her a half-smile. 'Hey, same old, same old – we're just a couple of bores, I guess.' He sat forward until he was very close to her face. 'Aimee, the disease was always here – you were just the unlucky one to find it. Everyone thought the biggest problem you had was the attacks on the rig by cross-border rebels. That's why the Green Berets were sent down, as your shield. No one expected the contamination or the resulting quarantine order. And no one could have expected the GBs would be neutralized. We also strongly doubt any local bandits or rebels could have taken them out. We think there's something else down here, Aimee. Something strange that no one was prepared for.'

'Something strange? Yes, I think I've known that for days. Did you know all the animals have disappeared? And then there's the priest – Father González. Apparently he has a church close by and has been ministering to the locals for some time. He walked into our camp one evening and just bewitched the men. They followed him and never came back.' She took a sip of water and turned her mouth down. 'Or maybe the men were just bored and depressed from not being able to work and decided to keep on going after the mass. Perhaps Father González turned up at the time when they were looking for some sort of spiritual guidance, or ... I don't know ... some kind of intervention maybe.'

'Hmm. I'd like to speak to him, ask him what he knows about the missing men – yours and ours. He has a church close by, you say?' Alex asked.

'Yes. Come dusk he'll more than likely turn up here again, persuading more of the men to follow him.' Aimee sipped more water then pointed with the bottle at the slim gauntlet attached to Alex's arm. 'Should I ask?'

Alex lifted his arm, hand out flat, then made a fist. A stream of clear spikes created a furrow through the mound of dirty clothing and punctured the cabin's floor and wall. After a second, the spikes melted and disappeared.

Aimee shook her head. 'Must be a big seller at Christmas. I'll send you the bill for the clothing.'

Alex smiled and placed his hand over hers again. 'The guys have managed to get the water purification back online, also lights and some of the running water systems. There's no hot water, but I reckon an air-temperature shower around here isn't exactly going to be cold, is it? You'll feel better afterwards, then we can talk some more.'

She smiled. 'Okay, okay, a girl can take a hint. I know I stink.' She leaned forward and kissed his cheek.

A hundred memories flooded Alex's mind and his senses, and, without thinking, he turned his face towards her. She kissed him again, this time for longer, parting her lips slightly. Alex reached up and held the back of her head, pulling her to him and feeling the warm softness of her tongue in his mouth.

Part of him knew this wasn't the right time or place. But still his hand slid from her head and neck and traveled down her back. He felt the slick warmth of her skin beneath her shirt and her racing heartbeat. He grabbed her shirt and lifted it over her head. His own shirt quickly followed, and then he allowed himself to explore the body he could never forget – the small breasts, nipples hard under his fingers, the flat belly that fluttered when he touched it.

Aimee lay back on the small bunk and his heart ached at her beauty, and vulnerability. He saw that her blue eyes were dark, but this time it was not from anger. His searching found she was ready for him. She pulled him down on top of her and the cot squealed in protest at their combined weight.

'I've missed you,' she said.

'I never left you.' His mouth found hers again.

TWENTY-THREE

Inside the CDC lab, Maria's computer screen was completely dark now, no human blood cells discernible among the black sea of bacteria.

'Remove the slide,' she told her son. 'We'll use those live samples as our test bed.'

Michael nodded and slipped his hands into the gauntlets either side of the isolation cube. As his gloves gripped the glass slide, Maria saw the image alter.

'Hold it.' She leaned in close to the screen, her brow furrowed. 'Remove your fingers from the slide.'

'What's up? What is it?' Michael's voice was worried.

Maria ignored him. 'Place your fingers near the slide again … slowly. That's it …' She fiddled with the magnification on the screen and took still images of the movement progression.

'Amazing. I've never seen anything like it.'

The dark sea on the screen had parted into two groups either side of the slide – right where Michael's fingers gripped its edges.

'Michael, this is simply astounding – I've seen microorganisms exhibiting chemotaxis before, but nothing like this. We know that bacteria with motility structures can direct their movements according to certain chemicals in their environment – so, find food by swimming towards the highest concentration of attractive molecules, or flee from toxins. But these things aren't using a random walk or corkscrew motion; they're actually lining up like army ants.'

Maria replayed the images. At first, the Hades Bug was just a mass of micro-scale bodies; then Michael grasped the sample slide. The cells immediately formed into two clumps, each swarming towards his fingers. When Michael removed his hands, as Maria had asked, the bacteria floated back to a central clump. His hands appeared again, and they instantly coalesced into two halves and swarmed towards his fingers.

Michael looked pale behind his protective lenses. 'What does this mean? How could they even detect me through the gauntlets? How could a microorganism *be* that socially responsive and organized?'

Maria replayed the images again. 'Traces of body heat, the pulse of your blood through your fingertips, sensitivity to movement; or maybe something we're not even aware of. What concerns me is the way they suddenly acted cooperatively. In my time, I've see all manner of clumping, fusion and bacterial agglutination, but never have I witnessed this much coordination in a bacterial population.'

Maria sat back and stared at the screen, not conscious of Michael's voice until he touched her shoulder.

'You think the cells may be sentient? Or at least be able to communicate?' He sat down beside her.

'No, impossible. They don't *think*. More likely it's some form of chemical signalling, quorum sensing, or some other pathway … I just don't know yet. Dr. Weir brought this strain of bacteria up from over a mile below the Earth's surface. It's likely it's traveled through a billion billion generations without ever encountering animate life. It could have evolved all sorts of abilities for detecting carbon food sources, its own genotype, and maybe even abilities for defense.'

Maria got to her feet, walked to the cabin door and pushed it open a crack. New humid air flowed in to replace the stale humid air. She mentally added in the new pieces of this microbiological jigsaw puzzle: one hundred percent lethality, high communicability, rapid transmission to a terminal stage, no known vaccine or treatment. And at this point she wasn't even sure if they had it contained within the quarantine zone or whether it was already spreading out into the jungle through the local fauna.

She turned back to her son. 'We've got forty-eight hours – by then we need to have developed a vaccine.'

While Michael worked on the vaccine, there were a few other precautions to put in place around the camp. Maria searched through the bags they'd brought with them, found what she was looking for, and went outside. She saw Alex Hunter coming out of Aimee Weir's cabin and waved him over.

'Captain Hunter …' She pulled the facemask down off her nose and mouth. 'How do you do it?'

'Excuse me?'

'How do you manage to look so fresh all the time? I know you've had as little sleep as the rest of us, and you carried most of the equipment. Do you take stimulants?'

He gave her a hard stare. 'Just training. Is there anything I can do for you? Have you got everything you need?'

Maria narrowed her eyes. 'Whatever you say, Captain. I'd just hate to see you or any of your team collapse because they're taking uppers in this heat. It can cause respiratory shock, you know.'

Alex just grunted, and she decided to get the point.

'Michael and I are going to attempt to create a vaccine, but, given the limited resources and time, we're going to need a lot of luck. In the meantime, we need to do all we can to limit new outbreaks. We don't know yet how the infection spreads, but we can guard against one of the most common vectors – insects.' She pulled two large unlabelled spray cans from the bag at her feet. 'I need your people to fumigate all the dwellings, and under the cabin floor areas too. May be a good idea to take it right up to the edges of the clearing.'

Alex nodded. 'Makes sense.' He took the cans, sniffed and recoiled, holding them slightly away from his body. 'Is this DDT?'

'Stop being a big baby; of course it is. For tropical regions, it's still the most effective, long-lasting chemical for dealing with blood-sucking insects. Don't worry, Captain, I'm sure it's not going to end up in blue whale blubber or babies' milk down here. And right now, our priority issue is to prevent the microbes' transmission – wouldn't you agree?'

Alex didn't look convinced. 'Hmm, okay. Anything else?'

'I think, for insurance, we should also set up braziers burning damp jungle foliage every ten feet to create a smoke curtain to dissuade the higher flying insects from entering the camp. It won't be very pleasant, but it means we'll be able to move around in the evenings without having to reapply insect repellent every hour.'

'Consider it done. Anything else?'

Maria smiled. 'Done for now, but come back later and I'll give you a briefing on our progress.'

As she stepped back, Michael's voice could be heard calling to her from inside the lab. He sounded concerned.

*

When Maria re-entered the cabin, Michael was standing with his hands on his hips gazing at a sealed Petri dish suspended over a portable heat pad in the isolation cube. Maria could see that the dish's contents had been reduced to ash.

'*Mitéra*, I think we've got a problem,' he said.

'The attenuation process? What's happened?'

'It's not working. I've tried three different samples – all resisted the increasing temperature until they reached a critical point, and then they just incinerated. I expected this to be a heat-tolerant microbe given its pedigree, but this little horror is amazing. Normally, microorganism attenuation occurs from about 120 to 160 degrees. But at 180 degrees, it showed no visible sign of any change to its form, shell or contents of its cells. So I kept going higher …'

Michael replayed the last few minutes of his work on Maria's computer screen; as they watched, the temperature gauge increased to 500 degrees.

'Oh my God,' whispered Maria.

The gauge continued to rise, its red line passing 600, then 700, then 800. At 1000 degrees, the dish started to register activity.

'This is past the tolerance of any known microbial thermophile,' Maria said. 'Or even any previously encountered extremophile. It should be totally denatured now, but we seem to be seeing the exact opposite. In fact, I think the heat's causing some sort of cellular bud acceleration.'

At 1200 degrees, the bacteria in the Petri dish turned into a boiling broth, then exploded with activity. Areas of the dish that were once devoid of the twisting dark bacteria were quickly filled. Maria could see that the temperature gauge was rising rapidly; the red line moved past 1500 degrees and the isolation cube, built to withstand enormous heat, started to swirl with color as the panels expanded. The bacteria in the dish all pulsed at once, then thickened. Individual cells lost definition – the broth had started to solidify.

Michael spoke softly. 'Agglutination after five minutes at 1800 degrees. Activity, but hard to discern as the light won't pass through the solid single object. The dish has now doubled its weight ... and increased its mass by 1000 times.'

'What the hell is happening here? Is it changing form somehow?' Maria couldn't take her eyes from the glutinous mass in the dish that pulsed like a living organ. The red line of the temperature gauge approached 2000 degrees.

'I'm reaching maximum temperature with the heat disc,' Michael said wearily. 'I would have needed to swap to an open flame to go any higher, but ...' He paused, and, like a spoiled cake, the mass collapsed, shrivelled and turned to a powdery, dust-like substance. 'Eleven minutes, seventeen seconds ... then total incineration. There's nothing left – no shell walls, nothing. Not even DNA fragments. Just a fine mineral substance that's akin to something like carbon or diamond dust.'

Maria's mind was racing: *2000 degrees – that's atmosphere-entry temperature.* She thought again of Aimee's comment about iridium in the original sample; and recalled the description of the "bleeding" stone discovered miles under the earth at the Egoli mine. She stared at the cooling cube, her mind testing different hypotheses, turning over the options.

'I've tried this several times now,' Michael said, 'always with the same result. There's a collar temperature, which, once pushed through, results in the bacteria being immediately destroyed. Up until then, it's not only extremely vibrant, it almost looks like it's turning from individual bacterium into some sort of coalesced multicellular life form.'

Maria swung around in her seat to look at him and he rushed to qualify his comments. 'I know, I know – that's impossible. But maybe Dr. Weir's right; perhaps we should be considering radiation to destroy the cells.'

'No,' Maria said quickly. 'We continue with the heat process. It's just a very robust and vigorous thermophile. It's utilising heat the same way as a food source – just a little more energetically.' She thought for a moment. 'We can't keep pushing it to 2000 degrees for every attempt at attenuation – slows the retesting process too much.' She stood up and walked to the isolation box. 'We've got power now, and therefore the cooling systems are working. So … use heat-shock – means you shouldn't need to push it up to such a high temperature to achieve your results. Cool it with ice for thirty minutes then immediately place it onto the preheated disc. The thermal displacement shock should destroy it. Not even viruses with armored protein coats can stand up to that.'

She looked down at the cube and frowned, leaned forward and sniffed. 'And check the seals when it's cool. I think I can smell a heat-production vapor.'

TWENTY-FOUR

The sun had fallen behind the tall trees hours ago; as it dipped now towards the horizon, the shadows merged into twilight. Barrels of slow-burning vegetation had been spaced around the edges of the clearing and the heavy humid air kept the smoke low to the ground, giving the campsite a Gothic feel.

Alex felt something approaching. Small sounds carried infinitesimal vibrations that could be felt deep in the inner ear, light carried colors and wavelengths not seen by normal human vision; even the skin contained remnants of Pacinian corpuscles that could detect the slightest movement – all these were like superior senses within Alex's system. And now they kicked into action: he felt the shift in atmosphere like a bow wave preceding a ship. He tried to reach out with his senses and form some kind of image, but it refused to take shape in his mind. *Must be still too far out*, he thought.

Then his head snapped around and he frowned in disbelief. *Amazing – so quiet.* A man stood silently at the edge of the clearing, as if waiting for a sign, or an invitation. He was wearing priest's vestments.

Aimee appeared beside Alex and unnecessarily nudged his arm to get his attention. He nodded towards the man. 'I take it that's your priest?'

'Yeah, Father Alonso González – he gives me the creeps.'

She folded her arms and stared at the man from under lowered brows. Alex smiled; he could tell the priest would get no invitation from her. Something about him made Alex extremely uneasy too. He was no taller than Alex, and not physically imposing, but Alex's unique vision detected a cold radiation emanating from him that would have better suited a corpse.

He pressed the stud in his ear and spoke softly. 'HAWCs, we got company. Give me a perimeter.'

In a few seconds, Mak and Franks appeared just at the edge of the jungle, one on either side of the priest, guns cradled in their arms, barrels loosely pointed at González. Sam took up a position a few steps behind Alex; he could feel his second-in-command's eyes boring into the newcomer.

Alex looked around; he sensed other presences now, close by, but he couldn't distinguish them yet, or identify their positions. He winced slightly – despite their indistinct physical presence, they screamed for attention inside his head.

The remaining drill workers were gathering close to the priest. They stood still, not speaking, just watching him as if waiting for some signal. Tomás came up behind Aimee and stood just behind her right shoulder. He was bumped out of the way by Captain Garmadia, who took up position between her and Alex.

The priest fixed his eyes on Alex and glided forwards. He stopped about five feet away, but didn't speak. It was if he was waiting for them to make the first move. It was Garmadia who obliged.

'I am not aware of you having authorization to be in this area, *padre*. Where are you from, and on whose instruction were you sent to Paraguay?'

The priest's eyes flicked to Garmadia for an instant, then he turned his head to the HAWCs on either side of him, took in Sam, then switched his gaze back to Alex. His mouth lowered slightly behind his beard. 'You are a North American, *señor*?'

Alex ignored the question. 'You must be Father González. Where are our men, Father? We'd like to speak to them.'

The priest's mouth had remained open and the deep voice spilled out again. 'Many men decided to return home. The others are safe with me.'

'We will be the judges of that, *padre.*' Captain Garmadia stepped in front of Alex, possibly feeling insulted that the priest had chosen to address the HAWC. 'I am Captain Fernando Garmadia of the Paraguayan military forces. I am in charge of this district. I insist on seeing our men immediately.'

The priest replied to the Paraguayan soldier, but kept his eyes on Alex. 'Do you fear the God? That one day He will rise up?'

Garmadia frowned. '*Perdón?*'

'It is a fearful thing to fall into the hands of the living God,' the priest said, his stance as still as stone.

'Hebrews 10:31,' Sam said, coming up beside Aimee, his eyes fixed on the black-clad priest. 'God is not the author of confusion, but of peace – Isaiah 4:25.'

The priest's left eye bulged slightly and swivelled towards Sam. Then he seemed to relax and held out his hand to Alex. 'Isaiah has words of the greatest beauty. I am sorry, I have been too long without educated company. Please allow me to formally introduce myself.'

As Alex held out his own hand, Sam said to the priest, 'That was actually Corinthians 14:33. I thought you might have known that.'

Two things happened: the priest seized Alex's hand, and Aimee screamed.

An explosion went off in Alex's mind, then blackness, darker than night, engulfed him. An alien roar tore through his head, and he saw screaming human beings trapped in a blood-red web as a hellish nightmare of sharp teeth slowly descended upon them.

He heard a thousand voices, shouting in triumph now, not fear. *One day He will rise up!* The words came from all around him, and from deep, deep below the earth. A thousand voices, a million, that were separate and then one, as if a single mind shared a billion mouths. It was his dream playing over again.

*

From a dark cave, miles below ground, he heard his name – *Alex, Alex ...* It had to be Aimee – she was calling to him from the surface. He floated upwards, happy that he could fly through the ice and stone. She was calling him and he sped towards her.

He opened his eyes. His head was resting on a soft pillow, but it still hurt like hell. There was dried blood caking his nose.

Aimee was bathing his forehead. She leaned in close to his face. 'Alex, are you okay? You blacked out when the priest grabbed your hand, and blood started gushing from your nose. You scared the hell out of me ... uhh, all of us.'

He grabbed her hand and sat up quickly. 'Where is he?'

Sam pushed forward from where he stood at the rear of the crowded cabin. Alex could see Maria and Michael Vargis behind the lieutenant's large frame.

'Gone,' Sam reported. 'It was weird – he grabbed your hand and you looked like you'd been poleaxed. You fell, and there was blood everywhere. I was watching the priest until you fell, then when I looked up again, he just wasn't there – can't have been more than a second or two. No one can move that quickly – not even you. I sent Mak and Franks out, but after an hour they gave up without finding a trace.'

Alex swung his legs over the side of the bed and stood up quickly; he swayed for a second. 'I'm okay.' He looked at Aimee's expression and gave her a smile. 'Really. I must be dehydrated, that's all.'

He looked around the room, but his eyes weren't focused on its interior; he was seeing much further than its four walls. 'He's gone now,' he said softly, then, 'Sam, with me.'

He was out of the cabin before anyone could say another word.

*

Sam was one of the few below the rank of general who was aware of Alex Hunter's abilities. He had been on missions where he had seen his commanding officer do things that no other human being was capable of. He knew Alex had a second sense that opened to him a world that was inaccessible to other people. He also knew that Alex didn't black out because he was dehydrated.

'What did you see, boss?' He had to take long strides to keep up as Alex moved quickly.

'I don't know, Sam. As soon as I touched the guy's hand, everything turned upside down. The images I got were bizarre, openly hostile and definitely not priestly.'

Alex stopped when they reached the center of the camp. It was completely dark and the perimeter lights were struggling with the limited power supply. In addition, the burning braziers now only gave off a dull red glow, looking like portholes to the bowels of hell.

'I want a watch tonight,' Alex ordered. 'You and I first, then Franks and Mak can relieve us in six hours. Keep everyone inside the perimeter. At first light, we'll pay a visit to the *padre* at home. I've got a bad feeling about all the men that went with him.'

Sam nodded. 'You got it, boss. Hey, take it easy.'

He recognized the look in Alex's eyes – it wouldn't take much of a push before the furies were let loose, and then … Alex Hunter was capable of a lot of good, but when the rage took hold, then sometimes *good* wasn't the priority.

*

'Yes, Maria, no, Maria, of course I verified the results, Maria, and no, I didn't make a mistake.' Michael mimicked his mother's voice as he checked the results of the thermal-shock process. 'Hey, don't like the cold, do you?'

The Hades bacteria had been rendered dormant at the low temperature. Michael also noticed that the cells in a state of dormancy had developed a protein coat, but had quickly germinated and reactivated when the temperature was increased. At 2000 degrees, as if a switch had been flipped, the same results manifested – black, inanimate, useless dust.

'*Skata*! No fucking difference. Got any other great ideas, Maria?'

Michael stood with his hands on his hips, staring into the isolation cube as its walls swirled with color while it cooled. He sniffed – Maria had been right; he could smell something too. He removed his glove and placed his fingers on the glass, pulling them away almost instantly – it was still too hot to touch safely. But he was sure he'd felt a slight roughness on the normally smooth surface.

He bent down to look closer, but could see nothing. He searched in one of the equipment boxes they had brought with them, removed a small but powerful magnifying glass and held it up to the box, moving it in and out to adjust the focus until he could see the surface of the box clearly. Fine, almost invisible cracks ran throughout the depth of its panes.

Michael stood up and looked towards the ceiling. 'So much for withstanding temperatures to 3000 degrees.' He rolled one hand into a fist and punched his forehead. 'She'll murder me!'

He bent to examine the box again, then frowned, and turned back to the equipment pack. He took out a glass slide and swab, replaced his gloves, then wiped the swab down the side of the glass cube. He transferred the sample to the slide, squeezed a drop of sterile water onto it, and placed it under a manual microscope. He twirled the focus dial several revolutions until he had his desired clarity. *Hmm, that's not good.* The solution showed traces of the Hades Bug dust – somehow its incinerated fragments had extruded through the thick glass of the isolation cube.

Michael sat back, thought for a moment, then shook his head. 'Well, I'm out of ideas.' He exhaled and stood up slowly. Much as he hated it, he needed to ask Maria what to do next, and inform her of the failing isolation cube.

He stretched his back and turned to the door, pushing the hood of his suit back to expose his perspiration-slicked hair. He pulled off his gloves and, with one hand, opened the door. With the other, he wiped his brow, transferring a small black smudge from his finger to his forehead.

If he had looked one last time through the microscope, he would have seen something that might have worried him more than a broken piece of equipment. On the glass slide, among the floating fragments, sub-microscopic buds were beginning to appear on some of the biological splinters. Gradually, the buds opened and extended cytoplasmic stalks; a moment later, cell division restarted.

*

Maria listened to her son with an impassive face as he told her about the bacteria's development of a protein seed coating at lower temperatures. She knew that their options had been limited to start with; and were now probably exhausted. Without any form of realistic, natural or derived immunological defense, the human race had no hope of winning a microscopic physiological war with the Hades Bug. And losing to this particular microorganism meant a very unpleasant death. For the first time in her life as a scientist, Maria considered euthanasia as an option.

Michael broke her concentration. 'What now? Should I try to chemically attenuate? We didn't bring many compounds. I'm still thinking the radiation option would —'

'No!' Maria yelled, and Michael recoiled as though slapped.

She immediately regretted using the sharp tone, and exhaled wearily. She wished she could tell him. The radioactive material she had brought wasn't the simple shortwave Röntgen radiation used for X-rays. Instead, it was the infinitely more powerful lithium-deuterium particles required for an elastic collision – a million times too much energy for simple bacterial attenuation.

She softened her voice. 'No, Michael, for now we document our results and concentrate on other, less elegant defensive mechanisms. We can still consider gross amputation for extremity contamination, and, out of the body, surely it must be vulnerable. Let's look at what kills it – sodium hypochlorite should at least explode the cell walls.'

She reached over and rubbed her son's arm, smiling into his face. She was often brusque with him, but in her heart she knew he was the only good thing to come out of her marriage. One day she'd tell him that. He frowned, probably not understanding the reason for the sudden show of maternal affection.

'You've done a good job,' she went on. 'But I think its rapid transmission is a good thing – as long as we can totally isolate the infected men, then we can let the disease run its course; let it burn itself out.'

She knew that probably wasn't true anymore – the genie was out of the bottle. Unlike South Africa, there would be no simple sealing of a hole in the ground here. This wound had ruptured and cauterisation would not be enough; total excision of the necrotic flesh was needed. There was no way of knowing for how long the Hades Bug could go dormant; it could remain in that state for weeks, years … centuries? They still knew next to nothing about it.

She felt she was being pushed towards a precipice. A paragraph from Protocol 9 leapt into her mind: *In the event of possible border or boundary extrusion, initiate total CZS.* Comprehensive Zone Sterilisation meant leaving behind no hosts, no vectors, no transmission – and no survivors.

She looked at Michael, her only child. *There must be another way*, she thought.

TWENTY-FIVE

While Alex went to talk to Franks and Mak at the start of their rotation, Sam performed one last outer perimeter sweep of the camp. The jungle was making all its usual chirps, whistles and squeaks, and small creatures scuttled from his path as he pushed through the damp foliage. Though the constant noise made it difficult to detect an intruder, Sam didn't mind – it was somehow comforting. Silence in a jungle was unnatural and unwelcome, usually heralding predation.

Only a few dozen feet out from the camp, the light was completely swallowed by the jungle. That, the cloud cover and an intermittent rain meant Sam moved more by feel and instinct than sight. He used his flashlight for rapid observations only, and not at all if he could help it. He stopped and stood silently, a hulking figure in tiger-stripe camouflage, just as invisible as other creatures of the forest. *Nothing – all good.*

He turned back to the camp for a few hours' downtime; he needed it. He trod cautiously to minimise noise, but instead of the regular spongy green carpet underfoot, he felt something hard and flat – too flat to be natural. 'Hello.' He bent and retrieved the object: an ancient-looking leather-bound book with what seemed to be a faded gilt crucifix carved into the front.

He opened it and flicked on his slim flashlight for second. The pages were handwritten … *in a combination of Spanish and Latin,* he thought. They also contained some detailed illustrations.

Hmm, not a Bible then – maybe somebody's journal. The priest's?

He tucked it under his arm, looking forward to pitting his formidable language skills against its contents.

'You're quiet tonight, big guy,' Franks said, popping her gum.

'This is not a good place.' Mak stared into the dark jungle.

'It's just a fucking jungle, Mak. Jeez, be a big boy now.' She raised her eyebrows briefly. 'Let's do another perimeter sweep. Rendezvous back here in twenty.'

Mak ignored the jibe. 'It is not the jungle. It is what I feel *in* the jungle that concerns me.' He frowned again, then said quickly, 'Copy that. Twenty, and back here … and you should not swear so much.'

*

Casey watched him go. Every now and then, he'd stand stock-still for a few moments and listen to the sounds of the dense green around him. She shook her head and said softly to herself, 'For fuck's sake, stop doing that – you're freaking me out.'

She turned her back and started off in the opposite direction. The camp clearing was fairly large, designed to accommodate over a hundred men, their equipment, a few cabins and assorted makeshift offices. It was like a mini-town carved out of the jungle. Without their constant attention, it would only take about two seasons for the jungle to totally reclaim it.

Casey scanned the jungle – listening and looking for anything out of the ordinary. She breathed in heavily through her nose, searching out smells too. She was good, she knew it; she never missed anything. Like all HAWCs, Casey Franks was completely focused at her job; and when that job became combat – armed or unarmed – she reveled in the physical challenge.

She couldn't see Mak anymore; he was shielded by a row of cabins. She expected him to reappear in a few moments. The skin on her neck crawled and she looked over her shoulder … there was something … She stood still and waited, not even breathing. There was nothing. She frowned – *that fucking Mak had her freaked out; soon she'd be seeing witches on broomsticks and dancing goblins.* She looked across to where he should have come into sight again – there was still just empty clearing. *Huh, what's going on?*

She pressed her ear stud. 'Hey, Mak, you takin' a leak? Where are you?' She waited in annoyed silence. 'Mak, come in. Over.'

The line opened, signalling a response, but instead of Mak's voice she heard a grunt and gurgle.

'Fuck!' Casey sprinted across the clearing.

*

Alex sat upright in his bunk as though jolted by electricity. That sensation of dark desolation he had felt before blacking out had returned.

There were faint sounds of a skirmish taking place on the far side of the camp.

He pressed the stud at his ear. 'Uncle, we got contact.' Before he had finished the last words, he was out the door.

*

Casey saw Mak struggling with a single combatant. She pulled her sidearm and a blade and rushed to support him. At forty feet, she saw Mak get smashed to his knees; even in the dark she could see his face was battered and bloody. She could hardly believe anyone could take down the big man so easily – Mak was a HAWC, and a good one.

The Iraqi attempted to raise his gauntleted arm and bring it around into his attacker's face. With impossible speed, the assailant grabbed his arm and twisted, fast and hard. The crack of bone and tendon echoed across the quiet camp. A spray of needle-sharp ice projectiles raked the ground beside Casey and she had to swerve to avoid being shredded by the deadly thorns. The spray stopped abruptly as Mak's attacker ripped the gauntlet free and threw it away.

Twenty feet out and still moving, she lifted her gun arm – just as the man brought his fist down onto Mak's face. The front of the HAWC's skull crumpled as if he'd been hit by a sledgehammer. The man pulled his hand free from the broken flesh and watched as the Iraqi's large body fell to one side.

'Motherfucker!' Casey fired three times, with three strikes to the upper torso – at such close range she was never going to miss.

The man didn't fall. *Must have a vest*, she thought.

She stopped and planted her short, muscular legs wide apart in a shooter's stance, preparing to put another volley into the man – this one targeting his head. Instead, the last ten feet separating them became one in the blink of an eye. The man moved up into Casey's face almost supernaturally and tore the gun from her grip as easily as an adult would take an annoying toy from an infant. A large hand closed around her neck.

Her eyes went wide in alarm. *It's the fucking priest.*

She brought the Ka-Bar blade around and embedded it in his torso – and got as much reaction as if she'd stabbed a hanging side of beef. The hand at her neck tightened and she felt her eyes start to bulge as the blood flow to her brain was cut off.

The man smiled at her. Or, rather, his mouth split unnaturally wide into a shark-like grin. A black hole ringed with needles leaned in towards her. She mouthed the word *motherfucker* and found the strength to twist her blade. The mouth opened wider. As her vision started to cloud, she saw something in the depths of his gullet; something waiting inside that needle-ringed cavern. It was the first time in her life she'd ever been frightened.

As her misty vision started to turn from red to black, something hit the priest. Hit him hard.

*

Alex raced across the clearing so quickly, those trying to follow him must have wondered whether his feet even touched the ground. He took in the scene with a single glance: Mak was down, dead, and Franks was under attack by a single powerful assailant. He knew who it was – the priest. González had Franks by the neck, crushing her throat, as he leaned in towards her.

Alex's great strength was usually more than an adversary's physical frame could withstand, and he'd learned to pull his punches. Not this time. He wanted this man dead, destroyed.

The blow knocked González's head sideways.

But the priest didn't go down, as Alex had expected. Instead, he dropped Franks and turned to stare at Alex. From the angle of the man's head where it flopped against his shoulder, Alex could tell his neck was broken. The mouth dropped open and a roar emanated from its black hole – a howl from the depths of hell itself. Alex had heard the sound before: on the recording of Captain Michaels' last transmission.

González moved far quicker than Alex anticipated, striking him in the center of the chest with such force that Alex felt the impact deep in his ribs. He was thrown back ten feet to land on the dried fronds that Tomás and the men had been spreading over the mud.

Fool! Alex screamed at his own stupidity. He had let himself be taken by surprise.

He rolled quickly to get to one knee … and into the waiting hands of González. The blows raining down on his head were clearly meant to crush his face and skull. They came hard and fast, and Alex only had time to catch the fists in his own hands. He grunted from the effort. *This guy is far too strong for a normal man; far too strong for anything on two legs*, he thought.

He released one hand and swung a fist towards the priest's mid-section, intending to break most of the ribs underneath the dark cassock and make it impossible for him to breathe. Instead, his hand was caught in the air before the punch connected, and crushed in what felt like a steel vice.

Each man struggled against the other's strength. Alex looked sideways into the priest's face, which lay at that sickening angle on his shoulder. It was composed; no strain, no pressure – it was as though he was wearing a mask. Then he noticed that only one of the priest's eyes was fixed on him – and it bulged and strained as if wanting to join the fight by itself.

Alex pushed and pulled, but for every ounce of force he applied, an equal or greater measure was pushed back. He was locked in an embrace that was sapping his immense strength.

Slowly, the priest forced one of Alex's hands towards his face; the mouth behind the beard dropped open and a gray tendril snaked out between the bristles. Alex's eyes widened as he saw needle-sharp teeth surrounding an almost totally spherical orifice – like the mouth on a lamprey eel or a leech. His hand was being drawn towards this disgusting maw.

Alex became aware of sounds all around him – some emanating, strangely, from the core of the priest; some from the cabins, and also the ground beneath his feet. It was a chorus of mewling desire and hunger – for him, for his flesh. The calling he had heard in his dream.

He gritted his teeth, grunted and managed to halt the slow pull on his hand, but his shoulder ached from the exertion. The priest had his other arm held tight, so it was out of action – for now, at least. Alex brought his knee up into the priest's side and was satisfied to feel bones crunch. But it had little effect – the man didn't even seem to register the strike.

The gray tendril had unfurled further from the priest's mouth and was now touching Alex's exposed flesh just behind his glove. Revolted, he pulled with all his strength and brought his knee up again. At the same time, he heard a shout from beside him. A stream of razor-sharp ice projectiles raked up the side of the priest's body – and also through Alex's thigh. Alex jolted from the pain and, in the brief second he was distracted, the priest let go – and was gone.

Alex couldn't believe it. The man had somehow ripped himself from Alex's grip and disappeared back into the jungle as fast as a lightning flash.

TWENTY-SIX

'We need to cut her,' Sam said.

He hadn't needed to check on Alex – the HAWC leader was up and sprinting into the jungle after the priest the moment he realized he'd disappeared. Sam's priority was Franks and her crushed windpipe. Her tongue protruded like a fat slug between lips colored a deep crimson-blue. Sam could tell she was suffocating.

The drill workers crowded around, Maria and Michael Vargis hovering behind them. Aimee, after taking one look at the female HAWC's condition, had rushed back to her cabin. She returned now with a length of rubber pipe, tape, a scalpel and a small brown bottle. She knelt down beside Sam, who had drawn a shortened Ka-Bar blade and was feeling Franks's neck for a position just below her larynx.

Aimee gently grabbed his knife hand. 'You've done this before?'

'A few times – not exactly a perk of the job, or one I enjoy. And my work wouldn't be as tidy as yours.' He sat back, happy to let her take over.

Aimee splashed the contents of the bottle onto Casey's neck and Sam's eyes stung from the smell of the surgical cleanser. She expertly sliced into the flesh, and was immediately rewarded with the wet sound of air being sucked into the wound. Franks's chest inflated and she started to struggle beneath them.

'Hold her down,' Aimee said.

Sam held the HAWC's shoulders as she writhed on the ground; the return of consciousness was rapidly bringing pain and memory with it. Aimee pushed the tip of the tube into the wound and cut the end off with the scalpel, leaving just an inch protruding. She covered the tube and wound with tape.

The crowd parted to let Alex through. He kneeled next to them and looked at the wound and the rise and fall of the HAWC's chest, his face blank of emotion.

Casey Franks opened her eyes. Her lips moved but no sound came out; a small red bubble popped on her lower lip.

Alex reached down and squeezed her shoulder. 'Don't speak … he's gone now. But don't worry, we'll find him and finish him – that I promise. You just concentrate on getting better; we need you.'

Alex took Sam by the arm and led him out of the group. 'That wasn't a man, Sam. It looked like a man, but it wasn't. It was too strong, too fast, and I couldn't hurt it.' He shook his head as though in disbelief. 'Did you see what it did to Mak?'

Sam looked around, then back to Alex, his eyes wide. There was no sign of Mak's body.

*

Alex was shaking with rage and disbelief. His soldier's body had been stolen – and while they were all just a few dozen feet away. There was a short slide mark into the foliage, then nothing. It was as if the body had been consumed by the jungle itself. It had taken all Sam's and Aimee's combined influence to prevent Alex from charging after it – even though he had no idea where to look.

Now, he tried to calm himself as he focused on the jungle, trying to sense some trace of Mak's body and the creature that called itself González. But there was nothing; the priest was either too far away, or gone for good. Alex didn't believe the latter. He hadn't hurt the man at all, and, if not for Sam, he might have ended up as dead as Mak.

Alex rubbed his forehead hard. He had underestimated the exchange – an amateurish and near suicidal mistake for any soldier to make, let alone a HAWC leader. As soon as he'd touched the priest's flesh he had sensed something strange. A human physical presence … and then something no longer human. And the thing hiding in his mouth – *a parasite*?

Alex felt Sam and Garmadia watching him as he paced. He could hear them talking. Sam held Mak's gauntlet in his hands; other than some bloodstains, it was all that remained of the soldier. Alex swore at the green wall of the jungle.

A light rain started to fall and he looked up into it, letting it cool his face and calm his anger. He knew that in this region it could rain for days on end – any tracks would be obliterated. It was still hours before sunrise. They'd need some rest.

'Lieutenant Reid, Captain Garmadia.'

Sam strode over, Garmadia following behind. Alex saw Garmadia looking at the line of puncture wounds in his leg; perhaps he was noticing that they hadn't bled.

He held out his hand for the gauntlet and studied it for a few seconds before looking up at the two men. 'Get some sleep.' He saw Sam about to argue and cut him off. 'That's an order. I'll take the rest of the watch. At 0600 we're going to find Mak's body and bring him back.' He pulled the gauntlet onto his free arm and said softly, 'Along with the priest's head.'

Michael was hot and thirsty, and had a headache that felt like a small ball of fire in the center of his brain. He had been looking through the microscope for an hour and his vision was starting to blur. He sat back to rub his temples. 'My God, my head is killing me. I've just about had enough of this place. When do we get to go home?'

Maria was filling two syringes with a clear fluid. She looked up at her son briefly before bending back to her task. 'What's that, darling? Home? We could all do with getting out of here. Don't worry – everything will be fine soon.'

She set down the second syringe very carefully.

*

'How is she?' Alex asked Aimee.

Franks's unconscious figure lay on the low bunk in Aimee's cabin. In the opposite corner of the room, Chaco and Saqueo sat huddled together, long ago having given up the struggle to sleep. Both boys watched Alex – Saqueo with curiosity, Chaco with distrust.

'She's fine,' Aimee said. 'If I hadn't sedated her, she'd be up and trying to resume duties. I put a temporary balloon stent into her windpipe to re-dilate it, and I've removed the tube and stitched the wound. It'll hurt like hell for a few days, and she won't be able to manage solid foods, but at least she can breathe easily now. She was very lucky.'

Alex kneeled down beside the sleeping HAWC and tilted her head. Her entire neck was bathed in dark iodine, even though the wound itself was tiny. But Alex wasn't interested in the field tracheotomy – he'd seen plenty before; instead, he examined the large bruises all around her throat. He remembered the immense strength of the man, or thing, that he'd fought. *Not a man*, he'd told Sam. *But what then?* he wondered.

Aimee kneeled down beside him and placed her hand on his arm. 'I saw him, Alex – González – he looked like he was trying to bite you. I think he's gone insane. I'm scared for all the men he's taken. There's a rare condition called porphyria that can affect sufferers in different ways. In acute cases, the symptoms are sensitivity to sunlight, muscle- and bone-lengthening, especially around the skull and teeth, and, in the extreme cases, psychopathic behavior. There are medical records linking the condition to the original legends of werewolves and vampires. You know, we've never seen González during the day.'

'Porphyria … vampires?' Alex continued to stare at the marks on his HAWC's neck. He knew that madness, and some drugs, could give a person almost superhuman strength, but he had felt something else lurking within the man. The tiny gray tendril that had extruded from the strange mouth to … what? Taste his flesh? He shuddered and looked at the cracked ceramic plating on his right glove. The priest should have been dead after his first strike. *Not a man*, he thought again.

'We're going out tomorrow to find the priest and bring all your men back,' he told Aimee. 'I'll need you to —'

'Good. I'm coming with you.' Aimee stood up and folded her arms.

Oh, great, he thought. 'Okay, but get some rest. Sam and I are leaving at about 0700 hours. I'll call in for you then.'

Aimee's eyes went diamond hard. 'Like crap you will. You'll leave earlier than that and leave me behind. I know you Alex. I'm coming and that's that. You'll have to tie me up to make me stay here.' She paused, perhaps thinking she shouldn't have mentioned that idea. 'Look, I can show you where we found the Green Berets' bodies,' she went on. 'And besides, you know I'll just follow you anyway.'

Alex thought for a few seconds; he believed her – she would follow them. He stood and tilted his head back with resignation. '0600, be ready.'

Aimee stood on her tiptoes and kissed his cheek. 'See, that wasn't so hard now, was it, Captain Hunter?'

Alex smiled. 'You win this time, Miss Pushy, but I reserve the right to take you up on that offer to tie you up if you get us into trouble.'

Aimee smiled and her blue eyes seemed to darken. 'Get me home first.'

*

Alex needed to call Hammerson; the satellite would be in a transmission intersect now and he had to meet its sweep window. There would be no rest for him after that; he'd stand watch until it was time to depart. His body was on fire with energy, and sleep would not come, or be needed, for days.

He scanned the surrounding wall of dense vegetation and tried to *feel* for the presence of González. There was nothing. The jungle was loud with the sounds of the night – which was good. It was when the creatures shut down that he needed to worry.

He had one last stop to make before the contact with Hammerson. At the door of the Vargises' laboratory cabin, he took a disposable face mask off a hook and pulled it over his face. He paused for one last look around the smoke-filled clearing. The rain was still falling, and he was glad for the frond mat that Tomás and the men had laid down.

He knocked and pushed open the door. The two scientists were still in their biohazard gear. Maria greeted him, but returned immediately to the microscope. She looked tired and her normally perfect hair was in slight disarray.

Michael sat back in his chair and gave Alex a weak smile. He looked pale, Alex thought; too pale.

'Progress?' He didn't have time for pleasantries; events were moving too fast for politeness or politics.

There was silence for a few moments, then Maria pushed her chair back and ran her hands over her hair. 'The bacteria is immune to significant heat, and moves far too rapidly for a natural immunological response. We're not even close to a vaccine. We need a full-sized lab and about a month.'

'Is there *anything* we can use?' Alex asked.

Maria shrugged. 'There are no more infections, so we figure it's spread by insect vectors – the smoke and DDT did their job. And the men in the isolation cabin are all dead and ... gone.' She went back to looking through her microscope.

Alex felt a small ball of annoyance in his gut. He inhaled slowly, calming himself.

'I think cold slows it down,' Michael said. 'Maybe at low enough temperatures, it could even kill it.' His voice sounded phlegmy.

'That's something – how can we use it?'

Maria looked up. 'We can't. The temperatures needed to terminate the bacteria would also explode human cell walls. You'd die about the same time as the Hades Bug did.'

Michael coughed and Maria looked across at him, as if really noticing him for the first time. 'Michael?'

Alex stared hard at the man, using his enhanced senses to pick up the poison in his system. 'He's sick ... infected.'

'What? No!' Maria jumped to her feet so fast her chair toppled over backwards. She moved quickly to Michael and tore off her glove, intending to place her hand on his forehead.

Alex grabbed her wrist. Close up, he could see the dark veins in the young man's eyes.

Michael held up his hands to ward Maria off. 'Forget it; I'll be dead in a day.' He dropped his head into his hands for a moment, then sat up, sniffing back tears. 'I knew it wasn't just fatigue, but I hoped ...' He looked miserably at his mother. 'I don't want to end up like the men in the cabin. Can you give me something ... so I just go to sleep?'

Maria turned to Alex. 'How are the generators holding up?'

Alex realized what she was thinking. 'Sedate him,' he said.

'No, please,' Michael said. 'There's no cure – just kill me.' He went to get to his feet, but Alex put one hand on his shoulder.

Maria had filled a syringe from a small amber bottle; now she plunged it into Michael's arm. In a few seconds, he was slumped back in his chair. Alex wrapped him in a sheet from one of the cots, lifted him like he weighed nothing, and took him to what had once been the camp's mess cabin. Nestled between a coffee machine and a soda machine was an ice chest. Alex used one hand to lift the lid and shoved the unconscious scientist in among the ice. As Michael's body settled, Alex sensed the deadly bacteria coursing through the young man's system; he doubted he'd make it.

Maria stood staring down at her son for many minutes. Alex could hear her saying something under her breath; Greek, he assumed. Finally, she turned to him with a look of weariness on her face. 'Twenty-four hours and there'll be a solution. I guarantee it.'

*

As the rain continued, puddles formed beneath the mat of fronds covering the campsite. The dried black stains moistened, then thickened. After another hour of the soaking rain, the black shapes were able to slide across the wet ground to find each other.

The viscous puddles became pools. Living pools.

A hungry mewling swelled the air, inaudible to human ears.

A tall cassocked figure lurked just beyond the foliage surrounding the camp, its head moving in time to the ultrasonic chorus.

TWENTY-SEVEN

Hammerson listened to Alex's update with growing alarm. 'Lieutenant Makhdoum dead, and Franks down. And by some insane priest with super-fucking-powers who doesn't exist in anyone's records? Jesus Christ, Alex!' He got to his feet and began pacing his office.

'That's not all.' Alex's tone brought Hammerson to a sudden halt. 'The CDC don't believe they can control the necrotising bacteria. It's one hundred percent lethal. Maria Vargis's son is now infected.'

'One hundred percent lethality – that bad, huh?' Might need some different people down there to take a look-see at that little baby. 'Is it contained?'

'Yes, for now. Maria Vargis believes it was being spread by insect vectors, which have been eradicated in the area. Its rapid rate of infection means the hosts don't live long enough to be good carriers.'

Hammerson nodded. 'Good. Secure the site, Arcadian; we need that drilling operation back online. As for that priest responsible for Mak's death and our missing GBs, find him and terminate him. I'm sure God will forgive us later.'

'We'll catch up with him tomorrow, I guarantee it.' Alex paused for a second. 'Jack, one more thing: what do you know of a Protocol 9?'

Hammerson frowned. 'Say again, Arcadian.'

'Maria Vargis mentioned a secured set of international instructions – protocols, she called them – for dealing with unexpected or unusual encounters. Apparently, Protocol 9 relates to global life-threatening microorganisms. One minute Vargis is saying this is a terminal outbreak and there's no way she can control it, and in the next she's telling me she'll have a solution in twenty-four hours. It doesn't make sense. I reckon she's not telling me everything.' There was another silence before Alex said, 'Did you know about these protocols, Jack?'

Hammerson tapped his chin with one large, gnarled fist. 'No, but I don't like the sound of it. I'll get back to you. Over, Arcadian.'

*

Hammerson replaced the phone, sat down and switched on his computer. After entering his passwords, he selected an option on the secured military intranet that showed no identifying text or numbers, just three colored boxes. He chose the first. The screen went black and stayed that way. To anyone else, it would have seemed a technological error or unfinished code-corridor. However, to Hammerson and a few others with special operational clearance, it was a sign that the system was waiting for the next step.

Hammerson pressed his palm against the screen. A red line traced the shape of his hand, then disappeared. After a few more seconds, two words appeared on the screen: *ASK MUSE*. He typed in *UN Security Council*, then *Protocol 9*, and waited.

He could have got the information he needed by calling in a favor from any number of generals, but that would have taken time and he was an impatient man. Besides, the Military Universal Search Engine didn't just rely on the United States' vast warehouses of data; it accessed just about every other site on the planet too. Decades ago, the US military's strategy and logistics division had forecast that the first strike of any modern war would come from a computer lab. Everything in the world was computerised now, from televisions to the most sophisticated defense systems; and with such complex

software came vulnerabilities that could be exploited in either offensive or counteroffensive attacks. The US military was spending
billions of dollars protecting itself from external hackers while sim-
ultaneously diving into foreign networks and data warehouses.

After another few seconds, an eyes-only document entitled 'The
Protocols' appeared on the screen. There were ten of them – *Ten
Commandments for the modern age*, thought Hammerson, as he
opened the document and paged down to Protocol 9. His coffee cup
stopped midair on its way to his lips when he came to a paragraph in
the 'Recommended Actions' section. He scrolled down and quickly
read the words under 'Terminal Outbreaks'.

'Oh shit, she wouldn't.'

He downloaded the entire document and reached for the phone.
He needed to swivel a communication satellite, now.

*

Despite Sam's difficulty in drawing meaning from the ornate script
that filled the heavy fibrous pages of the journal, he was enjoying
its beauty. The cursive style was a relic of a time when penmanship
had been lifted to an art form; each letter was perfect in its slope
and precision. The outside leaves of the book were damp, but the
inside leaves were surprisingly dry, indicating it had been only recently been dropped to the moist jungle floor. Each page was dated,
and the year was 1617 – *in the year of the Holy Father, Pope Paul
V*, as the chronicler, a young Jesuit by the name of Father Juan de
Castillo, put it.

Sam moved quickly through the early section, which was concerned with the voyage to the Southern American continent, then
through its primitive towns and on into the deep jungle. From
here, the almost clinical descriptions leapt to colorful life, with
accompanying illustrations. Sam smiled as he felt the priest's excitement and good humor. Pictures crowded nearly every page
now: the local Indians cooking, clearing ground, children playing;
another Jesuit drawn from behind, holding an outdoor mass, his
arms held wide.

Sam turned another page and frowned. Here, the text described the new church's bell tower, and a drawing of a smiling man polishing a large bell covered half the page. Sam recognized the broad shoulders, the square beard with the gray at the jawline. It was the priest, their priest: Father Alonso González.

He looked again at the date at the top of the page: 1617 – nearly 400 years ago. Impossible.

But so was a non-military trained man taking out two HAWCs and nearly doing the same to Alex Hunter.

Sam snapped the book shut and looked at his wristwatch: 0530. No sleep after all. He headed for the door.

TWENTY-EIGHT

A lex prowled the camp, stopping from time to time at the edge of the jungle to reach out with his senses, trying to get an impression of anything lurking and watching from behind the dark green curtain. His head throbbed with a dull pain as he pushed his awareness out as far as he could. He could feel something there, but, strangely, it was all around him rather than in one specific location. And it felt like González, but … He focused harder and got the sense of some kind of living essence, big and getting bigger, like a massive life form stirring or waking. He shook his head as the pain threatened to overwhelm him. There was too much life out there in the jungle to pull out individual details easily.

In less than an hour, he, Sam, Captain Garmadia and Aimee would track down the priest, and this time they wouldn't underestimate him. Alex ached to get within reach of the killer of his HAWC. He had lost too many good men and women in battles above and below ground to let one be taken so cheaply.

He noticed that Maria's laboratory light was still on, and drifted over to peer in the window. The CDC woman sat at her desk unmoving. Laid out before her were two syringes. *Maybe she developed a vaccine after all*, he thought. He looked again and thought, *Perhaps not.* Misery filled the room like a dark cloud.

He backed away from the window and saw a light come on in Aimee's cabin. Before he got to the door, it was pulled open and a fully kitted Casey Franks stepped out. She had been sharing Aimee's quarters so Aimee could change her bandages.

Boss, she managed to breathe.

The bandage at her throat was still a little discolored, and purple bruising stretched from the base of one ear to the other. She looked as fit as ever though, her arms bulging with power, and her eyes carried a restless energy.

Alex nodded to her. 'We're going after the priest and the missing men. You'll cover base camp until we return. Need anything?'

'Sir, I'm fit for duty. I can …' Her words were barely audible, and Alex knew they must have hurt.

'Negative soldier. You will cover the camp as ordered.' Alex held her gaze.

After a moment she nodded slowly and breathed out more words: 'Just bring me his head.'

She lifted her clenched fist, her eyes burning with anger. Alex brought his own fist against hers; the armored plating of their gloves clacked together.

Aimee's hand alighted on Franks's shoulder and the HAWC turned sideways to let her past.

'Drink plenty of water in small sips,' Aimee said, 'and apply the antibiotic powder and change the bandage every four hours. You're lucky, you heal quickly.' She looked at Alex and raised her eyebrow. 'Seems to be a HAWC trait.'

Casey rolled her eyes and mouthed, *Yes, Mommy*. Then, as Aimee stepped past her, she raised one hand flat against Aimee's chest and looked her in the eye. Her face became very serious as she said, 'Be careful.'

Aimee half-turned to show the gun butt sticking out of her back pocket. Franks dropped her hand, nodded and turned to Alex. *You don't deserve her*, her look said.

I know. She's a heartbreaker, thought Alex.

He caught a glimpse of Chaco and Saqueo huddled in the corner of Aimee's cabin. Both were awake. Chaco rubbed his eyes while Saqueo gave Alex a thumbs-up.

Alex held up his hand to them. 'You boys stay here, okay?'

They looked at him blankly.

'Here, let me. Umm, *quédense aquí, sí?*' Aimee pointed at the ground for emphasis.

The boys looked at each other briefly and then nodded.

'See, I told you I'd come in handy,' she said with a grin.

'You sure did tell me, many times.' Alex checked his watch – fifteen minutes to go.

*

Alex studied the sketch of the priest in the journal. After a while he grunted. 'Same name, same face – could be our man. But based on these dates, he should have been dead nearly 400 years ago.'

Sam shrugged. 'If it was just the face and name, I'd say it was a coincidence. But his strength and speed, the way his head lay on his shoulder after you hit him … I've seen men with broken necks before, boss. He shoulda gone down – a normal man *would* have gone down.'

Alex remembered the unnervingly calm expression on the priest's face while they'd fought. And then there was the thing in his mouth …

'So what's keeping him propped up?' he asked.

'That's the multimillion-dollar question,' Sam said with a shrug. 'And what's he doing with the men he's taking?'

He snapped the book shut as Aimee approached.

Alex put his hand on the big man's shoulder. 'See if there's anything else in there we can use. And let's not share this info just yet.' He indicated Aimee with a flick of his eyes.

Sam nodded and slid the journal over his shoulder into his harness backpack.

*

Captain Garmadia lit a cigar and exhaled blue smoke into the dawn air. Sunrise – if that's what it could be called in a dense jungle – had provided them with a misty light for the last few minutes, but it would be several hours before the sun made its way above the canopy to give them any real daylight.

The rain had eased during the night, but the vegetation matting Tomás and his co-workers had laid down squelched under his feet. It was starting to feel more like a raft than a ground covering. For now it continued to do its job of keeping them above the mud, but in a day or so it would be overwhelmed.

Garmadia squinted at the photograph in his hand: a plump woman with a wide smile and large brown eyes. He kissed it and tucked it back in his pocket. He had decided in the night that, given the circumstances, his job had been completed. The disease seemed to have been contained, but the number of desertions meant there weren't enough men to restart the rig. His recommendation to Colonel Lugo would be to relocate the campsite, send in another drilling team, and put Captain Hunter and his team on a plane home.

He would like to leave now, but it would take another day or so to assist in sewing up the last loose end – apprehending the man who called himself González. Garmadia didn't believe for a second that the man was an actual priest; more likely he was directing the rebel activity in the area. *After all, how does a man of the cloth learn to fight with such strength and speed*, he wondered as he remembered the skirmish with the HAWC leader. These North American Special Forces soldiers obviously weren't as good as they believed.

The Paraguayan officer watched the two big HAWCs and the North American woman discussing the map the woman held. He shook his head, his mouth turning down in disdain. Why did the North Americans always want to have a woman with them, even when they were heading into potential danger? Maybe the *gringos* couldn't perform without an audience. He looked at Aimee from behind. Too skinny for his taste.

The small group seemed to have come to a decision. He sauntered over, and Alex Hunter nodded a greeting and made a space for him.

'We're going to head to the drill site then make a sweep back towards the camp,' Hunter said. 'Dr. Weir believes the trouble with the priest might have originated in that area.'

Garmadia shrugged and drew the cigar from his mouth, blowing smoke towards the group. 'Captain Hunter, I will accompany you on your search, but after today I will be heading back to my base. I think you will agree, there are not enough men here now to operate the machinery. I have spoken to Dr. Vargis and she has told me there are no new outbreaks of the infection, and she believes there will be a solution to the disease within a day. There is nothing more for me to do but make a final report and depart.'

The two HAWCs and the woman stared at him for a moment, then Hunter turned away and spoke to Aimee.

'He's right – there's not much more we can do here. We'll stay on another couple days to find the priest, but getting you home would be the best thing right now.'

Aimee looked as though she was about to object, then changed her mind.

Garmadia grunted and turned away. *Make the right decision, señors and señorita, because when I will leave I will be taking the truck with me. It will be a very long walk home without it.*

*

The boys watched the small team head off into the jungle, the dark vegetation closing around them almost immediately. The woman HAWC with the bandage around her neck stood like stone in the center of the camp watching them go. After a while, she reached up to feel her neck then headed towards the cabin where the other lady doctor always worked.

Chaco pulled on his grimy T-shirt. 'I'm not staying here. That old woman doctor scares me even more than the Hawkmano. I'm going to follow them.'

Saqueo pointed a threatening finger at his little brother's chest. 'No, you will stay here … Chaco, I warn you, do not open that door … Chaco, do not dare go outside … Chaco, wait for me!'

Saqueo pulled on his own shirt and followed his brother out into the warm dawn air.

TWENTY-NINE

Aimee pushed yet another frond out of the way as she squelched along the track. It had narrowed even in the few days since she had last traversed it. *The jungle swallows everything*, she thought.

She walked a few paces behind Alex, who led them out, watching his broad shoulders roll as he stepped smoothly through the green. She had seen more scars on his body, and there was more pain in his eyes, but he was still the man she remembered. She felt good being near him, but found it hard to look into his eyes. Every time she did, she felt the old attraction – and she saw it reflected in his gaze as well. She tried to analyze whether it was the situation that was making her want him again. If she were safe at home, clean, not tired or scared half to death, would she feel the need to have her Black Knight standing guard? Perhaps she was misleading him … or misleading herself.

She looked up at his back again just as a broad leaf flapped back behind him and whacked her in the face.

Yep, thanks, I needed that! Wake up, girl. Are you thinking you're just going to walk back into his life?

She smiled. *You bet*, she thought.

*

Alex looked again at Aimee's map – less than an hour to the mining site. It felt good to get out of the camp, away from the pervasive feeling of illness, and whatever else it was that made his skin crawl and clouded his senses.

Despite his relief, he was distracted. He could feel Aimee's eyes on him, as if she were constantly tapping him on the shoulder. He needed to concentrate; the jungle was growing quiet again – he could sense something closing in on them.

They were being watched.

*

At last Aimee led them to the small clearing where she, Francisco and Alfraedo had discovered the soldiers' remains several days before. Little of the bloody mess was left, and the ground was churned up as though it had been worked over by a pickaxe.

'*Insectos de la carne*,' Garmadia said, looking first at the churned soil, then higher into the trees.

Sam translated, 'Meat insects.'

Garmadia toed a piece of white-looking shell; when he lifted it free they could see it had once been the top of a skull. 'The pigs take most of it,' he said. 'What they leave, the insects consume.' He looked around, his face pale. 'By the size of the kill zone, I would say a lot of blood was spilt here. This is not good.'

'It was horrible,' Aimee said. 'A massacre. Francisco wanted to know if the Green Berets themselves had done it. I told him no human being could be savage enough to do what we saw here.'

Sam leaned into the bushes and withdrew a mangled piece of black steel. He turned it over in his hands before handing it to Alex. 'Special Forces SCAR rifle; or was.'

Alex sniffed the muzzle; it had been fired, and the smell of gun oil was still strong. He looked at the metal barrel curled back on itself – took a lot of strength to bend high-grade steel. He remembered the fist marks in the heavy metal plate in the communications cabin back at the camp, and the great strength of the man they tracked. *Just who, or what, the hell are you?* he thought.

The feeling of being watched was overwhelming … his senses tingled.

He swung around quickly. Garmadia crouched as if he were about to be struck a physical blow.

The presence was right here. Alex lunged into the jungle …

Garmadia swore in Spanish as Alex dragged a squirming Chaco and Saqueo into the clearing. Sam laughed and cradled his weapon.

'This is not what I would call following instructions,' Alex said with a sigh.

Chaco sniggered, and Saqueo rapped him on the head with his knuckles. He spoke rapidly to Alex, who shrugged and looked to Sam for help.

'I'll tell them they must go back to the camp,' Garmadia cut in. 'They will slow us down.' He started to speak rapidly to the boys in a tone that immediately quietened them.

Alex shook his head with resignation. 'No, too late now. It's too dangerous to send them back alone. Captain, notice anything?' Garmadia stopped talking and half-turned to Alex. 'Listen – no sounds – I think we're close. They'll just have to keep up.' Alex nodded to Aimee.

Aimee spoke in her mangled Spanish to the boys. They leaned around Garmadia and Chaco clapped his hands and Saqueo nodded. In turn, Garmadia shook his head, and stooped to speak into Saqueo's face with even more venom. He talked quickly, but managed to keep the cigar wedged between his teeth. Chaco had fully retreated behind his older brother, and glanced briefly at the jungle behind him, possibly contemplating a dash for cover. The smaller boy's bottom lip trembled.

'Hey! Lighten up Castro. I'll take care of them.' Aimee walked between Garmadia and the boys, and said a few words more in mangled Spanish to them. It was enough to have both boys nodding warily and smiling … and only briefly looking over their shoulder at the Paraguayan soldier.

Garmadia threw his hands in the air and turned away. '*Mierda! Mujeres y niños. Gringos estúpidos.*'

Alex grinned. He didn't need to understand Spanish to know that Garmadia was giving his opinion on the wisdom of bringing women and children along on their search.

THIRTY

'Power's dying,' Casey Franks said. 'The lights draw the least juice, but I reckon in an hour or so they're going to drop out as well. Be dark soon – have you got enough lanterns in here?'

She rubbed her throat; it was moist and she knew the bandage needed changing again. She winced – still felt like she'd swallowed a fork, but at least she could talk above a whisper now. She had just completed a quick walk-through of the camp. The place was eerily quiet. Most of the men seemed to prefer the inside of their tents, and the ones that ventured out darted away from her in the gloom.

'Dr. Vargis? Did you hear me? I said ...' She winced and swallowed the pain.

Maria Vargis was hunched over a small electronic box on her table. 'Yes, yes,' she said without turning. 'Please leave me alone.'

Casey looked around the room. Everything had been cleared off the bench tops save for a silver case, a small electronic box and some hypodermic needles. The laboratory resembled a messy storage shed; progress had obviously slowed.

She shrugged and turned to leave. 'Very well, ma'am.'

'Do you have children?'

The question stopped Casey in her tracks. 'Ahh, pardon, ma'am?'

Maria swivelled and looked at her with red-rimmed eyes. 'Do you have any children, Ms. Franks?'

No one had called her 'Ms' for years – *doesn't sound right*, she thought. She didn't bother correcting the scientist, just shook her head slowly in response.

Maria Vargis looked at her hard for a few more seconds, then nodded and dropped her eyes back to the silver case and small black electronic box. Casey thought she hadn't seen anyone look that tired outside of a battle zone.

She left, closing the door behind her. As she stepped down onto the woven matting, water squeezed up between the fronds, soaking her boots almost to her laces. *Nice*, she thought.

*

The authorization was being formalised and the initiation codes would be sent to her within the next few hours.

A while back, Maria had also walked through the silent camp. Unlike Casey, she had peered briefly into several of the tents – and what she had seen had horrified her. Nearly every man lay sweating dark rivulets. The Hades Bug was continuing to spread, even though the vector controls had been deployed. There was no time to begin to determine how.

Maria sat at her desk, thinking. Only a few people in the world would ever know what was about to occur deep in the Paraguayan jungle. Many of the world's satellites would be conveniently turned away; false data on earth tremors was already manufactured and awaiting distribution to any interested media outlets. Now, it all came down to her.

She sighed, feeling dead inside. She turned her head to look out the greasy window. *It was never meant to get this bad*, she thought.

Dusk usually triggered the sensors that switched on the lights around the camp's perimeter. Tonight, however, instead of their white halos, the lights glowed a dull yellow for a few minutes then weakened to a shadowy golden-brown.

Maria grabbed a flashlight and rose wearily to her feet. She felt at least a hundred years old; dead tired but unable to switch off and sleep.

There'll be plenty of that soon enough, she thought grimly.

She walked down the steps from her cabin and, like a ghost, Casey Franks appeared behind her. A man trotted towards them, the one who had organized the laying of the mat of fronds. He looked from Maria to Franks and seemed to decide that Maria was the point of authority.

'Ahh, *señora*, many of the men will not come out of their tents. Those that do cannot find the dry wood, for the fires. *Repelente contra insectos* – you understand?'

She kept walking. 'Yes, I understand. Use the wood from the cabins.'

It doesn't matter, she thought. *There's only one way to stop it.*

He frowned. '*Las cabañas?*'

'Yes. *Si, si.*' She waved him away and squelched on. The matting was seriously taking on water now.

She made her way to the refrigeration unit, stopping a few feet short of the metal box. There was no hum emanating from it. She squared her shoulders and flipped the lid open quickly.

She backed away involuntarily, into Casey Franks, and a shivery gasp escaped her lips. Michael was still there – but not all of him. He should have remained comatose from the drugs she had given him, but at some point he must have woken as his head was thrown back and his mouth open in a silent scream. The ice was gone, along with his extremities. His remains floated in a gray soup, and she was glad for the small mercy of the murky water.

She leaned forward to touch his forehead one last time, or at least close his dark, oily eyes. As a contagious disease specialist, she knew it was wrong even as she was reaching to do it. Her hand was inches away when a powerful grip on her forearm stopped her. Casey Franks pulled her back quickly, the force nearly spinning her around. The lid of the now useless refrigeration unit banged shut.

Maria collapsed into the powerful young woman's arms and sobbed. Franks held her close, and Maria was grateful for the physical contact.

After a while, she stepped back and pushed the tangled hair from her face. 'He was my only child,' she said to the ground, unable to meet the HAWC's gaze.

'I liked him,' was all Casey said.

Maria managed to look up and into the woman's face. 'Thank you.'

She turned and headed to her cabin. The decision was made. There was more at stake than just a few miserable lives in a jungle.

THIRTY-ONE

A lex walked just ahead of Aimee and the boys. He could sense danger looming up around them like an evil maelstrom. A continual background noise filled his ears: a cross between the mewling of an infant and a boiling swarm of locusts – continuous, hungry and getting louder with each passing moment. Alex was now sure that the thing they knew as González was its focal point; and the infection spreading throughout the camp was somehow linked to the priest.

He saw Sam was holding the journal open as he walked. He dropped back to his second-in-command. 'Anything more about our friend?'

Sam gave a small shrug. 'Seems this González got hit in the eye and blinded by something – but our man seems to have two good eyes. Anyway, soon after he went from being at death's door to making a miraculous recovery.' He gave Alex a half-smile. 'God works in mysterious ways.' Sam closed the book. 'Oh, one more thing – seems all the animals disappeared from around their camp.'

Alex turned quickly. 'What?'

'Yeah, the Guarani Indians were complaining the hunting had gone bad, then their domesticated animals went missing as well.'

Alex's expression became darker. 'That's exactly what Aimee told me happened at the camp – the animals in the forest disappeared … and then the men.'

'Great,' said Sam. 'Anyone else see a recurring pattern here?'

Alex nodded at the journal. 'Keep reading, but one eye only. I get the feeling our friend's not far away.'

He was looking back to check on Garmadia's position when his ear stud gave the double vibration that indicated a message from headquarters. He frowned and slowed, gave his call sign and listened.

Hammerson spoke quickly. 'Arcadian, I have an urgent update. Can you receive?'

Alex dropped back a step. 'Go ahead, sir.'

'We may have a significant problem. Are either of the CDC representatives carrying any radioactive material?'

'Yes. Maria Vargis has stated she is carrying X-ray-grade isotopes. I can verify the radioactive material, but cannot substantiate its primary use or design.'

He heard Hammerson exhale. 'Shit damn – as I suspected. Alex, you asked about Protocol 9, and I've found it. In effect, it's an instruction manual on how to deal with everything from alien invasion and meteor strikes to a potential bio-terminal event. Be advised that the Protocol 9-nominated action for a significant terminal outbreak is a total site cleanse.' Hammerson paused for a second. 'I'm afraid the recommended cleanser is nuclear, or a scaled incendiary instrument. Arcadian, I believe that radioactive equipment they are carrying is likely to be a single-megaton nuclear device.'

Alex rubbed his forehead. 'Jesus Christ, Jack, wha—'

Hammerson cut him off. 'That's not all. She's sought immediate authorization for a burn. I believe she'll get it … very soon.'

Alex looked over to where Aimee and the boys were standing. Chaco gave him a thumbs-up and Alex winked in return.

'Can you stop it?' he asked Hammerson.

'Negative, Arcadian, I've already tried. This is way above my pay grade – they literally told me to go to hell. There's no time to go skating over people's heads. Are you clear of the camp?'

Alex turned his back on Aimee who was watching him closely. 'No, not all of us; Franks is still there. How much time do you think we have?'

'I'm not sure. Vargis should get authorization for initiation within a few hours, and then it's up to her – could be anything from immediate detonation to several hours. You'll need to be at least five miles from the blast zone. Alex, if I were a betting man, I'd say you have between two and four hours.'

Alex thought over the options before he spoke again. 'I can have Franks delay the outcome; maybe even stop Vargis. Give us time to get everyone clear of —'

'I say again: negative, Arcadian,' Hammerson interrupted. 'This has presidential authorization. And, unfortunately, Vargis is the right person to make the call. Her brief also authorizes her to use deadly force to execute a ratified cleanse. Franks would have to kill her to stop her … and we don't want that. Arcadian, on my command, all other orders are rescinded. I've already dispatched a V22. We can't put it down anywhere close, but it'll drop some air hooks to pull you out. It'll be coming in from the northeast coast. But be advised, I cannot order those men to place themselves within five miles of ground zero. I'll send the pick-up coordinates, but you'll have to get to them. God speed, Arcadian. Over.'

Alex turned back to Aimee, who mouthed, *what's up?* He tried to think, but too many problems and options spun in his head. He just stared at her, like a robot temporarily stuck between gears. He needed more time. They had been traveling all day, and the sun was starting to set. Traveling all day – and they hadn't gone that far. Certainly nothing like five miles from the detonation zone.

He'd call Franks and tell her to evac immediately. She was injured, but she was tough; she'd run till she dropped if he ordered it.

Aimee spoke his name and he focused on her face, noticing the creases of worry etched into it. He nodded and smiled at her, but his mind still raced. He couldn't do anything for anyone else at the camp, and he shouldn't try. Still, even though he personally couldn't buy them more time, he could get Casey Franks to ask Maria Vargis to allow a few extra hours to get clear. Then he and Sam needed to start steering their group away from the blast zone and towards their rendezvous point without their Paraguayan chaperone realising what was going on. Alex could imagine the response of any soldier if they found out a foreigner was planning to detonate a nuke in their back-yard. It'd get ugly, and he had enough problems.

He'd update Sam, but that was all; he'd need the big man's calm intellect if they were all going to make it out alive.

He called his second-in-command over, then pulled his GPS unit from his pocket pouch and checked their coordinates. If they changed course now, they'd make it.

*

Casey Franks listened calmly to Alex's clinical briefing on the situation. She'd experienced all manner of things in her career with the HAWCs, and currently being in the vicinity of some wild necrotising bug, an insane priest and a potential nuclear explosion was just another situation to be dealt with.

'Got the coordinates, boss,' she confirmed. 'By the by, Michael Vargis is dead, and Maria Vargis is zoning out. I'll try to buy us some time and then move to rendezvous with you at …' She checked her watch: it was just on 1800 hours. 'Approximately 2200 hours. But you know what traffic's like around these parts.'

She allowed herself a small smile. Alex would know what she meant: *Don't wait around.* The chances of her making it were slim.

She didn't need to pack; she didn't need food, more water or further armaments. If need be, she could live off the land. But she didn't expect to be out there for long. The only thing she really needed was time. Her first call would be to Maria.

*

Maria wiped her eyes and sniffed. Any moment she expected to hear the peep of her secure comm device informing her that the initiation codes had been received. Then it was a matter of plugging them in and setting a countdown.

She felt a knot in her stomach and wondered whether she'd have the strength and courage to detonate. There would be innocent casualties. She wiped the steamy window to look out across the darkening camp. The braziers were glowing dark red and smoke was once again curling along the ground – it looked Gothic. If not for the heat, she might have expected Dracula to appear out of the mist.

This waiting was excruciating.

She got slowly to her feet. Maybe she'd take a walk over to say goodbye to Michael. It'd be her last chance.

*

Casey Franks spotted Maria standing in front of one of the isolation cabins. She wondered why; its last patient had long since succumbed to the foul disease.

Casey walked closer, and was about to clear her throat so as not to give the woman a start when the CDC scientist spoke without turning – as if expecting her.

'I shouldn't tell you this but you need to get out of here … now.'

Casey kept her expression flat as Maria turned to face her. The scientist's hair hung in dripping bundles of rats' tails and her face looked to have aged a generation in a day.

'I'm going to burn it all,' she said. 'You need to be a *long* way away.'

Casey didn't move. 'I know.'

Maria frowned for a moment, then closed her eyes briefly and nodded in understanding. She turned back to look at the cabin.

Casey spoke as gently as she knew how. 'How much time can you give me?'

Maria snorted. 'Unfortunately, that's not up to me anymore. I'm afraid the question should be: how much time will *it* give *us*.' She nodded towards the rounded beams that kept the cabin raised up above the muddy ground.

At first Casey couldn't see anything in the camp's gloomy lighting, but then she detected movement. There was a black, jelly-like substance inching its way up the support beams. 'What the fuck is that?'

'Seems our little Hades Bug is quite sociable – likes to join with its family. It's not content to wait for a chance interaction with its food source anymore; I believe it's about to start looking for it.'

The jelly bulged in dozens of places to form small black globes like glistening, dark grapes. They split vertically to reveal opaque pupils that bulged obscenely towards the women.

Maria turned back to Casey. 'I can give you four hours. After that, everything will be ash. God speed, Lieutenant Franks.'

Casey looked from the slime to Maria and back again. She'd seen what that stuff could do to a human being when it was microscopic. If it was now growing and about to go hunting – *bring on the fucking nuke*, she thought.

She had her extra time; now to use it. She turned away, bumping into Tomás who had come up behind her.

'*Señora*, the men that are not sick have all gone now. They would not wait for your *amigos* to return.'

Casey grabbed the little man by the shoulders and looked hard into his face. 'Doesn't matter – you need to go home now too, Tomás. You need to go fast. Understand?'

He frowned. 'Go home, *señora* ... now?'

Casey gestured around the camp, then made two fists and opened them with an explosion sound. 'Big bang coming – go home now!'

Tomás looked around the camp too, confusion showing on his face.

'Oh, come on, Friday,' Casey muttered, more to herself than to the little man in front of her. 'Ahh, *el grande dangera. Explodea ...* Oh, fuck it. Just go. Go!' She pushed him towards the jungle.

He walked slowly towards the green wall but kept looking back over his shoulder at her. She nodded, made shooing motions with her hands, and gave a final wave goodbye.

She pulled her GPS from her pocket and used it to locate Alex. *Hmm, lot of miles*, she thought.

She sucked in a deep breath and winced at the pain in her throat. She tied a bandana cloth around the bandage, pulled out her longest knife, and then jogged to the edge of the clearing. She looked back at the scientist still standing in front of the hut. She waved, but couldn't tell if Maria Vargis hadn't seen her or was choosing to ignore her.

Casey Franks began to run, bullocking branches and fronds out of the way, and slashing at others with the razor sharp blade, as she picked up speed. Her feet kicked up sodden debris and mud as she sprinted through the darkening jungle. The mud stuck to her boots, some of it red … and some of it black.

*

After the strange soldier woman had left, Tomás stepped back into the clearing. He looked around and saw the other doctor woman standing in the drizzle. He decided not to interrupt her; she frightened him a little. It was just him and her now. All the men who were physically able to leave had over the last few hours. He would have left with them, but he knew that when *señora* Aimee returned she would need him.

He smoothed out the now illegible piece of paper pinned to his chest. He'd wait for her. She would want that.

THIRTY-TWO

Aimee knew something was troubling Alex; had been troubling him ever since he'd taken a call from Hammerson. His mood had darkened and he was on edge – he seemed to be turning inwards. She let the two boys walk slightly ahead and dropped back to talk to him. She could see Sam further back, half-turning so he could keep an eye on Aimee's position in front and also Garmadia's in the rear.

'Alex, it's too dark,' she said. 'Maybe we should head back.'

'We can't go back.' He continued walking.

'Huh? Why, what's happening? What aren't you telling me?' She stepped up beside him and leaned around into his face.

He let out an exasperated sigh. 'The CDC has decided that little bug of yours represents too great a threat to the human race. They've also decided they need a thorough burn to ensure a safe and complete sterilisation.' He shrugged. 'Nothing I can do about it – other than get us safely away.'

'What?' Her raised voice made the boys stop in their tracks. 'That's ludicrous. Everything's soaking wet – just how much do you think is going to burn? Besides, we already know the Hades Bug is heat tolerant. For Chrissakes, if the top-ranking scientist in the CDC made that call, she's a lot less qualified than I first thought. No, nix that; I think she's insane.' Aimee folded her arms, her jaw jutting and her eyes boring into him. 'Well?'

'Nuclear burn by a compact single-megaton package,' he said in a flat tone. 'Possibly an advanced W54 or W55 type device. Immediate vaporisation of surrounding material, and detonation expansion results in the formation of an atmospheric-displacing shock wave. Temperatures of ten to the power of seven Kelvin form in the hypocenter of a fireball columning up into a mushroom cloud.' He looked at her, his eyes weary. 'Aimee, what can burn, will burn. We need about a five-mile clearance so we're clear of the shock wave and any short-term fallout.'

Aimee's mouth dropped open. 'But ... but what about Michael, her son? Tomás, and all the men? What about Casey Franks?' She balled her fists and shook her head in disbelief.

'Franks is on her way; the men are all gone. Michael Vargis is dead, and Maria is —' Alex stopped abruptly, his head whipping around to look down the trail at Sam.

Aimee put her fingers to her temples, rubbing them for a second. Then she gasped. 'Oh, no. The drill site was never capped! The gas bed is enormous ... If Maria sets off a nuke, she's liable to light up the entire continent.'

She realized Alex wasn't listening. His eyes were alert and focused back down the trail. She had seen that look on his face before and didn't like it. It meant imminent danger.

Suddenly Aimee could hear her own breathing. The jungle had fallen silent.

*

Things seemed to be occurring in slow motion. Alex knew Aimee was speaking to him, but her voice was smothered by all his senses screaming at him. The danger he had felt all around exploded into his mind like a klaxon alarm.

It's here. The priest is here.

Sam noticed the change in his leader's expression and stance and immediately went on high alert himself. As he began to swing around, there was a deafening roar all around them. Chaco and Saqueo dropped to the ground and covered their ears. Aimee threw her pack to the ground and flung herself over the boys.

Alex instantly recognized the sound and leapt to cover the huddled group.

'Where's Garmadia?' he yelled to Sam.

This wasn't how or where Alex wanted the encounter to take place: boxed in on a narrow jungle trail, darkness closing all around them, and Aimee and two children in his care.

He opened his senses to the jungle and received an impression of something circling them, faster than any normal man or beast could possibly move. He pushed out harder, trying to see the thing that stalked them and anticipate its next position. He managed an image of something dark and misshapen before a bolt of agony smashed through his head. It was coming, but not for him.

He threw himself to the ground in front of Aimee and yelled to his second-in-command. 'Sam, get back here.'

Sam took up position on the other side of the huddled group. Alex pointed both his gauntleted arms at different angles into the jungle.

'It's González,' he said. 'He's moving around us … he's going to come in. Wait for it … on my mark.'

Sam was looking back and forth into the darkness. 'I don't see or hear him. I can't get a bead.'

'Fire!' Alex made two fists and triggered a double stream of ice needles into the jungle. Sam did the same with his single gauntlet. The silent projectiles flew out in three supersonic streams, shredding leaves and branches. Plant material showered down around them.

'He's on the move!' Alex yelled.

A deformed face broke free of the jungle near to Sam and roared again. Its jaws opened wider and lower than was humanly possible. Rows of spiked teeth circled the entire maw.

For the first time in his life, Alex heard his tough-as-nails second-in-command swear in fright.

Aimee screamed as Alex leapt across her to join Sam in directing blasts of ice spikes at the creature. But the moment he was in position and raised his gauntlet, the face withdrew.

Perhaps it's only testing our speed and weaponry, Alex thought.

A breeze seemed to pass behind them and two gunshots rang out.

'Cease fire,' Alex ordered.

He could sense the priest had gone. Slowly, he moved his head one way then the other, trying to pick up the evil that emanated from the man. Another shot punctured the silence and he turned quickly to see Aimee kneeling upright, a pistol in her steady hands. She slowly lowered the gun.

Sam rubbed his shoulder, trying to ease the pain from the gauntlet's recoil. He looked at Alex with a mix of shock and disbelief written large on his face. '*That thing* was González? Shit. You can forget about me ever going to confession with that guy.'

Alex grimaced. 'Maybe it was González once. But I doubt it's him now.'

Sam looked down at Aimee who was pushing her gun back into her waistband. 'Boys okay?'

She glanced down. 'Yeah, they're both ...' Her face immediately creased in shock. She roughly pulled Saqueo up and flipped her pack out of the way. 'No, no, no ...'

Saqueo stood holding a scrap of his brother's T-shirt, a frown of confusion on his face. Chaco had been ripped from right next to them without them even knowing.

The boy grabbed Aimee's arm and shook it. '*Dónde está Chaco?*' He held out the scrap, his voice rising. '*Dónde está mi hermano?*'

He screamed his brother's name until Aimee grabbed him and hugged him to her, her own face a mask of anguish.

Alex remembered the breeze that had passed over them. *Nothing from our world can move that quickly*, he thought as he looked around slowly. There was a large moon rising, and the surrounding jungle was taking on a silvery shadowed glow. But there was nothing to see other than the dense jungle all around them.

He turned back to Aimee. 'He's been taken.' He closed his eyes for a few seconds, casting out with his senses. When he re-opened them, his face was grim. 'The priest has him. He's alive, but hurt ...'

Garmadia approached slowly, his handgun held loosely by his side. Alex rounded on him. 'Where were you?'

Garmadia shrugged. 'I was trying to get behind our attacker, but I am afraid I got lost. I am not familiar with this part of the jungle, Captain Hunter – no one is.' He holstered his gun and looked away.

Aimee let go of Saqueo and walked quickly to Alex. 'We have to get him back. Now!'

Sam moved slowly into Alex's line of sight. 'Boss, I wouldn't advise it. There's a lot of hot rain about to fall.'

Aimee glared at him. 'What? Sam … no.'

Garmadia held out his hands, palms up. 'Sorry, *señora* Weir, but the *soldado* is right. It is not advisable. Besides, the boy probably ran away. He will be home before we are.'

'Shut the fuck up,' Aimee yelled, making Saqueo jump. She rounded on Alex, ignoring both Garmadia and Sam. 'Alex, you're better than that.'

No, I'm not, he thought. He looked at Sam, who just shrugged and turned away, keeping his eyes on the surrounding jungle. Alex stood motionless for a few seconds, until he thought of the way González had ruthlessness crushed Mak's face and then tried to do the same to him and Franks. A small fire lit in his belly.

He pulled a small black box from a pouch at his waist and looked at the tiny glowing screen. The approaching V22 was one red dot, and the rendezvous point another. Their position was shown in blue – they weren't that far away. He made his decision.

'Let's find him.'

Even Alex himself wasn't sure whether he referred to the boy or the priest.

THIRTY-THREE

The lighting around the camp's perimeter had died long ago, and even the dull red glow of the fires had become just a few wisps of smoke leaking over the rims of the barrels. Maria sat in the dark cabin, her face lit by a green screen inside the silver case she had open on the desk before her. Beside it was a small communication device showing six rows of five alphanumeric characters. Nothing else; no effusive thank you, or religious references, or even the promise of a small brass plaque stuck to a park bench somewhere.

Her eyes blurred. She wiped them clear and sighed as she began to type. A question appeared on the screen before her: *Countdown Duration?* The field was three spaces long and measured in minutes. She wanted to type '1' and then just close her eyes. She was tired of it all.

'Last promise I ever have to keep,' she said to the screen.

She entered 240, the maximum available, and closed the case. Its electronic locks engaged and sealed it from the world. The countdown would be relayed back to CDC headquarters. It was all out of her hands now.

She got to her feet and went to the bunk she had made up. She lay down and stared at the ceiling. Despite the thick, humid air enveloping her, she shivered as she crossed her arms over her chest.

*

The miasma of evil was so thick, Alex felt as though it was coating his nose and throat. He looked ahead at Sam – the large HAWC seemed oblivious. Perhaps he couldn't sense the *wrongness* they were walking into.

Sam froze like a hunting dog, and motioned with his head at something just through the branches. When Alex nodded his understanding, Sam proceeded for another dozen paces, then stopped behind a veil of heavy fronds. A glint of gold was visible behind the greenery. Aimee and Saqueo came up beside Sam, Garmadia on his other side. Alex pulled aside the ferns. It was a bell – heavily tarnished, but still shining gold in patches. Alex heard Saqueo suck in his breath and whisper something in his mix of Spanish and Indian. Sam looked at him and put a finger to his lips. The boy was silent again.

Sam whispered without turning. 'Remember when we saw those people leaving the area? They spoke about a legend – *cuidado debajo de la flor de oro*. It translated as *beware the golden flower*. You know what? I think the bell is the golden flower.'

Alex nodded slowly. 'They also said that when it bloomed, the devil would rise. Just like in Castillo's journal. And that bell has been recently moved, judging by the tracks across the clearing. The *blooming* could mean that it's suddenly become visible again.'

Sam nodded. 'Uh-huh, and, boss, just before the journal ends, Castillo wrote that he thought the old priest was *poseído por el demonio* – possessed by the devil.'

'He's possessed by *something*, that's for sure.'

Alex took another cautious step forward and pulled more of the heavy fronds out of the way. A large clearing was revealed, covered in scattered debris. The silver moonlight made a pathway to a stone building huddled beneath an enormous banyan tree.

Dull pain flared in Alex's head as he tried to determine if the priest was inside the structure. Normally he could pinpoint a living entity if he concentrated, but all he was getting was chaos – the swarming white noise turning to a roar. To Aimee and Sam, the building probably looked silvery and silent; to Alex, it was enveloped by a mass of swirling souls, howling in confusion and terror. He shook his head to clear it and sucked in a deep breath.

In a standard approach, Garmadia and Sam would have advanced from one side of the clearing, and he would have taken the other. Aimee and the boy would have remained behind, under cover. Instead, the pervasive feelings of danger made him order a different tactic. He wanted open ground – the heavy green curtain concealed too much, even for his advanced senses.

'We'll go in together, nice and tight – straight up the middle.' He looked at Aimee. 'Ready?'

She mouthed *yes* back to him, gave a small smile in the dark and raised her handgun.

Alex turned to Sam, nodded once and pushed through the last fronds.

*

Casey Franks had been running hard for an hour, only able to ignore the burning pain in her calves and thighs because of the greater agony in her throat. She slowed to a jog and pulled the bandana cloth from around her neck. She wiped it over her face, neck and hair, then held it up over her open mouth and squeezed hard – a small stream of salty fluid dribbled down between her lips and she swallowed greedily.

She pulled in a giant breath and quickly checked her coordinates in relation to her current position, destination, and Alex Hunter. She frowned: her commanding officer was traveling west, away from the designated meeting point.

She grunted and shrugged. *Orders unchanged*, she thought as she re-tied the cloth around her neck.

From a pouch at her side she removed a small foil-covered capsule. She tore open the foil and snapped the pellet in half under her nose, inhaling sharply, then screwing up her eyes and throwing her head back from the jolt. After another second, she exhaled and opened her eyes, their pupils now enormously dilated. She stood a little straighter, the chemical stimulant giving her a burst of artificial energy.

'Fuck, yeah!'

She drew in another lungful of the warm, fetid air and started running again. She still had a long way to go.

THIRTY-FOUR

The small group had covered half of the clearing when Alex held up his hand then lowered it, palm downwards. Everyone sank to the ground.

Aimee stared at the broken earth and picked up one of the pieces of debris. It was bone, fairly fresh, still discolored by blood and sinew. She glanced around the clearing – it wasn't littered with pieces of sharp rock as she'd first thought; now she saw shards of bone, skull fragments and tufts of hair. A nauseating jolt ran through her as she realized this was probably all that remained of their missing workers.

She whispered to Alex, 'It's bone, not rocks … all around us.'

Garmadia's voice was nervously loud in the clearing. 'I don't like this, Captain Hunter.' Aimee noticed how round his eyes were in the moonlight. He looked ready to bolt.

Alex half-turned and spoke softly. 'I don't like it either, but we're here.' He faced back the other way. 'We've got company – can't tell from where yet.'

As soon as Alex said the words, Aimee sensed the presence, like a dark pressure wave closing in on all sides.

Sam, who had been bringing up the rear, turned his back on the small group, pulled free his sidearm and held up his gauntleted arm. Both weapons pointed at the wall of green, ready to fire.

Aimee swallowed; her mouth was dry. Any other time she might have laughed at the almost comical way Saqueo clung to her back. But, huddled in the center of a killing field with something evil tracking them in the darkness, humor was the last thing on her mind.

'Incoming!'

Alex's shout felt like an electrical shock to her already stressed system.

*

Alex stood and held both gauntlets up, his head whipping back and forth. He could feel it – almost right in front of him – but still couldn't determine its exact location.

The jungle had once again fallen into a vacuum-like silence – not a chirrup, croak or rustle; everything was either holding its breath or in hiding. But now, cutting through it, came the sound of something airborne sailing towards them. A shadow briefly fell across the moon and Alex swiveled to point one arm up at the sky, before yelling, 'Move!'

As the group scattered, something struck the ground wetly where they had been huddled. It bounced once, then lay lifeless in the dirt.

Alex could see it clearly in the moonlight. It was Chaco. His little body had been savaged, his throat torn out, leaving flaps of ragged skin and a small line of crushed cartilage. He looked unnaturally floppy, as if every one of his bones had been pulverised or removed.

Alex moved to stand between the mutilated body and Aimee and Saqueo. Sam didn't say a word when he saw the body, simply crouched and scanned with his weapons the direction it had come from. Garmadia, however, threw up onto the dry soil.

He reached over to grasp Alex's arm, his voice nearly hysterical. 'You must get us out of here immediately. This thing will kill us all. That is an order!'

When Alex didn't acknowledge him, he tried again, half-turning towards Aimee so she could hear. 'I'm sure *señorita* Weir does not want this boy to share his brother's fate.'

'Keep Saqueo away,' Alex told Aimee quickly.

Garmadia spoke again, but Alex's brain refused to assemble the sounds into words. There was something circling them, at such speed that it seemed to be all around them at once. He looked down at the tiny, mutilated corpse and felt his body begin to shake as a red wave of anger washed over him.

He pushed the Paraguayan aside and stood with his legs planted wide apart, his face lifted to the air as though sniffing it. *Where the fuck are you?* He was boiling with frustration – he couldn't fight what he couldn't see.

Then he froze with indecision as he processed Garmadia's attempted command. *He's right, we should leave.* With the boy dead, the missing drill-site workers all obliterated, the reasons for being here had fallen away. He should get them out of the clearing and head for their rendezvous with the chopper. Time was against them.

His logical mind knew that, but there was another voice in him that demanded something different. It wanted the confrontation; it screamed for vengeance for the attacks on his people. It wanted him to take on González again; it wanted blood.

He still couldn't move. What if he was killed? What chance would Sam have, let alone Aimee and the boys? They'd all be doomed. Perspiration beaded his brow, and he groaned as a wave of pain rippled from behind his eyes, up and over his forehead, then down his spine. *Why can't I decide? The decision should be easy.*

Alex already knew the answer: the rage inside wouldn't let him.

To the others, he would have seemed like a statue, silent and still as stone. But inside, he was already fighting; wrestling with his furies, pushing back their lust for destruction, even if only for a time.

We cannot stay!

He blinked and felt like he was breaking free of a slab of ice that had formed around his body.

He looked at Aimee. She had one hand on Saqueo's back, keeping him flat on the ground, and in the other held the gun. She was looking directly at him and there was terror on her face.

'We're leaving,' he said, and smiled at her.

She continued to stare at him, then started to speak, but her words stretched and her mouth moved so slowly. As he watched, the sensation of being just outside of time grew stronger. Aimee, Sam and Garmadia looked like they were in a movie that been set to slow play.

Then he realized that the world wasn't slowing around him; *he* was speeding up. His heart rate had increased to over 400 beats per minute; his body had taken over. In the instant it took him to wonder why, the thing came at him from the jungle's edge, crossing the thirty feet of clearing before he had a chance to turn.

He felt a blow to his head that was like an explosion; he actually saw stars, just like in a comic book. Something lifted him bodily and threw him backwards into the undergrowth, where he slammed sickeningly into a tree trunk.

González had arrived.

*

Sam was only aware that they were being attacked when he heard the crash of Alex's body striking the tree. He saw Garmadia on all fours, his movements unsteady, as though he'd been knocked to the ground and was suffering a concussion.

Sam spun quickly with the honed reflexes of a Special Forces operative, but where their opponent should have been, there was nothing. The man moved too quickly for them to engage him. Sam struck out time and again, but González disappeared and reappeared beside him as though materializing from the air. The tall priest smiled, and Sam saw the rows of needle-teeth shine wetly in the moonlight.

Sam brought his arm around towards the leering face, firing off a stream of frozen spikes, aiming to saw the black-clad figure in half. But González easily caught his arm and, with a brief jerk, pulled the gauntlet free and threw it deep into the foliage. With his other hand, he grasped Sam by the upper arm and lifted, flinging him backwards as though he were weightless.

Sam hit the ground hard, but managed to roll and come to his feet with his handgun pointed at the priest, who was standing over Aimee and Saqueo. The boy was curled into a foetal position. Just as Sam was about to fire, González's attention was drawn to Captain Garmadia, who was staggering groggily from the clearing. Perhaps a fleeing prey was too attractive to ignore. González was a blur of dark movement as he scooped up Garmadia and returned with him to stand again over Aimee and Saqueo. The struggling captain cried out as the fingers that held him buried deeper into his flesh. With one hand, he tried to prise away the grip around his throat; the other brought his handgun up towards González's face.

González smiled, and took hold of the captain's arm at the elbow, almost gently. He looked down at Aimee and Saqueo, his mouth behind the red-streaked beard lifting as though in a smile, and jerked once on the arm. The bones of the clavicle splintered within the shoulder, and the large flat deltoid muscles tore free from the upper back and chest. The sickening sound made Sam grit his teeth.

Garmadia was silent, his mouth opening and closing in shock. The priest dropped him to the ground and watched as blood pulsed from the terrible wound, splashing like black oil onto the dry soil.

González looked down at Aimee and Saqueo again. As he reached for them, Sam charged, gun and knife raised.

He knew the advance was futile, but he hoped it would offer Aimee a few seconds' diversion to try to flee into the jungle.

Just as before, the priest moved so quickly, it made Sam feel he was standing still. One minute the creature was kneeling over Aimee and the boy; the next, he had closed the few feet between them and held Sam in his grip.

González seemed to be enjoying himself. He nodded at Sam and smiled. Sam smiled back, determined not to show fear or pain. He knew that the human body could survive fifty percent blood loss, removal of several organs and limbs, and blinding pain, but the real killer was shock. Sam gritted his teeth hard and prepared for the pain.

Steel-like fingers dug deep into the muscle of his upper arm and grated on the bone. The only thing that prevented them piercing flesh was the tough synthetic suit he wore – but Sam knew that wouldn't hold for long.

Shots rang out from behind him: Aimee. Sam saw bullet holes pit the black-clad torso. They distracted González and he turned towards their source, giving Sam a few seconds. He'd dropped his sidearm, but was able to swing his blade up and into the nexus between the man's neck and shoulder, deep into the trapezius muscle bunching. A good strike – fatal if deep enough, and certainly debilitating in combat.

González didn't even flinch. His attention remained firmly on Aimee and the boy, as if he'd remembered what he really wanted all along.

Sam tugged the knife free. No blood spurted from the deep rent in the dead flesh. He drew his arm back again, this time planning to drive the laser-sharpened blade into the creature's face. But, as if tiring of his antics, González shook him hard to disorient him, then, in a blur of strength and speed, threw him backwards like a discarded bag of trash.

As Sam hit the tree line, he regretted he hadn't give Aimee her time. González hadn't taken his eyes off her.

*

Alex burst from the undergrowth, enraged by the way the priest had knocked him aside so easily, causing him to leave those under his protection exposed. He was just in time to see Sam's large body flung into the jungle as if it were weightless. Small-arms fire rang out, and he saw Aimee firing point-blank into the chest of this thing that looked like a man but wasn't.

Alex raised one arm, pointing the gauntlet at the monster's chest. González lifted Aimee and Saqueo, one in each hand, and held them close to his face and body. Alex didn't know if he was shielding himself from the ice gun, or savoring the smell of their sweating flesh.

Almost faster than Alex's eyes could follow, the priest was at the door of the small stone building. He looked back once over his shoulder, his dark eyes issuing a challenge, then vanished into the darkness beyond the opening. There was a deep grinding sound, and by the time Alex had made it to the top of the steps, a giant stone blocked the doorway. The priest was sealed inside – with Aimee and Saqueo.

THIRTY-FIVE

Alex struck the stone with his shoulder but it didn't move. He placed both hands against its surface and strained. The granite block weighed many tons and resisted his herculean efforts. He examined it, wondering at its thickness and searching for points of weakness.

'Boss.' Sam had struggled back to his leader's side. Abrasions covered one side of his face and his suit was torn to shreds, like Alex's. He had recovered his ice gun from the jungle where the priest had thrown it.

'We need a plan.'

'I'll get them out; don't worry.' Alex stepped back, preparing to charge at the block of stone again.

Sam repeated his words a little louder and grabbed hold of Alex's arm. 'Boss – we've got to have a plan. We just shot and stabbed at that thing and it still knocked us outta the park. It's quicker and stronger than both of us.'

Alex didn't answer; he just shook Sam's hand off and threw himself at the granite. His body shuddered at the impact, but the stone remained in place. He stepped back, ready to continue hurling himself at the rock until he or it gave way. Aimee was trapped in there with that monster. He wouldn't stop until he'd got her out.

*

Sam knew that look on his leader's face; that single-minded focus: it meant logic was seeping away and the rage was taking over. He also knew that with Aimee sealed off behind that stone, Alex's only priority was to be in there as well. Nothing else mattered. But if Alex did manage to gain entrance, the priest would have him right where he wanted him. It would be sure suicide.

His mind jumped back to the private briefing the HAWC commander, Jack Hammerson, had given him before they left on this mission. Sam had sat in stunned silence while the Hammer told him about Alex's medical history, the treatment that had saved his life, and how uncontrollable rages were now threatening his control over his enhanced abilities. He had also explained what lay in wait for Alex if he was ever delivered back to the Medical Division.

Hammerson had a task for Sam: to make sure Alex didn't fall. If he did, and was disabled or couldn't be quickly revived, then he was to be terminated. The HAWC commander was determined the Arcadian would never see the inside of a military hospital again, anywhere, anytime. It had taken Hammerson all afternoon to convince Sam to be Alex Hunter's executioner should the need arise, but the thought of Alex ending up as so many slices of tissue in a test tube had finally convinced him. They had agreed on one concession, however: if the Arcadian's full recovery was anticipated, and they could locate a safe place to conceal him, the termination would be deferred. They shook hands on it, both men knowing such a concession was potentially meaningless. In the twenty-first century, US surveillance technology meant there was no such thing as a safe place anymore.

This was exactly the type of situation Hammerson had explained to him, and Sam had feared, where the rage his leader suffered could push him beyond rationality and control. He would never be able to stop Alex physically, but he could at least try to persuade him to rethink actions that were plain suicidal – like the one he was attempting now.

'Alex!' Sam stepped in front of him.

Alex yelled in frustration, not even looking at him. 'Move aside, soldier.'

Sam didn't move; instead, he pushed hard into Alex's chest. 'What is the plan?'

'To get her out!' Alex roared, pushing back hard on Sam's chest.

Sam's entire 250-pound frame staggered back uncontrollably. He stepped forward again and grabbed Alex's wrist.

'What is the plan?' he yelled into Alex's face. 'Arcadian – without a plan, she will die.'

Alex screamed and punched his free hand into the granite block beside Sam's head. Sam felt stone chips strike the side of his face. Thank God the blow hadn't been directed at his skull.

He yelled louder. 'Arcadian – insertion, engagement, extraction. What is the plan?'

Alex blinked and shook his head, the words seeming to puncture the rage that had overtaken him. He rested his hand and forehead against the cool stone. Sam watched as the bones in his smashed hand slid around under the skin, lifting back into place. He recoiled slightly at his leader's unnatural ability.

Alex stood straight and looked into Sam's face. 'She won't die today.'

He seemed to have stepped back from the abyss of fury, but Sam could see his eyes still burned with an intensity that bordered on the insane.

He said quietly, 'No, boss, she won't die today. Now, what's the plan?'

Alex's eyes bored into Sam. 'The plan? I'll take González; you get Aimee and the boy out of there and head to the rendezvous point. If anything goes wrong, you will not wait for me. Clear?'

Sam looked at Alex for a long moment, then shrugged. That was probably as good as he was going to get right now. He rested his hand on his recovered sidearm. 'All right, boss – let's get 'em out of there.'

THIRTY-SIX

Aimee kept one arm around Saqueo and held the other over her lower face. The stench in the dark, airless space was almost a living thing.

González had thrown them roughly to the ground as soon as they stepped through the doorway, and then moved back to slide a huge granite block across the opening. She shivered, remembering the ease with which he had moved the stone. She only knew one other man that might have been capable of performing such a feat, and he was now locked on the other side of the rock.

When González had secured the doorway, he had also shut out the last faint traces of light; the darkness was now absolute. Aimee held her breath and willed her heartbeat to slow. González had not returned to them, and she guessed he was waiting for Alex to try to enter. She had no doubt that he could see them; from time to time, she felt a chill run across her neck and knew he was casting his gaze in her direction.

Aimee had no weapons, bar one – her intellect. Perhaps she could reason with him, negotiate. Or at least slow him down and buy Alex some time.

'*Padre?*' Her voice sounded tiny, like that of the little girl who used to cry when her hair was pulled by the boy next door over twenty-five years ago. She tried again. '*Padre?* Are you there?'

The reply was a roar – so close and so agonizingly loud that she found herself screaming in terror and pain. A charnel-house odor washed over her – the hot breath of some carnivorous beast. She tried hard not to retch.

Beside her, she felt Saqueo tremble, and he pressed his face into her side. *Please hurry, Alex*, she wished into the darkness.

*

When Alex heard the roar and Aimee's muffled scream, his vision blurred with fury. His lips drew back and he bared his teeth.

Sam turned and said something, but Alex didn't hear. Everything around him had disappeared the moment Aimee had cried out. Once more, he placed his hands against the stone and pushed. Nothing. He ground his teeth and strained, the muscles across his back and shoulders screaming from the exertion. The stone moved a half-inch, but when he adjusted his grip, it grated back into place.

He's pushing back – he knows I can open it. The realization gave Alex a surge of confidence. *I can get in, and then I will destroy you!* he silently screamed.

Unexpectedly, a voice answered him. *Yes, come. And we will consume you, as we will every living thing in this world.*

Cold washed through Alex's mind and rocked him momentarily. He took his hands off the stone and stared hard at its gray surface. He frowned and pushed his mind out once again. *What are you?*

A sound that could have been a grating laugh preceded the deep voice that replied. *What are we? Or what is the shell you see? But of course, unlike others of your kind, you perceive more, don't you? We should ask, what are you, Alex Hunter, child of science? Are you a man, or simply a creation of man?*

Alex was stunned. *How could the creature know these things about him?*

The harsh voice ground out once more. *This shell, this being, was once like you: afflicted by mortality. It believed in a god – something all powerful, all knowing and immortal. We are far older than your entire race, and have the power to consume your world. Are we not then those very gods?*

We? That tiny word unsettled Alex more than anything else he had seen or heard. *Are there more like you?* he sent. *Where are they?*

The dry rasp came again. *More than you could count in a thousand lifetimes, Alex Hunter. The seed has waited patiently to rise up, and now it grows. It will be your extinction.*

Alex frowned; Aimee had suggested that the bacteria that had devastated the men at the camp seemed to have been waiting for them to dig it up – *waiting to rise up*, the thing had said. Was the thing that used to be González somehow linked to the Hades Bug?

The idea reminded him of something he'd learned back in his earliest days in the Special Forces: they'd been warned not to build jungle shelters or bivouacs near certain types of trees as they were favored by army ants. The thing Alex had found fascinating about the ants was the way they always sent out scouts, or advance guards, before invading a territory. The scouts were the heralds of a ravenous tide of destruction. Was the priest the herald of the Hades Bug's army of cells? Or was he a product of them?

Suddenly, Alex thought the nuke was looking like a brilliant idea.

The voice leaked into his mind again, and he cleared his thoughts in case it was able to pick images from his brain.

We need all of you. Join me willingly; or flee now, before you become no more than a few scraps of new tissue on this rotting frame.

Alex closed his eyes, a smile forming at the corners of his lips. He had just learned two things: first, the creature had an ego and craved an audience; second, and more importantly, it didn't want to confront him. For all its incredible strength, it had limitations; it knew fear.

He studied the edges of the slab; he wouldn't be able to shift it while another force, one possibly stronger than he was, pushed back from the other side. He needed more leverage.

He lifted his hands from the stone. *I'm coming in … to talk further.*

There was a pause. *Like the lamb may talk with the lion … Come, then.*

Alex guessed the creature knew what he planned, but if it bought him one extra second, then good. He wedged his fingers into the small space where the hewn block didn't quite sit flush with the stone doorframe, and heaved. There was a begrudging movement of the stone.

'Sam. Shoulder to it,' Alex ordered.

Sam's contribution would only give him an extra few hundred pounds of thrust, but it should be enough to gain the advantage he needed. Alex thought again of Aimee's scream, and heaved. Six inches of dark space opened up. Now he could set both hands to work. He sucked in a deep breath and ground his teeth together as he moved his arms apart – like Samson between the two pillars of the Philistine temple. Slowly, the massive stone block, and the creature holding it, gave way to the greater force.

'Alex!' came Aimee's cry from within the darkened space.

The gap was little more than a foot wide but it was enough. Before Sam could stop him, Alex leapt through.

THIRTY-SEVEN

Even with the small gap open to the night, the inside of the stone room was impossibly black. Alex, with his enhanced vision, could make out the warm body glow of Aimee and Saqueo. She stood, her back to a wall, facing out into the darkness. Saqueo was cowering behind her, his face pressed into her back.

Close to her, there was a colder image; as still as a pillar of stone, and even darker than the surrounding blackness. Alex knew the priest could easily see him – clearly, the darkness was his preferred element. A smile parted a mouth that was far too wide for a human face.

Alex held out one arm and feigned a slight stumble, not wanting the priest to realize he also had excellent vision in darkness.

González reached up to stroke Aimee's face, evidently wanting her to scream to draw Alex towards him. Aimee flinched but didn't make a noise.

Alex needed the creature to move away from her so he could use his ice gun; at this close range, and with a double stream, the creature would be cut in half in a matter of seconds. He continued to play his part, moving to the left and holding one hand up to the wall, his other arm out in front, like a blind man who had lost his cane.

González smiled again, perhaps confident that he alone could see in the darkness. He moved around behind Alex, silent as he came up from behind. Alex could almost feel the wide smile looming towards him, revelling in the trap it thought it was about to spring.

Just a little closer, he thought.

*

Sam had given up trying to widen the gap between stone and doorframe. Instead, he removed some of his equipment to slim down his frame; if the stone wouldn't give for him, he'd give for the stone. He pulled a battered silver cigarette lighter from his pocket and looked briefly at the bald eagle engraved on its side. *Long time between cigars*, he thought, then sucked in his breath, flattened his body and started squeezing through the gap.

*

Alex kept his senses open to the priest's presence, while keeping his back turned to his approach. In a few more paces he would have moved to a position farthest from the door ... and the priest would be closest to it – dangerous for Alex, and giving the priest access to the only exit. But it meant González was farthest from Aimee and Saqueo, and a clear target.

Keep coming, just keep coming, Alex prayed.

Then he saw Sam was forcing his way into the dark room – almost right in front of the priest. Alex wouldn't be able to use his guns. *No! Not yet*, he silently screamed.

González stopped and waited.

Sam's head and shoulders came through the gap; there was a click and a small orange flame sparked into life. The game was up: no more hiding; no more pretending in the dark.

González's roar reverberated around the room and he turned towards Sam.

Alex charged – his own roar of anger barely audible above the priest's unearthly howl.

*

In the flickering orange glow of the tiny flame, Sam saw a vision that made him gasp and throw his arm up. Just as he was about to fire, González changed course to meet Alex's attack.

Sam yelled his frustration and tried to force more of his body through the narrow gap. In the weak light, he saw González and Alex crash together, the expression on his leader's face matching the ferocity of his enemy. The impact in the small room was thunderous, and dust rained down around them. The flickering shadows from the lighter flame gave the battle the quality of an old Lumière stop-motion film.

Sam grinned humorlessly. This time, González wasn't just dealing with the weak flesh of a man. The priest would find this world had its own monsters.

*

González flew at Alex, his black robes flapping like a pair of large, dark wings. His mouth hung open in anticipation of sinking those dozens of rows of teeth into Alex's flesh.

Alex met the thing mid-flight, the impact loud in the small room. This wasn't a human he faced and he didn't pull any blows. His first strike was into the priest's face, and he was satisfied with the resulting crack of bone and the indentation in the side of his skull.

The blow should have killed González instantly, but he wasn't even slowed.

Alex briefly caught sight of Aimee, who was screaming something to him as she edged towards the door. *Good, they'll be safe now*, he thought, and then the priest was on him again. In only a few seconds, Alex's face was a battered and bloody mask. A blow in his midsection felt as though it had come from a steel battering ram.

He swung his arm once more, putting all his strength into the punch. Instead of connecting with the dead flesh, he found only air. The creature moved faster than Alex could strike. He spun, preparing to launch a volley of ice spikes at the darting form, but it was now a mere shadow within shadows.

The next attack was the priest's – the side of Alex's head exploded with pain, and he went down. Bloodied pieces of his shattered communication pellet fell from his ear.

He heard Aimee scream, and saw Sam leap over his fallen form with his sidearm in his hand. Bullets thwacked into the priest, every one hitting its target, but his flesh absorbed them without any sign of the impact.

Sam's full clip had emptied. He raised the empty gun over his head and swung his arm down hard. It never found its intended target. González spun and swatted Sam down like he was an annoying insect. Then he bent, grabbed the HAWC's large body and raised it above his head in two hands. A yell of excruciating pain escaped Sam's lips as González brought his hands together and snapped his back with a crack like a rifle report.

González launched the HAWC's loose frame at the stone block in front of the door. Sam was a big man, and his body struck the rock with such force that the gap almost closed, shutting them inside. Even in his dazed state, Alex knew his friend was either dead or crippled, and they were all trapped.

González stood unnaturally still in the center of the room, smiling again. Behind him, Aimee and Saqueo stood blindly in the darkness.

Alex felt like he was at the bottom of a deep pit where sounds and images were indistinct. Voices began to scream at him, cutting through the fog, furious vapors that swirled round him. It wasn't Aimee; she and the boy were mute with terror. He grunted with pain as the voices increased in volume and ferocity, abusing him for his weakness, his cowardice, his dishonor. His second-in-command had been crushed before his eyes; the woman he loved was frightened and vulnerable in the darkness; and all he could do was grovel in the dirt.

Get up, the voices roared at him.

Alex punched his fist into the ground, and shook his head to clear it – of the voices and the fog of concussion.

Aimee and Saqueo were too close to the priest to use his gauntlets, so he pulled both his short- and long-bladed Ka-Bars from their sheaths. He shook his head again, this time to clear blood from his eyes, sucked in a deep breath and got to his feet. Summoning his last reserves of strength, he launched himself at González.

The priest caught him in midair and held both his forearms fast, the smile never leaving his bearded face. In his mind, Alex heard the dry, grating laugh again. González forced him backwards, exerting enormous pressure on his arms, trying to wrench them apart. It would have torn a lesser man down the middle, but Alex resisted. For a few seconds, it seemed they were in balance locked in their deadly embrace.

González surged forward and slammed Alex back so hard, his head bounced off the heavy stone wall. His vision swam again. The priest seized the opportunity to lean in towards him and open his mouth, bringing it close to Alex's face. Even in the dark, Alex could see the small gray thing rise in the back of the priest's throat. Hair-like tendrils fluttered in anticipation of its feast and it mewled softly. As Alex watched, the priest's right eye shrank in its socket then vanished, reappearing in his mouth on the end of a gray stalk. Something living inside the priest was emerging to feed.

Alex strained against the priest's grip, and the creature slammed him into the wall again and again. Alex screamed his defiance and strained even harder. He brought his knee up into the priest's groin with a force that should have exploded his testicles. There was no response, other than the inexorable forward movement of that hellish face towards his own.

Alex roared in rage, frustration and revulsion. All he could think of was Aimee; how she was trapped in this dark room. How, if he died, she would be doomed.

The small, questing tendril unfurled towards his eye. He couldn't move; couldn't do anything but wait for it to latch onto his face.

He heard the click of Sam's lighter, then hundreds of spikes punctured one side of the priest's face, exiting his skull on the other side. González roared in pain and turned, and another stream took off the top of his head. He shrieked and disappeared down a small hole in the center of the room, his dark robes swirling behind him.

Alex fell to his hands and knees, sucking in enormous breaths. 'Oh God, that was a close one, buddy.'

He turned in the direction the ice spikes had come from, expecting to see his second-in-command's lopsided, aw-shucks, ain't-nothing-type grin. Instead, he saw Aimee sitting on the floor holding Sam's arm up like a cannon; she had one arm wrapped around the gauntlet for aim and the other was curling his hand into a fist. Behind her sat Saqueo, holding the lighter.

She gave him an exhausted grin. 'Anything else you need … buddy?'

THIRTY-EIGHT

Casey Franks crashed into a tree, and wrapped her arms around it to stay upright. The heat and humidity were exhausting her despite her physical capabilities. She wiped her face; it was wet with perspiration and blood, and crisscrossed with scratches from her charge through the dense green jungle.

With hands shaking from fatigue, she pulled the small GPS device from her pocket. She checked her positioning. Not far now: two of the dots had grown closer – hers and the chopper's. But the third …

'Ah, what? Fuck!'

Alex was still way too far west, and hadn't moved much since she'd last checked over an hour ago. A moment of indecision washed over her as she considered changing course.

'Fuck, fuck!' she yelled into the dark, momentarily silencing the surrounding wildlife.

She took a swing at a large leaf, and looked again at the GPS. It was too far to make it to Alex and then get back to the rendezvous site – her heart would simply explode.

She pulled the last foil-covered pellet from her pouch, broke it under her nose and shuddered as the chemicals punched her up another level.

'Orders, fucking, unchanged.'

She ran on.

*

Hammerson sat in his office watching his computer screen. Arcadian had been en route to the rendezvous but had diverted – something had changed. A short while ago his communication device had ceased working. Sam Reid and Franks were still in go mode, but their signals were a long way apart.

What the hell is going on?

He pinched his lower lip and looked at a small timer in the corner of his screen – just a little more under-the-table information courtesy of MUSE. The timer ticked down in hundredths of a second; he checked it against his watch – sixty minutes to detonation, and just forty-five minutes until rendezvous. Franks should make it, but Alex and Sam? They needed to leave *now*.

He sent another pulse to Sam's comm pellet and waited. In the field, even in the thick of combat, HAWCs were able to acknowledge a message with a single returned pulse ... but nothing.

Hammerson sucked at his teeth, then slammed his hand down on the large desk. 'Come on, boys, going to be a red hot dawn today.'

He ran both hands up through his cropped hair, then tried Sam again. Still nothing. Now all he could do was wait. And, God, how he hated waiting.

There was a commotion outside his door; the next instant, it flew open and he saw Adira Senesh standing there. His assistant, Margaret, was right next to her, her hand on the captain's arm. Senesh looked down at the hand and Margaret took a step back from the ferocity of the woman's glare. She gave Hammerson a look that said both *I'm sorry* and *she frightens me*.

Hammerson nodded to his assistant, who backed out of the office and pulled the door closed.

'Not a good time, Captain,' Hammerson said.

Adira strode towards him, pointing a finger like a gun directly at his face. Hammerson noticed the knuckles on her hand were abraded. He'd read the report on the two HAWC recruits she'd injured: one left severely incapacitated, the other still on life support. Both out-thought and out-fought; he'd be rejecting both of them as

HAWCs following that performance. He sat back and folded his arms, keeping his face expressionless. Senesh was becoming a problem – a clever, highly trained and explosive one. He needed to be smart and careful.

'Will Arcadian be free from the blast radius?' she spat.

Hammerson groaned inwardly. *Damn Mossad's information networks – probably better than our own.* He didn't respond, just looked slightly bored.

Adira's hand curled into a fist and she leaned forward on it over his desk. 'If the best soldier your country has ever produced is vaporized in the next few minutes, will you be rewarded for that? I think not.' She narrowed her eyes. 'Billions of dollars spent on the so-called Arcadian Project, all for it to be destroyed in minutes.'

So, there it was. *She did know about the Arcadian,* he mused. Hammerson had known from the outset that there was a double mission thrust in Captain Senesh's secondment to him and the HAWCs. He knew the Israelis; and he knew his old friend Meir Shavit too well to think he did anything without an ulterior motive. Damn shame really, the woman was skilled. He'd immediately recognized her potential and had tried to turn her, but her resolve was iron hard and her subterfuge skills world-class. In the end he'd simply quarantined her from the frontline and she had taken it as a personal affront. She'd also been getting way too nosy.

He smiled grimly at her, leaned forward himself and keyed a few commands into his computer. He turned the screen around so she could see it and pressed a key.

A nighttime CCTV loop commenced. A figure in black, moving low to the ground, climbed up and over an eight-feet concrete wall like a dark and silent spider. The face was black-masked and a single lens jutted out from the head. Somehow the intruder managed to deactivate the electronic countermeasures, then entered an upper silo of Deep Storage, one of the access vents to the most secure military storehouse facilities in the United States. The film switched to the inside of the complex, but only for an instant before it was blacked out by the infiltrator.

Hammerson sat back and folded his arms again. 'We'll get 'em next time. And no need for rendition here; we'll grind the information out of them, then throw what's left into the chemical furnace.'

He stared into the woman's face, his eyes like twin lasers, and watched with satisfaction as her jaw tightened aggressively. Both her fists balled and he readied himself. Adira picked up an old tank shell he kept on his desk as a paperweight and threw it with enough force to smash through the plaster wall. He felt the impact under his feet.

Hammerson's office door immediately opened and Margaret stood there with a small-calibre handgun by her side. He held up his hand to her and she paused in the doorway, keeping her eyes on the Israeli woman.

Adira spoke through gritted teeth. 'I could have had a jump jet down there by now – Hunter would be already on his way back. My country hasn't burnt its bridges in South America like yours has.'

Hammerson kept his gaze flat. 'Not your problem, Captain.' He motioned sharply with his head to the door.

She glared at him for a few seconds, looking as if she was going to say something else, but then spun and went out, her shoulders hunched in fury, Hebrew curses filling the air around her.

Hammerson raised his eyebrows at Margaret. She looked over her shoulder, then back to him and nodded – she was gone.

'Thanks, Margie. And have security double-sweep my office again – it's getting a little crowded in here.'

*

Adira stood on the landing of the military office block and sucked in a few deep breaths to calm her pounding blood.

It is my problem ... and I am not finished yet, you bastard goyim, she thought.

She stood like stone, staring off into the distance as she listened to the small pellet inside her ear. Then she glanced up at the building where Hammerson's office was located; there was an almost imperceptible black dot on the outside of his windowsill.

And sweep inside your office as much as you like, old man.

THIRTY-NINE

Aimee heard Alex groan as he shifted the massive block further across the doorway. His hands were red with blood – this time, mostly his own. The wounds were already healing, but she knew he felt every one of them.

Moonlight filtered in through the wider opening. Alex kneeled and felt Sam's neck; he exhaled and nodded slowly.

Aimee was relieved. She knew Alex would be devastated if the closest person he had to a friend died.

'Get Sam and Saqueo outside,' he told her. 'I won't be long.'

Aimee noticed he wouldn't look at her. She knew exactly what was on his mind – *unfinished business*. She put her hands on her hips. 'Uh-uh, no way, buster. If you go down there, I'm going with you.'

Alex looked at her for a moment then shrugged. 'Sure. Just help me get Sam outside.'

'Yeah, right,' she scoffed. 'And as soon as I step out there, you'll push the door shut.'

Alex shook his head slowly. 'Aimee —'

She cut him off. 'I've seen what that thing can do, Alex. If you get killed, then we'll all end up as more bones on its killing field.' She looked briefly at Saqueo, then back into his eyes. 'And if you shut me out, and you win, when you *do* step outside ... then I'll damn well kill you myself!'

Alex looked up at the roof and exhaled. 'Aimee ... Ahh, Jesus.'

He wiped one hand through his hair and looked down at Sam's unconscious form. 'Saqueo ...' He pointed to the doorway, then grabbed his HAWC by the shoulders and pulled the large man through the gap, the boy following him.

Aimee smiled and nodded her satisfaction ... but only for a moment. The hairs on the back of her neck prickled and she turned to peer at the black hole in the floor. No light, sound or movement came up from its depths, but something was leaking out nonetheless; she could feel it – and it was pure evil. There was something down there, waiting for them in the black depths.

'Alex, please hurry,' she whispered.

*

Alex heard Aimee's plea and tried to work as quickly as possible. He removed one of his gauntlets, then ripped off Sam's shirt sleeves; the material was tough to tear, but he needed the padding. When he re-entered the small room, he found her wide-eyed and pale, pressed as close to the doorway as was possible without actually being wedged in the gap. He knew what she felt: there was a darkness here that had nothing to do with lack of light.

He grasped her arm and pulled her to him. 'We'll be okay,' he said.

'We will now,' she responded with a smile when she saw the weapon, the color coming back into her face. 'I'll look after you.'

Alex wrapped one of Sam's sleeves around her elbow and halfway down her forearm, then slid the gauntlet over the padding. He left her wrist free, and spent a few seconds adjusting the weapon so the sensors would pick up her brachioradial muscle movements for the triggering mechanism.

He pointed her arm towards the far wall. 'Try it.'

Aimee nodded and drew her eyebrows together in concentration. Nothing happened for a few seconds, then a small stream of ice spikes hissed from the gun in a wild spray and her body fell back from the recoil. Alex grabbed her before she hit the ground.

'You have to be ready for it. Short bursts, or you'll either be blown off your feet or dislocate your arm.'

She lifted her trembling arm again. This time, she managed a two-second burst that hit the wall in a straight line. She lowered her arm and rubbed her shoulder. 'Got it, and *ouch*.'

Alex kneeled down, drew his longest blade and wrapped Sam's other sleeve around it. He pulled a small canister from his belt and squirted some acrid liquid on the toughened material, then used the big man's lighter to ignite it. He stood up and handed the torch to Aimee. 'Let there be light.'

She took it and looked towards the black pit. 'And let there be luck.' The massive gauntlet covered most of her slim arm, its weight pulling the limb down to her side. Her eyes were wide behind the torch flames. 'Let's finish this, and go home.'

'There are steps … about eight,' Alex told her. 'Aimee, if you get the chance for a shot, you take it. Do not wait for me to get out of the way. You shoot, and you shoot to kill. Understand?' He waited a second, watching her. When she didn't respond, he peered closer into her face. 'You promise me that?'

'Yes, yes. Don't worry about me. Just remember who it was that saved *your* ass up here.' She moved forward quickly and kissed him.

Alex smiled and shook his head. She was brave, but her lips were cold with fear. He drew his short blade and disappeared down into the impenetrable darkness.

FORTY

Aimee followed quickly, holding the burning torch and gauntlet before her. Even with the light from the flame, the room remained dark. It seemed to consume light. She felt a spongy mass under her feet, and could see the wall nearest her was stained a dark brown and pierced by hairy roots that looked like tentacles reaching for their prey. She shuddered at an old memory.

Alex was in the center of the room, down on one knee, his head turning slowly. She saw that his eyes were half-closed – he was relying on a different type of vision.

'I can't …' he said, turning to her and frowning. 'It's overwhelming.'

His face registered shock just before a howl tore through the small room. Aimee staggered at the sudden, overwhelming noise, and then everything went crazy.

The priest dropped from the roof like a giant spider, his mouth open in that terrible roar, and flung himself onto Alex, smothering him with his black robes. The creature's sudden descent created a draught that made Aimee's torch waver and dance; for one heart-stopping moment, she thought it was going out.

She raised her gauntlet, hesitating as the jumping light made the movements of the priest even more erratic. It was hard for her to tell where Alex was in the jumbled mass. *Short bursts only – do not wait for me*, he'd said. She gritted her teeth and made a fist.

At exactly that moment, the tangle unfolded and the priest held Alex up in front of him, one arm round his throat, the other exposing his chest and abdomen to the spray of spikes that was already on its way.

*

Alex felt the penetrations run from his waist to shoulder. What was left of his suit was tough, but not designed for protection against that sort of assault. The pain was hot at first, then cold, as his body recognized the frozen water penetrating his flesh and attempted to deal with the trauma.

Alex ignored the pain; his vital organs were undamaged and he knew his body had the recuperative capability to deal with the injuries. It responded with a severe jolt to his system and a resulting flush of chemicals that burst through him. He jerked backwards and reached behind his head to grab the priest by the robe, then pulled with all his strength. The creature hung on, its claws digging into Alex's flesh.

Alex grunted with a last herculean effort and slammed backwards. The thing on his back was enormously powerful, but, like Alex, was encased in a human body and bound by the same skeletal and muscular limitations. He tore it over his shoulder, ripping free the black robes and slamming it into the wall. González stuck to the stones like an enormous dark growth, then grinned before dropping lightly to the floor. He straightened and opened his arms wide.

Alex heard Aimee gasp. The priest's body was crisscrossed with weird veins and bulges, and his skin didn't look right. It sagged in some places and was overly tight in others – as if a wrong-sized suit had been pulled too quickly over the frame.

González's hands curled into claws and he crouched, ready to spring. Alex saw some of the ropy tendrils slide around under his skin and tighten, as though they were the strings of a giant marionette.

'Now!' Alex yelled.

He hoped Aimee understood his intent as he raised his arm and fired a stream of projectiles at the thing. From behind him, another stream shot out, hitting González in the neck and head before sliding up towards the roof and dying out.

Alex directed his spray at the priest's shoulder, keeping it focused for as long as he could before González spun away … long enough to nearly sever the arm. González howled again and leapt towards the steps – and potential escape. He was fast, but he was also damaged, and had underestimated Alex.

Alex leapt too, colliding with the priest's naked torso. He heard a satisfying crunch of cartilage as he slammed the body backwards onto the stone floor. When González got to his feet again, his arm was hanging loosely by his side. He snarled.

'Hurts, doesn't it?' Alex said, and charged again.

He cannoned into the man, hurling him backwards into the far wall. Before the body even hit, Alex had his arm up, directing another deadly accurate stream at the thing's leg. The thousands of high-speed spikes cut through the thigh, partially severing it.

González stuck to the wall again, but this time there was no grin. With a sickening, sticky sound, the limb fell away from his body. There was no spurt of blood; instead, strings of dark mucilaginous tendrils stretched from the severed leg back up to its ragged stump. Alex watched in horror and disgust as the threads tightened and began to reel in the limb.

Aimee directed another short burst at the man's torso, the dark holes that appeared in his chest testifying to the hits. The priest grew still and silent. His bulging eyes swivelled to Aimee, one moving more slowly than the other. His mouth opened and he slurred, 'I am sick, child. Please forgive me.'

'He's trying to buy himself time,' Alex warned. 'He's —'

He didn't need to finish. Aimee's slim arm lifted again, wavering slightly from the strain.

'Fuck forgiveness. This is for Francisco, you demon from hell.'

The spikes shot into the thing's face, slicing flesh from its skull. Alex fired again too, cutting through the tendrils that were recovering the injured leg, then severing the other leg. González fell to the ground.

Alex walked over and placed his foot on the priest's chest. There was no blood, despite the massive trauma. The skull, where it was exposed, was gray instead of white, like that of a skeleton in a museum.

González reached up with his remaining arm and grabbed Alex's ankle, but could get no leverage to throw the HAWC off. Alex felt the crushing strength that still remained in the man's arm and lifted the gauntlet slowly, pointing it at González's face.

The priest began to laugh, the words coming thickly from behind his gore-soaked beard. 'Creature of the dirt, we will meet again.'

Alex smiled back. 'I doubt that … your holiness.'

He fired at the other shoulder, severing the final limb. Still the hand continued to grip his ankle. He finished by cutting through the neck and kicking the misshapen head away to the far wall. The odor of the thing's open flesh was vile.

'Yuck.' Aimee covered her mouth and nose.

Alex shook off the talon around his ankle and kicked the limbs away from the body. He pulled a small canister of liquid fuel from a pouch at his side and doused the torso, then stepped back and nodded to Aimee. She threw the flaming torch onto the carcass and stepped back too.

Alex waited mere seconds to make sure the corpse was fully alight before grabbing her arm and leading her up and out of the pit.

*

Behind them, in the shadows, the priest's severed head lay in the dirt. One of its eyes swivelled to watch them go.

FORTY-ONE

Up in the main room, Alex looked back at the pit, now glowing red-hot from the burning remains, and over to the massive block that was partially covering the doorway. 'Just one more thing,' he said.

As he put his hands on the stone, a small face appeared in the gap.

'*Encontró a Chaco, señora?*' Saqueo asked, looking from Aimee to Alex and then back again.

Ah shit, thought Alex. They had protected Saqueo from seeing the small body out in the clearing; he was probably hoping his little brother had been trapped somewhere inside the old church. He exhaled, suddenly feeling his fatigue. *And the pain never ends …*

He turned to Aimee. 'Take him outside … and talk to him.'

He could hear Aimee speaking softly to the boy in halting Spanish as she led him from the church, but he shut it from his mind. He placed both hands on the corner of the stone and his foot against the wall, sucked in a deep breath and gritted his teeth. At first, nothing, but then a minuscule tilt. Alex screamed with the exertion; he felt his muscles protesting, and one of the healing wounds on his chest ripped open.

The giant stone balanced on its corner for a second, then, in slow motion, began to topple. Alex leapt back and lifted one arm up to protect his eyes.

With a thunderous noise, the stone fell across the hole.

Alex nodded. 'Just in case.'

He walked around the slab, noticing only the tiniest of gaps where it rested against the stone floor.

*

'You okay?' Aimee nodded towards the cuts, punctures and bruises on Alex's face and body as he kneeled down next to her beside Sam.

He grimaced and raised his arm to feel his ribs. 'You did shoot me by accident back there, didn't you?'

Aimee gave him a half-smile. 'Of course. If I'd *wanted* to shoot you, I'd have aimed better.'

Alex tore open a small foil packet and broke the capsule inside under Sam's nose. Sam spluttered then groaned. Alex pulled him to a sitting position, but Aimee put her hand out.

'Wait! Should we be moving him?'

'Move him or leave him,' Alex said. 'Seconds count now.'

After a moment, she gave an almost imperceptible nod and held out a canteen. Alex took it and splashed some water over the HAWC's head.

'Come on, big fella, we've got miles to go and not much time.'

Sam drank deeply, and then blinked several times. 'What happened? Are we still in the desert, or are we …? Oh yeah, I remember. Where's González?'

'Ashes by now, we hope,' Alex said.

Sam smiled, but then his face dropped. Alex knew he'd remembered his last few seconds of consciousness and was performing an inventory of his injuries. Sam exhaled and his frame seemed to shrink slightly. 'Sorry, boss, don't think I'm going anywhere today.' He reached down and squeezed his legs, then closed his eyes. 'Might just stay here awhile … enjoy the night air.'

Alex clasped his friend hard by the shoulder. 'Is that right?'

Sam shook his head. 'Legs don't work.'

'Mine do,' Alex said. 'No time to argue, soldier; you're coming.'

He tore open another silver capsule and held it out to Aimee. 'Hyper-stimulant aerosol; it'll give you about another hour's energy.' She hesitated and he pushed it at her. 'Go on, you'll need it.'

Aimee inhaled, and her head shot back as if she'd been kicked in the face. 'Ow, that stings.' She scowled at Alex before sneezing twice.

Alex pulled his satellite-positioning device from a side pouch and checked where they were. He called Saqueo over and turned to Sam. 'Tell him we need to move very fast and he *must* keep up.'

Sam spoke quickly. Saqueo asked a question while pointing at himself.

Sam nodded. '*Si, si, rápidamente.*'

Saqueo looked back at the dark interior of the church and his mouth turned down at the corners. '*Chaco era de lo más rapido corriendo.*'

Sam nodded. 'Yeah, I bet he was a fast runner. Let's just get you out of here.' He looked up at Alex. 'You drive, I'll navigate.'

'Deal. And you can do the talking – my comm unit's busted. Tell the Hammer we're on our way; and get on to Franks too. Tell her she's not to leave the party without us.'

Alex lifted his second-in-command onto his back and Sam wrapped his bear-like arms around Alex's shoulders and chest. His legs hung down uselessly, so Alex bound them together with cord in front of his waist to stop Sam's large frame slipping off as he ran.

Sam pointed east and Alex set off. Aimee and Saqueo had to sprint to keep up with the HAWC leader as he raced through the jungle, their way made slightly easier because of the green tunnel he forged for them.

*

'For Chrissakes, Reid, they don't have the fuel to hang around in the air. Tell Captain Hunter to damn well be there, or be prepared to walk home.'

Hammerson paced to the other side of his office, swearing while the voice on the line spoke again. What he heard made him curse even louder before he was calm enough to reply.

'Look, I'll see what I can do – just goddamn get there.'

He finished with a final incendiary blast at First Lieutenant Samuel Reid, then signed off and flung himself down in front of his computer screen. The three dots were converging. Franks was already in position; the big V22 chopper was over land and closing fast – it would get to Franks in approximately twenty minutes. It was dot three, Alex and his team, that made him groan out loud. They were still miles away.

Then a small grin appeared on his lined face as he picked up the phone and punched in some numbers. *Arcadian's alive.*

*

'Ha! Now you know why I let you make the call,' Alex shouted over his shoulder.

Sam laughed. His leader never ceased to amaze him. Here he was, carrying a big ox like himself on his back without showing the slightest fatigue, and at the same time overhearing the Hammer's blasting being delivered to the inside of Sam's ear.

Sam pulled his head to one side as yet another branch threatened to whip him across the face, then held the GPS up to see the small screen. He indicated a slight shift in their direction, and Alex veered towards where he pointed, punching a new hole through the damp, green curtain of vegetation.

*

Inside the church, a mewling sound came from underneath the granite slab that now covered the dark hole. The red glow of the fire had died down and black greasy smoke leaked out through the gap between the rock and the floor.

A thin tendril unfurled from the smoke, and a round gray blob appeared at its tip. The blob split down the middle to reveal an opaque eye, which hung motionless for a moment, before the tendril bulged and thickened and burst open in a knot of gray worms that pulsed and flopped free of the gap. The gray rubbery mass lay still, the eye on the stalk waving back and forth, as if examining its surroundings. Satisfied that it was safe, the creature lifted itself up on tiny sucker-tipped legs and, grub-like, made its way towards the door.

FORTY-TWO

The V22 sped over the treetops, its twin Rolls-Royce Liberty turbo shafts emitting little more than a high-pitched whine. Despite its size, the machine moved gracefully at a speed twice that of anything comparable. Stripped down as it was, it could also get more than five times the range. Hammerson had begged, bullied and bartered to get access to the giant helicopter in the first place. But getting the US Navy to turn a ship around and close in on another country's territorial waters just to give the giant machine another ten minutes' airtime had used up every last ounce of goodwill he was owed, along with all his poker credits.

The pilot knew little of the mission or the pick-up. He had co-ordinates – GPS dots – but only the Hammer could talk to the people on the ground. The chopper's cargo bay was designed to carry twenty-four fully equipped combat troops, but today there was only one man sitting there. Their orders had just been amended: they'd been given ten extra minutes of hover time at the rendezvous point.

The pilot shook his head. Though the country was fairly benign to the United States, if there was a flyover, they'd instantly be spotted sitting in the air like a giant dragonfly over a pond – and, at this point, he didn't have any good answers as to why they were there.

He looked at his screen: five minutes to destination.

*

Saqueo stuck his tongue out in a mock panting action at the speed they were having to run at to keep pace with Alex. Aimee couldn't manage more than a smile in response; every ounce of her energy was being directed to her legs, which felt like rubber … damned heavy rubber. The chemical stimulant was wearing off and she had red-hot cramps in a tightening band around her diaphragm.

Alex yelled over his shoulder to Sam, 'Time to arrival?'

Sam looked at the small unit, yelled back, 'Eleven minutes', then gave the coordinates of both Franks and the V22.

Shit, another eleven minutes, Aimee thought. *Might as well be eleven hours.* She swallowed thick saliva, and her vision swam for a few seconds.

Alex called her name. Her mouth tried to form words but there was no air left in her lungs. He slowed, then turned, and she wobbled towards him. He grabbed her and pushed her hair back so he could look at her face. She grasped hold of his shoulder for balance, and took a small sip of water.

Saqueo was bent over sucking in huge breaths, but he seemed okay.

She moved her hand to Alex's collar and pulled him a little closer. 'Give me another blast.'

Sam reached over from his position on Alex's back and felt her neck. 'About 160 beats per minute – another hit could kill her.'

'Just do it!' Aimee exhaled the words as forcefully as she could, then gritted her teeth and stood a little straighter.

Alex thought for a second and nodded. Sam grunted and broke the last capsule, giving her the full dose. She inhaled deeply, feeling giddy as her heart fluttered in her chest and the deathly fatigue evaporated from her muscles. She grabbed Saqueo and waved the capsule under his nose for a second. He yelped and pulled away.

They started running again. Aimee noticed that Alex had increased his speed.

*

Casey Franks wrapped the belt around her waist and groin, and pressed the button to lift her from the jungle floor. As soon as she broke clear of the canopy, she sucked in a lungful of cooler air.

'Jesus!' The crewman's mouth dropped open when he saw her walk up the lowered rear ramp of the giant helicopter. She knew she had a hundred grazes and scratches on her face and arms, and sap, twigs and dead bugs stuck in her close-cropped hair. She shrugged out of the harness and headed straight for him, causing him to take a half-step back.

'Boo,' she said, and winked as he handed her a set of head mics and a water canteen. She nodded her thanks and drained the canteen in seconds.

She pulled on the headset and turned her back to check her GPS unit. *They're close.*

Grabbing a roof handle, she walked a few paces down the open ramp, pulled a small monoscope from a pouch and scanned the thick jungle for any sign of her team. An impossible task really, given the amount of cover.

'We can only wait five more minutes, then we've been ordered to evac,' the crewman said.

Casey turned narrowed eyes on the young man then returned her attention to the forest floor. *I'll let you know if you can obey that order in four minutes, fifty-nine seconds*, she thought.

*

Alex sensed the chopper before he heard it. The huge dual props displaced a lot of downward air pressure and the density changes moved through the still forest, felt by some of the local wildlife and him.

'We're here,' he yelled.

In another minute, they all heard the chopper, and then in a few more they could see it.

Alex picked up Hammerson's message as it was delivered into Sam's communication pellet: *Four minutes until detonation.*

Two cables dangled from the rear of the hovering behemoth. Alex didn't stop until he had one belt secured around Aimee and

Saqueo, and the other around his own waist. Sam held onto the cable above Alex's head. There wouldn't be two lifts – they would all go up at once, or not at all.

Even as they rose above the canopy, the giant helicopter started to move off.

*

Adira stood hidden behind the tree line some distance from the USSTRATCOM base. Though she faced the rows of administration buildings, her eyes were screwed shut as she listened to the small pellet in her ear. She'd heard Hammerson's communication of the countdown's final minutes, and her lips had moved silently in an ancient Hebrew prayer as she willed Alex Hunter to make the critical rendezvous.

Now, she exhaled and leaned back against a tree. She brought one hand to her lips and kissed the small blue star inked on the meat between her thumb and forefinger. *Thank you*, she whispered before melting back into the woodland.

FORTY-THREE

Tomás pushed open the cabin door. '*Perdóneme, señora.*'
He had brought the doctor a small cup of water. He kneeled beside her cot and saw that her eyes were still open, but she didn't move or acknowledge him in any way.

He spoke again, this time in English. 'Excuse me, please.'

Still nothing.

He put the cup down on the floor and touched her shoulder, then shook it gently. The woman's head turned towards him in a dreamy, slow motion, and an empty syringe clattered to the floor.

A small bell sounded behind him, and he turned towards the source of the chime – a silver case.

The chiming stopped, and he heard the woman whisper one word, a name: *Michael.* Then Tomás's world turned white.

*

'Stay away from the windows,' the pilot ordered.

His voice cut out in a blast of white noise as a searing light flooded the cabin through the port and starboard windows.

Aimee put her hand on Sam's arm, as though to help brace him. Sam patted her hand and smiled, the light from the windows turning his face from X-ray white to a darker reddish glow. Aimee'd wanted him strapped down and immobilized on a makeshift spinal board, but he had protested furiously on the grounds that he'd just been carried through miles of jungle on the back of a galloping, two-legged horse. How much more damage could he sustain from sitting up now? They'd compromised by belting him, in a sitting position, to one of the metal benches in the long fuselage.

The pilot spoke again. 'Okay, everyone, we're gonna get a little push shortly, but we've got good distance now and a lot of shielding. I'd like a bit more height as the shock wave tends to kick up more debris down low, but then we'd become visible. Not that a megaton of nuke going off is as easy to hide as a firecracker in a letterbox.' He chuckled. 'Just take it easy back there folks and enjoy —' There was a sickening jolt and his laidback tone vanished. 'Holy fuck. What the … what *is* that?'

Everyone looked out through the toughened-glass windows.

'Over here,' Aimee said at portside, moving so Alex could see. A small mountain was growing out of the jungle a few miles from where the detonation had taken place. It looked like a giant green boil, swelling then starting to split. 'It's the gas bed – trillions of cubic feet of natural gas and primitive petrocarbons. The nuke must have ignited it. It's massive – covers a big part of this country and the next. I doubt we'll be able to outrun it.'

The mountain burst and a column of orange flame, half a mile wide, shot into the atmosphere. Chunks of jungle – some as big as battleships – sailed into the air, and hung for a second, like enormous tree-covered dirigibles, before falling back to the earth.

This time there would be no little 'push'. This time they would be smashed.

Aimee couldn't stop her mouth dropping open. Millions of tons of explosive pressure forced the ignited gas straight up and out of the widening hole. Even at their distance, the occupants of the helicopter had to cover their ears against the deafening cataclysm.

This is what the end of the world will look like, she thought.

*

Alex could see the brutal wall of blast pressure rushing towards them.

'Brace!' he yelled, and grabbed hold of Aimee.

Casey did the same to Saqueo, and Sam wrapped his arms around some cargo netting on the walls. Thirty-five thousand pounds of flying machine was kicked from the rear so violently that it turned sideways and seemed to skid in midair.

The V22's multi-directional propellers were computer assisted by gyroscopic sensors that allowed the blades literally to bend and contort, so it could stabilize in everything from a hurricane to a force 8 blast shock wave. Every one of these technological capabilities was tested to its limit by the wall of violently moving air.

In the back of the chopper, there was chaos. Bodies were thrown around like tenpins, and Alex and Casey Franks struggled to protect Aimee and Saqueo as they were all bounced from the floor to the ceiling and around the walls. Alex had one arm wrapped around Aimee's head and face; the other, he stuck out to ward off flying debris and grab on to anything secure. He'd managed to grasp and hold a seat railing when his head connected with Casey Frank's left boot. The toughened sole, still caked with black mud, left a perfect imprint across his forehead.

The V22 stabilized as the shock wave passed them by and traveled in a circle away from the huge red wound that had broken open in the Paraguayan landscape. Alex rolled onto his back on the cabin floor, and let Aimee do the same, both of them gasping for air.

'We're still alive,' Aimee said, wincing as she sat up. 'I guess the entire gas chamber didn't ignite.'

Saqueo pushed free of Franks's arms and leapt up to press his face against one of the windows, where he pointed and chattered at the devastation to the jungle, and his home.

Sam rolled his shoulders, grimaced, then reached into his pack behind him and pulled free the heavy journal. He dropped it onto the bench, then relaxed back. 'Never a dull moment in the HAWCs.'

'Fucking A-right, Uncle,' Franks said, while she stretched her back.

She offered her hand to Aimee, who took it and got to her feet. She went over to Saqueo and looked out the window. A curtain of flame and black smoke, many miles wide, rose into the upper atmosphere. She shook her head.

The mega blast had creased and ruptured the landscape for miles in every direction, but instead of the colossal plume blowing into the upper atmosphere, the rapidly expanding gases had lifted the skin of the earth, and then dropped it back to sink hundreds of feet into a massive bowl-shaped crater. The gas bed had collapsed in on itself, and, like a cork being forced back into a bottle, had stopped any more of the primitive fuel being fed to the eruption.

'The gas bed must have collapsed somehow, or sealed itself before the entire chamber went up. Thank God for that.'

The pilot spoke calmly through their earphones. 'Just relax now, folks. We're out over open water, and will be landing on the USS *Bataan* in … exactly twenty-nine minutes. Cocktails will be served,' he finished with a chuckle.

Alex smiled and ran his hands up through his hair that was still sticky with sap and debris, and wiped them on his trousers. He knew the *Bataan*: a Commando-class aircraft carrier – one of the new, smaller and faster carriers the US Navy had in operation. It would be a fast trip home.

He rubbed some grit from his eye. It stung like hell.

FORTY-FOUR

Aimee sat with Sam on the deck of the aircraft carrier. The on-board surgeon had placed him in a spinal brace-chair, and now his bottom half was strapped up with dozens of belts, braces and wires to hold his lower spine as rigid as iron. She thought it looked uncomfortable as hell, but also knew that Sam probably no longer had much sensation below his waist.

He was translating Father Juan de Castillo's journal for her. Saqueo sat squashed up against Sam's other side, oohing and ahhing at the detailed drawings. The brittle, yellowed pages revealed the young priest's hope and joy when they first arrived in the jungle, but later descended into sadness and despair as his companion and mentor, Father Alonso González, was injured, fell sick and then began to change into something strange and unholy.

Sam looked up from his translation as Alex and Casey Franks approached, and Aimee took the opportunity to flick back to a line drawing of a native girl. The artistry was beautiful: the girl's eyes were almost alive as they stared liquidly back at her. Pressed into the page beside the likeness was a dried flower; its now wrinkled petals had made a blue star-shaped stain on the thick paper. Aimee briefly wondered what had become of the little dark-haired girl.

'At ease, everyone,' Alex said. 'Still a few hours before we get choppered into Key West. Might as well enjoy the downtime. We're all still very tired.'

He sat down heavily next to Aimee, then lay back, his face turned to the sun, and closed his eyes. Aimee was about to show him the portrait of the girl when she saw how pale he was.

She frowned. 'Alex? Are you okay?'

He breathed in and out deeply, then sat up slowly. 'I've felt better. I'm so tired, and another headache isn't helping.'

Aimee gasped and tears sprang into her eyes. 'No!' She grabbed his sleeve and pulled him closer. His eyes were streaked with black veins.

'Get the doctor!' she screamed to Franks. 'And get some ice.'

*

Jack Hammerson pushed his thumb and forefinger into his eyes, screwing up his face in disbelief, as he listened to Sam Reid's assessment of Alex Hunter's condition. Sam had refused the execution order point-blank, and had vowed to kill anyone who tried to carry it out – wheelchair or not. When it finally came down to it, Hammerson felt the same.

He swore again. Alex Hunter, the Arcadian, brought down by something smaller than the eye could see. *Bullshit!* He opened his eyes. *Brought down, but not killed, not yet,* he thought.

'I'm sending a cryo-cylinder,' he told Sam. 'You ensure Hunter goes in there ASAP. And you report to me and no one else on this, understand? If anyone asks, you're transporting Makhdoum's body. Got that?'

Hammerson lowered his head when he heard Sam's next report. 'I see. Have Dr. Weir sedated – that's an order! When she wakes, I'll speak to her.' *And tell her Alex Hunter is dead, whether he is or not,* he thought glumly as he disconnected the call. He hated doing this sort of stuff.

He fell back into his chair and contemplated the situation. The cryo-therapy would lower Alex's thermal range to minus 150 degrees, putting him – *and* the Hades Bug – in suspended animation. Any lower and Alex's cell walls would freeze and then burst. The downside was that when his body was warmed again, his brain would probably be jelly. At present, there were only two paths available for Alex Hunter – both terminal. One: Medical Division would get him – alive or dead – for immediate autopsical analysis. He'd end up in a hundred different sample jars and test tubes – just little bits floating in formaldehyde. The second path was no better: the bacteria would lie dormant until its host was warmed, and then turn him to mush – an ignoble end for a near invincible warrior.

Alex Hunter needed medical treatment – *just not ours*, Hammerson thought. He brought his fist to his chin and tapped for a moment. Only two paths unless we engineer a third … He stopped tapping and narrowed his eyes. Right now, Alex needed a guardian angel – one who could get him out of the country and into level-1 medical treatment. He sat still for another few moments, his mind working, then he leapt forward, reached for his comm unit and selected a name from his list of HAWCs. There was a notation beside the name: 'UA/AAO'; it meant 'Unauthorized Absence; Armed Approach Only'. *A hard case*, he thought as he placed a call to the secret number.

'I have some news,' he said, the instant it was answered. 'It concerns Captain Alex Hunter.' He paused, then spat, 'I know you know, and I couldn't give a fireman's fuck what you think. You want to help Hunter, you get here ASAP.'

He hung up and swivelled his chair to sit staring out through the window. *This'll either work beautifully or get very ugly*, he thought with a grim smile as he clasped his large, rough hands across his chest.

FORTY-FIVE

Hammerson switched off the engine of the drab armored truck and waited as its thirty-kilowatt powerplant whined down to silence. With the window down, he listened for a few seconds, then shouldered open the door and stepped out, placing his hands on his hips as he surveyed his surroundings. Cicadas thrummed in the late morning's warmth, and the secluded road was like a green tunnel with towering ponderosa pines lining each side of the pavement. Colonel Jack Hammerson was alone, dressed in plain black combat coveralls, fully armored and alert.

Contact, he thought, and dropped his hands to his sides, his fingers loose and open.

The transport pulled up a hundred feet down the road. It was a full minute before a figure stepped out, dressed almost exactly like Hammerson. The figure looked slowly left and right, taking in the surrounding woods and the deserted forest road for a few moments, then walked towards him and stopped.

'Do you have my furniture?'

Hammerson hadn't expected any warmth or camaraderie from the Mossad agent, even though she had worked with him for over six months, but he was surprised by the look of barely contained fury on her face. He kept his movements to a minimum. In his day, he'd been the most outstanding HAWC in the field; he was a survivor, smart and aggressive. But the woman before him was something else again. She was one of Mossad's elite Kidon agents, and he had personally enhanced those skills even further with HAWC techniques. A hostile Adira Senesh was pure lethality, something even he knew to be wary of.

'Yes, I have him,' he replied, keeping his voice level and his gaze direct. 'Along with all the information you need about him – his genesis, treatment, the unusual side effects. We've also included samples of the treatment compounds. Be advised: if he wakes, he may not be the same person. He may not know you or any of us.'

He looked briefly towards the truck. Alex Hunter had been kept in suspended animation in a special cryo-cylinder. The bacteria had been halted, but not stopped; it was still in his system – and possibly now in his brain. He knew the Israelis would try to eradicate it. They wanted the Arcadian alive; none more so than Adira Senesh.

Hammerson knew Senesh had been placed with them to uncover details of the Arcadian Project, but he'd always suspected that, for her, the mission was a vehicle to keep her near Alex Hunter. He had thwarted that desire throughout her time with the HAWCs. She had requested to work with Alex; he had denied it. She had demanded to go with the team on the Paraguayan mission; also denied. But he hadn't anticipated that her fury would reach an incendiary level when her sources informed her that Alex had been near fatally injured on the mission. When Hammerson had shared with her the information that the US military wanted to cut their elite soldier up for analysis instead of curing him, her rage had exploded.

Adira's eyes slid away from him and she turned to her own truck and nodded. From its rear came an electronic whine as a ramp lowered. Two large men jumped from the cabin and walked towards Hammerson's truck. Without looking at the HAWC commander, they opened the rear door and pulled free the coffin-shaped metal cylinder. A gurney unfolded underneath it to take the weight, and the men pushed it to the rear of their truck. Moments later, Hammerson heard the whine of the ramp closing.

Throughout it all, he'd kept his eyes on Adira. Her hands rested on twin guns strapped in a 'V' shape down across her groin. She had well and truly returned to the Mossad fold.

'Take care of him,' he said. 'No one knows he's still alive.'

The ferocity of her glare stopped him saying any more. *Probably shouldn't try and give advice right now*, he thought. He held his breath as he saw her fingers flex, and calculated the odds of winning if she decided to engage. He was armored, so was she … but she was quicker.

He waited.

Her eyes burned into his. 'If Alex Hunter dies, it is on your head,' she said slowly. 'And I will not forget.'

She turned away without another word.

Jack Hammerson only exhaled once the transport was reversing down the road.

*

Adira sat silently in the back of the truck with the steel cylinder. Slowly, she reached out to place a hand on its casing. She could feel the cold emanating through the solid metal.

She had achieved her primary mission of securing the Arcadian data and now she was going home – she should have been elated. But she had failed in her personal objective to keep Alex Hunter safe and that dispirited her. Adira rarely had time for friendships; never really liked or respected anyone enough to allow them to get close to her in any shape or form. Now the one person she had respected, the one person she had ever … what?

She withdrew her hand from the steel and sat staring at the coffin-like container. Her palm still felt cold.

*

Hammerson watched a satellite feed of Adira's truck speeding across the country. He was relieved: the 'furniture' had been successfully removed and there had been no firefight. He was out of practice, and going up against Senesh wouldn't have been a great way to see if he still had his edge. He felt no remorse for what was essentially his act of treason, or for manipulating Captain

Senesh or lying to Aimee Weir. He couldn't have protected Alex from Medical Division. Arcadian's only chance of survival was to get out of the country and under General Shavit's secure umbrella in Israel.

He opened his email and selected a small group as recipients of the message he was about to send. They were some of USSTRATCOM's most senior military people, including the US Vice-President and the head of the Medical Division. He began to type:

MILITARY DEATH NOTIFICATION 121 – EYES ONLY
DECEASED: *CAPTAIN ALEX HUNTER*
CAUSE OF DEATH: *AGGRESSIVE TIER-1 BIOLOGICAL CONTAMINATION*
ACTION: *BODY INCINERATED*

He looked at the message for a moment, then typed another line underneath:

NOTE: *TIER-1 MICROORGANISM SAMPLE OF HIGH MILITARY VALUE OBTAINED. RECOMMEND IMMEDIATE STUDY FOR WEAPONIZATION POTENTIAL*

Might as well throw them a bone, he thought.

He sent the message, then sat back, closing his eyes and clasping his hands behind his head. The Arcadian had been off the grid for years. There would be no letter of condolence from the President, or notification to the next of kin, his mother, Kathleen Hunter. She had been told years ago that Alex had died in action. There would be no further communication with Aimee Weir either; now she thought him gone too. The man was a ghost.

Hammerson spoke to the ceiling, his voice tinged with grief. 'You're free now, Arcadian. Maybe I'll see you again some day.'

He leaned forward and tapped a few keys on his computer. A satellite feed of the coast showed a blue dot moving out over the water. The micro-tracker he had planted in Alex's heel was non-metallic and undetectable without surgery. He was the only person who knew it was there. He smiled.

'Nope, I *know* I'll see you again some day.'

Author's Note

Many readers ask me about the underlying details in my novels – is the science real or fiction? Where do the situations, equipment, characters or their expertise come from, and just how much of any legend has a basis in fact? So, starting with *This Green Hell*, I've decided to share some of my research. I'm sure you'll see why it caught my attention.

Saint Roque González (1576–1628); the Martyrs of the River Plate

Roque González de Santa Cruz was born in 1576 and ordained at the age of twenty-two. By thirty-two, he had become a well traveled missionary in South America, converting the natives to Catholicism and settling them in townships. In 1628, González was joined by two young Spanish Jesuits, Alonso Rodriguez and Juan de Castillo. The three men trekked into the jungle of South America and founded a new settlement near the Ijuhi River. Their mission was to bring the local natives together in a single place, so they could be converted to Christianity, and also saving them from becoming laborers for the Portuguese army. Soon, González and Rodriguez moved on to Caaro, in the south of what is now Brazil, leaving Castillo at Ijuhi River. Unfortunately for the priests, the Guarani Indians in the new location resisted being converted and attacked the mission under the leadership of a powerful 'medicine man', Nezu. Father González was killed by blows to the head with a tomahawk as he was preparing to hang the new church bell. The new chapel the priests were building was set on fire and the Jesuits' bodies thrown into the flames. Father Castillo was soon tracked down and also killed; he was savagely beaten and then stoned to death.

The three Jesuits died in November 1628. Six months later a written account was prepared as evidence in the process of their beatification; the original documents were lost but copies were found many years later in the Argentine. Roque González, Alonso Rodrigues and Juan de Castillo were declared blessed in 1934, and canonised by Pope John Paul II in 1988. The three Jesuits remain the earliest beatified martyrs of America.

Carbon-hungry bacteria: methanogenesis

In my story, I have Aimee Weir looking for the key to a process called methanogenesis. She looks for the unique bacteria that actually ingests carbons and produces natural gas, miles below the earth. This is a real biochemical occurrence, and although science today understands how the methanogenesis process works, and also understands the time scales and transition characteristics, the full range of the microorganic zoology (types of bacteria) involved is still a mystery. Consider this piece from the US Geological Survey:

Natural gas generated from microbial activity in natural organic deposits (coal, black shale, petroleum) represents an increasingly important natural resource … It is estimated that natural gas from microbial activity (methanogenesis) accounts for about twenty percent of the world's natural gas resource. Since this gas is biologically produced, it also represents a possible renewable resource. Examples of microbial-produced natural gas deposits in the United States include: the organic-rich Antrim shale deposits in northern Michigan, and the shallow eastern edge of the Powder River Basin coal [sic] in Wyoming.

Although a considerable body of research exists on the biology of methanogenesis, there is much less known about the microbial-mediated conversion of geopolymers such as coal, black shale and petroleum to methane. Methanogenesis involves a large consortium of microorganisms in order to convert the geopolymers in fossil fuels to methane. Methanogenic archaea are the end producers of methane, but the consortia also includes fermenting bacteria that biodegrade geopolymers in the organic deposit to simpler molecules utilized by methanogenic archaea. The nature of the microorganisms, enzyme systems and decomposition pathways involved in the production of microbial natural gas from organic deposits is actually poorly understood.

Porphyria; the 'vampire' disease

Were vampires real? Sensitivity to sunlight, lengthening teeth, and unusual hair growth; not to mention blood drinking and an aversion to religious symbols. Unbelievable? Perhaps, but read on and see what you think.

This article was created and made available by Mr. Lawrence Koppy, a gentleman writer. Full details of this, and other articles, can be found on: http://www.suite101.com/writer_articles.cfm/lkoppy:

Porphyria, sometimes called 'the vampire disease', is a collection of rare, genetic blood disorders. Extreme cases of the disease can manifest gruesome symptoms where victims accumulate pigments called porphyrins in the skin, bones and teeth. While harmless in the dark, porphyrins become caustic, flesh eating toxins that can cause gruesome facial disfigurement when exposed to the ultraviolet rays of sunshine. Noses and ears can be eaten away with lips exhibiting a red, burned effect until they peel back from the gums that in turn recede, exposing the teeth in an unnatural way with a frightening, fang-like appearance (compare these symptoms with the description of Stoker's Dracula below).

> His eyebrows were very massive, almost meeting
> over the nose, and with bushy hair that seemed to

> curl in its own profusion. The mouth … was fixed
> and rather cruel-looking, with peculiarly sharp teeth;
> and these protruded over the lips.

Like the vampires of legend who can be weakened or even destroyed by the rays of the sun, real life victims of porphyria do indeed need to exercise great caution when venturing out into ordinary sunlight. This is due to the way porphyria cause changes in heme, a component of blood that carries oxygen throughout the body and is used to remove carbon dioxide.

Heme is turned into a toxic substance by porphyria, which the body then tries to break down. Lacking the ability to dispose of these toxic substances the body deposits them on the skin, gums and teeth. As the disease grows worse, the skin blackens, swells, and ruptures when exposed to the sun with hair growing from the sores. This hair growth could have made the victim appear to be changing into some sort of wolf-like beast and become woven into the fabric of vampire/werewolf legend.

One of the most well known myths associated with vampires, the drinking of human blood, can also be attributed to porphyria. It has been theorised that people afflicted with porphyria centuries ago may have used the folk remedy of drinking animal blood as a way to relieve their pain and the associated anemia. Add to this the fact that blood-drinking would have taken place during the night when porphyria victims did not have to worry about reactions to sunlight and it is easy to see how these unusual practices could well have been incorporated by people of that era into a crucial part of vampire lore.

Victims of porphyria, due to fear and superstition, subsequently became victims of the law during the 16th century, a time when the Inquisition was flourishing. Individuals suffering from revolting disfigurement faced doctors who wouldn't or didn't know how to treat the disease. This left them at the mercy of church officials who demanded they confess their sins or face death by fire.

Approximately 600 people suffering from porphyria during this time were burned at the stake. This could explain folklore that has vampires repelled by crucifix-wearing priests. Porphyria victims of that era would likely have associated the church with danger and have had an aversion to religious symbols.

Life from deep space

This article is included with thanks to Lucy Sherriff and *The Register* online magazine, and can be found at http://theregister.co.uk/2006/12/04/organic_rain/.

Scientists have found evidence that the seeds of life may indeed have fallen from the sky. Analysis of a meteorite that fell onto the frozen Tagish Lake in Canada in 2000 has shown the space rock to be riddled with organic material that is billions of years old, and at least as old as the solar system itself. Researchers speculate that this kind of matter could have played a vital role in the development of early life on Earth.

The Tagish Lake meteorite is unusual because it is so well preserved. Most meteorites, although usefully frozen in space, thaw or become contaminated when they arrive on Earth. This has frustrated researchers' attempts to test the hypothesis that organic material could have arrived on the primordial Earth on comets, asteroids, and meteors.

A team of NASA scientists, led by Keiko Nakamura-Messenger, scanned the Tagish meteorite in slices with a transmission electron microscope. This revealed sub-microscopic 'globules', which consisted largely of carbon, hydrogen, nitrogen, and oxygen, the researchers report.

To have captured such exotic isotope mixes, the meteorite must have formed much further from the sun than the Earth, Nakamura-Messenger says, which confirms that the chemicals are not contaminants, but are native to the space rock. They were most likely part of the cloud of material from which the planets themselves formed.

The team suggests two possible ways that the globules formed: in both cases they began life as icy grains that formed on the rock in the outer reaches of a very young solar system. It is possible that the grains then formed a hardened shell when bombarded by radiation. The center would later have evaporated, leaving a hollow shell of organic matter. Alternatively, the grains were exposed to alkali compounds in the meteor itself, which could have hollowed out the centers. The research, which is published in the journal *Science*, cites 26 such globules. But Nakamura-Messenger says the meteorite could contain billions of them.

Legends of the missing Inca gold

In *This Green Hell*, I had Ramón and Hector searching the jungle for lost gold. There are real reasons for this, and even today there are probably hundreds of men and women hacking through the South American jungle in search of the missing riches of the Incas.

This is because there are so many legends about Incan gold, and the great wealth that was hidden at the fall of their empire. As an example, there was the Great Golden Chain (a thousand feet long), that needed two hundred of the strongest warriors to carry it. The ceremonial chain was supposed to have been cast into a lake … but more likely, something that huge (and heavy!) would have been buried. Another was a Golden Sun, giving off magnificent rays of pure gold that occupied the Temple of the Sun at Cuzco. In addition, the Incas delighted in fashioning objects and everyday scenes from beaten gold – an extraordinary example would have been the Garden Courtyard, or Garden of the Sun. It was a life-sized garden, complete with rows of corn, sheep and shepherds – all fashioned from gold. The crops were sown with maize – the stalks, leaves and ears of which were all gold. There were golden shepherds who guarded the sheep, armed with slings and staves made of gold and silver. And lastly, but not finally, there were the mummies of thirteen past Incan emperors coated with gold, studded with jewels and seated on golden chairs – all of which vanished at the time of King Atahualpa's death in 1533.

These artifacts have never been recovered from the jungle – their dollar value is estimated in the billions, but their historical value is priceless. The list is extensive, but perhaps the subject is best summarized by Pedro Cieza de Léon (1520 – 1554) in a small excerpt from one of the volumes of his significant *Chronicles of Peru*.

> If all the gold that is buried in Peru … were collected, it would be impossible to coin it, so great the quantity; and yet the Spaniards of the conquest got very little, compared with what remains … If, when the Spaniards entered Cuzco they had not committed other tricks, and had not so soon executed their cruelty in putting Atahualpa to death, I do not know how many great ships would have been required to bring such treasure to old Spain, as is now lost in the bowels of the earth and will remain so because those who buried it are now dead.

Thank you to author Robert Lebling and *Mysteries Magazine* for allowing use of portions of his article. The full article can be found at *Mysteries Magazine*: http://www.scribd.com/doc/22717756/Locating-the-Lost-Chain-of-the-Inca-Mysteries-Magazine-05 [PDF].

Acknowledgements

Thank you Lucy Sherriff – geeks truly will inherit the earth, and to Lawrence, Rob and the US GEO for allowing me to share some of their research. To Kathleen, Cory and Brad – my biggest supporters … and critics! To my publisher, Cate.

And finally to my editors, Joel and Nicola – wordsmiths, inter-rogators, and counselors, I thank you.

Hell is not hot, or cold.

Nor is it deep below ground, or somewhere in the sky.

Instead it is a place on Earth filled with sucking bogs, disfiguring diseases and millions of tiny flesh-eating creatures.

Hell is a jungle, and it is monstrously green.